THE COMPLETE SERIES

KENDALL RYAN

About the Book

Knox Bauer's life has unraveled to the point of no return. Fighting to fill the emptiness inside himself, he seeks solace in unfamiliar beds with unfamiliar women. As guardian to his three younger brothers, he can't seem to do anything right. But this can't go on…they look up to him in every way, and all he's done lately is prove how messed up he really is. Needing a change, he attends a local Sex Addicts Anonymous meeting, where he finds himself tempted by the wholesome yet alluring instructor, McKenna.

Twenty-one-year-old McKenna is trying to make amends. After losing her parents in a horrific accident, she knows if she can just be good enough, maybe she can forgive herself for what happened. With her newly acquired degree in counseling, she begins leading a sex addicts group where she meets the troubled Knox, and her life takes on complications she never bargained for. She doesn't have time for a bad boy who only wants to take her to bed, even if her body disagrees. The fixer in her wants to help, but trusting Knox's true motivations might take more courage than she has.

Chapter One

KNOX

Pain exploded in my hand and I fell back onto the scuffed wooden floor. I stared down at the blood dripping from my shredded knuckles, and it took me a moment to place the shrill noise coming from behind me.

"Knox!" a girl screamed.

She knew my name, but I couldn't remember hers.

The girl's voice wasn't familiar. Probably because we hadn't done much talking when I brought her home last night. I wondered if the screams and moans she let out during sex would be more familiar to me. Probably not; I was pretty wasted when we'd gotten here.

Through blurry eyes, I looked at the girl for the first time, trying to remember where I'd picked her up. At the moment she was topless and wearing only a glittery pink thong. Images of her shaking her ass in that thong flooded my brain.

Tears welled in her eyes and she crept closer to me. "Are you okay?"

The G-string she wore jogged my memory. Lap dance...dollar bills...shots of Cuervo burning a wicked path down my throat until my mind was just where I needed it. Oblivion.

"Knox, oh my God. What did you do?" She looked down, inspecting my hand more closely.

I closed my eyes for a moment, willing her to quiet down before she woke up my brothers. When I opened them again, I looked down and took stock of myself, naked and sitting sprawled on my bedroom floor. It wasn't one of my finer moments. I straightened my fingers, then hissed through clenched teeth as I inspected my injured hand in the dim light. *Shit.* I wasn't sure if it was broken, but it throbbed like a bitch.

"I'm fine," I bit out. My heart pounded in my chest and I was breathless, as if I'd just finished running a sprint. Blood smears painted the wall where I'd taken out my aggression, and a ragged hole gaped in the drywall. As I took deep breaths, trying to calm myself, I realized I'd been having a dream about what I would do to my father if I ever saw him again.

"Do you want me to get you something for the pain?" the girl asked.

A distant memory flooded my brain, probably what brought on the nightmare in the first place. Images of my leg, broken and twisted when I'd fallen from a tree as a boy, suddenly came back to me. I remember putting on a brave face when my dad referred to pain pills as "bitch mints."

I shook my head. "No, I'm fine." I didn't need them then and I didn't need them now.

The girl sucked her lower lip into her mouth, her eyes welling with tears. There was nothing I hated more than seeing a girl cry.

"Come here." I reached my good hand toward her.

Her expression wary, she crawled over to where I sat on the floor. When I rose to my knees and stroked my lengthening dick, her eyes locked onto my movements, darting back and forth between my face, my bloodied hand, and my cock, trying to understand what I wanted.

"Come suck me off." Yeah, it was a dick move, but it was the only thing that would calm me down right now. It was either that or liquor, and I knew my cabinets would be empty. If I'd gone out earlier, it was most likely for alcohol, pussy, or both.

She frowned. "What about your hand?"

"Fuck my hand," I ground out. "I want your lips around my cock."

Wordlessly she obeyed, crawling the rest of the way toward me and leaning down to take me in her mouth. I fisted my bloodied hand in her hair, watching the curve of her back as she moved up and down over me, liking the feel of raw power and satisfaction it gave me.

Within minutes, I tapped her on the shoulder and she moved away as I finished with my hand, spurting into her open mouth. "Good girl." I petted her hair and she blinked up at me.

I rose and headed into the bathroom to clean myself off. "You can go now," I called out to her where she still sat on the floor, looking confused.

"But it's three in the morning."

"I don't care. Get the fuck out. You got what you came for." I tossed the bloodied towel to the bathroom floor and inspected my hand. The skin was torn at the knuckles, but nothing felt broken as I spread my fingers apart and rotated my wrist. I'd live.

"You don't have to be such an asshole," she yelled, gathering up her clothes and dressing hastily. "There's something wrong with you, you know that?"

Her hurt expression should have caused me to feel something. Remorse, regret, sympathy…something. But my battered body and fucked-up mind had stopped responding to normal human emotions years ago. I lived according to my baser instincts now. It was just easier that way.

"I know," I murmured. There was more wrong with me than she'd ever know.

The following morning I woke up late, my hand still throbbing. Crawling from bed, I twisted open a bottle of Jack that I'd found conveniently tucked under my pillow and took a healthy swig, then tucked it back under my pillow for safekeeping. I might be a mess, but I didn't want my younger brothers to pick up my nasty habits.

My cell phone vibrated from the rickety table by the door. The cell phone was new, as was my number, so I couldn't figure out who might be calling me. I glanced at the screen. *Fuck.* It was my therapist's office, reminding me of my appointment that afternoon. The last thing I wanted to do was go in and talk to some dickhead therapist about my feelings. But it was all part of my plea bargain. I had my choice: therapy or jail. Fucking DUI.

It just didn't seem fair. I'd tried to do all the right things since our father left—I worked hard all week, took care of my brothers, and paid the bills. But when I sought a little relief during my free time, I always found myself in a pile of shit.

But I couldn't think about that right now. If I did, I'd start drinking and either show up drunk to my first appointment, or not show up at all. Neither of which was a good option.

━━━━━━━━

When I arrived at the office, the soft music and scattered couches in the waiting room already had me on edge. I didn't want to be here. Knowing I didn't have much of a choice, I approached the receptionist at the desk, a meek little thing with brown hair pulled into a ponytail. Big green eyes looked straight up at me. "Knox Bauer. I have an appointment at three o'clock."

"Hi. Could you sign in right here?" She tapped the clipboard on the counter.

I signed my name and took a seat. A moment later, she scurried around the desk and handed me a clipboard of forms. "Since it's your first time here, can you fill these out ?"

I took the papers without a word and watched as she sauntered away, her ass bouncing in the most delectable way in her knee-length skirt. I hadn't seen a girl dress like that in a while. All prim and proper. She was sending off schoolmarm vibes, which my dick told me I found refreshing. I guess I'd been hanging out with strippers too much, not that I was about to reevaluate the company I kept. No, they served a distinct and necessary purpose in my life.

I shook the thoughts away and focused on the forms. Once I turned them in, I was escorted by the receptionist with the nice ass into the therapist's office.

"Knox?" An aging woman with gray hair greeted me, rising from behind her desk.

"Yup." I strode into the office, hearing the soft click as the receptionist closed the door behind me.

"I'm Dr. Claudia Lowe. Have a seat."

I obeyed, lowering myself to the stiff leather arm chair in front of her desk. No sense in pissing off the good doctor straight away. I'd play nice. For now.

We sat facing each other, her appraising me coolly over the rim of lowered spectacles. "I trust you know why you're here?"

I nodded.

"I see a lot of anger management cases. Most are men with a history of fighting or domestic abuse. Your case is something altogether different. I trust you know that too."

I nodded again. Oh yeah, I'd gotten myself in a pile of shit, all right. After a night out drinking last summer, I'd stupidly driven home and gotten a DUI. Because it was my first offense and my court-appointed attorney played the sympathy card, explaining to the judge I was caring for my minor siblings, I was let off easy with fines and community service. Then after I'd brilliantly smarted off to the judge, he'd tacked on an order to see a counselor for anger management.

The first shrink I'd seen had dug into my brain, and concluded pretty quickly that my issues weren't related to anger. After a battery of questions about my past and how I dealt with the stress in my life, she became convinced I had an issue with sex and referred me to Dr. Lowe. I didn't think fucking was a crime, but apparently the counselor had felt differently. She'd written up some shit about stress being relived in sexual ways, and that I lacked the ability to form and maintain healthy relationships with the opposite sex. Bullshit. I was just horny.

I glanced up at Dr. Lowe, who was reading from a page in front of her. "When you were fifteen, you got kicked out of school for engaging in indecent acts with a female student."

"I don't see how my high school flings have anything to do with this."

She smiled tightly. "Nothing is off-limits in our sessions together, Mr. Bauer. Just because it's not officially on your record doesn't mean we're not going to discuss it."

I ground my teeth, and she pushed on. "When you were seventeen, you were sent to a boot-camp-style high school during your senior year. Three months later, you were arrested for public drunkenness and lewd behavior."

I sighed. "My buddies and I had our first night out in months. I got drunk and I took a girl out in the back alleyway. I wasn't hurting anyone, just blowing off some steam. And trust me, she was willing." The woman probably wouldn't care that it was around that same time that my father had left us, so I didn't mention it.

She leaned forward, removing her glasses and resting her elbows on the desk. "I know you feel these instances can be explained away, but you have a history of using sex to cope. And after gaining legal custody of your brothers—"

"I'm not discussing that with you."

She nodded. "Not yet."

Motherfu— I cursed under my breath. No one needed to know our family business. I took good care of the boys. They weren't part of this. I intentionally kept this side of myself from them.

"I'm recommending something a bit unconventional for your treatment. I would like you to join a local Sex Addicts Anonymous support group."

Sex addict? My jaw tightened. I wasn't a fucking sex addict. I liked pussy. There was a difference. A big fucking difference.

"Your sexual past has been noted, and according to your own admissions, you've had more partners than you can recall and you use sex as an escape."

She glared at me, waiting for me to disagree. I bit my cheek and stayed quiet. It was true I thought about sex a lot. All the time, actually. But I thought most guys did. Though, if I were being honest, I knew I was worse than my buddies. When I was younger they'd nicknamed me Worm, because of how many girl's panties I'd wormed my way into over the years. I wasn't an addict, though; I was an opportunist. I'd never turn down a willing female.

"This field of study is just emerging but most researchers agree, the definition of a sex addict is someone whose deviant sexual

13

behavior interferes with daily life—their relationships, job, et cetera."

Well, shit. I wouldn't fight her on this. I was radioactive. An asshole. A user of women, but shit, they'd all been willing. Maybe she was right, though. I hated the tears and drama that came with my less-than-stellar behavior toward the opposite sex. And the last thing I wanted was my behavior to rub off on my brothers. I wanted better for them.

Dr. Lowe scribbled something on a piece of paper. "Here's the group you'll be attending. First meeting is tomorrow morning and they meet weekly. I'll receive reports on your progress and what you're learning about yourself during these group sessions. If you progress well, I'll be able to note that in my letter to the judge. The choice is yours."

She shoved the paper at me.

"Okay." I kept my voice neutral as I picked up the paper, but inside? Inside, I was fighting the urge to curse and crumple it into a ball.

This was bullshit.

Chapter Two

McKenna

I closed my eyes and said a silent prayer. I needed to stop my hands from shaking. This was going to be fine. I could do this. My pep talk did little good, though; I knew how pathetic I was. A sexual addiction counselor and technically still a virgin.

It wasn't from lack of effort on my part. I'd made up my mind my sophomore year of college and decided to have sex with my boyfriend at the time, Jason. He'd been thrilled, of course; I'd made him wait six long months with only heavy make-out sessions to sustain him. He'd been weird about sex—often leaving me to initiate things and tell him when I was ready for more—which only made me feel undesired and insecure. I didn't know what I was doing. I wanted him to take the lead, but never had the courage to tell him.

When I finally told him I was ready, we were in the backseat of his Toyota Prius, since we were both too embarrassed to tell our dorm roommates that we needed some privacy. He'd done it before but seemed almost more timid than me, repositioning us over and over in the tiny car, and then losing his erection when he'd finally slipped on the condom. I felt like a failure. Like it was somehow my fault, and it wasn't an experience I wanted to repeat. So I hadn't.

The only part of being a virgin that bugged me was that if anyone here knew, I was sure I'd be a laughingstock.

But I thrust my shoulders back, ready, or at least ready to fake it for my first solo group session without my mentor, Belinda. I could do this. I'd be fine. It was a different group than the one I'd trained with. Belinda had recommended that, which I thought was good advice.

I'd gotten to know the roughly dozen or so regulars who attended her Tuesday night meeting. I'd become familiar with their stories—like Pamela, the sweet Italian girl who was always looking for love, trying to make up for her father's rejection. Or Ted, the middle-aged businessman who'd become addicted to Internet porn during the economic downturn when he was laid off and home alone every day. Bored and horny.

Today I'd have a whole new group to get to know, the Saturday morning group. As scary as it was, this was a fresh start. This group wouldn't see me as just the trainee. I was the group leader. I'd studied for this, gone to school for this. But that didn't mean my stomach wasn't flipping violently when the doors opened and the first person entered the room.

An older man with hair graying at his temples.

I smiled warmly, then averted my eyes and went back to organizing the papers on my desk. I didn't want him to feel watched or uncomfortable in my presence. There was a fine line between being friendly and open, and giving people their space. I certainly never wanted anyone here to feel judged.

The room began to fill, people mingling near the coffeepot, making small talk about the weather or local sports teams—discussing anything but the reason we were all gathered here. Most were middle-aged men, not surprising there, it was the same with my last group. But a few younger people and women made it a little more diverse.

When everyone had taken a seat in one of the chairs arranged into a semicircle in the center of the room, I was just about to take the spot at the front when a guy about my age, looking tense and unsure, opened the door and just stood there.

He was tall and extremely fit with wide shoulders and a toned chest, hinted at by the way his T-shirt clung to him. His hair was cropped close, just long enough to be messy in the front. But his deep, expressive eyes were his most stunning feature—a mix of dark hazel and warm brown framed in thick lashes and bright with intelligence.

For a split second I struggled to pull my gaze away from his. I'd appreciated attractive men before, but this man possessed a magnetism that made it impossible for me to look away. My heart thundered in my chest while I stared, mouth open, watching him.

His hand curled around the doorknob, but he made no move to enter. He was obviously new here. And by the looks of it, about to flee.

"Are you here for SAA?" Our abbreviation for sex addicts anonymous. "Come on in, we're just about to start." I found my voice and motioned him forward.

He swallowed hard, his throat contracting as emotions flashed across his face. Then his expression hardened and he entered the room, letting the heavy door fall closed behind him with a thud.

Mister Tall, Dark, and Devastatingly Handsome took the last open seat, the one directly across from me, and raked his gaze over my skin. A hot shudder passed through me and I fought to control my nerves. Something about having to address the group with his dark eyes on me made me incredibly nervous.

I cleared my throat and began. "Welcome. This is a support group for people with sexual addiction. I've been working with another group, so I wanted to take a moment to introduce myself, and then I'll ask you to do the same."

I folded my hands in my lap and began, my eyes looking anywhere but at the guy across from me. He was too distracting.

"My name is McKenna, and I've been leading another SAA group for six months. I have a bachelor's degree in counseling and I also work at a center for troubled teens. In my free time, I like volunteering and watching scary movies."

I smiled warmly. "I'd like everyone to introduce themselves, tell us a bit about yourself, and if you're comfortable, why you're here." I turned to the gentlemen to my left and nodded, thankful that I'd gotten through that with my voice steady and composed.

One by one each person introduced themselves, most giving a brief snippet about why they were here. Their revelations were vague and general, saying only things like *I need help to get my life back on track*. That was to be expected; we'd work our way up to the more personal confessions as time went on.

When everyone else had spoken, my eyes went to the beautiful stranger seated across from me. He cleared his throat and fidgeted in the chair, eliciting a loud squeal as the metal legs shifted against the tile floor. Something in his posture told me he had no plans to share anything about himself. Active group participation was a strong indicator of belief in the program, and one's ability to successfully overcome their addiction.

I frowned, realizing he might be here for the wrong reasons. A college kid on a dare from his friends, or a way to pick up easy women. I wasn't sure, so I fixed him with a stare.

"To be part of this meeting you must admit you have a problem, and that your life has become unmanageable and you need help. You must commit to attending the meetings and to sharing with the group."

The newcomer rolled his eyes. "My name's Knox Bauer. I'm a Virgo and I like long walks on the beach."

I released the little breath I'd been holding. It seemed we might have a problem, one I'd have to address after group. I'd seen Belinda do the same thing before, to make sure everyone was here for the right reason.

I pushed on, ignoring his blatant disregard for the group—for now. Finally the clock on the wall indicated our hour was up, which was good because I couldn't take another second of his eyes watching my every move. I felt distracted and itchy, and fought the urge to run—to flee this room and Knox's heated stare. But I told myself to calm down. I could handle this. Too bad my training in no way prepared me for a super-hot alpha male invading my space.

After putting on a sincere smile, I wrapped up the meeting with, "Thank you, everyone. I'll see you next Saturday and in the meantime, stay strong. And remember you can call me or your sponsor at any time."

I breathed a sigh of relief. My first solo group had gone pretty well. All except for the newcomer, Knox, who seemed reluctant to take part in the group. It was time to address the issue head-on.

My eyes went to Knox, who was already rising from his chair. "Knox, can you stay behind a minute?"

He hesitated briefly, obviously thinking it over, and then lowered himself back to the metal folding chair.

The room was too small, too warm, and I crossed the room to adjust the ancient thermostat on the far wall. I didn't even know if it worked, but the chance to get out of Knox's line of vision for just a moment was a welcome reprieve. I pushed the switch to the coolest setting and sucked in a few deep breaths.

I returned to stand in front of Knox. His smile was playful as his eyes wandered the length of my body. His look was so sexual, so erotic, that my stomach twirled into a series of intricate knots and my knees trembled where I stood.

Chapter Three

KNOX

The overpowering scent of citrus floor polish was giving me a headache. I wanted nothing more than to escape, but I nodded in response to McKenna's request, lowering myself back down to the seat. Evidently I was about to catch shit for not sharing my feelings in this damn circle jerk of a meeting.

The people around me rose and filed from the room. I didn't know what I expected sex addicts to look like, but it certainly wasn't this. They looked like regular people, for the most part. Guys like me.

McKenna crossed the room to fiddle with the thermostat on the wall, seeming to buy her time, and then approached me once again.

I couldn't resist letting my gaze slip down over her curves. Her confidence wavered as her eyes dropped from mine to the floor between her feet. There was something about me that threw her off her game. As confident as she'd been during the meeting, her self-assurance wavered as she stood before me.

Petite, but with nice curves, she was stunning. She had long glossy hair hanging down her back and delicate features—a small nose, wide eyes, and high cheekbones. I'd be blind not to notice how attractive she was. Her eyes darted everywhere but on me, letting me take my fill uninterrupted. Wasn't there some saying about never trust a skinny chef? Well, never trust a beautiful sex-addiction counselor either. Or perhaps it was that I didn't trust myself around her.

As I studied her, I realized she wasn't like the girls I hung around. She was beautiful. Educated. Intelligent. Submissive. It was that last part that got my blood pumping south. Introducing her to the business end of my dick became priority number one, but then my lurid thoughts screeched to a halt. I cursed under my breath. That wasn't in the cards. I needed to remember why I was here.

McKenna sat down in the chair beside me, her hands moving restlessly in her lap. "I think we got off on the wrong foot," she murmured. "I'm here to help. That's all." She held up her hands, palms out in a placating gesture, and her eyes met mine.

Her hands were small and looked soft. It had been a while since I'd been around a girl as innocent and pure as she seemed to be. I nodded, acknowledging her statement, then cleared my throat and asked, "Did you need something?" She had asked me to stay behind, after all.

She took a deep breath, inhaling slowly, as if to steady herself. "Success in this program hinges on one's ability to admit they have a problem with sexual activity, and that they need help."

Although I could surely use her help with some sexual activity, I had a feeling that wasn't what she meant.

"I'm here at the request of my counselor." My voice was bland, indicating my lack of passion regarding her little meetings.

She looked down at the floor to the space between our feet once again, momentarily falling silent before raising her gaze to mine once again. "What do you do for fun, Mr. Bauer? To blow off steam."

Mr. Bauer. I liked the sound of that falling from her pink lips way too much. My gaze zeroed in on her mouth, and McKenna bit down on her lower lip.

I stuffed my hands into my pockets, forcing my eyes away. "What do you want to know?"

"Your hobbies."

My hobbies? Drinking, getting arrested, fucking pretty little things like her. Since the truth would shock her, I just shrugged. "Nothing that concerns you, angel."

"You're awfully…dominant, aren't you?" Her words were direct, but her gaze remained glued to the floor, as if she was unable to be so bold while holding my eyes. It set off something inside me.

I didn't like the label. *Dominant.* I'd read a little bit about it online, and I'd be lying if some of the shit I read didn't ring true. I liked to take control in the bedroom. Give orders. Be pleased by a girl eager to submit, or give pleasure to someone so willing to receive it. I liked the control it gave. The heady feeling of power. Especially

24

because there was so much in my life I couldn't control. And something about McKenna's gentle nature told me if I could get past her walls, she would submit to me beautifully.

I was even sicker and more fucked up than she knew. I'd own her. But as fun as it might be, I wouldn't let myself break her. She was my sexual addiction counselor. She was off-limits. And it wasn't like I had an actual problem. I liked sex. I was a red-blooded American male, but I could control myself.

"Your reaction is very common, Mr. Bauer," she went on. "With all due respect, it sounds like you may be in denial, especially if you continue to engage in destructive sexual activities."

I let out a snort. "You think you're going to cure me of wanting sex, angel? Not a chance." The nickname slid from my lips with ease. She was a sweet, blue-eyed, petite little thing. Soft and innocent looking too. An angel amongst devils.

"We don't preach celibacy. That's not what I'm asking of you." Her voice wavered ever so slightly.

"Damn good thing too." No way in fuck was I taking a vow of abstinence. I felt itchy and uncomfortable just thinking about it, like a caged animal ready to rebel. Why was I letting her get under my skin? *Shit*.

"We operate under the same approach as many twelve-step programs. We don't expect abstinence, but my goal is to help you engage in healthy sexual activity. To work with you to stay away from people or images that might trigger compulsive sexual behavior."

This was insane. I wasn't some sicko, some sexual deviant. I just really, really liked women. I shouldn't have even come here today. I should have told that counselor to fuck off instead of agreeing to this bullshit interrogation. My heartbeat pounded in my ears, and I crossed my arms over my chest to hide my clenched fists.

"Our group members often have unresolved emotional issues, things from their pasts that bring on PTSD, anxiety, depression. Eighty percent of sex addicts were abused as children…" McKenna prattled on like she was reading from a textbook.

My past had nothing to do with my liking sex. The only thing that kept me in my seat was watching McKenna's pretty blue eyes looking so solemnly at mine. She held me captive, even if I didn't want to listen to what she had to say.

McKenna licked her lips slightly, which made my dick twitch, and said, "Only once you deal with your sexual dysfunction can you form true, loving relationships, and break the cycle."

No thanks. Been there, done that. And I had the battle scars to prove it. I shifted in my seat, becoming more agitated by the second.

She leaned forward, her expression sincere. "You can't do this alone, in private by yourself, Knox. I'm here to help."

"Sex feels good, McKenna," I spat out. "You should try it. It releases endorphins."

"So does jogging."

I couldn't help the throaty chuckle that tore from my chest. Jogging as a replacement for sex? This girl was crazy.

"I have to go." I shot to my feet, needing out of this room where her sweet scent was invading my senses and making my head spin.

McKenna opened her mouth to argue, but closed it once I stood.

We were done. At least for now.

Chapter Four

McKenna

That night while lying in bed, I couldn't stop myself from thinking about him. Knox Bauer. Even his name rolling off my lips sent my pulse racing.

I pulled the freshly washed sheets up to my chin and closed my eyes, trying to clear the thoughts swirling inside my head. I knew all too well that morning would come too soon, and I needed my rest. Tomorrow I was on call at the teen shelter; I'd volunteered to be put into their regular rotation of staffers. It was a big commitment but it kept me busy, which I preferred.

Even as I lay warm and cozy in my big empty bed, my thoughts flitted back to the gorgeous stranger who had given off such a mysterious and commanding vibe. I thought about how wounded he was. How high he'd built up his walls. I plotted various ways to reach him, to get through to him and help. Of course, I knew from years of schooling that successful treatment hinged on the patient actually wanting to get better. And something told me Knox didn't. He seemed comfortable with himself and his sexuality.

I'd be lying to myself if I said I didn't notice him physically. My undersexed body was highly aware of him. His masculine scent—crisp cotton and spicy aftershave with hints of sandalwood and leather. The five o'clock shadow that I was sure would rasp against my skin if he kissed me, and the deep timbre of his rough voice. It was a lethal combination that did something to me. The man was trouble, a sexy-as-hell troublemaker, but still. It bothered me that I couldn't turn off my thoughts.

Most of the night I tossed and turned, unable to forget the way Knox's messy disheveled hair made him look both sexy and dangerous at the same time. The way his dark eyes pierced mine, forcing the air from my lungs.

It was my job to help him, not lust after him. I'd need to follow the advice from my own lessons when he was near—counting backward from ten, taking deep, calming breaths. That is, if he ever showed up again. He seemed adamant that he didn't belong there, and I wouldn't be at all surprised if he dropped out altogether.

What seemed like only minutes later, my alarm went off, startling me awake.

While the water heated for my shower, I dragged myself to the sink to brush my teeth. I was nothing if not efficient. After stepping into the steaming water, I cranked it as hot as I could stand. The heat enveloped me and soothed my aching shoulders. I was exhausted and struggled to remember why, what I did yesterday to wear me out.

A vision of Knox's chiseled features invaded my mind. Oh yeah. I suppressed a shiver racing down my spine and through my belly and pressed a hand against the wet tile wall, supporting the sudden jolt at the memory of him. I'd never had that weak-in-the-knees, butterflies-in-the-stomach feeling before. I'd thought it was all a myth. But it seemed Knox was the one man who had broken through my defenses.

Too bad he was off-limits and I could do nothing about it.

Chapter Five

How your life could change so drastically over the course of a few years was crazy. I could have never imagined that at age eighteen I'd be financially and legally responsible for my three younger brothers.

But when my dad left four years ago, there was no way in fuck I was letting us get split up and sent into the foster care system. We'd been through enough. After losing Mom, and then Dad turning out to be a selfish prick, we had to stick together. Tucker had only been four, and Luke and Jaxon just thirteen and fourteen at the time. I'd graduated early from high school and began working full-time to meet our rent, utilities, and grocery bills. That first year was a blur. We had peanut butter sandwiches for dinner when money was tight, and endured the heat and electricity getting turned off more than once that first year. Things had gotten a little better since then, but it was still hard.

I knew I used girls to forget pain, to mask my emotions, and of course to feel pleasure. That had begun when I was still in high school. I also knew I had no plans to change it. Just because I was in some ridiculous sex addicts group didn't mean I need to go all holier-than-thou and reform myself. Fuck that. My lifestyle was the only thing keeping me sane at the moment. The only thing keeping me out of jail, most likely. I might tone it down for my brothers' sake, but I wasn't about to change who I was.

All week long I'd worked, hit the gym, hung out at home with my brothers, and looked forward to seeing McKenna again. I knew it was stupid. She was my sexual addiction counselor, for fuck's sake. I was delusional thinking there could be something between us, yet I knew she felt the raw magnetism just like I had. I'd seen it in her eyes. Her curiosity had been unmistakable. The soft inhalation of breath, her fluttering pulse, calling me "Mr. Bauer." Shit, I had liked that way too much.

After a late-afternoon jog where I'd let the smoggy heat of Chicago drench me in sweat, I showered, dressed, then made the boys a snack just as they were arriving home from school. It was one of the rules I enforced—straight home after school, homework and family dinner, and then friends or other social activities. The front door burst open and a pile of backpacks, shoes, and lunch boxes hit the foyer floor. Jaxon disappeared up the stairs as Luke and Tucker tore into the kitchen, stealing crackers and slices of cheese from the counter where I'd placed them.

"What's wrong with Jaxon?" I asked.

"He has to poop." Tucker giggled.

I smiled. Sometimes I felt pretty damn lucky to live with only guys. We said what was on our minds, took care of business, and didn't overanalyze things. It was a pretty sweet deal.

Minutes later Jaxon appeared, looking sullen. Even though he was the oldest, I worried about him more than the other two. He was in his final year of high school with no clue what he wanted to do afterward.

I leaned against the counter, watching them munch on crackers and listening to stories about school. Tucker wandered away after having his fill, and I brushed the crumbs he left behind into the sink.

"Is everything okay, Knox? I heard screaming coming from your room the other night," Jaxon asked.

Jaxon was the most like me, which meant he was also the most suspicious, especially after my arrest for a DUI. I could understand their concern. I was the only guardian they had—I couldn't go off the deep end like that again. And I refused to let them down; that would make me no better than our father.

Embarrassed, I scrubbed a hand over my face. "No. But it will be. In fact, I wanted to tell you that I've begun attending a class Saturday mornings to put my life back on track."

"Is it the anger management class the judge wanted you to take?" Luke, my seventeen-year-old brother asked. His watchful eyes waited for my response.

With Tucker in his bedroom, playing superheroes by the sound of it, I figured Luke and Jaxon were old enough to know the truth. I didn't shield them from much. To me, that was no different than lying. My father was a liar, and I didn't care to walk in his footsteps in any regard.

I took a deep breath. The first step was admitting you had a problem, right? "The counselor actually wants me to attend a group for people with sexual addiction. She thought my history with girls was…too much."

"And that's a bad thing?" Jaxon asked, a hint of a smile playing at the edges of his mouth. He was way too much like me. And the several high school girls I'd found crying at our doorstep proved his track record was already eerily similar to mine.

I needed to find a way to get through to him. But I guess getting my own life on track was the first step.

Chapter Six

McKenna

Friday nights were the hardest for me. I had thought moving to Chicago would be my chance to break free, the beginning of a grand and exciting adventure. But so far, my life here had been anything but.

I worked, I volunteered, and I went home to the quiet little apartment I shared with Brian. Then I'd change into my pajamas and heat up a can of soup for dinner each night while watching sitcom reruns in my bedroom. When I thought about how different my life was from that of other girls my age, it didn't even seem like we were on the same planet. Going out dancing, dating, going to clubs…all of it felt so far out of reach for me.

I had always thought there would be time for fun later, like I was in a holding pattern waiting for my real life to start. As if all this was temporary. Someday I'd meet someone, forgive myself, and all the stress and guilt I carried around with me would suddenly vanish. I knew it didn't work that way, but it was a pretty thought.

While I was growing up, school and grades had always been more important than boys and parties. Plus, I was what you'd call a late bloomer. Braces and glasses hampered my social life throughout high school, as well as a layer of acne, thanks to the greasy pizza place I worked at after school. After the accident, a social life and dates to dances were the last things I cared about. It had all been about surviving.

Needing some independence from the little Indiana town where I grew up, I'd jumped at the chance when I was offered a job in Chicago to counsel troubled teens. Besides, there was nothing for me back in Indiana anymore.

After my parents passed away tragically in a car accident my senior year of high school, I'd stayed with my friend Brian and his parents so I could finish the school year. Each day I kept my head down and did what was expected of me, then each night I cried myself to sleep. After graduation, I attended a local community college and continued living with Brian's parents, even when he moved two hours away to go to Indiana University.

I had moved to Chicago to be free, to start over. But of course that wasn't possible. My past followed me, just like it always would. Brian decided to relocate along with me, saying he would never let me fend for myself alone in the big city. Even though that had been exactly what I'd wanted. A fresh start where no one knew me as the sad little orphaned girl.

Did I want to live with Brian? No, but affording my own place in Chicago was out of the question. We'd found a two-bedroom, two-bathroom apartment, so at least we each had our own space. There was also a large kitchen and living room, and a small den where we put a breakfast table and my bookshelves. Brian had painted it a sunny yellow for me, even though we'd have to change it back to white when we moved out, per the landlord's orders.

I should have been grateful, but his presence was a constant reminder of what had happened. Of who I'd become. I was living as a shell of my former self without any idea how to break free.

I pushed all that from my mind when I heard Brian knock at my bedroom door. Fixing on a pleasant smile, I pulled it open and stepped out into the hall. "Hi."

"Hey, you." He pulled me warmly into a hug, and I didn't fight it. It was the only physical affection I got. And Brian was comfortable, like your favorite tennis shoes. "You ready?" he asked.

"Yep." I grabbed my purse from the counter and looped it around my body.

Brian had bought a Groupon for a painting class tonight, and invited me along. He knew I wasn't a go-out-and-party type, and his attempts at taking me out to dinner had failed too. It felt too much like a date, so we stuck to simple activities like this. Safe. Platonic. The story of my life.

When I thought about my meeting in the morning, the prospect of seeing Knox again sent a little thrill through me, making my belly dance with nerves. All week while I worked with the teen girls at the center, I'd felt like a hypocrite. I counseled them about not making their whole life about a guy, yet here I was, all my waking thoughts consumed by the mystery that was Knox Bauer.

"You okay?" Brian squinted at me.

"Fine." I squirmed, forcing the thoughts of Knox's raw masculinity from my brain. "Let's go get our painting on."

Chapter Seven

After a trying week with my brothers, the last thing I wanted to do was go to my Sex Addicts Anonymous meeting—but the promise of seeing McKenna there forced my hand. I wanted to watch the way her eyes gravitated toward mine, and the soft flush of pink that warmed her cheeks when she spoke. She was a curiosity. A fun plaything to entertain me since I had to sit through the torture of being there.

I stepped into a pair of jeans and shoved my feet into my worn boots before making my way downstairs. Tucker sped past me, tearing through the kitchen with a bowl of cereal in hand, sloshing milk on the wooden floor right at my feet. He beelined it for the TV to watch his Saturday morning cartoons. It was the only time I let him eat in front of the television, so instead of scolding him for the spilled milk, I dropped a kitchen rag to the floor and began mopping it up with my foot. The TV switched on and a roar of canned laughter came from the other room as I flung the milk-soaked cloth into the sink.

Our house wasn't clean. It wasn't organized. But we tried to keep it somewhat tidy. We each took turns washing the dishes and doing the laundry. The floors weren't mopped and the bathroom was often neglected, but we managed. We had clean dishes to eat from and fresh clothes to wear. It was all we needed.

During the week while the boys were at school, I managed a hardware store, and at night I occasionally picked up bartending shifts for the extra money. It provided enough to pay the bills, but bigger things weighed on me—paying for college, buying cell phones, and cars for the guys. I had no idea how any of that would be possible.

I tried to push those thoughts from my mind as I drove to my sex addicts meeting. I would deal with one problem at a time. It was all I could do.

When I arrived, the chairs were already filling up in a semicircle around McKenna. I grabbed a paper cup of weak coffee and sat down just as she was getting started. Her eyes flashed to mine and a tiny smile lifted her mouth. She hadn't thought I would show up, and her relief was visible. I couldn't help but give her my best panty-dropping grin and watched as her chest and neck flushed pink.

McKenna's eyes dropped down to the notes on her lap and she took a moment to steady herself before beginning. "Sex addicts are very me-centric. Your addiction isn't meant to serve anyone else. It's a selfish pursuit. You get what you want, when you want it. And that's why it can be so difficult to break. You're not used to having to delay gratification. Today I want you to think about how you first became dependent on sex."

She paused for a moment, her gaze drifting around the faces in the group. I couldn't help but notice she deliberately avoided looking my way. Apparently I rattled her and she needed her composure to continue the meeting.

How did I become dependent on sex? I wasn't sure I could pinpoint when it happened, but sure, I used sex to numb my pain and manage stress. Listening to McKenna, I was starting to believe that maybe it wasn't totally normal.

"Over time, people develop a tolerance for sex. They need more and more of it to feel okay, and they experience withdrawal if they can't have it. Eventually, it can destroy your relationships—your marriage, your job. I know we've previously talked about being fired for looking at Internet porn at work, or marriages ending when a spouse discovered an affair. Your risky behaviors put you in danger for contracting a life-threatening STD. Or put you in debt, paying for strip clubs and prostitutes. None of these things lead to good outcomes. Can anyone share some of the techniques they've developed to work through their cravings?"

Shit. She actually wanted people to share how they avoided sex? It would be more useful to share techniques on how I seduced girls from nightclubs, coffee shops, the grocery store, or how to fuck standing up in a tiny bathroom stall. Doggie style. It was really the only option.

A timid girl directly across from me cleared her throat. "I count backward from ten and practice deep, calming breaths."

"That's great, Mia. Anyone else?" McKenna asked, looking straight at me this time.

I wasn't saying shit.

Watching McKenna was hypnotic. After our last little exchange, I hadn't been able to get her out of my mind, and seeing her in person, I completely got why. She was soft and pretty. Her voice was light, clear, and appealing. Listening to her and watching the way her mouth moved around her words penetrated my walls, reached deep inside me and went straight to my dick. I had no idea why she'd have such a profound effect on me—unless it was a simple case of wanting what I couldn't have. I wanted to unbutton her white shirt, push it open, and rub my fingertips over her nipples until she sucked in a deep, shuddery breath. I wanted to see what kind of panties she wore and break down her walls, like she was doing to me.

Holy shit. Maybe I did have a problem. I was sitting in a sex addicts meeting with a hard-on. I was pretty sure that couldn't be filed under *N* for normal.

But shit, I wasn't like these people. Was I? The fucking jackass next to me was dressed in sweatpants with a hole in the crotch, and he'd just spent twenty minutes confessing about how he'd jacked off in the car to porn downloaded on his phone before coming into the meeting. I scooted my chair farther away from him and caught a glare from McKenna.

McKenna continued providing prompts in the conversation and several more people opened up. By the time the hour was up, I knew far more about the people sitting around me than I wanted to.

A few group members still lingered as I approached McKenna at the front of the room, where she was leaning against a table near the window. I wondered if she was going to chastise me for not talking again.

"Still afraid to open up?" she asked, peeking up at me through thick lashes.

I wasn't afraid, but I knew what she was trying to do. She wanted to goad me into talking.

"I don't like this sharing bullshit in the group. I'm not saying I won't talk to you—I will. Me and you. Someplace else. Private."

She narrowed her eyes, searching mine. "You think you're the first guy in this group to hit on me? Not by a long shot. I'm here to do a job, Knox. That's all."

I chuckled. She thought I was asking her out? That was ridiculous; I didn't take girls out.

"Don't judge me. You and your charmed life you lead—you don't know anything about my life, sweetheart. And P.S. I'm here because I choose to be here."

"McKenna?" a tall, lanky guy called out from the doorway. "Everything okay?"

I looked his way, noting that I hadn't seen him in the group before, yet he seemed pretty familiar with McKenna.

"Brian? What are you doing here?"

"I thought you might like a ride home. Is everything all right?" His gaze moved between me and her, his expression radiating concern.

McKenna swallowed and glanced at me before answering. "It's fine." She nodded. "And I told you, I'm fine taking the bus."

"Are you sure?"

McKenna fixed her friend with an icy stare, sending her message loud and clear without words.

"Okay," he said, stuffing his hands in his pockets. "I guess I'll see you at home later."

"'Bye, Brian."

Brian nodded and left reluctantly, leaving McKenna and me alone once again.

When she turned to face me again, I could see judgment written all over her pretty face. I was beneath her. She'd labeled me and stuck me in some damn box. Hell, I knew I wasn't good enough for a girl like her, but I hadn't expected for her to actually call me out on it.

I fixed a sneer on my face. "Better go get home safe and sound, away from all us fuck-ups, McKenna." Then I turned for the door and strode away.

Chapter Eight

McKenna

I could not have handled that worse. I hated the idea that I'd offended Knox; that was never my intention. Maybe he'd been serious about opening up one-on-one with me—perhaps it hadn't been a pick-up line at all. And I'd overreacted. Horribly. A sour pit sank low in my stomach and settled there.

I noticed a small leather-bound notebook resting against the desktop where Knox had been leaning. Crossing the room to retrieve the book, I wondered if there was a way to find him, to apologize and return his journal. I should have just waited to return it to him next Saturday, assuming he came back, but I knew that wasn't what I wanted.

This group was supposed to be anonymous, but Knox gave his last name at the first meeting—Bauer. And his first name wasn't all that common, so perhaps I'd have some luck finding him. I pulled out my smartphone and typed his name into Google: KNOX BAUER + CHICAGO, and was rewarded with an address. A home in the South Loop, not too far from where I lived.

Since I hadn't yet gotten around to buying a car, I took the city bus to a stop that would let me off two blocks from his neighborhood. Along the way, my mind drifted to Brian and the overprotective nature he'd been exhibiting lately. I knew I needed to have a talk with him soon.

After moving to Chicago, Brian had interviewed at several accounting firms in the city and quickly got multiple offers. He insisted that he wouldn't have me living by myself in a strange city, and changed his entire career plan for me. Living here alone was part of the appeal, but of course I hadn't argued. I had someone to hang out with Friday nights or go to the Laundromat with on Sundays. It was nice. And he was someone steady I could rely on. I couldn't really complain; he looked after me and I wasn't naive enough to think that a young girl alone in the city didn't need a friend.

Of course there was a chance he might read things wrong between us if we lived together. Sometimes the way he looked at me for too long made me wonder if he and I were on the same page about our friends-only relationship status. But he'd insisted, and I hadn't refused, even though I knew I'd never reciprocate any deeper feelings he might have. Maybe he was too safe a choice—he wasn't broken—there was nothing for me to fix, so he held no appeal. But either way, I just wasn't attracted to him that way.

My thoughts drifted as I stared out the window of the bus. Cars whizzed past and tall buildings loomed in the distance. There was a whole bustling world out there that I wasn't a part of. My life had become something almost unrecognizable. I knew how I'd gotten this way: one tiny step at a time. A few months after I lost my parents, I began volunteering. The grief counselor I saw at school thought it might help, and she was right. Caring for others got my mind off my grief and reminded me that not everyone led a charmed life. I spent time at the soup kitchen, the homeless shelter, a center for special needs kids. It became somewhat of an obsession. It was my escape from the harsh reality my life had become.

My parents' deaths had been my fault. Not literally, of course; I wasn't foolish enough to believe that. But in a small way, I was responsible, and that was all that mattered. There was no un-doing what I'd done. They'd died in a terrible car accident at the hands of a drunk driver on their way to church one Sunday. I still remembered every vivid detail about that morning.

I'd wanted to sleep in, as I often wanted to do on Sundays. It became a sticking point for me and my mom. We'd fight every weekend because I didn't care about going to church. I was too old for Sunday school and didn't see the importance of going. We'd argued that morning, and I'd screamed at them from my room and slammed the door in my mother's face. They'd left late because of me, much later than usual, and when they drove through the intersection of Main Street and Fourth, the drunk driver was there, running the red light just in time to slam into the passenger side door, killing my mom instantly and banging up my dad pretty badly. He was airlifted to a nearby hospital and died from bleeding inside his brain two days later.

If I'd just been selfless enough that Sunday morning and put my own needs aside, I would have gone with my parents. They wouldn't have left late, and they'd still be alive. But they weren't, which was why I worked so hard to make amends for their deaths. It couldn't be all for nothing.

Glancing at nearby passengers, I brushed at my cheeks, wiping away a few tears that had sneaked past my defenses. I took a few deep breaths, willing myself to think about something different, and clasped the journal tightly on my lap.

The journal. I hadn't intended to look inside Knox's notebook, but the boring bus ride, a desperate need to avoid my own depressing thoughts, and my overwhelming curiosity were a lethal combination, and within seconds my fingers were itching to open its pages. I glanced around again at the passengers around me, like they'd somehow know I was snooping. But of course no one was paying me any attention. I took a deep breath and unthreaded the little leather tie securing the book, then opened the book slowly, as if it held a great secret that I wanted to savor.

Inside the pages was anything but what I expected. Outside it looked like a journal, but there were no journal entries. Just sketch after sketch of the same woman. She was incredibly lifelike and beautiful with long dark hair curled in soft tendrils around her shoulders, wide yet sad eyes, and a graceful neck that led to a delicate collarbone. The simple pencil sketches with smudges of gray and black against the stark whiteness of the page gave the drawings a gritty, realistic feeling.

I could almost see Knox bent over this notebook, pencil in hand, a furrow of concentration slashed between his eyebrows. I wondered who the woman was. A former lover? His girlfriend? For the first time, I wondered about the man beyond his sexual addiction. I knew from my training that a sexual addition was often masking some other issue. With Knox, I had no idea what that might be. He seemed healthy and in control. But perhaps that was just a mask he put on.

I was so engrossed in the sketches that when the bus rolled to a stop, I barely noticed. Startled by other passengers rising and exiting the bus, I quickly wrapped the notebook with its leather ties and joined them when I realized it was my stop.

Huddling into my jacket for warmth, I walked through the neighborhood, noting the older homes, likely built in the early 1900s. Most were in need of a fresh coat of paint, and some needed a whole lot more—new windows, a replacement roof, or even a bulldozer.

When I found the house that bore his address, I stopped and looked up at the three-story home to see peeling pale yellow paint, a slanted front porch, and a heavy wooden door. It should have looked cold and uninviting, but some unspecified characteristic gave it charm. It felt homey and inviting, even if it was a strange home for a guy who appeared to be in his early twenties. Maybe he shared the big space with several roommates.

Clutching the leather-bound notebook in my hands, I climbed up the front steps and knocked on the door. Voices sounded from inside, but no one came. I waited several long moments and knocked again, more firmly this time.

A young boy with messy dark hair answered the door. "Hi," he said simply, his smile revealing two missing front teeth.

"Hi. Um, is Knox here?" I asked uncertainly, all traces of confidence vanishing.

"Uh-huh." He turned from the front door, leaving it wide open, presumably for me to follow him inside. With my heart slamming nervously into my ribs, I crossed the threshold and followed the little boy, sensing that everything I thought I knew was about to be challenged.

The scene in front of me took a moment to process. Knox was holding a baby girl in his arms and two teenage boys were wrestling on the living room couch. With all the commotion, they'd yet to notice me.

Knox looked completely at ease with the baby resting in his strong arms, and she was happily engrossed watching the wrestling match, blowing bubbles and cooing at the sight. I took all this in within a matter of seconds, trying to place what exactly I was seeing.

All three boys looked like mini versions of Knox. Dark hair, soulful caramel-colored eyes, and all of them were tall. Even the little boy who'd answered the door nearly reached my height of five foot two. But the baby had me baffled. She had light golden-blonde hair that hung in tiny ringlets around her face and big bright blue eyes.

Knox and the other guys still hadn't noticed me, and the little boy who'd answered the door had busied himself with a giant pile of Legos in the center of the living room floor, while the others continued arguing. I took the opportunity to glance around at the rooms around me. The house was decorated with mismatched furnishings that had seen better days. But it was cozy and fairly neat. A large blue couch sat atop a woven brown rug and was flanked by wooden end tables scattered with papers and a baby bottle. A set of shelves held an array of toys and books, and straight ahead I could see the kitchen and dining room, along with a set of stairs that went off to my right. The home felt lived-in, not at all like my cramped, industrial-feeling apartment where everything was beige.

"Luke, Jaxon, cool it, would you? Grab me a diaper and some wipes," Knox said, hoisting the baby up higher in his grasp.

"Oh fuck. Do you smell that?" The taller of the two boys rose to his feet, sniffing the air. "We've got a code green!"

"Don't curse around Bailee, you dipshit." The slightly shorter boy rose from the couch and shoved the other in the shoulder.

I cleared my throat and four sets of expressive brown eyes swung over to mine.

"McKenna?" Knox asked, his eyebrows rising. "What are you doing here?"

A bundle of nerves rose in my stomach and lodged in my throat. The grand plan I'd hatched about coming here to face him suddenly felt immature and idiotic. He had his own life and responsibilities, and here I was tracking him down like a schoolgirl with a crush.

"I—" My voice squeaked and I started again. "I just wanted to apologize for earlier." I held up his notebook. "And return this to you."

His eyes searched mine and his face softened. The little girl in his arms let out a short cry, pulling our gazes apart. "It's okay, baby girl." He bounced the little thing on his hip to quiet her like he'd done it a million times before.

"These are my brothers. Tucker." He pointed to the little boy on the floor. "Jaxon and Luke." Jaxon was the next tallest after Knox, probably six feet and had longish hair that hung in his eyes, and Luke was just a fraction shorter. "And this is Bailee." He looked down at the little girl in his arms, but offered no further explanation.

"Guys, will one of you change Bailee so McKenna and I can go talk?"

"Hi, I'm Luke." The shorter boy offered me his hand and I shook it. His entire hand closed around mine. I'd guess that he and Jaxon were both in high school, and I also guessed with their thick hair and gorgeous eyes fringed in dark lashes, they were both popular with the girls. Just like their older brother.

"Hi, Luke. It's nice to meet you."

"Who are you?" Jaxon asked, his mouth in a crooked grin as he looked me up and down.

"I'm a...friend of your brother's."

"Knox doesn't have friends who are girls," he challenged.

My mouth hung open. I was clueless about how to respond.

Knox stepped between us. "Enough, guys. Go take care of Bailee." After handing the baby off to Luke, Knox turned to fully face me. I took in his chest-hugging thermal tee, dark denim, and bare feet. It was a side of him I wouldn't have guessed at. Softer, paternal. It made my stomach tighten. I was used to things in my life being neat and orderly; I liked knowing what to expect. Knox challenged everything I thought I knew, and left me wanting to piece it all together.

"Join me in the kitchen?" he asked.

"Sure." I waited for him to lead the way. I should have felt intimidated around him, with his broad shoulders and height, but I didn't. Seeing him around his brothers made me feel completely comfortable.

His jaw tensed as he noticed the boys still watching us. "On second thought, there's too many little ears down here. Are you okay if we go upstairs?" His dark honey eyes latched on to mine and I was rendered speechless. Join him in his bedroom? I should probably say no. But my head bobbed up and down in a nod.

Knox motioned me in front of him and I started up the stairs.

I could feel his hot gaze on my backside the entire way up the stairs. I wanted to spin around and catch him looking, but then what would I say? *Like what you see?* I wasn't that brazen, so I continued climbing while my body heated under his stare that I could feel all the way to my core.

When we reached the second floor, his hand went to my lower back with a feather-light touch to silently guide me, indicating that I should continue up the third flight of stairs to the attic. From the way his fingertips lightly raked against my spine, I could tell he knew his way around a woman's body. The thought both excited and frustrated me. How many women had he led up these stairs in the exact same manner?

I desperately needed to keep my perspective about why I was here. To help him as a member of my group. That was all. *Right, McKenna, that's why you haven't stopped thinking about him once…and bussed it across the city just to return a notebook.*

When we reached the third floor, the wooden planks creaked as I crossed the large bedroom, light streaming in on both sides from dormer windows set deeply into the vaulted ceiling. His bedroom was set up more like a mini apartment, with a sofa and TV on one side of the room, and queen-sized bed at the far end where the ceilings pitched their lowest.

I couldn't help but notice the half-empty bottle of whiskey on his bedside table, and the hole punched through the wall a few feet from his bed. A pang of unease about being up here alone with him sliced right through my middle. I didn't know him. Not at all. Yet here I was, alone in his bedroom. I'd never been so reckless and inquisitive, but something about Knox's quiet intensity pushed me outside my comfort zone. I wanted to learn everything there was to know about this troubled, beautiful man.

He motioned me over to the sofa and I sat down, my back straight as an arrow with the notebook resting in my lap. I wondered if his bedroom was where Knox took his conquests. I knew the darker side of this addiction and the impulsive behaviors that drove people to sex in public restrooms, alleyways, backseats of cars, and all sorts of strange places. But I didn't like the idea that Knox's attic bedroom, where I currently sat with him, might also be the place he lost himself in other women.

"Relax, McKenna," he whispered and smiled before sitting down

56

across from me in an old leather armchair.

I released a silent exhale and handed him the notebook. "You left this."

He took it from my hands, his thumb brushing mine and sending a small thrill up my arm. "Thanks." He waited, silently watching me, like he knew if he just waited me out, I would explain what I was really doing here.

I took my time, looking around the room, from the gray sheets that were tangled on his bed to a little desk that sat in the corner, complete with a stack of unpaid bills. My unease about Knox, about his life obviously so very different from my own, ratcheted a little higher.

"Did you look inside?" he asked, looking down at the journal in his hands.

"No," I blurted too quickly, my face flushing with heat. We both knew it was a hasty lie.

He untied the leather string fastened around the notebook and opened the pages to me, turning the book so I could see. He glanced up to watch my reaction, and I brought my hand to the open page, lightly tracing the shadows he'd captured so realistically under her wide eyes. She looked tired and so lifelike.

"You're very talented," I murmured. "She must be someone

important to you."

"My mother," he confirmed.

I met his eyes and smiled. He clearly loved his mother to devote so many hours to sketching her likeness. He flipped through a few of the pages for me to see, and then set the book on the table between us. Again, he waited for me to fill the silence.

My curiosity was too much. "So, Bailee's your…" I left him to fill in the blank.

"Neighbor's daughter. We babysit her sometimes for Nikki while she works. Plus it's probably good for her to have some male role models since her dad's not in the picture."

"Oh."

Knox cracked a lopsided grin. "You thought she was mine?"

"I wasn't sure. You seemed pretty comfortable with her."

He shrugged. "I guess I am. I mean, I'm comfortable around kids. I have three younger brothers I helped raise. And Bailee's here enough. She's a pretty easy baby."

"Except for that code green stuff?"

He shrugged. "It's good for the guys to learn to change diapers and warm up bottles. It teaches them responsibility."

"So you all live here…with your parents?" My voice rose on the question.

"Mom passed away seven years ago, and my dad took off with a waitress a few years after that. I have custody of the boys."

"Oh." Everything I thought I knew about Knox, the sex-addicted playboy, was lost in that instant. He was a man who worked hard and loved his family enough to step up and provide for them, putting his own dreams and goals aside. He was a real person, not just one of the bodies who filled a chair at my little group Saturday mornings. And now that I'd gotten a glimpse, I wanted to know more.

"So…" I looked around his room, my uncertainty about being here obvious. "This is your life."

"This is it," he confirmed. "Not what you expected?"

His raising his brothers and babysitting for a neighbor? No. Not at all. I glanced to his bedside table again, my eyes seeking the bottle of amber-colored liquor that sat there. I wondered what demons lurked just under the surface of his controlled demeanor. Why he needed the vices he did.

Perhaps we had more similarities than I realized. We were both on our own without our parents. Knox's load of responsibility was heavier than mine, but my guilt over how I lost my parents might have made up for that deficit. We were each wise beyond our years, burdened with things at a young age. Maybe we recognized that in each other. Something to draw us together. Because I certainly felt drawn to him. More than anyone.

Annoyed, I gave myself a mental kick in the pants, forcing myself to remember I was here to help him, not to pry into every facet of his life.

"Why won't you open up in group, Knox?" When he shrugged and made a non-committal noise in his throat, I pushed a little harder. "What are you afraid of?"

His gaze leapt to mine. "I'm not afraid. I'm just private. I don't particularly want to air my dirty laundry in front of a bunch of strangers. Can you blame me?"

"That's a very normal feeling. But most people find that once they cross that hurdle and open up, there's a certain comfort in knowing there are others out there with the same struggles. You're not alone, Knox. The first step is just admitting you have a problem."

My little speech was met with silence while Knox looked deep in thought. "How about this...I'll tell you some things that you want to know, if you'll do the same."

"You want to know about me?" I asked, surprise evident in my voice.

He shrugged. "Fair's fair."

If that would get him talking, I didn't see any harm. "I'm game. Who starts?"

"I do." Knox's dark eyes searched mine, and I fought a little shiver that prickled the skin at the back of my neck. "How did you become a sex addict counselor? Do you have experience with addiction yourself?" Interest flickered in his gaze.

I chewed on my lip again. The story was nothing as dark or interesting as that. The truth was the grief counselor I began seeing in high school led me down this path.

"I went to school for counseling and after I graduated with my bachelor's degree, I took a part-time position at a center for troubled teens here in the city. I had extra time, so I looked into what other opportunities I could get involved in, and I got linked up with this lady Belinda. She leads SAA and became my mentor. Then after a while of sitting in with her groups, I got my own group."

Sheesh, I was rambling, but something about the intent way Knox watched me while I spoke, looking between my mouth and my eyes, left me distracted and warm. I drew a deep breath, trying to clear my head. Knox was still watching me, waiting for me to ask him something. It was my turn.

"So…" I drew out the word, buying time. I could go for the obvious, asking him how he ended up with this addiction, but something told me not to push him. I wanted him to open up and feel comfortable, so I couldn't interrogate him from the start. I liked talking to him and I wasn't ready for it to end. "Tell me about your brothers," I said at last.

Knox leaned back into the armchair, crossing one ankle over his knee. Gosh, he was so big, so male, that it was impossible not to notice how completely he filled the small space between us. My pulse jumped and quickened in response.

"Tucker's eight and in the third grade. He's a good kid, listens to his teachers, and keeps his room clean." He released a heavy sigh. "He has an amazing capacity for love. He was so little when we lost her and when Dad took off, that I think he's the least affected by it."

Listening to him talk made me wonder what the little boy had been through. I couldn't imagine losing my mom at such a tender age, and then having to watch my dad run off and abandon the family. My heart ached for him.

"Luke is seventeen and he's a junior. He's smart. Like *smart*-smart. He wants to go to college and he studies hard so he can qualify for a scholarship when the time comes. And Jaxon…" He shook his head. "Jaxon is too much like I was. He's eighteen and will graduate in the spring. I thought I'd feel relieved once he turned eighteen, knowing that he could ensure the boys didn't get split up if something ever happened to me…"

He hesitated, and something in his eyes made me sad. I could see how much he worried about them.

"I'm sure he'd step up if he needed to," he went on. "But for now, he has no plan of what to do when he graduates, no job, no money, and he chases after girls just like I did at that age."

It surprised me how much Knox was sharing. As uncertain as I'd felt, I was glad I'd followed my instincts and came here today. Maybe he just needed someone to talk to. Not that I'd been thinking about my background in counseling a moment ago. I'd been thinking about his sad eyes, and the way my heart slammed into my ribs when he was near.

Knox grew quiet, like he'd said too much. His eyes slowly lifted to mine. "Your turn, angel."

Something about seeing McKenna in my space was surreal. I couldn't believe she was actually here, sitting in my bedroom. My messy-ass bedroom.

When she'd refused my offer for coffee, I'd seen the momentary indecision in her eyes. She'd wanted to say yes. But something had kept her from acting on it. So I'd left my notebook behind on the table, wondering if would propel her to find me. She had. And now she wanted me to spill my secrets, to psychoanalyze me. Too bad. I wasn't opening up until she did the same. I didn't know shit about this girl; I didn't have to tell her anything. She wasn't my court-appointed counselor. But if she took the first step, showed me I could trust her, I wasn't opposed to talking. Something about her intrigued me.

And now, after just a few minutes, I was sitting here spilling my guts like a pussy. I needed to switch us to a lighter topic. She wanted to be let in, but I was pretty sure she'd hate me once she really knew all of it.

Her back was still ramrod straight and she totally looked out of place. It was adorable and struck something inside me. I wanted to see her pretty, unsure smile again. "Is your boyfriend going to be mad you came here?" I asked with the hint of a smile playing on my lips. Her denying that he was her boyfriend would definitely make the alpha male in me happy.

"Brian?" Her brows pulled together. "He's just a friend."

"No boyfriend then?"

She shook her head. "No. No boyfriend. What about you?"

"I prefer females. I thought we'd established that was my main problem." Her cheeks flushed ever so slightly. "And no, angel, I don't have a girlfriend."

"Knox," she started, then stopped herself, chewing on her lower lip before continuing. "I'm sorry I'm here taking up your time, I just came to apologize for how I reacted today. I thought you were blowing off the group and trying to pick me up."

That might have been my intention at the time, but now it was anything but. McKenna wasn't like the girls I was used to. If I pressured her into going out with me, something told me I'd only push her away. And I wasn't ready for that to happen.

"I was serious about being more comfortable talking one-on-one versus in a roomful of people."

She nodded. "I get that. I'm sorry again. I figured it was a come-on."

I shook my head. "Not my intention, angel."

She frowned, like the idea that I wasn't coming on to her was a slight disappointment. This girl just got more and more interesting the more time I spent with her. I shifted in the chair so I was leaning a little closer to McKenna. Her scent was light and crisp, with the warmth of vanilla and a hint of soap. Not too overpowering, but subtle and pleasant. Just like the girl herself.

The stairs creaked and I glanced over to see Tucker peeking around the corner to spy on us. I'd purposefully left my bedroom door open; I didn't want any confusion over what was happening between me and McKenna.

"Would you like to stay for lunch?" I asked her. A healthy relationship with a female might be just the kind of normal thing my brothers needed to see from me. And after Jaxon's wise-ass comment that *Knox doesn't have friends who are girls*, I wanted to show them I did. Or at least I could.

McKenna met my eyes and nodded uncertainly. "Okay. That sounds…nice."

"Cool. But you have to help me cook."

She smiled warmly at me, a smile too nice and genuine for someone like me, and I felt a stab of regret about luring her into my world. Something in me wanted her, and that was very dangerous.

Downstairs, we found the guys rummaging through the cabinets and munching on handfuls of crackers and chips.

"McKenna's staying for lunch." I urged them to put the junk food away and motioned for McKenna to have a seat up on the counter while I gathered ingredients for spaghetti. It was a staple meal around here—inexpensive, easy, and filling. I piled a box of pasta, a jar of sauce, and a package of ground beef on the counter, then grabbed a skillet from the cabinet between McKenna's legs. She gasped at the unexpected invasion and I rose to my feet, smiling innocently.

"So, how do you know Knox?" Luke asked, looking back and forth between the two of us.

As she paused, obviously struggling to answer his question. "I met her at group," I interrupted, and she tossed me a grateful smile. I took the opportunity to study her again. Even I had to admit there was something about McKenna that seemed out of place in my life. She was wearing dark jeans that hugged her ass nicely, a white button-down shirt that looked really soft, and little diamond earrings. She looked sweet and wholesome.

Looking down at myself, I took in my worn jeans, a faded black T-shirt, and socks with a hole in the toe. My brothers were no better off. Most of their clothes were secondhand too. Not that we minded; we had what we needed. Something told me McKenna came from money, but I also had the sense she was more than okay slumming here with us. I just wished I knew why. Was she running from something in her life too?

67

After we ate, the guys headed outside to play basketball, and McKenna and I settled on the living room sofa together. She was different than I would have guessed—not at all stuck-up. She'd laughed and joked with my brothers while eating a big helping of my spaghetti, which was little more than overcooked noodles and runny tomato sauce, and then had helped with the dishes. And now she was sitting cross-legged on my couch looking delectable as fuck. The desire to kiss her shot through me like an arrow.

Knowing I couldn't do a thing about it was a special kind of torture.

"It's getting dark," Knox commented, looking toward the front windows.

Following his gaze, I noted the way the late-afternoon sun was sinking into the horizon, leaving the sky with an eerie glow. "Are you worried about the boys being out after dark?"

"No. They'll be fine." He was quiet for a moment, but still looked lost in his thoughts. "When night comes and everything is quiet…" He paused, reluctant to continue. I waited, holding my breath and hoping that he'd open up to me. "I realize it's just me, with all this pressure riding on me, and I need someone. Some company to make me feel whole again." He cleared his throat and looked down at his hands.

I didn't like nighttime either, but I wanted to know more about what he meant. "Is that why you go out at night?" I ventured.

"I need that place where I become numb to the world and can forget everything for a little while," he admitted, his gaze still fixed on the fading afternoon sun.

He was actually letting me in. Even if it was just a peek, seeing inside the mind of this man was like opening a window and sucking in a deep breath of fresh air. It was enlightening.

Nights were the hardest for me too. I wondered if that was part of the reason I found myself here, reluctant to go home. In the darkness, my guilt was its thickest. I lay in bed and thought about my parents, and the feelings of guilt and despair almost drowned me. But I'd never considered throwing myself at a man to make me forget. Volunteering was my escape. I lost myself in the servitude of others. I used their problems and misfortunes to remind myself that people out there had it worse. Perhaps Knox and I weren't so different, after all. He just medicated himself in a very different way.

He turned back to face me, his dark gaze deep and penetrating. We watched each other for several heartbeats while delicious tension swirled between us. I wondered what had happened to lead him here. I knew he'd lost his mother, and his father had left, but how had he become this lust-filled version of himself?

Watching his sad eyes, I thought I understood what he was saying about the darkness. It was the same feeling that haunted me. I didn't have bills and siblings to worry about, but my parents' deaths had left a hole in my heart. I couldn't stand to be alone with my grief, so I threw myself into work. Knox threw himself into the arms of women. We forced our pain away by chasing after distractions. Sleeping around was his version of my volunteering.

"Sorry, that was probably a weird thing to say." He shook his head, as if trying to clear the thoughts.

I wanted to take his hand, but instead my hand came to a stop beside his, not quite touching, but sending my message all the same. He hadn't pushed me away. And I wanted him to know I appreciated it, and that we shared more than he knew.

Turning to face me yet again, Knox's voice dropped lower, taking on a serious tone. "Are you sure it was wise coming here? Hanging out with me alone?"

"Why wouldn't it be?"

He swallowed, his lips moving in a distracting way. "I'm a sex addict."

My heart sped up as his words ricocheted through me. "Should I be afraid of you?"

"I wouldn't hurt you, but that doesn't mean I don't want to do some other things."

"L-like what other things?" I unconsciously leaned closer, drawn forward by his magnetism.

Knox let out a low, throaty chuckle and leaned back against the couch, stared straight up at the ceiling, and let out a heavy exhale. "Oh, McKenna." He patted my head like I was a naive little girl.

Maybe I was foolish and naive for coming here today, but I could handle myself. It wasn't like I was at risk for falling for this man, was I?

The trio of boys burst in through the front door, ending our strained silence. I could tell that Knox was as pleased as I was at their timing. Knox scooted further away from me on the sofa to make room for the littlest, Tucker, and soon we were in an intense racing game on their Xbox. They all took turns beating me and laughing at the way my entire body moved as I tried to steer my race car.

I had stayed at Knox's far longer than I'd intended, nearly five hours. The time had flown by, laughing and eating with him and his brothers. I hadn't felt this relaxed and happy in a long time.

By the time darkness fell, it was pouring down rain outside. I was going to be soaked through by the time I made it home, but I had to suck it up. Somehow I knew calling Brian for a ride would be a bad idea. He'd never approve of my being at Knox's.

Reluctantly, I stood up. "I guess I should get going."

"All right." Knox stood next to me and crossed his arms over his chest. "Are you parked out front? I can walk you out." Before I could answer, he grabbed an umbrella from a closet by the front door.

I slowly turned to face him. "No, I don't have a car. I took the bus here."

A crease appeared between Knox's brows. "You took the city bus here?"

I nodded.

"Guys, I'll be back soon," he said, turning to address his brothers. "Come on, I'm driving you home. There's no way I'm letting you ride the bus after dark."

Letting me? He had a commanding way with words, but it had been a long time since I felt concern as genuine as Knox's seemed to be. Even if it was unexpected, it was nice.

The interior of Knox's Jeep smelled like him—sandalwood and warm leather. We rode the few miles to my apartment building while I pointed out the directions. I liked watching him drive. His long fingers curled around the wheel as his denim-covered thighs stretched out before him, drawing my eyes.

When Knox pulled to a stop outside the building, I wasn't ready to go. Reading my hesitation, he turned to face me. "Should I walk you up? Make sure everything's safe?"

"No, that's okay. Brian's home." I pointed to the black sedan parked three spaces down.

"Brian's that guy who came to your meeting to pick you up?"

I nodded.

"You live with him."

It wasn't a question, but I could see the uncertainty in his eyes.

"Yes, but he's just a friend, my roommate."

"Are you fucking him?"

"N-no," I choked out. Suddenly I felt hot and uncomfortable in the small, dark space with Knox, off-balance at the abrupt change in his tone. Why would he care if I was sleeping with Brian or not? "Do you have a date tonight?" I asked.

"I don't date."

I swallowed. "Fine. Will you be requiring company later?"

"Yes." His dark gazed pierced mine, looking hungry and full of desire. "I can't be expected to watch you parade around in your tight jeans all night and not need a release."

It was the first time he'd mentioned that my physical appearance had an effect on him. And I'd be lying if I said I didn't like it. God, what was wrong with me? He needed help, not another girl throwing herself at him. Besides, I should feel disgusted; he had just admitted he was going out looking for sex after spending the evening with me.

"Good night, McKenna," he said, his tone final and dismissive.

"Good night." I climbed from the Jeep, sliding from the seat until both feet touched the ground. Without looking back I headed inside, the cool rain a balm against my warm, flushed face.

Chapter Nine

McKenna

It had been a week since I'd seen Knox. Never in my life had I looked forward to my Saturday morning group so much.

All week I replayed in my mind the time we spent together at his house. I had felt a pull inside me, an indescribable urge to get closer to him. There were so many layers to his personality, so many sides to him. I wanted to know each one, to turn him like a crystal in the light, to inspect his many facets.

Knox entered the room and a slow smile tugged at my mouth. With his messy dark hair sticking up in several directions, he looked like he'd just rolled out of bed. He was dressed in jeans, work boots left unlaced, and a plain white T-shirt with a gray wool jacket slung over his arm. He looked rugged and beautiful. His eyes cut straight to mine. The way he looked at me was overwhelming; I could feel that penetrating gaze deep inside my body. And I liked it way too much.

I all but collapsed into my chair, needing to sit to steady my nerves. That week's group session was about making amends for your past wrongs. Basically it was about getting right with yourself and others in order to move forward.

We spent much of the hour talking about sexually transmitted diseases, how to notify past lovers of bad news, and the courage that took. A few people already had recent tests completed, and spoke about how nerve-wracking it was to get their results. Most of the others agreed to get testing done, and we agreed to talk next time about how to handle whatever their outcomes might be. I had the contact information for an AIDS/HIV support group at my desk, but I hoped I didn't need it. Thinking like that was probably juvenile, though. These people had exposed themselves and others to serious risk, and I feared theirs might not all be good news.

Throughout the entire conversation, Knox was quiet and contemplative as always. I wondered about his status and if he'd also pursue the testing this week. Something told me probably not. At least, not without a little shove.

I ended the group by passing out information on the local clinics that offered free testing. Knox took the flyer, but stuffed it inside his jacket pocket without reading it.

After everyone else had filtered out of the room, Knox stood and stretched, his arms lifting above his head. The movement lifted his T-shirt several inches to expose firm, sculpted abs. A bolt of heat raced through me. I really needed to have this thermostat checked.

I wandered over to where he stood, summoning my courage. "Have you been tested?"

His eyes flashed on mine, seemingly surprised I'd questioned him so directly. "I always use condoms."

I felt a small measure of comfort knowing that information. Of course it wasn't enough, but it was something. "Condoms can break. You should be tested."

"I have no weird symptoms. No burning sensation when I pee. I'm good." He smiled, trying to turn this into something lighthearted, but I stood my ground.

"You have your brothers to think about, Knox. Do it for them." It might have been an unfair move, playing his brothers against him, but I knew that would get through.

He pulled the rumpled flyer from his pocket and looked down at it. "Come with me?" he asked, his voice barely above a whisper.

"Of course."

His eyes lifted to meet mine. "Now?"

I hesitated, then relented. "Okay."

We waited at the clinic almost an hour before they could see Knox. They were busy on Saturdays, but still, I was glad we were here. I worried that if we postponed this, he'd never come back. He'd tried to encourage me to get tested too, handing me a clipboard when we checked in, but I'd refused. Little did Knox know, my sexual past was all but nonexistent. We were quite opposites in that way.

When he emerged from the doctor's office fifteen minutes later, his expression was sour, and his posture tense. "Let's go." He didn't bother stopping to wait for me to put my coat back on, so I jogged after him, stuffing my arms into the jacket as I tried to catch up.

"What happened?"

He turned to face me once we'd reached his Jeep in the parking lot. "I did it, all right?"

"Well, what's wrong?" I knew he wouldn't get his results for a week, so I was clueless about his sour mood.

"They jammed a giant Q-tip up my dick."

I giggled, relieved that it wasn't something worse. "I'm sure you'll live."

"You think that's funny?" The line between his brow softened as he looked me over.

I put on a straight face. "Sorry. No. I just…I'm glad you did this."

"Come on, I'm taking you home. Besides, I'm sure you're off to do more good in the world after this."

I didn't argue and climbed inside the Jeep, happy with my little breakthrough with him. Today had been a victory and I felt proud, though more than a little worried about his results.

Chapter Ten

McKenna

Later that week when I arrived home from the teen shelter, I was absolutely starving since I'd missed lunch. I pulled open the fridge and surveyed its disappointing contents. Brian's micro-brew beer, margarine, and a bag of baby carrots that were starting to petrify.

My parents had left me money. I didn't have to live this way, rooming with Brian, buying just the bare essentials and going without a car, but up to this point, I'd refused to give in. I wanted to be stronger than that, to stand on my own two feet and not use the blood money from their life insurance policies or my father's pension. It would feel like cheating and only twist the knife deeper in my chest to have to rely on that money.

And so far, I'd made it. Chicago was far more expensive than I'd anticipated and my meager salary didn't go far. But even if that meant my diet was mainly peanut butter and jelly sandwiches and forgoing a new coat this winter, it was worth it. Some days I thought about donating it all to one of the charities I loved, but something always held me back. My parents worked hard for what they had. They would have wanted me to have it. So I left it in a trust, just in case. But I hoped I was never desperate enough to touch it.

Abandoning the fridge to scan the cupboards didn't provide much in the way of options either. I needed to get to the store soon. It was times like this I missed my mom. She was an amazing cook and would have whipped me up something delicious from the simplest of ingredients. That was her talent. It didn't matter if all we had was boxed pasta and shredded cheese. I'd have an amazing hot meal in front of me in minutes. Before I could decide what to do, Brian came in behind me.

"Come sit down, McKenna." His voice was commanding and I wondered what was on his mind. I'd paid my share of the rent, and had even remembered to mail the electric bill on time this month.

I sat down on the sofa and Brian lowered himself down next to me.

"Are you doing okay?"

I fidgeted under his watchful stare. "Fine. Just a little tired. It was a long week."

"You work too hard. You're always running, always on the go. It doesn't have to be this way."

I blinked at him, wondering what had inspired his little speech. "I like staying busy, you know that." It helped me. I would hate to think what I'd do with an entire day alone with my thoughts. I shuddered at the idea.

"I'm your family now." Brian's hand came to rest on my knee.

I no longer had a family. Brian might be a nice guy, but he didn't feel like family. Sure, we'd grown up together and I was totally comfortable around him, even in my holey sweatpants and my mom's ratty old slippers. But something was missing. It wasn't his shoulder I wanted to lean on when things got tough. The image of Knox cradling baby Bailee against his shoulder rushed into my brain. She'd rested her head on him and let out the softest little sigh. I hadn't felt that kind of comfort in ages.

"I could take care of you, McKenna. My job pays enough, you could stop working around the clock. You could just be happy."

I stared at him, dumbfounded. Happy? How could I ever be happy not working? And I certainly didn't do it for the money. Most of my hours were unpaid volunteer work. Brian didn't really know me at all if he thought that. His words reminded me that I had no one, no family, and a rush of wetness filled my eyes. Perhaps it was because I was starving and bone tired, but I couldn't handle this conversation right now. Silent tears threatened to overflow, so I excused myself to the bathroom where I could cry alone like the loser I was.

Ignoring Brian's hurt expression, I scurried away and shut myself in the small room. I locked the door firmly behind me, then closed the toilet lid and sank down. I had spent all day pretending everything was fine, that I was in control, but one tiny conversation about the current state of my life and I broke down, sobbing like a baby.

I'd taken my parents for granted, but now that they were gone, I realized just how much they meant to me. I was an only child, their miracle baby, since they were told they'd never have kids. It broke my heart even more for them. All the years of struggle, all they went through to have me, and I was so oblivious, totally ungrateful and self-centered in the years before they died. A voice of reason chimed in, reminding me a lot of teens were that way, but I forced the thought away. I deserved to feel every bit as sad and lonely as I was in that moment.

I wiped the tears away with the back of my hand and grabbed a wad of toilet paper to blow my nose. All day I had been cheerful and helpful, fixing a brave face firmly in place as I helped others. But the harsh truth was that I was totally and completely helpless.

Watching Knox interact with his brothers only reinforced what I already knew. Family was everything. Without one, I felt like I didn't fit in anywhere. And definitely not here in Chicago, with Brian as my only friend and pseudo family.

The crazy thing was, when I was near Knox that painful ache in my chest vanished. It was like his presence alone had some strange impact on me. I could stop worrying and planning my next move. I could just *be*. It was a feeling of total relief. Maybe the craziness of his life balanced out my own. He certainly had a lot on his plate and a truckload of issues to work through. Those were things I recognized. They made sense to me.

I was struck by the sudden realization that I wanted to see him. I wanted to spend time with him and his brothers. I wanted the distraction and company they provided. Their loud, messy household and camaraderie. A pang of guilt hit me as I realized it was for entirely selfish reasons, but I didn't care. Not enough to keep me away from him.

Making a plan in my head, I blew my nose one more time and splashed cool water on my cheeks. I straightened my shoulders and leaned over to inspect myself in the mirror, only to see splotchy pink marks had discolored my cheeks and neck, and my eyes were rimmed in red. *Crap.*

I dabbed on some concealer and ran a brush through my hair. If I was going to catch them before they made other plans for dinner, I needed to get moving and go buy some groceries.

By the time I left the grocery store, the sky was a pretty pink color as the sun was starting its descent. I was hopeful and excited for the first time that week.

Guilt had stabbed me as I'd lied to Brian about where I was headed, but something told me he wouldn't have taken the news well that I was going to Knox's. The label of *sex addict* was enough to immediately dissuade him from liking Knox. I was willing to suspend judgment. There seemed to be so many more sides to him.

I didn't even notice the cooling night air. A bit of chill would do nothing to dampen my mood as I strolled purposefully toward Knox's place. I hadn't realized how badly I'd needed to see him after lusting after him these last several days.

Anticipation gave me a little rush as I climbed the steps leading up to his house, balancing a big bag of groceries on my hip. I'd gotten a package of chicken, potatoes, bread, frozen peas, and a cake mix too, hoping it would be enough to feed all the boys. I briefly wondered if they were watching Bailee again, and imagined Knox smashing up some of the peas and potatoes for her dinner. Was she even big enough to eat vegetables yet?

As I started up the steps, it occurred to me how dark the house was. There were no lights burning inside and a pang of nerves hit me. I didn't know what I'd do if they weren't home. My entire mood hinged on getting to see Knox tonight. Not healthy, I know.

I knocked twice and rang the bell, but the house remained utterly silent. My stomach sank to my toes as I waited, hoping someone would answer. The tears from earlier threatened to make another appearance as bitter disappointment coursed through me. No one was home. I wondered if Knox was out with a girl right now and the idea stung.

A commotion in the street caught my attention and I turned. Knox and the two younger boys strolled up the street, cheering and hollering and generally being rambunctious boys. My heart jumped at the sight of Knox balancing three large pizza boxes in one hand, and Tucker hoisted up on his shoulder.

"McKenna?" Knox set Tucker on his feet and stopped directly in front of me. His large form overwhelmed me and even though I'd been hungry to see him, I now found myself a little unsure about showing up here unannounced again. "Is everything okay?" he asked, inspecting me from head to toe.

I liked the way his gaze slid over me way too much. He saw the real me, the one I hid from everyone else. He knew I wasn't here for anything related to the group. I was here because I wanted to be.

Knowing he could read my expression—I never did have much of a poker face—I lifted my mouth in a smile and held up the bag of groceries. "I came to make dinner." My gaze floated over to the pizza boxes he was holding.

"Tucker won his soccer game. We're celebrating with his favorite—ham and pineapple pizza. You're welcome to join us." His eyes appraised me coolly, as if waiting to see what I'd do.

"I...I don't know."

"Come on, who can say no to pizza?" He grinned and waved the boxes tantalizingly in front of me.

He was right, my stomach grumbled at the scent. Pizza with Knox and his brothers sounded perfect right now. Much better than taking the bus back home alone and sitting there with Brian watching me all night while he pretended to be working on his laptop.

"That'd be great." I hoisted the bag of groceries on my hip, immediately feeling better as my previous disappointment faded into the background.

"What's all that?" Knox tipped his head to the bag while unlocking the front door.

"I was, um…" *Spit it out, McKenna.* "Going to make you guys dinner. Sort of as a thank-you for inviting me to eat with you last time."

Knox's smile lit up his whole face. He peeked inside the bag. "You'll just have to come back another time then to cook this up."

"Deal." I breathed a sigh of relief and followed him inside.

"Jaxon?" Knox called, turning on lights as we crossed through the living and dining rooms en route to the kitchen. The house was dark and silent. I hadn't guessed that Jaxon was home. He hadn't answered the door when I knocked.

While Knox set the pizza boxes down on the kitchen table, I went with Tucker to grab paper plates, napkins, and drinks from the fridge. I rounded the corner just in time to see Jaxon shuffling a girl out the front door.

"Hey," he said, strolling up to join us at the kitchen table once the girl was gone.

"Who was that?" Luke asked.

"Lila," Jaxon said, offering no further explanation.

Knox didn't look happy; the easygoing attitude he had outside vanished as he turned to face Jaxon. "What the hell are you wearing?" Knox looked down at Jaxon with his eyebrows raised. "Looks like your jeans got into a fight with a lawn mower."

Jaxon's jeans weren't just ripped at the knees, they were practically shredded from the thighs down. I could easily see the print of his plaid boxer shorts. He grinned. "Lila can be a little rough."

"Go change. Throw those away. And I told you, I don't want girls here when I'm not home."

"Yeah, because you never have girls here, Knox. Your fucking bedroom practically has a revolving door. I'm surprised there's not a sign-up sheet out in the hall."

"Don't curse." Knox stepped closer, his posture tightening.

His eyes flashed to mine and I couldn't help but betray my curiosity. I chewed on my lip, wondering if what Jaxon said was true.

"Go. Change," Knox repeated. It was clear he didn't want Jaxon to say anything else to me.

As if remembering we were supposed to be celebrating Tucker's win, Knox hoisted him onto his shoulder before walking to the table. "You get the first slice, buddy." He slid Tucker into the chair at the head of the table and we all took our seats.

Over slices of pizza, Tucker recounted his victory to Jaxon and me. His entire face lit up when he talked about scoring his first-ever game-winning goal. As he chatted excitedly, Knox's gaze rested on me, watching me as I ate.

A tight knot formed in my throat and I had to remind myself how to swallow. While I sat reminding myself how to properly chew and swallow my food, I realized one thing. Knox was a good distraction.

Miraculously, for hours I hadn't thought about my parents, or my guilt, or my loneliness. Not once. Brian's earlier warning that I needed to get a life came to mind.

Well, this was me, getting a life. I doubted he'd approve of my methods.

Having McKenna here was strange, yet felt completely natural at the same time. I needed to keep it together in front of the guys, but I wanted to pull her aside and ask her why she came back. Once dinner was over, I sent McKenna into the living room to relax while the guys and I cleared the table. This was all new territory for me—but since she was a guest, she shouldn't have to clean up, right?

I carried the now-empty pizza boxes out to the garbage can and leaned against the side of the house, inhaling deep breaths of cool night air. It smelled like rain. I closed my eyes and tried to calm down. Why was she here? I never got rattled around a woman, but things were different with McKenna. Was it because she led the sex addicts group I was part of? No. I didn't think that was it. She made me feel aware and alive in a way I hadn't felt before, challenged things I thought I knew. She'd talked me into getting STD testing done, though I'd been adamant I didn't need it.

I'd be lying if I said I wasn't nervous for the results to arrive. McKenna thought I did the test for my brothers. The truth was that I did it for her, not for some altruistic purpose. I wanted her. Something told me if I pushed her, I could have her. And I'd never expose her to something I picked up from one of my exploits. I just wasn't ready to go there until I knew I could trust myself with her.

When I headed back inside, I found the boys in the kitchen cleaning up and jumped in to lend a hand, welcoming the distraction from the thoughts swirling inside my brain.

"So, what's McKenna doing back here? I thought she was just your counselor," Jaxon asked, looking down as he washed a glass in the sink. It was how guys worked. Sometimes we found it easier to have conversations when our hands were busy.

I bumped his shoulder as I pushed my way in to rinse. "She is. She's just my counselor. But she came to hang out too. That cool with you?"

"Sure. Why should I care?"

I could tell there was more to it than he was letting on. He'd brought it up for a reason. Maybe he was just curious about my having a normal relationship with a girl. Hell, I was too. I'd repeatedly told my brothers things weren't like that between McKenna and me, but apparently they knew my history with women too well.

"I like her," Luke said as he stuffed the paper plates into the overflowing trash can.

"Me too," Tucker chimed in. "She's nice."

"She's got a nice ass," Jaxon said, smirking down into the

91

dishwater.

Reaching back with a wet hand, I smacked the back of his head lightly. "Don't talk about her ass, dude."

Shit, he was right, though. Earlier when I'd watched her lift up onto her toes to reach the top shelf in the cupboard, her shirt had ridden up, revealing the milky skin of her lower back and a perfectly round ass I wanted to grip in my hands.

I'd fought the urge to walk up behind her and cage her in against the counter, and rub up against her like a dog in heat. It should be illegal to be that hot and be a sex addiction counselor. Seriously, they needed to outlaw that shit.

The guys wouldn't let me help clean up; apparently it was because they wanted to grill Knox about what my appearance here meant. Hearing him say I was just his counselor had stung. I was starting to wonder if I shouldn't have come. Maybe my being here was confusing.

I sat on the couch and flipped on the TV, wondering what to do. I hadn't felt like just his counselor. It had felt like hanging out with a friend. But apparently I needed to stop being delusional.

Soon the boys had finished their chores, and though Jaxon disappeared up the stairs, the others joined me in the living room. Before I knew it, I was surrounded on the couch by boys, Luke on one side and Tucker on the other. Tucker sat motionless, looking up at me in wonder. "You're really pretty," he said. "And you smell good. Like candy and soap."

"Thank you." I tousled his hair, running my fingers through the too-long strands. He was overdue for a haircut, but the look suited him.

He scooted his body closer and yawned. I patted my thigh and he laid his head down in my lap. My heart full, I reached down and pushed his hair back from his forehead, and he released a contented little sigh and closed his eyes. It seemed these boys were hungry for female attention, and it killed me to think they missed their mother so badly they were willing to accept attention from anyone. Even from me, someone they only met a couple of days ago.

After a little while, Knox went to help Tucker to change into his pajamas and brush his teeth, since it was clear he was wiped out from soccer. That left Luke and me still sitting together on the couch while the TV hummed quietly in the background.

Luke glanced over at me from his perch on the sofa, his expression all serious. "So, are you going to help my brother?"

"I'm trying to." I didn't know how much he knew about Knox's addiction. He knew that Knox saw a counselor, but I wasn't sure if he understood the full picture.

"Does that mean you'll be here more often?"

"I hope so."

"Me too."

After several minutes of comfortable silence, Luke looked over at me again. He was always so thoughtful and calm, his scrunched brows and creased forehead had me wondering what was on his mind.

"McKenna? Can I ask you a question?"

I wondered if it was related to my sudden presence in Knox's life.

And how I would explain it. "Sure, what's up?"

"It's kind of a private... You know what, never mind. It's stupid."

Now I was even more curious. "You can ask me anything, Luke."
If they didn't have regular access to a female in their lives, I wanted
to fulfill the role in any way I could.

"Well, I was just wondering. How do you, um, make a girl's first
time special?"

Oh my God. He was not asking me this. How the hell would I
know, with my utter lack of experience?

Knox had entered the room after putting Tucker to bed and he
glanced over at us briefly, acting disinterested, but I could see the
tension in his jaw as he plopped into the armchair and pretended
not to listen.

My heartbeat ticked in my throat and I fought to maintain slow,
even breaths. When I looked up again, I found Knox's eyes locked
on mine, looking straight into my soul. I met Luke's gaze again,
who was still waiting for an answer.

I gave him a little nod, as if I answered this type of question all the
time. "For a girl, her first time is really important. Probably more
so than a guy's." My voice was a little shaky and I cleared my
throat, starting again. "It's important to make sure she's really ready
and not just going along with it or feeling pressured."

Luke nodded, hanging on my every word. I didn't want to encourage him to have sex, but I also didn't want to counsel him too harshly and pretend this type of stuff didn't happen. He was a junior in high school, and many boys and girls his age were already sexually active. I couldn't turn a blind eye to that fact. Just because I wasn't getting any, didn't mean that other people weren't.

"Yeah, I get that," he said. "It's just, it's a lot of pressure on the guy to make it perfect, ya know?"

I smiled at him. It was sweet that he was worried about making it good for the girl. "No one's first time is perfect. Take your time, make sure you're both enjoying yourselves, and have fun. That's the best advice I can give you." It was the only advice I could give him, considering my own first time was over before it even started. I was a twenty-one-year-old virgin. A fact I wasn't necessarily proud of. Sometimes I felt like a freak.

"Okay, that makes sense." The crease in his forehead disappeared.

"Just be yourself, Luke. You're thoughtful and sweet. Oh, and make sure you have protection. And wear it."

"Yes, ma'am." His cheeks reddened slightly. "They give out condoms in health class."

I nodded. Curious, I wanted to ask him who the special girl was, but I thought more questions might make this conversation awkward and I didn't want to pry. "You can always ask me anything, I want you to know that." I smiled at him and patted his knee, all the while mentally cursing myself for implying I'd be around more, when the truth was I had no idea.

"So you know a lot about this sex stuff, huh?"

"Professionally speaking, I suppose so, but I'm not discussing my private life with you."

Luke's face broke into a wide smile. "That's okay, I don't wanna hear about my brother's sex life. Nasty."

"Your brother and I aren't—"

"I know." He smiled. "He likes you, I can tell." His eyes flashed on mine before he hopped up from the couch and retreated down the hallway.

What did that mean? Knox wasn't sleeping with me because he liked me? His logic seemed backward, but instead of trying to solve the puzzle in my head, I lifted my gaze to meet Knox's caramel-colored eyes, which was a big mistake.

I suppressed a hot shudder at the intensity I saw reflected back at me.

Fuck me. Listening to McKenna describe her perfect first time was a special kind of torture. My dick rose to attention, hanging on her every word.

She wanted a lover who took his time, and made sure she was enjoying herself? Sign me up. I'd gladly take the job, right fucking now. I wondered if she had enjoyed her first time. Given the chance, I would make sure she came and called out for more.

Even hotter than imagining myself in McKenna's little sex fantasy was watching the way she navigated a tough conversation with ease. I could tell she already cared about my brothers, and that did insane things to me. I had no clue whose virginity Luke was planning to take and honestly I didn't really care as long as he wrapped it up.

But listening to McKenna's advice, knowing she created a bond—a trust—with him to get him to open up, was pretty fucking cool. These kids didn't have a female role model in their lives. I was the closest thing they had to a mom or a dad, and I often did a shitty job of it. Especially with feelings and emotions. So it made me breathe a little easier knowing that they could rely on McKenna to fill that void. Even if it was just for now.

When Luke took off for his room, her eyes lifted to mine and I was overcome by a tight feeling in my chest as I watched her. Her cheeks were flushed pink and her breathing came in shallow little gasps. She was nervous and I had no idea why.

"I hope that was okay," she said hesitantly. "What I said to Luke. I don't want to overstep my bounds."

I got up from the chair and crossed the room to stand before her. Since it put my groin at her eye level, I was thankful my erection had faded. Even though things were purely platonic between us, there was a certain awareness we seemed to share when in each other's proximity. It grew stronger each time I saw her, and watching her now, seeing how her body responded when I was near, I couldn't help but believe she felt the same. We couldn't keep avoiding this chemistry between us forever.

Looking down at her, I couldn't stop myself from touching her, so I reached down and stroked my thumb along her cheek. Her skin felt incredibly soft, making me wonder if my skin, in contrast, felt rough and calloused to her.

Finally finding my words, I said, "That was amazing. Thank you for talking to him about that."

She looked up at me in silent gratitude and nodded once.

Reluctantly, I let my hand fall away and took a much-needed step back, trying to put some distance between the heat of her body and mine. Having her around, in my space, in these close quarters day after day was starting to become a challenge. I wanted her, but it was more than that—I didn't want to fuck her and move on like I normally did.

This was all uncharted territory for me, and I sensed it was for McKenna too. I needed to proceed with caution if I wanted to have a chance in hell with her. So I took another step back, watching her like she was an unpredictable wild animal I had no clue what to do with.

"What should we do now?" she asked, still looking up at me.

"Help me take down the fort?" I suggested.

I needed to do something to busy my hands before I disappeared into my room to jerk off. The box of tissues beside my bed was getting plenty of action lately.

McKenna's gaze wandered to the tent that was set up in the middle of the den. "Why is there a tent there?"

I shook my head. "Tucker. Bailee was over today and he thought she'd like it, but anytime he put her in there, she cried."

"Gotcha. Well, taking one down is easier than setting it up, right?"

"Right. Come on."

Watching the sway of her ass as she stood and crossed the room did nothing to help clean up my thoughts. I needed to relieve this sexual tension. If not with McKenna, then with someone else. And soon.

We sat side by side, collapsing poles and folding the tent while I thought about what to say to fill the silence that stretched between us. McKenna was concentrating on fitting the tent back into the bag, her tongue pressed into her lower lip as she worked. When she look up and caught me watching, her tongue darted back inside her mouth. I couldn't help but smirk.

When she looked at me, she didn't just look at me. She looked straight into me, like she could see into my soul. I liked being seen for the man I was on the inside, not just the fuck-up everyone saw on the outside. And since McKenna was here, it meant she wasn't judging me based on what she saw.

"Are you going out after this?" she asked, fiddling with the tie on the bag, deliberately avoiding looking at me while she waited for my answer.

"Why? Do you want to be my sponsor? Keep me on the straight and narrow?"

Her eyes met mine. "If that's what it takes."

"I wasn't planning on going out, no." I hadn't done that lately, and I intended to try to keep that record going. Actually, I hadn't done that in a while, despite what I let McKenna believe.

"That's really good, Knox."

Time for a new topic. I wasn't okay sitting here with a beautiful girl calmly discussing my last fuck.

I cleared my throat. "So, what's your story? Don't you have someplace you need to be?"

She flinched at my words.

Shit.

"That's not what I meant," I said quickly. "I'm sorry."

She shrugged, then looked away. "I heard what you said to your brothers. That I'm just your counselor. I'm sorry I keep showing up here."

"You are my counselor, but I shouldn't have said that."

She looked down, her confidence fading at my admission. Using two fingers, I lifted her chin. Her gaze slid intimately from my eyes to my mouth, and a warm feeling burned in my chest.

"What's that look for?" I asked, my voice coming out too thick. Her gaze slipped away from mine until once again my fingers under her chin reminded her not to hide from me. "You're beautiful," I whispered.

"Knox," she murmured, her voice a tiny plea. "I wish we'd met under different circumstances. My being your addiction counselor complicates things."

"Why can't I just be a man, and you just be a woman?"

"You're in recovery. I can't be a temptation to you."

I swallowed heavily. Too late for that. My balls were aching with the need to sink inside her.

"We all have certain wants and desires, McKenna. It doesn't make them wrong. We're only human."

Indecision flashed in her eyes and her gaze zeroed in on my mouth. If I had to guess, I'd say she was thinking about what it would be like to kiss me. It seemed that good-girl McKenna had a naughty side to her. Every ounce of her wanted that kiss. I could read it all over her, from her flushed chest to the thrumming pulse in her neck. I'd be willing to bet it had been a long time since a man touched her. Her body's responses were too obvious, and I could read the want and curiosity all over her.

I leaned forward just slightly, wetting my lips. She swallowed, her eyes tracking the movements. Angling my head to hers, I paused, stopping myself. Why? To prove a point. We were mammals, we reacted to the opposite sex. It was biology. We were born to breed, to reproduce. Men especially—to spread around our seed. Just the fact that I stopped myself proved that I didn't have a problem. Only I wasn't sure if I was trying to convince McKenna or myself.

She pulled back, just the slightest bit. "This can't happen, Knox."

"Then let me go about things the correct way then. Let me take you out. A proper date." As soon as I'd blurted it, I had no idea where that came from.

"I can't," she whispered, looking down at her hands in her lap.

"Can't or don't want to?"

"Isn't it the same thing?" She looked up and studied me with wide blue eyes.

"No. *Can't* means you won't jeopardize our professional relationship in group, and *don't want to* means you'd be lying by saying you don't feel this pull between us."

McKenna looked down and sighed. "Knox, don't do this."

"I won't push you. Not tonight. But we will talk about this."

"I should go," she murmured.

"Yeah, me too." I blew out a heavy sigh.

"You're leaving?" she asked, her voice wavering.

I shrugged.

"Where are you going?" McKenna rose to her feet, concern etching a line between her brows.

"Out," I said sharply.

104

"Don't do something you'll regret." She stepped closer and placed her warm palm against my chest.

She could probably feel the steady knock of my heartbeat, the indecision in my posture. But none of that mattered. I couldn't put myself in a position to get too close to McKenna. I wouldn't trick her into thinking I was somebody I wasn't. This was me. Rough around the edges and enough baggage to take down an airliner.

"Let me go, McKenna." I shrugged away from her touch.

"You know what, Knox?" she bit out, turning to face me. "Don't bother coming to group this week."

She left a few moments later and I was too wound up to even offer to drive her home. I felt rejected and angry. I wanted to put my fist through the wall. Instead, I checked to be sure all three boys were safe in their rooms, then shoved on my boots, grabbed my keys and a handful of condoms, and was out the door.

I'd pushed McKenna the slightest bit—just to test the waters—and she'd done exactly what I'd known she'd do. She ran. Left me with a pounding heart and a hot anger burning inside me that needed to be squelched. She might have been good at acting like she cared, but that was all it was. Some do-gooder act to soothe her conscience for whatever it was she'd done to deserve to counsel dickheads like me for a living.

Although I hadn't been here in weeks, I soon found myself pulling into the parking lot of the strip club, the neon signs bathing the dark interior of my Jeep in light, like a beacon pulling me forward.

I'd put myself out there, tried to go about things the legitimate way, and it had gotten me nowhere. McKenna was different, and I knew I had to do things her way if I wanted to be close to her. I was definitely willing to try.

But she'd turned me down without a second thought. It was always the same thing. Opening yourself up ended in rejection. Period. And tonight I needed a sure thing. The tension inside me evoked by being so near a beautiful woman and unable to do a damn thing about it had left me unsatisfied. I needed relief. At the same time, I knew that in the morning, whatever relief I felt would be marked with regret. But it was too late to turn back.

I entered the club and sank into the shadows, letting the bass-filled music drown out my own thoughts and reservations.

Chapter Eleven

McKenna

Realizing Knox was going out, that he was choosing his addiction over me, caused a stabbing sensation to pierce my chest. All I wanted was the safety and comfort of my own bed right now. I'd thought we were making progress. He'd invited me in for pizza, included me in their little celebration. The way he'd looked at me tonight when we were all alone told me he did feel something for me. But then just as quickly, his eyes had gone blank and he pulled back, closing himself off once again.

When I arrived home, I shoved my key in the lock and pushed open the door.

Brian rose from the couch, turning to face me, his expression pinched and angry. "Where the hell have you been? I called your cell six times."

Oops. I'd left my phone at the bottom of my purse all evening. There was no one I'd wanted to talk to when I was with the Bauer brothers. I smiled, remembering the way Tucker had curled himself against my side and Luke had opened up. Tonight had felt like something special. A tiny connection that I hadn't felt in a long time.

Knowing I was terrible at lying, I took a deep breath, dropped my purse on the counter, and turned to face Brian. "I was over at Knox's, having dinner."

His eyes widened and his jaw dropped open. "Are you insane? You went to that—that animal's house? Alone?" I'd made the mistake of mentioning Knox's name after Brian had seen me talking to him after group. "Do you have any idea what could have happened— what does happen to girls like you? Watch the evening news more often, because that was stupid and reckless."

"Girls like me?" My hand went defensively to my hip.

"Yes, girls like you—young, attractive, and sweet. What were you thinking, McKenna? Oh, let me guess, you thought you could get through to him, put him back together?" He huffed out an exasperated breath, like my helping someone was the most absurd thing he'd ever heard. I wanted to point out that I had a degree in counseling, but knew that wouldn't help my cause.

"We weren't alone. He lives with his brothers."

"Oh, that makes me feel so much better." His voice dripped in sarcasm.

"You're overreacting, Brian. Everything was fine." *Was.* Until the end when something in him snapped and he all but kicked me out.

"God, you're naive. I know you're trying to save the world and fix everyone and everything around you, but this is taking it too far.

I've tolerated your running all over the city, playing Miss Martyr, but this isn't healthy and you know it."

He's tolerated it? My heartbeat kicked up in my chest, my blood pressure jumping up. He didn't have any right to act this way.

"You could have been hurt," he said, softer this time.

"Yeah, well I wasn't." Not physically, anyway. "Stop acting like an overprotective older brother, Brian. Everything's under control." I pushed past him on my way to my room.

"That's all you see me as, isn't it?" he asked, his voice dropping an octave lower.

Rather than begin a conversation I so didn't want to have, I closed my bedroom door and mumbled a good-night in his direction. I was supposed to be getting my life together. Taking this job, moving to the city, all of it was supposed to be my fresh start. My do-over. Instead I felt more confused and alone than ever.

I regretted how I'd handled things with Knox tonight. I drove him away, told him not to come back to group. My feelings were too tangled up to properly be his counselor. I knew I was treating him different from anyone else. For all I knew, they could all be carrying on relations outside of class. I was holding him to a higher standard because I liked him. And I wanted him to like me back.

God, I was pathetic.

I had to force myself out of bed in the morning. Some days were tougher than others, and after last night, I wasn't feeling particularly put together and ready to face the day.

I didn't know why the sadness hit me harder some days. Maybe it was PMS. Maybe it was the sting of Knox's rejection, but I sat up in bed, my legs folded underneath me, fighting back tears and wishing I could talk to my mom. Knowing my parents no longer existed in this world was too much to process. The weight of their deaths crashed down on me and made it difficult to breathe. I felt like a massive dinosaur was sitting on my chest. A feeling that everyone told me should have faded by now, but was alive and present. I just needed to keep busy to block out the pain. It helped me carry on when I no longer wanted to.

That was what I focused on as I laced up my tennis shoes and threw my hair into a ponytail. I was meeting Belinda for coffee this morning to discuss the progress of my group, and then I was headed to a shelter to volunteer. I couldn't keep running off to see Knox. He wasn't someone to rely on. He was sick and needed help, and I would help him the best I could. I had only myself to rely on. Which was why I'd signed up to be part of a cleaning crew, wiping down cots and mattresses, scrubbing toilets, and mopping floors at the shelter today. If that didn't distract me from thoughts of Knox and this dangerous game I was playing with him, nothing would.

When I arrived at Cup O' Brew, I found Belinda already seated in a comfy armchair at the back of the café. I waved to her, and then ordered a hot chocolate at the counter. I even splurged and got whipped cream, hoping the extra sugar would help elevate my mood.

My insides were burning with curiosity, wondering if Knox had gone out looking for a girl after I'd left. Of course he had. Why wouldn't he? And I shouldn't feel the things I did. It would have been normal to be worried about his safety, his health, his mental wellness. Instead I felt a combination of jealousy and regret. Maybe if I'd stayed and talked to him, he'd have chosen me instead of the path he went down. It was all I'd thought about since last night, and I had the dark circles under my eyes to prove it.

Carrying my paper cup, I crossed the room to meet Belinda.

"You look well." She rose and gave me a brief hug.

I was good at hiding how miserable and alone I felt. And at knowing how to apply under-eye concealer to cover up the fact I'd spent the night tossing and turning.

"Thanks. You do too. I love your scarf."

The truth was Belinda went completely overboard with accessories. Bright pink hoop earrings, a rabbit brooch on her sweater, a colorful scarf wrapped around her neck, and a giant purple handbag. It was enough color to give me a headache. I slid into the wide leather armchair across from her and took a sip of my hot chocolate.

"Tell me how it's going leading the new group."

I fidgeted with my cup, like Belinda would somehow read my thoughts and know all I thought about these days was Knox. "It's going well. I have about twelve regular members and occasionally get drop-ins too." I wasn't quite sure what she wanted to hear. Did she want updates on each individual and their progress?

"Good. And how about participation?"

"Participation in class is average. Some talk more than others, those who are quiet pay attention thought and often nod along." *Except Knox; he only shares when we're alone together.*

Belinda took a notebook from her giant purse and flipped it open to scribble something down. "And engagement with fellow group members? How's that?"

"Engagement?" I had no idea what she meant.

"Do they support each other, do they mingle after group is over and talk? Exchange phone numbers? Things like that."

"Oh. Um, no, not really." Most people fled the room as soon as the hour was up, like they were desperate to get away.

"It's something I'd like you to encourage. This is their group. They are there to support each other. It's your job to connect them, encourage them to build friendships inside the group."

I looked at Belinda, wondering how I'd accomplish that. My mind flashed to Knox again and I imagined partnering him up with Bill or Donald for sharing time, and knew that wouldn't work. But why was I even thinking of that when I'd told Knox not to bother coming back? Feelings of overwhelming guilt pierced through me, and I struggled to remain composed.

Belinda leaned forward in her chair. "We can provide the structure of a one-hour weekly meeting, but for most people that's not enough. They need a support system of others who care about their progress and success. It also teaches them there is a way to get their social needs met through healthy interactions, rather than just with sex."

She was talking about friendship, and suddenly I realized that I was that person for Knox. Before I ruined things, he was slowly starting to open up. I had hoped over time it would lead to his recovery, though it wasn't my motivator for spending time with him. The truth was, I liked him. I liked being near him. I didn't think Belinda would approve of that, though. Just the thought of telling her I'd been to his house, spent time alone with him, made my chest flush. No, I would need to keep that to myself.

"I'll work on it," I promised.

"Good. We'll meet again in a few weeks, and I want to hear about your progress and who you've connected in the group."

I made a move to get up, but Belinda held up a hand to stop me.

"There's one more thing. I'm sending a young woman to your group. Amanda's a little different from our usual case. I've been individually counseling her, but I think she could benefit from a group setting. She has a sex and love addiction. She looks for Mr. Right in all the wrong places. She even tried to trap her last hookup into a relationship by getting pregnant. It obviously didn't work out the way she wanted—she's now pregnant and alone and has come forward for help."

"How far along is she?"

"Three months. She's not showing yet, but I wanted you to know her background. She's about your age, so I thought perhaps you two might connect. Tread lightly with this one. She's fragile."

Join the club. Maybe I wasn't in any position to be giving out counseling advice with the state of my own life, but I nodded. "I will. And thanks for believing in me." Her faith in me made me feel even guiltier about my growing feelings for Knox.

But I needed to put that out of my mind. I was due at the shelter and had a day of hard work ahead of me.

Chapter Twelve

As I lay in bed tossing and turning, I worked over and over again in my mind what had happened between me and McKenna. I shouldn't want her. I wasn't the right man for her. She should be with someone educated, polite, and well-mannered. Not some asshole like me who had experienced enough loss to turn my heart into a hollow drum.

I knew one thing for sure—I wasn't good enough for her. And I'd been stupid to even fantasize that I might be. Last night had cemented the deal; she'd run and I had too. Straight into the arms of a stripper. Temporary bliss was all I had these days. Finding a willing, wet girl to sink into provided twenty minutes of mind-numbing sensation, and I couldn't give that up. Going out a couple of nights a week was my distraction. And thoughts of McKenna were starting to interfere with that. She was dangerous. I'd turned off my emotions a long time ago as my only source of protection, and I couldn't have her tearing those walls down.

But morning light brought a fresh perspective to everything and I wanted her. Why deny myself?

Tracking her down was harder than I thought it would be. Her asshole of a roommate hadn't wanted to help me; that was crystal clear. He looked at me through squinted eyes, presumably guessing that all I wanted was to get inside her panties. And while that might have been true, today I actually just wanted to apologize.

She'd taken a chance coming over last night, groceries in hand, offering to cook for us. I couldn't remember the last time someone had done anything like that for us. Not since my mother. And when I realized that I couldn't get what I wanted—her—I'd gone all macho caveman, running her out and heading to my old stomping grounds.

Little good it had done me. I'd sat there sulking like a pussy, unable to stop thinking about her, until I'd finally just gone home and crawled into bed alone.

But after I applied some pressure this morning, Brian had finally told me that she was volunteering at a shelter today, and said good luck finding her. It turned out the city of Chicago had dozens of shelters. I'd visited six of them already and was almost about to call off my mission when lucky number seven turned out to be the right one.

Letting myself inside the front doors, I was struck with the stench of sweat and mildew. I approached a woman seated behind what appeared to be bulletproof glass. This was the place McKenna came in her free time?

"Can I help you?" she asked.

"Yeah, I'm looking for a girl named McKenna. Is she here today?"

"I'm sorry, I can't tell you that." She crossed her arms over her chest.

I thought about describing her to the woman, but realized there'd be no way I could do that without sounding like a prick. *She's the perfect height to fit against me, curves that would bring a man to his knees, an ass you just want to admire, and tits to fit perfectly in the palm of your hand.*

So I lied. "I'm here to volunteer with my friend McKenna, but I'm not sure which shelter she's at today."

"Oh. You're here to volunteer? Well, come on then. I'll take you to her." The woman rose to her feet and motioned for me to follow her to a door just down the hall. Seconds later, it opened and I followed her inside. She led me through a series of hallways, and we passed by a large commercial kitchen and several bathrooms before finally entering a huge room filled with stacks and stacks of cots.

McKenna was sitting on the floor in the middle of the room, a bucket of soapy water at her side, wiping down a cot with a sponge. The woman turned and left me there at the entrance to the room, just staring at McKenna. I was too taken aback to say anything just yet. Who was this beautiful girl who gave so selflessly, who worked tirelessly to serve others?

As I watched her scrubbing down the cot, I was struck with the realization that McKenna was a good person, a rare find these days.

She looked so tiny and out of place in this dirty, windowless room on her hands and knees cleaning up other people's filth. Her hair was tied up in a hasty knot and her cheeks were rosy and pink from exertion. She looked like a blue-eyed, shimmering-haired angel in these grim surroundings.

"Need a hand?" I called out, stepping forward to enter the room.

"Knox?" She rose to her feet. "What are you doing here?"

"I came to help out today. Brian told me where to find you."

"You talked to Brian?"

I nodded, not bothering to mention that he hadn't wanted to help me, or that he'd been a complete asshole. Uneasy, I stood before her and surveyed our surroundings. "So, where do you need me?"

"Why are you here?"

"I'm sorry for last night; I was an ass." I stayed quiet while she looked me over. She was waiting for me to say more, so I took a step closer. "I'm not good at apologies and heartfelt displays, but I truly did come here today to help out. If you want me."

She chewed on her lip in indecision and for a second I thought she was going to push me away. "Okay," she said.

"Okay?"

She nodded, smiling at me. "I'm glad you're here. And I'm sorry about what I said last night. Of course I want you back in group."

"Don't worry. I knew you were bluffing about that." I rubbed my hands together. "So, what's our task?"

"See all those cots?" She pointed to several six-foot-high stacks of cots lining the far wall. "We need to wash all of them."

"All of them?" There had to be hundreds. "And you were going to do that all by yourself?"

She nodded. Shit, that would have taken her all day. Didn't she have anything better to do with her time than sit in a dank room cleaning for hours on end for no pay and little recognition?

I couldn't really picture her prioritizing going shopping at the mall or getting her nails done above this type of work, though. This was just who she was. I'd spent very little time with her, and I already knew that. She was a giver. Would she be as giving and accommodating in the bedroom? A pang of lust jabbed at my gut at the thought. *Down, boy.*

"I'll get you a bucket of soapy water and a sponge," she said, heading to the exit. I couldn't help but watch the sway of her ass encased in tight denim. She really was beautiful. Even in her jeans and T-shirt.

When she returned, I was unstacking the cots and lining them up in rows so we could wash each one. The thought of McKenna doing all this manual labor alone made me glad I came. This was a big job for one person.

McKenna returned, setting the bucket down beside me and splashing me with warm soapy water in the process. I considered engaging her in a water fight, but decided against it. She took this work seriously and I would show her that I could too.

We worked side by side for the better part of an hour, making only a small dent in the work ahead of us. I wondered if McKenna was set on getting through the entire bunch, or if I could talk her into going out to lunch. Looking over at her, I knew there was no way she was leaving until the job was done. She worked without pause or complaint as determination blazed in her eyes.

Dropping my sponge into the bucket of water, I went to unstack another set of cots for us to wash, moving the damp ones to the far side of the room where they could air dry while McKenna went to dump out our buckets of dirty water and refill them. My fingers were already pruned and my back was aching from sitting hunched over on the floor. But I wouldn't complain. Not while McKenna was still working so adamantly to clean these beds for people she didn't even know, would never meet. I had no idea why this was so important to her, but I could tell that it was.

We fell into a routine, my moving and unstacking cots, McKenna refilling our water, and each of us washing in silence. Seven hours later and finally we were down to the last couple of cots.

"Oh, Christ." I swore, pushing the filthy cot away from me. Someone had deliberately buried this one at the bottom of the stack.

"What's wrong?" She peered over at me from across the room.

There was shit smeared on the cot in front of me. If she really expected me to wipe up someone else's crap, she was crazy. "This one needs to be taken out back and burned."

"What?" She laughed, rising to her feet and crossing the room to stand over me. "Oh." She frowned, looking down at the brown stains.

"Someone shit the bed," I joked dryly.

"Just scrub it off."

"Hell no."

"You change Bailee's diapers. What's the difference?"

I cocked an eyebrow at her. "She's a baby. Babies shit their pants, this is different. This is probably from a grown-ass man. That's a whole different ball game."

"Fine, I'll do this one." She dropped to her knees to kneel beside me.

"No way I'm letting you do that. We seriously can't just throw this one away? Surely they have a dumpster out back."

121

"Knox, we're not throwing away the poop cot. It'll come clean. They're short on cots as it is."

Fuck me, the things I'd do for this girl. I soaked the sponge in soapy water and began scrubbing at the cot, fighting back the gagging in my throat.

When I was done, she giggled and said, "That wasn't so bad, was it?"

"I need a shower."

"They have showers here."

I rolled my eyes. The idea of showering here made me feel even dirtier somehow. "Come on. We're going out."

"We are? I was going to find the director and see if I could help with anything else."

"McKenna, we've been here all day. My hands are pruned, my knees are sore from kneeling on a concrete floor, and I was just subjected to human feces. We're leaving."

She giggled again. "Okay, I suppose you're right. We did enough for one day."

I was about to correct her and let her know I'd done enough for a lifetime, but I didn't want her to change her mind about leaving, so I shut my mouth and trailed behind her.

After a stop in the restroom, where I doused my hands, forearms, and even my face and neck in scalding hot soapy water, I waited in the hallway for McKenna in the hallway. While she washed up, I called home to check on my brothers and let them know I wouldn't be home for a while. When she emerged, McKenna had secured her hair in a neat braid hanging over her shoulder. How she could look pretty after the day we'd had, I had no idea.

Her eyes met mine and she tipped her head shyly. I needed to be careful about how I looked at her. I was watching her like I wanted to eat her alive. Hell, I wasn't opposed to it.

"Where are we going?" she asked as I led her out into the fading sunlight.

Chapter Thirteen

Knox

I held open the door for McKenna and we entered the small diner just blocks from the shelter. It was already after four, and after skipping breakfast and lunch, I was starving. Of course when I'd set out this morning to find McKenna, I hadn't known I was signing up for an all-day volunteer activity.

I asked the hostess for a table for two and noticed her gaze flicker between me and McKenna. Did she think we were here on a date? Shit, were we on a date? I never did things like this—take a girl out to eat. Even if it was just to a crappy diner. I hadn't done anything like this in years. Mostly because of the boys. I felt only mildly guilty about not being home when they got home from school. Something told me they'd approve of my being with McKenna, though.

McKenna surprised me by asking for a box of crayons at the hostess station. Then we slid into a squeaky leather booth and McKenna accepted her menu, smiling at me.

"What?" I asked.

"Thanks for helping today." She flipped over her place mat and began doodling on the back in purple crayon. The girl continued to surprise me.

I sensed that something between us had changed today. I'd shown her a different side of myself and put us on more equal footing. It wasn't what I had planned for my one day off from work this week, but I was glad I'd stayed and helped her. I couldn't imagine her doing all that alone today; she'd still be there. I knew people gave their time and resources to causes that were important to them, and I'll admit, it had felt good to give back today, but either McKenna had the soul of a saint, or her need to serve was something different.

"What drives you to volunteer, McKenna?"

Looking up from coloring, she chewed on her lower lip. "It's just what I do. I spend pretty much every free minute at the homeless shelter."

"You do this to avoid being at home?" If that dickhead Brian was making her uncomfortable, I'd head right over there and handle it.

"Not exactly. More like to fill my time. I don't like being alone with too much time to think. It's just…not good for me."

I wondered what worries could possibly be weighing on her mind. "What are you running from?"

She went back to coloring and I realized I didn't know much about this beautiful girl who sat in front of me. She grabbed the brown crayon and drew a two-story house, coloring in the windows with blue curtains, and then drew three stick figures in front of the house. On one of them she colored long dark brown hair and blue eyes, and I realized she was drawing me something from her childhood.

I watched her in silence, wondering if she was trying to give me a clue about her life. The thought of someone harming her rose the hairs on the back of my neck. Before she finished her drawing, the waitress delivered our orders—a salad and soup for her, and a burger for me. Setting her drawing aside for the moment, we dug into the food in silence, the weight of our conversation still hanging over us.

McKenna picked at her salad, using the tines of her fork to push a cherry tomato around the plate.

"What's on your mind?" I asked, wiping my mouth on the napkin.

Pretty blue eyes pierced mine as she hesitated to answer.

"Say it, angel."

"When I met you…I don't know. I could feel your pain and knew you'd experienced more than your fair share of trauma too. I felt connected to you."

I knew what she meant, but that didn't mean I wanted to encourage her attachment to me. I would only end up hurting and disappointing her. Even if I did everything in my power not to, that was my track record with women.

I pushed my plate away, my appetite all but vanishing. "McKenna, I'm not going to deny that we have a connection. We do."

"But?" she supplied, a trace of sarcasm in her voice.

"But…I fuck random girls. I use them for sex. I'm not a good guy. You shouldn't be so nice to me."

"You've made bad choices. You've messed up. But you're not a bad guy. I see the way you are with your brothers, and attending group, that's your way of trying to get better. You're not going to scare me off so easily, Knox."

My participation in her little meetings was practically court-mandated, and honestly, the only reason I'd continued going was because of my attraction to her. The waitress appeared again, this time to collect our half-eaten meals.

"Will you tell me more about how this all started," she asked.

"What do you want to know?"

She shrugged, looking down at the vinyl-covered table. "Whatever you want to share."

McKenna passed me the box of crayons and I chuckled, flipping over my own place mat to the blank white side. "Is this some type of counseling technique, drawing out your feelings?"

"No." She laughed, her tone light. "I just like to color."

I plucked a crayon from the box, noticing it was pink. But I wouldn't complain about the choice in color. If this was what she wanted, I would try to get in touch with my softer side. I wasn't ready to tell her everything, but after the day we'd shared—scrubbing shit off cots—I felt more open with her than anyone else.

"When my dad left, everything fell on me. I got a part-time job and took care of the boys. It would have been easier to drop out of school and get a full-time job, but I was set on finishing up my senior year. I knew I needed to graduate or I'd never be able to really provide for them."

I scribbled something on the paper in front of me, not really paying attention to what I was drawing. "All week I went to school, worked, put food on the table, and at night, I made sure homework got done, supervised bath time, enforced rules and curfews. And I had to put up with strange looks at parent-teacher conferences and doctors' appointments. Eventually I applied for legal guardianship."

McKenna's eyes stayed downcast on her own page, which made opening up easier somehow. She passed me another crayon, green this time, and I continued drawing – little crooked designs that made no sense but seemed to calm me.

"By the time Saturday night rolled around, I'd wait until the boys were in bed and I'd go down the road to the corner bar, where they never carded, and grab a few beers to relax. Then I'd find a pretty girl to sink into to forget my troubles." There was more, but I wasn't ready to talk about it.

McKenna sucked in a deep breath, temporarily pausing in her drawing.

I wouldn't sugarcoat this. If she wanted in, I would let her see the true me, faults and all.

"I did what was expected of me. I take care of my brothers, pay the bills, follow up on homework. But at night, after everyone goes to bed, the emptiness and loneliness become too much. I need relief and that's how I seek it."

McKenna

I couldn't believe he was telling me all this. In group, he was all penetrating gazes and silent intensity. But one-on-one, he was making himself vulnerable to me. I was straddling the line between being me—a regular girl who was interested in a guy, and a counselor who wanted to help him heal. I had no idea which one of us would win out.

Knox slapped a few bills down on the table, enough to cover both our meals.

"I can pay for myself." I reached inside my purse for my wallet.

"Next time."

I didn't know if there would be a next time, but I nodded. "Okay."

"Should we go?"

"Sure." I rose from the booth and stretched, my back straightening reluctantly. I smiled, realizing I would sleep well tonight from the day's manual labor.

I figured Knox was going to drive me straight home after we ate, but he surprised me by asking if I would go somewhere with him. I blindly agreed without knowing our destination. When he pulled to a stop in front of a deserted playground, I waited, unsure of what we were doing here.

"Come on. This place has the best slide in the world."

I watched in fascination as he climbed from the Jeep and headed toward the playground. I'd never seen him in a mood so playful and carefree. He was captivating.

"Knox! Wait up," I called, jogging behind him. He sat down on a swing and I joined him, each of us toeing the gravel to gain momentum.

He looked lost in his thoughts, and though there were a million questions I wanted to ask him, I waited, letting him enjoy the quiet moment he seemed to be having. We swung side by side, looking out at the park.

"I haven't been here in almost twenty years," he said finally. "I must have been about three when my mother worked in this part of town. She used to drop me off at this Russian lady's house while she went to work. Sometimes after work when she picked me up, we'd come here before going home."

I realized with Jaxon being four years younger, Knox would have been an only child at that time. It was sweet that he had memories of just him and his mom. I wondered if thinking of her made him sad, like it did for me. We sat in silence, swinging until the sky was growing pink with the impending sunset.

"So is that the famous slide?" I asked, tipping my head toward the monstrosity.

There didn't appear to be anything special about it. It was an old rusted-out metal slide, but I could tell in Knox's mind, it was somewhere sacred he'd built fond memories with his mom. And I wouldn't question it. I had my own version of this slide built up in my mind too.

"That's her." He smiled.

"Well, I've gotta try this out." I hopped off my swing in the middle of its upward arc and ventured toward the rusty contraption. "Are you sure this thing is safe?" I climbed up the bottom rung of the ladder and stopped, testing my weight.

He shrugged. "Should be fine as long as you're up-to-date on your tetanus shot."

Scampering up the ladder before I chickened out, I plopped my butt down so I was perched at the top, my legs stretched out in front of me. Knox positioned himself below me at the bottom of the slide, and grinned up at me playfully.

"Come on down, I'll catch you."

I pushed myself forward, expecting to slide down easily. Instead, my jeans rubbed against the dull metal and I scooted about two inches. We both cracked up laughing. "That was anticlimactic." With gravity proving to be no help, I used my feet to pull my pull myself down, scurrying the entire length of the slide until I came to an unsatisfying stop in front of Knox.

"It was better when I was three." He extended a hand and I accepted, letting him pull me to my feet.

"Such a letdown," I joked, nudging my shoulder with his.

"Hmm." His eyes lazily traveled over me. "I'll make it up to you."

"Oh yeah? How?"

He pointed across the street from the park. "See that coffee shop?" I nodded, and he said, "I'll buy you a hot chocolate."

"Deal."

While we sipped hot cocoa at a little café table, Knox called home once again to check on the boys. I loved how dedicated he was to them. It almost made me feel a little guilty for hogging him all day. But there was no denying I'd enjoyed today immensely.

"I have something to tell you," he said.

"What is it?" I waited, breathless. Anytime Knox let me in was a small win.

"My test results came today."

"And? Did you open them?"

He nodded, smiling crookedly. "I'm clean."

Wow. "That's amazing news." A contented little sigh escaped my lips.

"I'm glad you made me do it."

It was the little moments like this that made my job so rewarding. Knox wouldn't have gone on his own, and I was happy that I was the one to encourage him. I was even happier at the results.

I drank my hot chocolate slowly, savoring it, almost like I was afraid to take the last sip because it meant our day together would be over. As it neared time to leave, both of us grew quiet as the easy mood from earlier all but evaporated. I remembered what Knox said about the night, and I prayed he wasn't planning on going out to one of his usual haunts to pick up a woman. That thought crushed me.

"You okay?" he asked, setting down his own cup as if he sensed my somber mood.

"Fine," I lied.

"I should take you home." He might have voiced the words, but his body language wasn't on board. He was leaning toward me, his elbows on the table and his gaze piercing mine.

"Okay," I breathed. It was dark outside, nearly eight at night. Logic told me I should probably go home, even if the rest of me didn't want to.

As we neared my apartment, a feeling of sadness settled over me. It had been a magical day. I'd expected to work at the shelter all day and then go home to have dinner with Brian. *Oops.* I'd forgotten all about dinner with Bri. I'd just tell him my work at the shelter ran late. Never mind this glow to my cheeks and lightheartedness from spending the day with Knox.

Rather than just dropping me off at the curb, Knox switched the ignition off and walked me to the door. We stood together under the little yellow porch light, watching each other. I couldn't help glancing at his full lips and wondering if they'd taste like chocolate.

Knox shoved his hands into his pockets. He was stalling. Neither of us was ready to say good night.

"McKenna, I—"

Before Knox could finish whatever it was he was going to say, the door flew open and Brian stood between us, fuming. His eyes flashed from me to Knox and back again. Something told me he wasn't pissed that I'd missed dinner; it was finding me here with Knox that had him on edge.

I shoved past them into the foyer of the apartment. "Geez, Bri, relax. I'm sorry I missed dinner." I tossed my purse onto the counter and felt a pang of guilt seeing the plate of food he'd prepared and covered in plastic wrap for me.

"Where have you been?" Brian shouted, coming in behind me.

Knox bit out a curse, his posture stiffening as he stepped in front of me protectively. "She was with me. What's the problem?"

"The problem?" Brian crossed the room to stand directly in front of Knox. He was a fraction shorter and with much less definition in his arms and chest, but you wouldn't know it by the way he was puffing his chest out, acting like a caged gorilla. "The problem is that I know what you are. I saw you at that meeting."

"What I am? And what's that?" Knox asked, casually taking a step closer.

"Not good enough for her." Brian tipped his head toward me.

"And someone like you is? Why don't you let McKenna decide that for herself?"

"I've been protecting this girl from cocky assholes like you for years, and I'm not about to stop now."

"Brian!" I hissed through clenched teeth. I wouldn't have him insulting Knox.

Knox dropped his head back, looking up at the ceiling, and let out a short bark of laughter. "You want her for yourself."

Brian lunged at Knox, pushing both hands against his chest in a hard shove. Knox staggered two steps back into our living room.

"Be sure you want this." Knox's hands curled into fists at his sides, and my insides twisted violently. "McKenna?" Knox's narrowed eyes found mine. "Go to your room."

No way was I going in my room just then. They weren't actually going to fight over me, were they?

Brian rushed forward again and Knox sidestepped him, instinctively drawing him farther away from where I stood rooted in place, my jaw hanging open. Brian wasn't violent; he wasn't a fighter. Not even in high school when most boys had raging teenage hormones, he was calm and in control. But I'd also never seen that vein throbbing in his forehead.

"You know why she's with you, don't you?" Brian taunted. "She's a fixer. Always has been. Adopting stray dogs from the shelter, stopping to help wildlife cross the road, befriending the new kids at school…that's all this is. You're a problem"—he poked a provoking finger into Knox's chest—"that she wants to fix."

Knox's gaze flashed to mine and Brian took that split-second distraction to haul back and land a punch in the center of Knox's cheek.

I winced as the contact threw Knox's head back.

Not wasting a second, Knox rushed Brian, knocking him to the floor and landing several punishing hits to his face and body.

"Stop! You guys, stop it!" I clawed desperately at Knox's shoulders, trying to dislodge him from where he held Brian captive. Brian landed a quick hit to Knox's nose, sending blood pouring from both nostrils. Frightened, I cowered on the floor, scrambling backward on hands and knees as big soggy tears rolled down my cheeks.

Both men caught their breath, their fight seemingly over. Knox's eyes met mine and I read his expression as clear as if he'd voiced the words. *I'm sorry.*

His shoulders down and his gaze fixed on the floor, Knox left, closing the door quietly behind him. There was something about the way he'd shut the door that stuck with me. Had he slammed it closed, I would have felt better. I would understand his anger. He was just attacked verbally and physically in my apartment by my

roommate. His careful exit felt like defeat. Not a physical defeat—
he could have taken Brian—I saw that in the power of his punches
when he had Brian pinned down. No, it was more like he knew
he'd lost me before we'd even started anything, and he was quietly
walking away and letting Brian win.

The thought didn't sit well with me. I wanted him to fight for me,
to pull me from this corner and wipe my tears, tell me that no one
and nothing would keep us apart. But he hadn't. It was all a twisted
little fantasy. Knox didn't feel for me the way I did for him.

I remembered the way blood had erupted from his nose, and
wondered if he was okay to drive home. Sheesh, I hadn't even
offered to help him, given him a tissue, apologized for the brutal
way my roommate had behaved. Knox had been nothing but a
gentleman all day, and he deserved none of what Brian delivered.

"McKenna." Brian stood over me, hands on his hips. "I know you
want me to apologize—"

"Save it, Brian." I leaped to my feet and grabbed my purse from
the counter, slamming the apartment door behind me.

━━━━━━━━━━

When I arrived at Knox's place, all was quiet and dark. The
front door was unlocked and I let myself in, not wanting to wake
anyone who might be asleep. A lamp glowed softly next to the
couch, but no one was around, on the first floor at least. I crept up

the creaking staircase, my fingers grazing the wooden banister as I headed to the attic.

It was dark and silent on the third floor too, and I wondered if Knox was asleep. It had been almost an hour since he'd left my apartment, thanks to the city bus schedule, and it was entirely possible he was already asleep in bed. The thought of finding him, shirtless and stretched out on the mattress, sent a little thrill through me. I promised myself I wouldn't ogle him. Okay, maybe just for a second I'd allow myself to appreciate the view. Then I'd wake him and check on his injuries. See if he needed anything and apologize for my psycho roommate.

Tiptoeing across the creaky wooden floor, I felt like an intruder. I'd probably scare him half to death. "Knox," I whispered loudly. "It's me." The room was so dark, I couldn't even tell if there was movement from under the covers. "Knox?" I flipped on the lamp beside the small couch for light. Glancing up, I realized his bed was empty. Knox wasn't here.

Realization struck like a whack to the side of the head. He'd gone out. After spending all day bonding with me, showing me a sweet side to him by working at the shelter, he'd still chosen to go out. I didn't want to jump to conclusions, but really, what other possibilities were there? It was late and his brothers were asleep. He'd told me himself, this was how he operated. I just thought I'd be the one to get through to him, and it stung knowing that my efforts hadn't made one bit of difference.

I sat down on his bed, hating myself for how betrayed I felt. It wasn't fair to Knox. He was in treatment. He was bound to mess up now and then, and tonight with Brian had probably been a trigger for him. I knew he didn't handle stress well—that he turned straight to sex. What had I really expected when he left my apartment looking broken and defeated?

And it had nothing to do with being outmatched by Brian. I'd seen the restraint Knox displayed, the tension in his shoulders as he held himself back from doing any real damage. He'd spared Brian, and the only reason could have possibly been because of me. Because of my friendship with Bri.

I remained on Knox's bed waiting for him. I would wait all night if I had to; I needed to make things right between us. When my eyes grew droopy, I lay down, curling on my side against his pillow.

The sounds of running water and rustling coming from the hallway woke me. I crawled from bed, groggy and wondering what time it was. Since I was pretty sure only Knox used the bathroom on the third floor, I tapped my knuckles against the door. "Knox?"

"Not now, McKenna," Knox grumbled from inside.

No way was I letting him patch up Brian's handiwork alone. "I'm coming in." I pushed the door open and entered the tiny steam-filled bathroom. Blinking through the vapors, I found him slumped on the floor, his head hanging in his hands.

He stared up at me with unfocused eyes. "What are you doing here?" he slurred.

"Have you been drinking?"

He chuckled. "No, officer."

"Knox, this isn't funny. You're wasted. Did you drive home like this?"

"Relax. People get drunk, and no, I walked home."

"Where did you go?" I assumed it was somewhere local, since he'd walked home, but I was too afraid to ask my real question—*What did you do?*

"I went out. Had a few drinks." He shrugged.

"And?" I probed. I had to know; even if it crushed me.

"And I picked up a girl, and I couldn't even fuck her. Is that what you wanted to hear?"

My breath stuttered.

He pushed his hands into his hair, tangling it in disarray. "Your sad blue eyes wouldn't leave my brain. I couldn't stop comparing your subtle feminine scent to her harsh perfume. Your touchable soft waves to her too-stiff curls." Looking up to meet my eyes, confusion and distress was written all over his features. "I don't know what you've done to me. You've gotten inside my head, fucked with who I am." The pain and anguish in his eyes hit me straight in the chest.

Part of me felt proud—I'd actually gotten through to him. But most of me felt sad. Knowing I affected him just as much as he affected me was harrowing. And I'd never seen him so devastated and needy. It tugged at something deep inside me.

The pull between us was too strong. I wasn't sure how much longer I could hold out. "I just came to make sure you were okay," I choked out.

"I'm fine. Let me drive you home." He rose to his feet.

"You're in no condition to drive." And if there was one thing I couldn't tolerate, it was drunk drivers. Not after the way I'd lost my parents.

"Suit yourself. I'm going to shower then." With the water still running he began undressing, right there in front of me.

I slammed my eyes shut. Oh God. Knox. Naked. My heart banged against my ribs. I should turn around and march out of this bathroom, but my feet were frozen in place.

The shower door opened and Knox cursed as he stepped under what I assumed was scalding hot water. "What are you still doing here, McKenna?" he asked several moments later.

I peeked open one eye, and then the other. Knox stood in the small glass-enclosed shower stall underneath the spray of water, not even bothering to try to cover himself. He was beautiful. All male with sculpted muscles and rugged good looks. He had a dusting of dark hair in all the places a man should, but I forced my eyes up, not wanting to wander any lower than his defined abs and completely visually molest him.

"I-I came to help." *To take care of you.* I swallowed the thick lump in my throat and when I met his dark gaze, something inside me snapped. Without thinking, I pushed open the shower door and was suddenly under that warm spray of water with him. My hands stroked his cheek where it was already swelling, and my fingers pushed into his hair to soothe him. It was my fault he'd gotten hurt and therefore my responsibility to comfort him. Not that being so near him, enveloped in his heat, was any great burden. I felt more alive than ever before under his dark gaze.

"Kenna," he groaned, his eyes falling closed. The tortured cry of my name on his parted lips was the sweetest sound. He stepped closer until our bodies were flush together, brushing at the tops of our thighs, our abdomens, our chests. My heart slammed against my rib cage at the contact. He was pure male heat and my body responded greedily.

Desire raced through my veins, heating me from the inside out. I knew this was a bad idea—the worst. Knox was drunk and I was… I didn't know what I was, only that I'd never felt this way before, and I wasn't about to give it up.

We were so close his forehead rested against mine and his lips were just millimeters away from where I wanted them. I'd never wanted anything more than this kiss. We'd been unconsciously building toward this moment since the first time I'd laid eyes on this sinful man. My body knew then what my head could not.

"Kiss me," I whispered.

"And what if I can't stop?" he murmured, his lips brushing against mine.

Pure carnal need like I'd never experienced before shot through me. In that moment, nothing mattered but Knox's hot mouth on mine. "Then don't."

Our mouths were so close that we shared each breath. I breathed him in with each inhalation I drew. The only sounds were my thumping heartbeat crashing in my ears and the spray of water cascading down on us.

His male firmness pressed against my belly and my breath stuck in my throat. Struggling to breathe, my chest heaved with the effort and brushed against his bare chest. His hands found the hem of my shirt and he lifted the garment up and over my head, slinging the wet fabric to the shower floor where it landed with a smack.

I waited, breathless, to see what he would do. His lips delicately whispered against mine, sending little tingles radiating from my parted lips all the way down to the long-neglected ache in my core.

Feelings I'd never known, sensations long dormant, suddenly raged within me, lighting me up from head to toe. I felt awake, fully present for the first time.

I noticed everything, his tender mouth barely brushing mine, the way his dark, hooded eyes roamed from my lips down to the top of my breasts, the way his bare chest glistened in the steam, the tiny water droplets that clung to his eyelashes, and most of all, I noticed my body. I'd never felt more sexual than I did in that moment, standing there in a soaking wet pair of jeans and white bra that was now see-through.

His lips brushed mine a second time and a tiny groan escaped my throat. I'd never imagined he'd be so tender, and the wait was killing me. Knox's mouth came down against me, his warm tongue lightly touching my bottom lip. I opened to accommodate him as my heart rioted in my chest. That little encouragement was all he needed. His mouth pressed hard against mine, his tongue rhythmically stroking, teasing me in the most intimate way. When my tongue matched his, the sensations sent me spiraling out of control.

I lifted up on my toes, wrapping my arms around his strong shoulders, needing something sturdy to ground me. I'd never been kissed like this.

KNOX

She tasted like sunshine and candy and fucking perfection. I was fighting with myself to go slow, but temptation whispered in my ear, telling me I could have her.

She'd shown up here out of the blue, looking at my bruised cheek like she was the one in pain. It had been a long damn time since I'd been babied, but hell if it didn't feel good. I wanted to feel her soft hands on me, feel her pretty blue eyes caress me like I was someone worthy. But even as my tongue played with hers, my dick rock hard and aching, my fingers itched to touch her, to unclasp her bra and push her jeans down her legs. As the alcohol started to clear from my foggy brain, I knew I needed to slow this down.

I shut off the water and stepped out of the shower, wrapping a towel around my hips and tossing another at McKenna. "Dry off."

Her wide eyes flew to mine, questioning, hurting, but I headed to my room. Dressing quickly in a pair of boxer briefs and jeans, I grabbed a T-shirt and sweatpants for McKenna. They wouldn't fit, but at least she'd have something dry to cover herself with.

That part was critical. My willpower was hanging by a thread.

I tossed the clothes on the end of the bed and turned to see McKenna barefoot and wrapped in a thin white towel across from me. The straps of her wet bra were still peeking over her shoulders.

She dropped her gaze to the floor. "I'm sorry I came."

I crossed the room, fighting the urge to take her in my arms again. "I'm not."

Her face lifted, her eyes full of questions and shimmering with unshed tears. "But you just left me in there…"

"Because I won't take advantage of you."

"You weren't," she whispered, her voice husky.

Christ, she was killing me and she didn't even know it. "I fuck up everything I touch. If you're smart, you'll leave."

She stepped closer. "I must not be very smart then."

Never in my life had I thought so hard about a kiss, but this was McKenna. She wasn't a girl to use once and throw away. She struck a beautiful balance of being both vulnerable and strong.

I knew I shouldn't, that I should dress her and drive her home, but hell, I wanted to taste her sweet lips again. Fuck, I wanted to taste a lot more than that. She was all I'd thought about all night. Cupping her jaw in both hands, I pressed my mouth to hers, trying to be careful, slow, like she needed. But then she was lifting up on her toes and pushing her fingers into my hair, clawing at me to get closer, and I went instantly hard.

When my tongue touched hers again, I stifled a groan. She was like crack cocaine and I wanted more. Wrapping my arms around her to secure her body to mine, the towel around her opened and fell away.

I wanted to admire her gorgeous body, but that would require lifting my mouth from hers and that wasn't an option. I used my hands to explore while my tongue stroked hers. One hand roughly cupping the curve of her ass, and with the other I trailed my fingertips down her thigh.

Her breathing stuttered and I braced my thigh between her legs to support her. She began rubbing herself against me, her damp panties dragging over my thigh again and again.

"Can I touch you?" I asked against her lips.

"Yes," she breathed.

Cupping the generous weight of her breasts in my hands, my thumbs grazed the peaks, which instantly hardened and puckered under my touch. McKenna let out a soft little murmur. The sound sent a jab of lust straight to my balls. My erection was straining against my jeans, barely secured under the waistband, and I took a deep breath, fighting for control.

Still riding my leg, seeking friction between us, McKenna let out a frustrated groan.

She needed more, but I couldn't let us go too far. "Can I touch you over your panties?"

Wide eyes met mine and she nodded slowly. Her look was pure

trust and adoration. She was giving me the keys to the kingdom, and I wasn't going to waste this chance. I would make this good for her.

I didn't want to ask her if I could remove them, afraid she'd say yes, and that I'd take things too far. Besides, the little scrap of fabric wouldn't prevent me from taking care of her. Securing my left arm around her waist to hold her against me, I let my right hand trail down her belly. Little goose bumps erupted over her flesh and her breathing became erratic and much too fast. I loved watching her reactions to even the simplest of touches, although we both knew where my hand was headed, and it wasn't someplace innocent. I wanted to watch her come, to hear her stutter out my name as she gasped for oxygen.

My fingers met the hem of basic white cotton panties and continued lower, past the top of her pubic bone until I felt her warm, damp center. Finding the right spot, I caressed the little nub in circular motions and went back to kissing her, moving my tongue in time with my fingers so I could imagine it was the tip of my tongue swirling against her clit over and over. McKenna's hips bucked against my hand and her head dropped back. I sucked and kissed her throat as incoherent mumbles fell from her lips.

Her fingernails bit into my shoulders, and she sucked in a breath and held it as her body built toward release. Passion burned inside me and I longed to take her to my bed, lay her down and sink inside her warm body. But for once this wasn't about my release, it was all about McKenna, and watching her come apart was the most erotic sight of my life. She bit her lip, her eyes closed, and her pulse fluttered in her neck. She was beautiful. I continued stroking her most sensitive spot over her panties until I felt her body clenching, preparing for climax.

I held her, kissing her, pleasuring her until she was quivering with her release. She let out a loud gasp and her breath stuttered. Her eyes fell closed and she breathed my name again and again as she came apart in my arms. I held her while little tremors raced through her body, making her shiver.

After several moments she blinked up at me.

"Hi," I offered.

"Hi," she answered, still breathless.

"I set out some dry clothes for you." I tipped my head toward the bed and released her.

She nodded and crossed the room to grab them off the bed, then headed into the bathroom to change. Even after what we'd just done, she wasn't going to change in front of me. She was surprisingly modest for someone who'd just gotten off riding my hand.

I killed the lights, then crawled under the covers and waited.

Soon McKenna was wandering toward me in the dark. Even the

lack of light couldn't hide the healthy glow I'd put in her cheeks.

She lay down beside me, curling into a ball so that we lay facing each other. We were both quiet, likely both processing what had happened between us tonight. We just lay there watching each other in the dim light.

I had no idea how many laws or rules I'd broken getting it on with my sex addiction counselor, and I didn't want to know. I'd done a whole lot of sexy shit over the years, but I'd never had anything get me as hot as what I just did with McKenna.

The anticipation of it, knowing how hard I've had to work to win her over these past several weeks, getting her to trust me and let go. It felt huge, and I was happy. Leaving her panties in place like that and watching her writhe against my fingers, knowing she was soaking wet and ready for me, it made me wonder how good she tasted, how pink she would be, and it had made me so hard.

And the craziest thing was, I didn't want to rush her. I mean, yeah, I wanted to pull her panties down her legs, but in a way, I didn't. I liked that next time there would be more for us to discover.

I was going slow with a girl. And I liked it.

The shower and our little post-shower activities had seemed to sober Knox up. He lay there quietly watching me, his eyes clear and focused.

"Thank you for letting me stay over tonight," I said. I assumed this was a big deal for him—a girl in his bed who wasn't here for sex.

"It's not a problem," he whispered.

"I'm sorry about what happened tonight with Brian."

"You have nothing to be sorry for. I really don't like the idea of your living with that guy, though."

"He'd never do anything to hurt me."

"How did you end up living with him?"

I took a deep breath. Knox didn't know the story, and since I knew so much about him, I was starting to feel guilty for never telling him. "I lost my parents my senior year of high school." I wasn't ready to explain how it had happened or my role in the events, so I didn't. "My mom was an only child and my dad's only brother, my uncle Bob, had passed away two years before of a stroke. My aunt Linda, who I'm only related to because she was married to my uncle, lives in California and I didn't want to change schools, so I moved in with Brian's parents to finish my senior year of school."

"I'm sorry about your parents."

"Thank you," I murmured. I didn't want to dampen the evening by thinking about all that, so instead I pushed on. "And when I moved here after college, Brian came with me. He didn't want me to live in a new city all alone."

"Nice guy," Knox muttered flatly.

I swatted at his chest. "Thank you for…tonight." God, what had I been about to say, thank you for that orgasm? I'd never had an orgasm like that before. My cheeks heated.

Knox chuckled. "You can have that anytime you want. No need to thank me."

I chewed on my lip, working up my courage. "Isn't that hard for you, though? I mean, doing that with me, having me here and knowing it's not going to go any further?"

He was quiet for a second while he thought about it. "Yes and no. Trust me, I enjoyed it, and as far as it not going any further…I can manage."

"I like you so open and vulnerable like this," I whispered.

"Yeah? Well, enjoy it now then. I'm never like this."

"I know."

"Do you?"

"Yes, you're normally so intense, and dominant."

"Do you even understand what that word means, McKenna?"

"I think so." A crease lined my forehead. Maybe I didn't really know. At least, not in the context of how he thought of himself.

"I am dominant. Sexually. Does that scare you?"

"N-no?"

He chuckled lightly. I hadn't meant my answer to sound like a question. It only showed how unsure I felt around him.

"Good night, McKenna."

"'Night, Knox," I murmured, feeling sleepy and warm. And safe.

Chapter Fourteen

McKenna

When I arrived home the following morning, I thought it best that Knox not walk me inside. I said good-bye to him in the car and ventured in to face Brian alone.

Just as I suspected, Brian was waiting for me. Probably waiting to ambush me. He flipped off the TV and rose from the couch, coming to meet me near the door.

"Did you stay the night with him?"

"Brian," I pleaded. My tone was a warning. He didn't get to act the way he did last night and then give me the third degree this morning. Besides, I didn't want to crush him or make him angry by confirming what he already knew. I'd slept in Knox's bed last night and it was one of the best night's sleep I'd had in years. I figured it was safer not to answer, so instead I released a heavy sigh.

"Tell me you're not stupid enough to fall for this guy. He's a goddamn sex addict, McKenna."

"Don't call me stupid." I pushed past him and entered the kitchen, grabbing the coffeepot and filling it with water.

"I'm sorry, I know you're not...it's just..." He rubbed the back of his neck, looking down at the scuffed tile floor. He looked tired, like he'd barely slept last night, and his face was pinched with worry.

It made my stomach cramp seeing him so distraught. Brian had always been there for me and he'd been a great friend for almost fifteen years. He'd messed up last night, but without him, I wouldn't have survived these past few years. I just didn't know why he was acting so ridiculous about Knox.

"I get it," he said. "You're a fixer, you always have been, and he's a project, but he's not like that cocker spaniel you found on the side of the road with a broken leg. You can't fix everything, and you sure as hell can't play house with him."

"Too late for that, isn't it, Bri?" I shoved the carafe back into the coffee machine and set it to brew. When I looked up at him, really looked at him, I noticed his lip was split and there was a bruise forming under his eye. Served him right for attacking Knox like he did.

Brian sighed. "I'm sorry I flipped out last night. I just don't want to lose you."

The sight of him and Knox fighting on our living room floor was burned into my retinas. I was glad neither was seriously hurt. Knox's cheek was still slightly swollen this morning, but nothing that a little ice and pain reliever wouldn't fix.

I tried to look at things from Brian's perspective. We'd moved here together and neither of us knew a soul, and now I was forming a relationship with another man. My anger faded just slightly. "I won't condone any more testosterone-fueled displays like last night. You're my best friend. Knox is my..." I stuttered, coming to a halt midsentence. What was Knox?

"He's your what, McKenna?" Brian challenged.

"Friend," I settled on finally. "So you have to be nice."

Stuffing his hands in his pockets, Brian nodded. "For you, I'll try. But just be careful with that guy."

"I will," I promised. I would be careful with him, I just hoped he would be careful with me too. I was terrified of feeling something real for him, unsure if he was capable of returning those feelings.

Chapter Fifteen

McKenna

The rest of the week passed quickly. Brian seemed to chill out a little, not mentioning Knox again and being overly helpful at home. He was trying to make up for how he had acted, though I wondered if his change in mood was because I hadn't seen Knox again.

Things had gotten busy at the center for troubled teens, and even though I only worked there part-time during the week, I found myself going in early and staying late. They were short staffed, so I'd added extra hours to my schedule without having to be asked. And since I still had my weekly commitments at the homeless shelter, soup kitchen, and others, I was exhausted at the end of the day.

Knox and I had texted a few times, and I wondered if both of us were subconsciously trying to slow things down between us after how heated they'd gotten the last time I saw him.

After sleeping in later than planned, I was running late for my Saturday morning meeting. The only thing that kept me from being really late was the bus had cooperated and been on time. When I entered the room, I found the members of our group already seated in a semicircle. Someone had even brewed the coffee. I breathed a sigh of relief. Everything was in order.

Crossing the room to the front, my eyes strayed to Knox. He'd turned to face the girl next to him—someone I'd never seen before. She appeared to be about our age, petite and very pretty with shiny coppery hair and big green eyes. Suddenly I realized that this must be Amanda.

Belinda was right. Despite being a few months pregnant, she wasn't showing at all. In fact, she had on a pair of skintight leggings that showed off how slender she was, and an off-the-shoulder white tee.

Tearing my eyes away from her, I realized Knox was still chatting with the girl and hadn't even noticed me. I slid into my seat and cleared my throat. Amanda and Knox ended their conversation, and I kicked off our session. But the little impish smile remained fixed on Amanda's lips long after her chat with Knox.

Somehow, seeing firsthand the effect he had on women bothered me even more than it should have. I wanted to separate their chairs, position myself between them, but of course I didn't. I just continued right on with group, trying to remain professional.

"Amanda, right?" I looked at the new girl and she nodded her head. "Welcome. I'm glad you're here." My voice sounded genuine, but if she was going to move in on Knox, that would change in a heartbeat. I would be the only one tempting him, thank you very much. "Why don't you introduce yourself and tell us whatever you're comfortable starting with."

"Sure. Hi, everyone. I'm Amanda." She looked around at the faces in the group and smiled. She went on to explain that she grew up in the foster care system, and no one had wanted her—or at least that was how she felt, and so she sought man after man to supplement those feelings. She used sex to cope—to feel wanted—if only for a short time. Then of course when it was over, she felt worse than ever.

It was a tragic cycle I'd heard before, and I honestly hoped I could help her break it. This work was hard, but I never gave up hope of actually getting through to someone. It made it all worthwhile. Amanda didn't mention her pregnancy, so I assumed she wanted to keep that to herself.

I moved on, asking what other updates people wanted to share. As Mia spoke about her recent breakthrough, I knew I should feel happy and proud. Instead I was struck with a sense of worry. The closer I got to Knox, the more I'd worry about his past with women, and if it was truly all in his past. The realization was harrowing. Would we ever really be able to move forward from the demons that haunted us?

The possibility that his sexual addiction could come between us terrified me. Would I be used and then tossed aside like so many before me? I was smarter than that, wasn't I? Brian's concerns had obviously gotten inside my head.

"McKenna?" Mia asked, her brows drawn together in question.

Twelve sets of eyes were peering right at me. How long had I been lost in my own thoughts? A quick glance at the clock told me far too long. Our hour was up, and a few people were already zipping up coats and jingling car keys in their hands. *Oops.*

"Thank you, everyone. See you next time."

Amanda turned right back to Knox, like she'd spent the entire hour just itching to strike up their conversation again.

Wiping the scowl from my face, I rose from my seat and went to the desk at the front of the room. As curious as I was about what they could be discussing, I forced myself to focus on something else. I wanted to talk to Knox, to tell him I hadn't stopped thinking about that night, but the more time that passed, the more foolish I felt.

Several minutes later, Amanda rose to her feet and slung her purse over her shoulder. She fished her cell phone from the bag and it appeared that she and Knox were exchanging phone numbers. A searing pain stabbed at my chest.

I shouldn't have been so hungry for his touch. It hadn't been my smartest moment. But I wasn't a normal girl. I was damaged emotionally and had felt so alone for the last few years that I craved physical touch. From a sex addict. A man like Knox wouldn't savor those simple touches like I did. He wouldn't be lying in bed tonight thinking about how his hand had felt brushing over my skin like I would be. He used women, took his pleasure and moved on.

Maybe it was time I did the same thing. I grabbed my purse from the desk and fled.

I dressed and ventured downstairs. Tucker was sitting cross-legged on the living room floor, watching a cartoon I knew he'd seen three hundred times. But his science project was done, so I wouldn't complain.

Jaxon and Luke were stationed together at the dining room table, and Luke was helping him with algebra. "Dude, what the fuck did you eat?" Jaxon asked, pushing Luke's shoulder to gain some distance between them.

"I don't know. I had Chinese earlier. Why?" Luke responded, sniffing his breath through a cupped palm.

"It smells like garlic and farts. It's fucking burning my nostrils, dude. Go get some gum or something. I can't concentrate on math when my eyes are watering."

Luke stuffed three sticks of gum into his mouth. "Happy?"

"Very," Jaxon said dryly.

"Guys, you're on your own tonight. I'll be at Gus's Pub till probably two. Call and order pizza." I handed Luke a twenty-dollar bill. "Lock the doors, and stay in. Got it?" They nodded in unison. "And call me if you need me."

I wondered if McKenna would still be stopping over, and what she'd think when the guys told her I wasn't here. I pushed the thoughts from my head. It wasn't my problem. We both probably needed to move on before things got even more complicated. I crossed the room and ruffled Tucker's hair to say good-bye. Then buttoned up my black dress shirt and headed out into the night.

Gus's was an Irish tavern that I tended bar at occasionally. Thursday nights were usually good for at least two hundred bucks in tips, and so when Rachel had called earlier and said they were short staffed, I'd jumped at the opportunity. We could use the cash, and I knew if I stayed in tonight, I'd end up calling McKenna.

"Hey, hot stuff." Rachel smacked my ass in greeting.

"What's up?" I nodded her way. She bent over at the waist, stocking the cooler with bottles of beer. Rachel was gorgeous and she knew it. She was tall and slender with long bleached-blonde hair and cherry-red lips. A series of girly tattoos made up a half sleeve on her right arm—butterflies, flowers, hearts, things like that. I was convinced a lot of our male patrons came in just to hit on Rachel.

"Sammy's out tonight and so is one of our bar backs, so we'll be busy. Hope you can handle it."

"I think you know I can." I'd been working here on and off for four years. I knew the place inside and out. Just because I didn't maintain regular shifts didn't mean shit. Tending bar was like riding a bike. Put a shaker and a bottle in my hand, and I knew what to do.

"Cocky much?" she teased, winking at me beneath thick black lashes.

"It's not cocky if it's true." I jumped into action, punching in at the register and grabbing a crate of glasses to stack beneath the bar.

The evening crowd began to filter in and take up seats at the bar and the nearby high-top tables. Rachel and I managed to keep up our easy banter while mixing drinks and pouring beers from the tap. She flicked a beer cap at my chest. "Hey, lover boy." She nodded her head toward the far end of the bar. "Looks like you have a visitor."

My eyes followed Rachel's stare to the end of the bar, where I spotted her. McKenna. Guilt burned in my subconscious for my actions the other night. I couldn't believe how far I'd let things go.

"Cover me for a second?" I called out to Rachel, already making my way toward the end of the bar.

McKenna looked completely out of place here. Her gaze darted around at the jostling bodies as her hands clutched at the shoulder strap of her purse, holding it securely around her body. When her eyes met mine, her expression softened just slightly. She stepped closer to the bar, sliding onto an open stool in front of her. The guy immediately to her left smiled and pushed himself closer.

When I approached, McKenna's eyes lifted to mine and she bit her lip, seemingly unsure about being here. Damn right, she should feel unsure. This place was a meat market and she was a delicious, juicy steak.

The douche bag next to her lifted his hand to get my attention. "Another beer and whatever this pretty young thing wants."

McKenna's eyes widened, as if she suddenly realized that coming alone to a bar might not have been the best call. But I wouldn't let anything happen to her.

I leaned closer, getting in the guy's face. "You're done here. I'm not serving you anything more, and you sure as shit aren't buying her a drink. I suggest you leave."

"What the—"

I slammed a fist onto the bar and the guy quickly rose and took off.

"Why'd you do that?" she asked, looking bewildered.

I wouldn't explain my actions to her. Not until she explained some things to me first. "Why did you come here?"

"Your brothers said you were out. I was worried you were—"

"Out drinking and picking up women?" I supplied.

She nodded.

"Nope. Just working." Christ, she was watching me with those pretty sapphire-blue eyes, looking at me like she was both hurt and disappointed. I turned to the guy next to us. "What can I get for you?"

"Bud Light," he called back. I cracked open a bottle and handed it to him, punching the order into the register to add it to his tab before turning back to McKenna.

"No freebies, honey. You want something to drink?" Rachel said to McKenna, suddenly standing next to me.

"She's a friend, Rachel. Back off."

Rachel laughed, throwing her head back. "Yeah, they're all your friends until morning. Right, Knox?"

Curiosity burned in McKenna's gaze as she appraised Rachel. Looking back and forth between us, I could see the wheels in McKenna's head spinning, wondering about my history with this feisty blonde. All it took was one little look from McKenna and I felt unworthy of her. This would never work. Why was she here? Didn't she get the memo after the other night? Unless she was back for more...

McKenna pulled her gaze from Rachel to focus back on me, and straightened her shoulders. "What time do you get off?"

"Two," I croaked, wondering what she was doing.

167

"I'll wait then. Give me a Diet Coke, please."

Rachel rolled her eyes and stormed away. Shit, I didn't know what her problem was with McKenna being here. As long as I did my job, she shouldn't care that McKenna was hanging out at the end of the bar.

"What are you planning to do? Stay here and babysit me, make sure I go straight home after my shift?" She didn't respond. In any other circumstance it might have angered me, but coming from McKenna, I knew her concern was genuine. "If we have any chance, you have to trust me, angel."

Her eyes flashed on mine. "Do you trust yourself?"

I leaned closer. "Around you? No."

Blush colored her cheeks. "I went to your house. I still owe you guys dinner, and when Luke told me you were here—at a bar— what was I supposed to think?"

"The worst, apparently."

Her gaze zeroed in on Rachel, who was still watching us with a scowl. "Have you slept with that girl?" She tipped her head toward the end of the bar where Rachel was polishing pint glasses.

Shit. "Once. A long time ago."

Her face fell.

"Hey…" I reached for her hand and brought it to my lips. "I'd be happy if you stayed tonight and waited for me."

She chewed on her lip, as if deciding.

The truth was, I trusted myself completely around Rachel. We'd had sex once, two years ago, shortly after she began working here. And despite her constant flirting with me, I saw it strictly as a one-time thing. If McKenna was willing to hang out here all night, I wouldn't deny myself the chance to be near her.

"Do you want me to order you some food? We have a full kitchen."

"Sure. What's good here?" She leaned toward me, settling in.

Just after one in the morning, Rachel told me to go ahead and punch out. The crowd had died down, but mostly I think she'd grown tired of watching me and McKenna steal glances at each other all night. Normally I'd feel bad leaving a coworker with all the end-of-shift cleaning, but I was itching to be alone with McKenna again.

I punched out in back and washed up before meeting McKenna. She slid off her stool and stretched. "Now what?"

I wanted to get her alone in my bedroom again, but I knew I needed to reel myself in before I pushed her too far. "Whatever you like."

169

"Can we just go back to your place?"

"The guys will be sleeping." I needed her to understand what she was asking me for. We'd be alone with nothing to distract me and no one to protect her.

She lifted up on her toes and leaned in until her lips brushed my ear. "I'll be quiet."

Blood raged south to my groin, making me instantly hard. "Come on."

Chapter Sixteen

McKenna

With my heart slamming into my ribs, I climbed the stairs to Knox's room, thinking about the first time I'd come here. Just like I could feel his gaze on me then, I could feel it now. Only this time, I knew what his hands felt like on my skin, what his hot mouth felt like moving against mine.

When I reached his bedroom, I wanted to be brave, to show him what I wanted, since I knew I wouldn't have the guts to tell him how I felt. Instead, I stopped awkwardly in the center of the room and stared at the big bed.

From behind me, Knox's warm hand came to rest on my shoulder. The heat from his body licked mine, warming me from head to toe. "Relax," he breathed behind my ear.

As if on command, my body instantly relaxed. This was Knox. He might have his issues, but he'd never hurt me. I opened my mouth to tell him I was fine, but let out a huge yawn instead. *Oops.* It seemed my body suddenly remembered the late hour.

"You're tired." Knox chuckled, coming around to face me.

I nodded. "I'm sleepy."

"Go lay down on my bed. I'm going to take a quick shower."

I obeyed, toeing off my shoes and padding across the room in my socks to crawl into his big bed. I pulled the covers around me and snuggled against his pillow. *Mmm.* That scent I'd come to love— sandalwood, leather, and male deliciousness—greeted me.

Sometime later, Knox crawled into bed beside me and I opened my eyes to watch him in the pale moonlight position himself on the pillow. He met my gaze and grinned. "Did I wake you?"

I nodded. "I dozed off waiting for you."

"It's okay. You can rest, sleepy girl. You're safe."

I did feel safe with him. Even the other night, things had only gone as far as I'd wanted them to. In fact, Knox had been somewhat reluctant, leaving me in the shower alone and dressing in the other room. Not that I'd had to convince him too much. His body had responded to the intensity between us just like mine had. His erection had been impossible not to notice. I hadn't been brave enough to touch him, even though I'd wanted to. In fact, it was all I'd thought about while lying in bed this week.

Knox was still watching me. He hadn't yet touched me, but he didn't have to. I could feel the heat from his body as his hot breath warmed a path across my skin. I nestled myself closer and he opened his arms for me, embracing me securely against his body.

"Knox?"

"Hmm?"

Losing my courage, I shrugged. "I'm not tired anymore." I wanted to ask him about his recovery, if he'd been abstaining from sex, but I knew I wasn't brave enough to hear the answer.

"What do you want?" He groaned, breathless.

Part of me couldn't believe I'd found myself in his bed again, tempting him. I shouldn't be here, even if it was exactly where I wanted to be. I didn't even know where he stood with his recovery. He kept that information closely guarded.

"Never mind. Maybe we should just sleep," I said, even though it was the last thing I wanted.

"You see, there's this girl who's making it a little *hard* at the moment."

When he emphasized the word *hard,* I giggled. "Knox?" I asked again.

"Yeah?"

I took a deep breath, drawing my courage. "How have you been doing with your addiction?"

He paused for several seconds, a long, awkward silence hanging between us. "I've cut back."

My stomach tightened into a knot. "Why don't you just stop?"

"Where's the fun in that?" he teased, poking me in the ribs underneath the covers.

"Recovering from an addiction isn't supposed to be fun." I arranged the blankets around me, feeling the sudden need to create a barrier between us.

"Who says I have an addiction? Maybe I just hang out with you on Saturday mornings because I want to."

"Your counselor, that's me, says you do, and I bet your brothers too if we asked them."

"McKenna…"

His tone held a warning, but I pressed on. "What, Knox?"

"I do what I need to do. Are you offering up your services?"

My breathing pattern changed. It was like my body forgot the simple process of drawing in air and releasing it back out. "I'm serious. I'm here, Knox. I believe in you, but…"

I swallowed down a lump in my throat. I couldn't take it to know he was still the same man he was before we met. I'd shared pieces of myself with him, made myself completely vulnerable, and I needed to know he was meeting me halfway.

"Listen, I'm not saying I'm a hundred percent, or that I'll never slip up, but I have been trying, McKenna."

My heart crashed violently against my ribs. It wasn't a promise, it wasn't any sort of guarantee, but nothing with him ever would be. I had to decide if I could accept that. My head said no, but my lonely heart was willing to try. I rolled closer, needing to feel the shelter his warm body provided.

Knox was trying. It might not be much, but knowing I'd inspired change in him meant everything. It meant maybe I was doing something right, that my hard work was beginning to pay off. As I lay there with him, warm and secure, I never wanted this moment to end. The vulnerability he showed me, his belief that things would turn out okay, it was all so fragile, but it was all I had.

Wrapping his arm around my middle to snuggle me in closer, his big palm came to a rest on my exposed hip, sending a tiny thrill zipping through me. My entire body buzzed with awareness. I wanted to pretend he was mine, that this was all normal—me and him alone in his bed. I wanted to touch him. We were so close, I could feel the heat from his skin and smell his scent—a combination of body wash and a slight hint of mint toothpaste. The urge to nuzzle into his neck and feel the stubble from his jaw scrape my skin rose up inside me. Instead I remained rooted in place, my breathing growing shallow and rapid as desire for him raced through my system.

I would never be able to sleep in this state. My heart slammed against my ribs, nearly knocking the breath from my lungs. "There's something I want to try."

175

"What's that?" he asked, his voice strained.

"Do you think I could…touch you?"

He swallowed heavily, his Adam's apple moving in the dim light. "You want to touch me?"

I knew this was hard for him—being physical without having sex—but maybe it was good for him too. Like stretching before a workout, he had to develop these muscles if he wanted to grow stronger, if he wanted to heal.

"Would that be bad?" I bit my lip, sort of liking the idea of being naughty after being good for so long. I wanted to feel his warmth, to make sure what I felt blooming inside me was real. That he was real.

"I'm pretty sure that would be really bad. One touch from you and I'd probably embarrass myself."

I pouted, though I was almost positive he couldn't see my expression. "What do you mean?"

He drew a breath and released it slowly through clenched teeth. "You have no idea how badly I want you. You're beautiful, smart, talented, kind, and good to your very core. Touching me will only taint you, as bad as I might want it."

He wouldn't decide this for me. Knox was a good man, despite his history. I placed my palm flat on his bare abs and felt him tense.

"Will you show me?"

"Show you?"

"What you like," I said, recovering. I didn't want him to know how inexperienced I really was.

"Fuck," he bit out. "McKenna, we shouldn't do this."

My hand curled into a fist, retracting away from him. "Do you not want to?"

He cursed again. "Trust me, that's not it. You get my dick so hard, but it's more than that. *You're* more than that."

My heart soared. Hearing him acknowledge that I was something special to him did strange things to me. And the fact that I turned him on despite my lack of knowledge…it made my heart pound like a drum and my panties grow damp.

Uncurling my fingers, I flattened my palm against his stomach and again felt his jerky inhale. I let my hand begin to trail south. A dusting of fine hairs tickled my palm as I lightly caressed him. When I reached the waistband of his boxer briefs, Knox sucked in a breath and held it. Not yet brave enough to feel him skin to skin, I brushed my hand against his erection and warmth flooded my panties.

I rubbed the length of his manhood as my heart thundered in my chest. My confidence growing, I rubbed him up and down, feeling

177

bold and powerful. He felt thick and long, and I wanted to see him.

"Kenna…" He groaned, sending a little rush of tingles skittering out over my skin.

As my endorphins kicked in, my inexperience no longer mattered. I felt alive, and I wanted this—to touch this beautiful, broken man, to be part of making him whole again.

My fingers edged into the waistband of his boxers and Knox lifted his hips slightly off the mattress, allowing me to pull them down and free his heavy cock.

Under the faintest glow of moonlight, I admired his body—his strength, masculinity, and the tender way he was watching me. He was making himself vulnerable to me, letting me take control and do things at my own pace. The emotional weight of the moment left me breathless. But then my gaze lowered and my breath caught in my throat. He was huge.

Curling my hand around him, I was surprised to feel how soft and smooth the skin was despite being rock hard and turgid beneath my grasp. As I ran my fingertips up and down the length of him, Knox let out a breathy groan. My core clenched. The idea of him filling me left me warm and achy. My palm slid lightly against him, gently massaging and caressing his considerable length as I savored the feel of him. Lightly rubbing smooth, hot flesh, I watched in fascination as he grew even harder.

Knox wrapped his hand over mine, increasing the pressure of my grip. "Like this." Our hands moving together, he dictated the pace of our movements until I was rhythmically stroking him from base to tip.

He released a shuddering breath and his head fell back against the pillow. "Fuck, your hand feels good."

My pace increased as I watched Knox's reactions. His warm breath puffed past his lips, his abs tensed, and his hand found my free one, intertwining our fingers. He pressed his palm to mine like he was sinking and I had the power to pull him back to safety. He gripped my hand and his dark gaze met mine. He communicated so much with that one look.

Emotion burned inside me. I was discovering him, but this moment meant more than that. We were healing each other in these little moments built on shared trust.

"Shit, I'm going to—" His teeth bit into his lower lip as his body went rigid. He growled my name as he came, milky-white fluid landing on his belly.

While our breathing slowed, Knox reached over the side of the bed for a box of tissues on the floor. He wiped my hand and his belly before curling his arms around me, caging me in. I melted into his embrace, loving the feel of his strong arms. He could hold me hostage in his bed anytime.

"Sorry about the mess," he apologized, whispering near my ear.

"I didn't mind." Watching Knox come apart and hearing his low husky voice growl my name had been worth it.

Meeting my eyes with an intense, passion-filled stare, he leaned closer, resting his forehead against mine. "You didn't have to do that."

I knew that. I'd wanted to. "Was it...okay?"

"That was fucking amazing." He pressed his lips softly to mine in a lingering kiss. "I like you in my bed," he whispered.

His admission meant the world to me. I kissed him back, my movements slow and deliberate, like every touch mattered.

During quiet times like this, I loved how open and exposed he made himself to me. I knew it was a side of himself he didn't share with anyone else, and that feeling was addicting.

Chapter Seventeen

Last night had been the most incredible experience of my life. I had slept soundly in Knox's arms all through the night. I smiled remembering our whispered conversation, and the way my heartbeat had thrummed so violently in my chest when I'd touched him. He was beautiful, and he wasn't broken like he thought. Then this morning was back to reality. We'd kissed good-bye early this morning. I wanted to go home to shower and change, and most importantly to arrive at our meeting separately. Even if I was breaking all the rules with Knox behind closed doors, I certainly wouldn't broadcast it in public.

I sat at my little wooden desk at the front of the room, having arrived several minutes early, unable to stop myself from daydreaming about him. The more time I spent with Knox, the less I noticed that hollow ache inside me. I sang in the shower, hummed when I cleaned the dishes, and felt lighter just knowing he was in my life.

But then I realized something even more terrifying than going back to my pre-Knox state. I was falling in love with him. With a deliciously flawed man I was supposed to be helping heal from sexual addiction.

Casting logic aside, I knew this was a dangerous game, and if I played I'd likely be burned. But falling for him hadn't been a choice. He wasn't just that haunted, intense man I'd glimpsed at first. He was different around his brothers, lighter, laughed easier, smiled that big smile that showed off his dimple. I liked that version of Knox. And I liked the version of myself when I was with him. I wasn't the broken shell of a girl I felt like most days. I felt vibrant and pretty and alive.

I wondered if my attraction to him was that our souls shared the same pain and loss. They could feel each other. When we were together I didn't feel any pain or guilt. I wondered if it was the same for him.

When he entered the room, my heart's rhythm changed, became erratic. His eyes met mine and while his face remained expressionless, I read the indecision, the confusion on him as clear as day. Did he feel guilty about what happened between us last night? It had been my idea to touch him, to push things further, and as much as I'd enjoyed it at the time, now I felt unsure and guilty.

Amanda patted the seat next to her, one that she'd clearly been saving just for him, and Knox crossed the room toward her.

Watching him and Amanda converse quietly, my stomach tightened and I felt hot. I was warm and flustered, and now I needed to start group.

I sat down in my seat and began the lecture I'd prepared. "Today we'll be working on openness and honesty with each other. We've been meeting for several weeks now, and it's time we progressed as a group. I'm going to ask each member of the group to share their progress, and this includes admitting to any slipups in a judgment-free, guilt-free environment. We're all human, and it's here that we don't have to hide."

I consulted the notebook on my lap to be sure I'd touched on all the key points I'd written out for myself. Knox watched me closely, his expression guarded and unsure. Guilt clawed at my stomach. I'd orchestrated today's entire conversation to flush out what he was too afraid to tell me. I needed to know.

I asked each member of the group to share how many days since their last sexual encounter. As each person spoke and Knox's turn got closer, my stomach coiled tight and nervous energy shot through my veins. Something was about to happen.

It was Amanda's turn next, so I forced my eyes from Knox, trying to be a good group leader and listen as she spoke. "I've been struggling with a lot of change in my life lately, and I'm not proud of it, but I slipped up last weekend. It's been one week of celibacy now for me."

I nodded and gave her a tender smile, and then my eyes swung back over to Knox.

"Same here. One week," he choked out.

Several things struck me at once and my brain fought to catch up. He wasn't counting our time together last night, probably because it hadn't led to sex, and his length of abstinence matched Amanda's perfectly. They'd exchanged phone numbers one week ago at the end of group and…what? Met up for sex that day? My body broke out in a cold sweat and my heartbeat rang in my ears.

With my windpipe threatening to close and tears shimmering in my eyes, I jumped from my seat and fled the room. I ran blindly down the hall, tears burning my vision and a rock-solid lump in my chest. It would have been one thing for him to drunkenly mess up with a stranger before we started really seeing each other, but planning a sex date with a member of our group?

I heard my name being called behind me and pushed my legs faster. I couldn't have anyone see me break down like this. I felt betrayed and humiliated. Why had I ever thought I could do this? Change this man and have something meaningful. I was an idiot. I'd been living in the fantasy of it. Being near Knox had made me feel better about my own life, but all of that had just come crashing to a close.

"McKenna! Stop!" Knox called behind me, closer this time.

I gripped the door handle to the stairwell, threw it open, and ran down two flights of stairs before I collapsed in a heap. I couldn't breathe, could only feel my heart clenching and dying inside my chest. I huddled against the wall, sobbing uncontrollably while tears and snot streaked my face.

Knox sank to his knees in front of me. "McKenna?"

I wiped my cheeks with the back of my hand and drew a short, shuddering breath. "When were you last with someone, Knox?"

"Other than you?" he asked, his brows pinched together as though he was the one angry about something.

I nodded.

He released a deep sigh and looked down. A thick, uncomfortable silence settled between us. My heart slammed against my ribs and with each second of his silence, my doubts only grew.

"She's pregnant, you know."

His eyes snapped up to mine. "Who?"

"Amanda," I croaked.

He didn't respond at first. He just sat there, silently blinking at me. "I know."

If he was still doing what he used to, I couldn't let it go. I couldn't move past it. Selfishly, I needed all of him. I needed him to be stronger because I most certainly was not strong enough for this. He was breaking me apart and I didn't even think he knew it.

"I thought I could do this. I thought I was strong enough, but I'm not. Not at all." A hiccup escaped my throat as I realized everything I'd be losing. Instead of constantly beating myself up, I'd focused on fixing Knox. And now I had no idea what good that had done me or where we stood.

"I can't stand by and watch you use random girls and then cuddle with me at night like everything is fine."

Angry hands tore through his hair, leaving it standing in disarray. Our happy memories of just last night seemed like so long ago. "You think this is a surprise for me? I told you I'd fuck this up."

I hated hearing him admitting defeat, for not fighting for this—for me. When he was ready to change and grow, he would. I'd wanted to be part of his growth process, but it seemed I hadn't been. I wasn't the girl to change him.

"I'm not right for you. I'm all hard edges and a mistake-riddled past. I'm too fucked up for someone like you. You have to see that. No amount of counseling or talking will fix the shit I've done, McKenna. You should leave while you can."

I was quiet while he spoke, my head empty and my heart in tatters. Knox was trouble; I should say good-bye and move on with my life. I needed to stop playing house with him and his brothers before it was too late.

I just didn't want to.

WHEN I SURRENDER

WHEN I BREAK, Book 2

KENDALL RYAN

About the Book

Undaunted by Knox's complicated history with sexual addiction, McKenna pushes forward in her relationship with this deliciously flawed man. She experiences the highest highs as they discover each other and the lowest lows worrying that his past may not be entirely behind him.

But when a complication from her own past demands attention, she is forced to decide where their relationship is headed and everything she thought she knew is questioned.

When I Surrender is book 2 in the *When I Break* series.

Chapter One

Knox

The girl, whose name I couldn't recall, writhed beneath me on the bed, ready and waiting. My pulse spiked as I watched her tempting curves move in the moonlight.

"Go down on me." She squirmed, wiggling her hips as if to entice me south.

"I'm not eating your pussy. You're a stripper, baby, I don't know where that thing's been." It was probably an asshole thing to say, but that shit was the truth.

She let out a short laugh, but didn't disagree.

"Roll over. I want you from behind." That way I wouldn't have to look into eyes that weren't McKenna's when I sank inside her. The darkness inside me had lain dormant for too long. Because of *her*. It was probably a good thing she figured out I was all wrong for her before I did something bad.

I reached for a condom, knowing that the dual sensations of relief and regret would soon be flooding my system. It was familiar to me, and a feeling I welcomed. Even as I rolled the condom on, I knew this dull ache inside wouldn't be satisfied by the girl in front of me. But this was who I was and I wasn't fighting it anymore. McKenna might have helped me see the light, but she wasn't here now. Just this warm, willing girl who wanted me. Sinking into her slick heat was the only thing I needed to numb my pain. Not to be psychoanalyzed by a girl who would probably never trust me anyhow. I'd lost McKenna anyway, so why was I even thinking about that? The truth was, she was still the only woman I thought about day and night, even when I was about to satisfy my needs with some random hookup.

The pattern was impossible to ignore – I'd lost every woman I cared for, beginning with my mother several years ago. That had been the start of my descent into becoming the man I was now. Thoughts of my mother did nothing to relax me. In fact, I felt on edge and wound tighter than ever.

"What's wrong? What are you waiting for?" The girl shifted to her side and gazed up at me, obviously looking for the same release as me. Blinking several times, I fought to understand what I was seeing – her dark hair and eyes made her resemble my mother. *What the fuck?* I scrambled away from her on my hands and knees.

With my heart hammering against my ribs, I opened my eyes to blackness all around me. I blinked again, struggling to see.

I was in my bed, alone, sweat glistening along my skin. It'd all been a dream. *Thank God.* My room was as dark and empty as my heart. I took a deep, shaky breath and scrubbed my hands over my face while adrenaline pulsed through my veins. I needed to calm the fuck down.

Knowing I wouldn't get back to sleep anytime soon, I climbed from bed and headed downstairs. I downed a glass of cool water and checked on the boys, who were all sleeping soundly, before returning to my own bed. I fell onto the mattress with a thud, my heartbeat still too fast to fully relax.

It'd been a week since I'd seen McKenna – sobbing and hysterical over the thought that I'd slept with Amanda. It still tore me up remembering her like that. I'd done my best to calm her, to try and make her see reason – that I was messed up and it was only a matter of time before I really hurt her – but I hadn't touched that girl. She'd fled the building without a backward glance. She either didn't believe me, didn't care, or both.

I stared up at the ceiling as the minutes ticked past. My mother's death left a cool, empty place inside of me, and McKenna running away only intensified that.

I hated this sick need that followed me into the night. The desperate wanting that tightened my balls against my stomach. I knew only one way to make it go away. I needed to forget, to bury myself deep in distraction and pleasure. I forced my eyes closed and tried to breathe through the craving. Sweat broke out over my skin and my heart sped. *Shit*. I hated this side of myself. Trying to quiet my swirling mind, I thought of McKenna, of her quiet confidence and wholesome beauty. Bad idea. My dick started to rise to attention, liking the new direction of my thoughts. I considered grabbing the bottle of Jack that sat untouched in my nightstand drawer and downing a healthy measure to force my brain into oblivion. Switching tactics, I focused instead on my brothers. I would do anything to protect them from the man I'd become. I had to fight these feelings inside myself.

The fact that I was even questioning all this, trying to calm my raging nerves without sex or alcohol, meant one thing. McKenna had gotten under my skin. And hell if a part of me didn't like it. She was a fascination, someone I wanted to understand. And I felt that way around very few people. I had the boys, and I rarely made time for others. Even friends I'd once been close with no longer counted on my list of priorities. Besides, most were busy being twenty-two years old while I was busy playing dad and sinking deeper and deeper into a hole.

Pulling in a deep breath, I began to relax. I pictured Tucker's uneven grin when he'd sunk that basket straight through the net earlier. I thought about my mother's upcoming birthday and made a mental note to buy flowers and take the boys to her grave. I thought about all the little things I needed to get done this week. Luke's upcoming college placement tests that we needed to register and pay for, Tucker's family tree that we needed to create for his history lesson, and Jaxon... I had no clue what was going on with my eighteen-year-old brother, only that he seemed to be becoming more and more like me. Which made my stomach cramp with fear. I wouldn't wish this life on anyone.

Rolling over and shoving my pillow into place, I released a heavy sigh and closed my eyes, praying for sleep to take me.

Chapter Two

McKenna

I hadn't planned to go on this retreat with Belinda, but given the current state of my life, running away for the weekend sounded like the exact thing I needed. The retreat was for addiction counselors in the Chicago area. There would be panels and lectures over the course of two days. We'd learn about advanced treatment techniques and also take much needed time to rejuvenate with yoga classes and meditation. It sounded a little silly to me and I hadn't wanted to go. I'd planned on staying home and throwing myself into my punishing routine of working and volunteering, but Belinda was my mentor and, well, basically I hated letting people down. So here I was, in the passenger seat of her minivan, watching the miles tick past while unease churned inside of me.

I regretted the way I'd broken down, sobbing, and fled from the group I was supposed to be leading last Saturday. I regretted how close I'd grown to Knox in such a short time, and that he'd been able to break me so easily. Ever since Knox Bauer had first walked into my sex addicts meeting, my life had been in one giant freefall. Despite his baggage, falling for him had been the easy part. Some of my best moments were the quiet ones shared alone with him. The times he'd made himself vulnerable and opened up to me had felt like something. Something real and important. And hanging out with him and his three younger brothers was a nice distraction from the guilt and pain of my everyday life.

But I'd been forced to see the harsh reality of the situation. Knox was a sex addict. Even if he was telling the truth and he hadn't slept with the girl from our group, Amanda, like I'd thought, he still had an addiction. Which meant he was dangerous for me, not someone to give my heart to.

"What's on your mind?" Belinda asked, peering over at me before letting her eyes drift back to the road.

I should have known she'd be perceptive. She was a counselor, trained in reading people and situations, just like me. And I had zero emotional energy left to try and act bubbly and personable, so there was no sense faking it. I'd been sitting here sulking for almost an hour. "Just some guy troubles," I admitted.

"Is this about your roommate Brian?" She had a good memory. In a moment of over-sharing I'd once admitted how I didn't think my long time best friend Brian was on the same page with our friends-only status.

"No. But Brian has complicated things a little." *Or a lot.* He and Knox had gotten into a fist fight because he didn't think Knox was good enough for me. "It doesn't matter now anyhow, I called things off with the new guy." I had to. Even though I hadn't known him long, Knox had the ability to turn me inside out and destroy me. And it wouldn't be fair to his brothers for me to parade through their lives and then disappear. Not to mention it'd be unfair to shred the broken fragments of my heart in the process.

"Hmmm," Belinda purred, squinting as she concentrated on the highway. "Have you ever given thought to why Brian was so upset?"

"Of course. He didn't like that there was suddenly another man in my life."

"And why do you think that was?"

I fixed my mouth into a polite smile. I could see what she was doing. My degree was in counseling, too. But the last thing I wanted to talk about was my lonely roommate Brian.

"Have you ever considered that Brian may be the better choice for you?" she pushed on.

"Belinda…." I gave her a mocking look. She needed to cut out the typical therapist questions. Everything about my body language screamed that I didn't want to talk. And no, Brian wasn't the better choice. I hated how everyone saw his rumpled blond hair and blue eyes and thought we'd look great together. He was cute – so what?

She chuckled. "Sorry. I didn't mean to pry. I can just tell something's bothering you."

Knox had already stolen my heart, was I really willing to risk my job too by telling Belinda I'd been seeing a man who was supposed to be in treatment? I thought better of it and shook away the thoughts. "I'll be fine. This weekend away came at just the right time."

She nodded. "Let me know if I can help."

Not unless she could go back in time and tell the old me not to get involved with a man so broken. But even as the thought filtered through my brain, I knew there'd be nothing she could have said that would have made me see reason. I'd been a goner right from the very beginning. His rugged beauty, masculine scent, those dark haunted eyes that spoke of his troubled past – all of it called to me. In his magnetic presence I felt fully alive. And I missed that feeling.

Those first two days were the hardest. I couldn't convince Brian that I was okay, no matter how many times I said it. His worried stare followed me around our shared apartment. Somehow I suspected he knew my foul mood was about Knox, but I didn't want to give him the satisfaction of knowing that was true. I didn't want to hear, 'I told you so.' So I would go into the bathroom and turn on the shower to cry. The scalding hot water would steam up the bathroom and fog over the mirror so I didn't have to see myself lose it. I cried for myself, for Knox, for everything we'd both lost. I cried over my parents like I hadn't in years. I guess feeling brutally alone and lonely would do that to you.

Despite the messed up circumstances surrounding how we met,

Knox and I shared a deep connection. I wasn't ready to give that up. But since my heart didn't know what was best for me, my head had to make that decision. I needed to keep my distance. And being two hundred miles away for the weekend was a start.

I checked my phone again. There was a text from Brian telling me to have fun, but nothing else from Knox. After my blowup last weekend, he'd sent one text, '*We should talk.*' That was it. I hadn't responded, afraid I'd run right over there to him again and not be able to walk away this time. He was my addiction and this time away was my treatment.

Meditation was pointless. Every time I closed my eyes, it was Knox's face that I saw. Every time the instructor told us to focus on something that made us happy, I thought about cuddling on the couch with Knox's littlest brother, Tucker. But I trudged through the lectures and seminars, intent on wiping my memory of all those stolen moments.

Chapter Three

Knox

A week had passed without any word from McKenna and I was starting to regret letting her walk away last weekend. At the time I figured she needed to cool down, take some time to process things, but now I saw that she'd been running. Away from me and my messed up pile of baggage just like I knew she'd end up doing eventually.

While she'd been wrong about Amanda, she'd been right about me. Even if I wasn't comfortable with the label, I had a problem with sex. I used girls to escape. I needed the pleasure to numb my feelings of pain and sadness. I just didn't know if I was capable of changing it.

I tucked a box of cereal under one arm and grabbed a gallon of milk before heading into the dining room. "Come on, Tuck. Breakfast time," I called to my youngest brother who was stumbling in from the living room sleepy-eyed. I just needed to get the boys on the bus then I could set out on my mission.

There was a line out the door and wrapping around the side of the building when I arrived. I took a chance and headed around to the back, hoping to find another entrance. With only an hour to spare before I had to be at work, I couldn't afford to waste time standing in a line. The heavy steel door at the back of the building was propped open by a large trash can. I was in luck.

I slipped inside, stepping into a huge commercial kitchen. I pulled a white apron over my head from one of the hooks on the wall. Unless I wanted to get thrown out of here before I found her, I needed to look the part. The kitchen bustled with activity – several apron-wearing volunteers were stationed behind a steel countertop, chopping and mixing, and a man with a white chef's hat was cooking something on an eight-burner gas stove. No sign of McKenna, though.

A dark skinned woman stepped in front of me, blocking my path. "Are you cooking or serving today?" She propped a hand on her ample hip, seemingly annoyed by the sight of me.

"Ah, serving," I said. Since I didn't see McKenna in the kitchen, I was hoping that meant she was in the dining room.

"Then where are your gloves and hair net?" she questioned, narrowing her eyes.

I glanced around the room and spotted a box of plastic gloves and hairnets on a table behind her. "Sorry." Shuffling past her, I grabbed my supplies and headed toward the dining hall. Shoving the net over my hair and slipping on the gloves, I searched for McKenna.

I spotted her several yards away filling little plastic cups of orange juice at a banquet table. She was deep in concentration and she'd yet to notice me. A line of tension creased her forehead and she looked tired. When she hadn't shown up for group on Saturday, I hated thinking it was because I'd driven her away.

She'd once told me that she came to this soup kitchen most mornings to serve breakfast, so I'd taken a chance coming here today. A chance that had paid off. Now I just needed to get her talking to me again. The doors opened and people began lining up with their trays in hand. I stationed myself at the table next to McKenna's. I felt her eyes on me, but rather than glance her way, I picked up the set of tongs and set an apple on each person's tray as they passed me.

"What are you doing?" McKenna hissed over at me.

Picking my head up, I glimpsed over at her, flashing a guilty smile. "Oh, hey. I'm just volunteering. You?"

Her eyebrows drew together and she let out a huff, obviously not buying my story. She was angry. Good. At least I was getting a reaction. Indifference would have been worse. Anger I could work with.

"Here you go, Mr. Bronson." Wiping away the scowl meant only for me, McKenna smiled at the older man in front of her, and placed a cup of orange juice in his trembling hands. We were at the

202

end of the line, and by the time they made their way over to us, their plates were loaded with oatmeal, scrambled eggs, and sausage links. It looked pretty damn good for a free breakfast. It smelled good, too. I would have never imagined there were so many people here in line so early for this. Of course McKenna had known, which was why she donated her time and efforts here. A quick glance at my watch told me I only had forty minutes left before I had to leave for my shift managing the hardware store. I needed to speed this process up.

I didn't grovel. I didn't beg, but shit if this girl didn't make me want to drop to my knees and plead for forgiveness. I must be getting soft. An elderly guy pushing a walker approached my table next. One of the staff members was holding his tray for him. "Apple?" I offered, picking up a fruit with the plastic tongs and holding it out to him.

"With these false teeth?" He smiled, a big gap-toothed grin. "I better not. I'm not feeling real adventurous today. But thanks for asking."

"Anytime, man." I set the apple back down on my table, feeling useless once again. "I could always go back to the kitchen, see if we have something else. A banana maybe?" I had no idea what they had back in their kitchen, but I was willing to try. This guy was someone's grandfather most likely. I didn't particularly like the idea of him going hungry.

He took my hand and gave it a shake. Misty blue eyes met mine as he grinned at me again. "Bless you for what you're doing. You're a good person."

"Trust me, I'm not. But I'm trying."

"Ah, what the hell. You only live once, hit me with one of those apples."

I placed a shiny red apple on his tray and felt McKenna watching. Glancing her way, I knew she'd overheard the entire exchange. I'd meant those words. I wasn't a good person. But I wanted to be. For her. "We need to talk," I said, low under my breath.

"Not now," she breathed, her eyes slipping closed. She looked like she was on the verge of tears. I wouldn't push her right now, but I didn't have much time left.

"I have to be at work soon."

She looked over at me again, confusion marking her features. "You came here before work?"

She knew it was a big deal that I'd taken the time to come here. Good. "Got up early, got the guys off to school, and yeah. I came to see you. You didn't return my text. I thought you were ignoring me."

Drawing a deep, but shaky breath, McKenna continued looking straight ahead. "Can we just enjoy this?"

I knew volunteering was important to her and I suddenly realized she thought I was interrupting. "Can we talk later, then?" I asked.

She nodded. "Okay."

"McKenna?"

"Yeah?" Pretty blue eyes flashed on mine.

"I didn't sleep with her."

She set down the cup of juice she was holding with trembling hands. A moment later she disappeared out of the room, treading down a long hallway, and I took off after her.

Shit. She'd agreed to talk later, and yet I kept pushing. But I needed her to believe that. I hadn't laid a hand on that girl. And after hurting her so badly the last time we were together, my own conscience needed clearing.

I heard soft sobs coming from the women's restroom and I pushed open the door and entered, securing the lock behind me. The stall door on the end was closed and I could see her gray tennis shoes beneath the opening. "McKenna?"

The cries stopped. "Go away, Knox."

Fuck. I slumped against the wall, fighting the urge the punch something. "I just needed to see you, make sure you were okay. The way we left things last time…."

"I'm fine, okay. Or at least I was going to be. Being here is my sanctuary, my escape. But now you've taken that from me, too."

She was hiding in the damn bathroom stall because of me. I should have felt sorry I'd come, but I didn't. I'd needed to see her with my own eyes or I was going to lose it. "When you didn't show up Saturday, I kind of freaked out. Are you done leading group?" *Because of me?*

"No, I was at a retreat with counseling seminars all weekend."

"Can I just tell you one thing?"

She sniffed. "And then we'll talk about the rest later?"

"Whatever you want."

"Okay."

"I never slept with Amanda. Not even close. I have no desire to sleep with her. We exchanged phone numbers because she wanted someone to talk to about raising a baby while recovering from addiction, and I'd told her I have custody of my three brothers. She's freaked out that she has a baby on the way and wanted someone to talk to." There was a long pause from McKenna. "Do you believe me?"

"If you weren't with her, then why did you answer that it'd only been one week since your last sexual encounter? Were you with other girls while we were...." A choked little sob escaped her

206

throat.

"Do you want to know why I said that it'd been one week since my last sexual encounter?"

Silence. She thought she didn't want to hear this. But she did.

"When I answered that question, it'd been one week since you'd come to me in the night, let me kiss and touch you. And even without sex, that was the most erotic encounter of my life. Touching you over your panties, knowing you trusted me, making you come… that meant everything to me. It wasn't even about sex. It was about trust. And after that, all other memories of girls I'd been with were wiped from my memory. There was only you. So that's why I said one week. And no, there's been no one else since."

The bathroom door unlatched, and McKenna stepped out slowly. Her eyes were watery and the tip of her nose was pink. She was still the most beautiful girl in the world. She'd pulled off her hair net and gloves at some point, reminding me that I still had mine on. I smiled weakly at her and pulled off the accessories, dropping them into the nearby wastebasket.

Crossing the room toward me, I opened my arms and McKenna folded herself against my chest. I held her and gently swayed with her in my arms. It'd been a tough week for her. Distress was written all over her features and she felt thin and frail. I wanted to take her home and put her in my bed and never let her go again. Instead I continued lightly rubbing her back, letting her calm down and collect herself. I'd wait as long as it took. I no longer cared about getting to work on time. If she needed me, I wasn't going anywhere.

A few moments later, she lifted her head from my chest and crossed the room to stand in front of the sink, inspecting herself in the mirror.

"You look beautiful," I murmured. She smirked at her reflection in the mirror. It was the truth. She splashed cool water on her cheeks and I handed her a paper towel. "You okay?"

She nodded. "Yeah. I'm okay. Thanks. And I know you have to get to work."

"Can we still talk later?"

"There's more?" she asked, pushing a chunk of hair behind her ear.

"We need to discuss you and me."

"There's a you and me?" she breathed.

"You know there is." My heart thumped steadily in my chest. My relationship with her was the only real thing in my life. Even if it wasn't a romantic relationship, I needed her presence. My brothers did, too. We'd figure the rest out later. "When are you free?"

"Tomorrow night. I'm attending a fundraiser at the library. It goes until 8:00."

"Come over after?"

"You'll be a gentleman?" The hint of a smile played on her full lips.

"If you like."

She exhaled a deep shuddering breath, like she was summoning her courage. "I'll come."

The urge to take her in my arms again was overwhelming, but I resisted it. As difficult as it was for me, I needed to learn to deal with shit without falling back on physical touch. "See you then."

Chapter Four
McKenna

I took my time getting ready, telling myself I wanted to look nice for the library fundraiser. It was an after-hours event with hor d'oeuvres and wine tasting. I should dress up a little, right? It had nothing to do with seeing Knox after. *Yeah, right.*

I was still reeling with the emotional turmoil stirred up by being near Knox. Getting away last weekend for the retreat was supposed to bring clarity, but all it did was make me miss him more. And then knowing he planned his work day around seeing me at the soup kitchen yesterday had torn down my final wall. Every time I thought I had Knox figured out, he surprised me and pulled me back in. With him, I knew the road was guaranteed to be bumpy, but at last I was moving forward.

I inspected myself in the mirror one final time. My dark hair fell in loose waves down my back and my fitted black pants and silky gray blouse looked simple, but chic. I puckered my lips in the mirror and added a dab of pink lip gloss. *Stop stalling, McKenna.* I grabbed my coat and purse and flipped off my bedroom light.

"You look nice," Brian said as I entered the living area. The football game was playing in the background. I found it sort of oddly endearing how he'd become a hardcore Chicago sports fan, now cheering for every local team. It was just another way he'd changed his life and habits to support me in this move.

"Thanks." I smoothed my hands over the fabric of my pants. "I have this fundraiser thingy at the library tonight."

"You look like you're going on a date." His eyes glanced over my curves and came to a stop on my face again. My cheeks heated.

"Nope. Just the library."

"Maybe I should join you."

"No!" He couldn't know I was going to Knox's after. I calmed my voice and started again. "I mean, no, that's not necessary. It'll probably be boring. A few speeches and sign up opportunities for volunteer work in the coming year. Nothing too exciting. Besides, I wouldn't want you to miss the Bears winning their big game."

"You know I would for you."

He was too good to me and I was hit with a pang of guilt about lying where I was headed. "Thanks, but no. You stay, enjoy your game." I slipped on my coat. If the chill in the fall air was any indication, winter was just around the corner.

"Hey, you wanna do something this weekend?"

"Uh, sure. Sounds great, Bri." It was probably time we put this awkwardness behind us and forget about his fight with Knox.

The closer I got to Knox's place, the more anxious I became. I was fidgety and distracted all during the fundraiser and watching the clock hadn't helped. The entire evening had dragged by at a snail's pace.

Knox was like a magnet drawing me to him. The pull was primitive and all consuming. And not because I was a fixer, like Brian said, but because our wounded souls found solace in the company of each other. He'd been like a balm to my unseen injuries. And I'd wanted to believe I was his healing balm, too. But I hated that I hadn't been. Despite his little speech in the bathroom, I worried he was still seeking nameless, faceless girls to soothe his aches, which was why I needed to face reality. Sex was his drug of choice. If I'd really meant something to him, he would give all that up, right? I questioned if he could have a relationship that wasn't based on sex. I needed to hear what he had to say tonight, even if it destroyed me in the process.

It was nearly 8:30 by the time I arrived and as I stood waiting on the porch for him to answer the door, I took a few deep breaths of cool air and promised myself that nothing would happen between us. Remembering how his tender kisses and skilled fingers had felt, I inwardly groaned. I needed to be strong.

The door swung open and Knox stood there in jeans, bare feet, and a white T-shirt looking sexy and sinful. "Change of plans," he growled.

I followed him inside and shut the door. It was dark and quiet inside. "Knox?" He continued to the stairs and began climbing them silently. I hurried to keep up with him. "What's wrong?" His sweet, gentle demeanor from yesterday morning had disappeared, but I wasn't about to let him shut down on me now. We'd come too far for that, hadn't we? We were supposed to talk tonight. "Knox, what happened?" I asked again as we entered his bedroom.

He opened a dresser drawer, digging through the pile of clothes until he pulled out a long sleeved black T-shirt. "We're going out. I need to blow off some steam."

I wondered what had changed his mood and turned him into this closed off version of himself. If he'd slipped up and been with someone, would he tell me? "Where are we going?"

"To the bar. I need a drink." He tugged the shirt on over his head and sat down on the bed to put on socks and his boots.

I'd never been to a bar. I was of legal age, but somehow it was just one of those things I hadn't gotten around to yet. The idea of going out with Knox made the skin of the back of my neck tingle pleasantly. "If I go out with you, will you tell me what happened?"

Dark eyes leapt up to mine as Knox finished lacing his boots.

"Jaxon got in a fight a school. He fucked…um, slept with the quarterback's girlfriend right before the big game."

"Oh. Did you talk to him, find out why he'd do that?"

"Of course I talked to him. He said the guy was a douche bag and they have gym class together and the guy was always an ass to him. So he wanted revenge. But the team lost their football game because the quarterback was so torn up."

"And then they fought?"

Knox shook his head. "No. He got jumped. Because once word got out what Jaxon had done, half the school was pissed at him."

"And the other half?"

"Thought he was a hero."

Wow. Talk about high school drama. "Is he okay?"

"He'll live. He's got some bruises and a fat lip."

"Is he here?" The nurturer in me wanted to go see if he was okay. Maybe bring him some pain reliever and some ice for the swelling, talk to him about his actions.

Knox nodded. "Yeah, but they're all in bed early tonight."

It sounded to me like he'd punished all three boys and sent them to bed early because of Jaxon's mistake, but I kept my mouth shut, unwilling to question him when he was in such a foul mood.

Knox rose from the bed and stalked toward me. "You ready?"

His plan worried me. Anytime his life got stressful, Knox turned to drinking and sex. I knew they went hand in hand for him. Sudden unease at what the night held in store settled in the pit of my stomach. "I don't know, Knox. Me? At a bar?"

He shot me a pointed stare. "What do you do to blow off steam?"

Without giving it a second thought, I rattled off my schedule. "Monday night I work at the food bank downtown, Tuesday I visit the youth shelter, Wednesdays I've been helping out on a Habitat for Humanity project, Thursdays I go to the Humane Society, and whenever I have time, I serve meals at the soup kitchen. Oh, and Saturday is group."

He shook his head at me. "My point exactly. Do you even know how to relax?"

I forced the rigid tension in my shoulders to ease. I could do this. And if I didn't babysit him tonight, who would? "So where are we going?"

We walked the several blocks to a nearby bar, huddled into our coats the entire time. Once night fell, so did the temperature. Drastically. But once we stepped inside the cozy warmth of the tavern, my spirits lifted. Knox led the way to a booth across from the long bar and we sat down facing each other. It felt intimate and foreign being out with him like this, and I liked it. Knox's eyes remained on mine as I slid out of my coat. He was wearing a dark leather jacket and coupled with the way his long-sleeved tee clung to his broad chest, it made my nipples tighten and rasp against my bra. My entire being took notice of his —on every level— both emotional and physical. It left me staggering for breath.

"So, are we going to talk?" I asked after several tense moments.

"Drinks first." His eyes cast over to the bar. "What do you want?"

My gaze followed his. Bottles of liquor were lined up along a glass wall behind the bar, overwhelming me. There were too many choices. "I- I'm not sure."

"You've never had a drink before?"

"I've had a drink. But I've never ordered something for myself at a bar before."

"Beer? Wine? Something fruity? I'll order for you, just tell me what sounds good."

I chewed on my lower lip. My parents died in a drunk driving accident. I'd never been big on drinking. "Something fruity I guess. But not too sweet."

He chuckled at me. "Got it."

A few moments later, Knox returned with a pale pink concoction in a tall glass for me, along with a bottle of beer and a shot of something for himself. He pushed the drink toward me and I took a sip from the straw. Mmm. It tasted like lemon-lime soda and cherries with a hint of something tart. Wait a second. "Is this a Shirley Temple?"

He chuckled and shrugged his shoulders. "There's alcohol in it."

"Are you mocking me?" I straightened my shoulders, locking eyes with him.

"Of course not, angel. Drink up."

I watched as Knox downed the shot in front of him, bringing it to his full lips and draining the glass in an easy swallow.

"Can we talk about what you said at the soup kitchen…about me and you…."

He nodded.

I paused, taking my time. I didn't know if I was really ready to go there with him yet. I decided on a different question that had been plaguing me for some time. "Knox I know you've told me about your addiction, but will you tell me how it first began? I need to understand. How did you get this way?

"It's second nature. I don't think about it." His eyes wandered away and he took a long sip of his beer.

"I know. But I'm asking you to. To really examine it. And open up and share with me." I knew I was asking a lot of him, and I didn't know if he was brave enough.

"I will. In time."

"What do I have to do for you to tell me?" I chewed on my lip, feeling brave.

He smiled. "You want inside my head that bad?"

I waited, silent.

"Fine. Take a shot with me."

I opened my mouth to argue, then snapped it closed again. I could handle one shot. Couldn't I?

This time Knox returned with two shot glasses, each with clear liquor inside. He set one down in front of me and kept the other in his hand. "This your first shot?" he asked. I nodded. "Cheers, angel."

"How do I...." I paused with the shot glass halfway to my lips.

"Tilt your head back. Open your throat. Let it slide down."

His voice was thick, laced with sexual tension, and my stomach knotted. But I did as he instructed, bringing the glass to my lips and tipping my head back. I felt his eyes on me the entire time, heating up the space between us. The stiff punch of liquor slid down easily, leaving only a slight bitter burn in the back of my throat. I quickly took a sip of my drink to clear away the taste.

"Good girl." He licked his lips and set his own empty glass down next to mine.

I had a theory that Knox been looking for love and closeness in all the wrong places. His mother died and his father had run off, abandoning the family. And I knew he said he found his peace, if only for a short time, with girl after girl. The feeling never lasted long, though, and so he sought the next girl. I don't think he knew he was stuck in that pattern until I'd come along and forced his eyes open. But I needed to hear Knox say it and connect the dots.

He grabbed his beer and took another swig, his eyebrows knitted together in deep concentration. "My mom and I were really close. I was a momma's boy and am not afraid to admit it." He smiled. I remembered the sketches he'd shown me. I knew he loved and missed her deeply. "When she died, it left this giant hole in me. I began chasing after girls in high school just to feel something. To feel alive. I dated in high school, and slept around a little, but after a while, it just wasn't enough anymore. I needed something more. I started going out to bars and girls were even easier to pick up outside of school. It was simple. I didn't really think about it. And when I was with them, I forgot all about my fucked up life. For a short time anyway. It was a coping mechanism."

"Didn't that bother you – using them that way? Those were

people's daughters."

"If you think they weren't using me too, you're more naïve than I thought." He smirked at me, challenging me to disagree.

I'd never thought about it that way, but I supposed he had a valid point. Knox wasn't the type to promise them the moon and stars. He was a take it or leave it kind of guy. And they freely took what he'd offered.

He'd been getting love the only way he knew how – by sleeping with anything with a vagina. It was sad, but on some strange level, I understood. Knox had spent many years feeling unloved and not capable of returning love. But I knew he was capable of more. I saw firsthand how sweet he was with his brothers. He'd stepped up to raise them and set aside his own goals and dreams. And I suspected he wanted to change. He'd been attending my sex addicts meetings for over a month now and hadn't pushed me away, despite my constant questions.

"Still, Knox, you had to know that wasn't right…."

"It's the only thing I know."

"Then discover something new." My eyes were pleading with his and I saw the moment my plea registered. His gaze turned hungry as his eyes flicked down to my mouth.

He leaned closer, his eyes soft and probing. "Meeting you has been interesting for me...."

My heart swelled in my chest and I wanted so badly to hear him continue. But he took a swig of his beer and let his eyes wander out onto the dance floor.

"So assuming you were still...that way, you'd be looking for a girl here tonight?"

"Most likely," he admitted.

The truth stung, but at least he was honest. We watched in silence as a group of girls, one wearing a tiara and a sash that declared her the *Bride*, shimmied on the dance floor to the beat of hip hop music.

"So if you were here to pick up a girl tonight – who's your type?" I looked on as a blond with large breasts thrust her hips back and forth, too embarrassed to meet Knox's eyes. I wondered if he'd go for someone so obvious about her body and looks. Someone so completely opposite of me.

"You really want me to answer that?" he asked. I nodded, still unable to meet his gaze. "Look at me," he commanded.

I did. And his heated stare lit me up from the inside out. I felt my chest and neck flush. I dropped my gaze, sliding my drink toward me and sucking down a big mouthful. "Yeah, I want to know," I said, finding my courage. The alcohol flowing through my veins was the likely contributor. When he was like this, so dominant and commanding, my body turned to a pile of mush, ready and waiting for his next command.

Knox's eyes reluctantly left mine and he scanned the dance floor with a bored expression. Not finding anyone of interest, his gaze turned toward the crowded bar. "I'll be back in a minute," he said, his eyes not returning to mine.

Unease churned inside me as I watched him cross the room and head down the back hallway alone. What was he doing? Had he already picked out a girl and given her a special wink? I couldn't believe he'd really disappeared and left me sitting here all alone. I sucked down more of my drink as tears blurred my vision.

I hated how I couldn't be what he needed and he chose instead to fulfill his needs without me. I sensed that Knox was developing real feelings, too. So why did he continue on with this charade of hussies? *Because even if he did have feelings for you, McKenna, you're a virgin. You can't satisfy his needs.* That realization sparked something inside me. Rebellion. It made me want to try.

A few moments later, Knox strolled back to the table, his expression unreadable. "McKenna?" Spotting the unshed tears shimmering in my eyes, he stood immobile in front of the table. "What happened?"

"You left me." I pressed my fingertips to my temples, willing the

222

tears away.

He slid into the booth next to me and pulled me close, pressing a kiss to my temple. "I went to take a piss. You didn't think…?"

I nodded slowly.

"Christ, McKenna. I wouldn't do that. I used the restroom, washed my hands, and came right back to the table." I suddenly felt foolish for freaking out. He hesitated for several long moments, his jaw clenching in the dim light. "What do you want from me? You know who I am."

"Friendship, Knox. I want your friendship."

"That's it? There's nothing more…." He smiled, crookedly, begging me to disagree.

He was hinting at the burning chemistry between us, brewing just below the surface. My obvious jealous reaction at thinking he'd gone after a girl. He felt this intensity between us and apparently he knew I did, too. I hadn't been hiding my true feelings well enough. He saw it in my lingering gazes, the way I cared for his brothers, and the ways my eyes always went to his while we were in group. There was no point denying it, since I knew eventually he'd see through my game. The truth was I wanted much more than friendship. I wouldn't have taken things physical with him if I hadn't. Something told me he understood that.

223

I took a deep breath, settling my nerves. "As for more…yes, I know who you are. You're a man who takes care of his family, who takes on the world for those boys, who works hard and plays harder…but you're also a man on the cusp of change. If you want anything more than friendship with me, then you'll have to show me."

"Show you what? I told you I don't do love."

"So change." I shrugged, flippantly, like it was the simplest thing in the world. Knox said he didn't do love, but he was wrong. He loved his brothers fiercely. He might not have done romantic relationships, but I believed in him, I believed anything was possible, as long as he wanted it bad enough. And selfishly, I wanted to be the one to change his mind about love. He was helping me and some little voice deep inside told me we could do this. It might have been foolish, but when everything else had been stripped away from me, I needed that hope. I would cling to it like a life raft until I was forced to admit he wasn't my savior and I wasn't his.

"What about Brian?" Knox asked, drawing another sip of his beer and signaling the bartender for another.

"What about him?"

"You and him. You ever thought about that? You guys could be good together."

Was he seriously encouraging my relationship with Brian? After all this? "First Belinda and now you, really?"

He shrugged. "Just pointing out your options."

Frustrated, I pushed a chunk of hair behind my ear. Brian had always been there for me. Would always be there for me. He was sweet and had cute boy next door looks to match. Would it really be the worst thing in the world to see if real feelings could develop between us? Sometimes I wondered about us, but I just didn't feel that way about him, despite what Knox or Belinda saw when they looked at us together. And his encouragement about Brian had the opposite effect, it only made me want to rebel. I took a big gulp from my grown-up Shirley Temple, finishing the drink. "I'm going to dance." I didn't dance, but being near him was too much of a roller coaster and I needed a minute to clear my head.

Knox moved aside to let me out of the booth and I headed to the center of the dance floor, ready to lose myself in the crowd. Squeezing my way past the writhing bodies, I found a spot for myself and closed my eyes, letting the thumping rhythm wash over me. Finding the beat, I swayed back and forth to the music. The alcohol had relaxed me enough that I felt totally unconcerned with how I looked to others. I moved and swayed, feeling loose and relaxed as the music took over.

I felt someone approach me from behind, but before my body had the chance to tense, I smelled his unique scent of warm leather and sandalwood and knew it was Knox. He placed both hands on my waist as his chest brushed against my back. A wave of heat crashed over me. He pressed his hips into my bottom and I forgot how to breathe. I spun to face him, needing to see his dark eyes. Was this part of his seduction efforts? He was used to things easily going his way with girls and that fact alone made me want to challenge him a little. He'd just suggested I be with Brian. Did he even really want me?

Knox's hands wandered from my waist to my hips, where his fingertips made contact with bare skin fractures of heat crackled across my abdomen. "Don't question this." He leaned down to breathe against my ear.

I danced with him, moving against him, working my hips in what I hoped was an enticing way. Knox's eyes followed my movements and his hands remained planted at my hips.

I'd just told him I wanted his friendship and now I was grinding against him on the dance floor. I knew I was sending mixed signals, but so was he. He'd suggested I be with Brian when all along he'd been possessive about the idea of my male roommate. I should have walked away, gotten some air, but air was the last thing I wanted.

The few disappointing experiences I'd had with a man made me pause. Knox's dominant side gave me hope that he could take control like I craved, allow me to feel like a woman and completely at ease in the bedroom. Was I really ready to walk away from that? I'd spent twenty-one years single, all while fielding questions from nosy friends and relatives about Brian and why I never had a boyfriend. God, I was delusional. Knox wasn't boyfriend material. He wasn't the type of man you gave your heart to. Still, I felt I owed it to myself to find out if he could make me feel this alive on the dance floor, what would it be like in the bedroom? Something in his nature called to mine, and I couldn't turn away.

Chapter Five
Knox

I watched McKenna sway and twist her hips to the beat of the music. She looked beautiful. Pink cheeks, soft curves, and waves of shiny hair flowing around her face. Her eyes were focused on me, and despite asking for my friendship, I knew she wanted more. And somehow I knew it wouldn't be hard to talk her into it. She felt this intensity between us just like I did.

The desire to explore her body, to fuck her until she cried out my name, was getting stronger. And the alcohol clouding my system wasn't helping. The more time I spent with her, the more difficult it became to resist her. And what scared me even more was that the more time I spent with her, the urge to fuck other girls evaporated. There was only McKenna. Her sweet scent, her gentle nature, and her quiet strength to make the world a better place were like a drug to me. I had to have her.

So why was I trying to push her into the arms of another guy? Because I knew it wasn't what she really wanted. She was here in my arms, grinding against *me*. She might have convinced herself that we wouldn't work, so why not let her see that neither would her and Mr. Perfect with his nice car and good job. She needed someone like me – someone fucked up and broken. She just wouldn't let herself believe that yet, so I was giving her a little shove, hoping to expedite the process. And shit, after she said tonight all she wanted from me was friendship – I might have been a little hurt and pissed off and this was my way of rebelling. None of that changed the fact that I had her in my arms and it was my thigh she was currently grinding on. I was taken straight back to that night in my bedroom when McKenna had done this same thing and I'd rubbed her clit until she came. I went instantly hard.

I curled my hands around her waist, pulling her body close to mine. "You're so fucking sexy." Her chin dropped down to her chest, and she fiddled with the little silver bracelet on her wrist. She didn't believe that she was sexy. But everything about her was turning me on. The fast inhalations causing her breasts to rise and fall, her flushed skin, the way she completely turned her body over to me… *Fuck*.

It wasn't lost on me that McKenna's interest in me – in my family – was likely because of her need to serve and take care of others. I still didn't know where that need came from. Right now, I didn't care. I needed this girl like I'd never needed anything. "Let's go," I growled. She took my hand and let me pull her from the dance floor.

I proceeded to have an internal argument with myself the entire walk home. The right thing to do was to keep my dick in my pants. But when had I ever done the right thing? It wasn't exactly my specialty and ignoring my instincts put me on edge. I wanted her. Badly.

When we reached the house, McKenna quietly toed off her shoes and followed me up the stairs. Once inside my dark bedroom, McKenna paused just inside the doorway, uncertainty written all over her in the pale glow of moonlight. Indecision coursed through me. My own needs would have to take a backseat. I just wanted to make her comfortable.

Wrapping her in my arms from behind, I pressed the brush of a kiss against the bare skin at the back of her neck. "You okay?" I whispered, letting my chin rest on her shoulder.

"Fine," she whispered. "Just…thinking…."

"Overthinking," I whispered back. "You tired?"

She nodded, her cheek resting against mine. "Am I sleeping over?"

"Do you want to?"

She hesitated and I spun her in my arms. As turned on as I'd been on the dance floor, I wanted her to see that she could trust me to go slow. She'd once requested that I be a gentleman with her and I wouldn't betray that trust. She'd done too much for me, taken a leap of faith on even being here and I couldn't fuck this up. Not for me and McKenna and not for my brothers either.

Brilliant sapphire eyes looked up into mine, so trusting and full of hope. She gave a tight nod. Even if she knew she shouldn't want this with someone like me – she did. That was all the reassurance I needed. I wouldn't lure her into my world or force anything on her. The fact that she was choosing to be here meant everything. She knew my fucked up past, and still she was here.

I placed a soft kiss on her forehead and gathered up some pajamas for her. A pair of a sweatpants and an oversized T-shirt I knew would be huge on her. "For you." I left the clothes in her hands and headed into the bathroom to give her some privacy. After brushing my teeth and waiting for McKenna to do the same, we crawled into bed together.

In the dim light from the moon and street lamps outside, only the faint outline of McKenna's curves were visible under the sheets. "Are you warm enough?" It didn't escape my notice that she'd forgone the sweatpants, dressing only in the T-shirt I'd left for her.

She nodded. "I'm perfect."

"I agree."

She chuckled in the darkness. "That's not what I meant."

"I know. But it's the truth. Sometimes I don't even know why you're here with me. Why you've never judged me the way others do."

"I'm no one to pass judgment," she said sadly.

She was the best, the most pure and selfless person I knew. How could she possibly think that about herself? Maybe it was time to learn about the inner demons that plagued her. "Will you tell me about your parents? How you lost them?" She stayed quiet. "You know so much about me and my past, and I want you to know that you can open up to me too, but only when you're ready. I won't force you."

She nodded. "No, it's okay. It's time you knew." She watched my eyes in the dim light as if deciding if she could trust me with the secret that burdened her. "When I was seventeen my parents died in a car accident. A drunk driver broadsided them on their way to church."

I found her hands under the blanket and laced my fingers with hers. "I'm sorry."

The shimmering hint of tears in her eyes made my heart clench.

"The worst part about it was knowing that it never should have happened. I fought with my mom that morning – I refused to go with them and I was the reason they got on the road late. It was my fault. And the last words I spoke to them were cruel and hurtful. I can never take that back, you know?"

I nodded. I knew about the finality of death and how it caused regrets and what-ifs to creep inside your brain and refuse to leave. "McKenna." I squeezed her tiny hands in mine. "That accident wasn't your fault." She blinked several times, trying to fight off the tears. It was the damn drunk driver, she had to know that. Seeing McKenna's pain made me feel guiltier than ever about my own drunk driving arrest. But without that wake up call, I doubted I would have ever met her.

"If I'd just been a good daughter that morning, put my own wants aside and gone with them…." A broken cry escaped her throat. "They'd still be here."

"Have you heard of survivor's guilt, McKenna?"

"Knox, don't," she warned.

"It wasn't your fault." I wish I had better words to say to soothe her pain, but I knew nothing ever would. It wasn't fair how she'd lost her parents. They hadn't deserved what happened to them, any more than my mom had deserved the cancer that took her. Instead, I pulled her closer, into the warmth of my body, and held her next to me and let her cry. Her body shook with silent sobs while I held her, wishing there was something I could do. I rubbed her back and let her soak my shirt with tears and whispered to her that it would be okay. Even if whispered softly and meant to soothe, my words were hollow. I knew from experience that a loss that great wasn't something that ever fully healed. The best I could do was hold her and be there for her. Death and loss made no sense. There wasn't any explaining it or rationalizing it. An accident like that wasn't logical, and neither was McKenna's view on her role.

She did nothing to cause their deaths. And I hoped in time I could help her to see that.

After what seemed like close to an hour, her sobs finally quieted and I continued to hold her until the little rasping hiccups stopped, too. She moved from the spot where she'd burrowed in against my neck. "I'm sorry," she whispered, and attempted to move back to her side of the bed.

My arms closed around her, keeping her close. "Never apologize for that. I'm here. And I know what it feels like to lose your parents."

She nodded. "Thank you for listening and for holding me…."

"Shh. No need to thank me."

"Knox?"

"Yeah?"

"This, us what does it mean?"

"What do you want it to mean?"

"More," she admitted softly.

I had no idea what more meant to her, but I could only assume it involved me fully opening myself up to this process. "I like you, McKenna. You have to know I'm not like this with anyone but you."

"I like you too, but this isn't going to be like one of your other relationships."

"So what do we do?" I traced her cheek and watched her eyes. She would have to take the lead, because I was at a total fucking loss for how to have a real relationship.

"I guess we see where this takes us."

"I've never had anything like this, how do you know I'm not going to mess it up?"

"Because you're a good man, Knox."

I pressed a kiss to her lips, surprising her. I hadn't meant the kiss as anything sexual, just a comforting endearment to show her I cared. But McKenna lifted her lips to mine and kissed me back. Her mouth was warm and soft and a jolt of pleasure shot straight to my dick. Now was not the time to get hard. McKenna's body was nestled in against mine, just the thin layer of her T-shirt and my gym shorts separating the heat of her body from mine. She tossed her top leg over my hip and pressed herself closer, no doubt feeling every hard inch of me. I wanted her, but not like this.

McKenna craved physical touch, but in a much different way than I did. She was seeking something real – a connection, something permanent. I never thought I'd be the one to offer her those things, but seeing how brave she was, how open she was with her needs, made me question everything. I wanted to be what she needed. I just didn't know how and was pretty certain I'd find a way to fuck it up. Hurting her was out of the question. She'd been through too much already.

We kissed for several long minutes, our tongues moving together, her breathing becoming ragged, and her lower half pressing clumsily into mine as though she was seeking something.

I hadn't wanted to push things between us tonight, but hell, she'd just broken down and told me she felt responsible for her parents' deaths. If there was ever a time she needed the distraction of pleasure, it was now. I knew that better than anyone.

"Knox...." she breathed, pressing her hips to mine.

I didn't respond, my lips moving to her neck to taste her and breathe in her sweet scent. Her hands scrambled along my abs until they reached the waistband of my shorts. I caught her roaming hands and moved them away just before they dipped inside. We'd just agreed to take the first steps toward a relationship and I didn't want her to think that had anything to do with sex. I wanted her, of course I did, but I wanted more, too.

Sex wasn't the way to show her how I felt about her. That meant nothing to me. But being near her kissing her, cooking for her, letting her sleep over in my bed. Those were the ways I told her how I felt about her. Only now as her fingers curled into my hair and her lips hovered above mine, I didn't think she got that. She wanted the physical, too. And it was killing me. Literally killing me not to take her and push her knees apart and sink into her slowly.

She let out a frustrated groan and rubbed her pelvis against mine. Even if I didn't want her to feel pressured to go further than she wanted, I wouldn't leave her in this state. Trailing my hand from her hip down to her pubic bone, my fingers brushed against her panties. The damp fabric clung to her skin. "Right here?" She whimpered softly. "Is this where you need me?" She pushed her hips closer, begging me silently. Lifting her panties aside, I pressed my fingertip against her firm little clit and she let out a ragged moan. Something told me I knew her body better than she did herself, and I liked hearing the responses I provoked from her. I liked knowing I was the one responsible for her pleasure. The one taking her over the edge. It did insane things to me. Even without touching me, she got me rock hard and aching. Half of me worried we should stop – we'd both been drinking – but none of me wanted to.

Removing my hand from her panties, I pressed a kiss to her parted lips and met her eyes. "Angel?" Disappointment flooded her pretty eyes. "How drunk are you?" She'd only had one drink plus the shot I'd made her try, but still, something told me she was unaccustomed to drinking.

She hesitated for a moment, blinking up at me. "Not drunk," she breathed. "Don't stop." Her mouth crashed against mine in a hungry kiss and I was done questioning this.

237

Restraint urged me to keep her panties on but I couldn't help lifting the baggy T-shirt she wore and kissing all over her breasts. Using both hands, I pressed her tits together and placed damp sucking kisses all over the rounded flesh, using my tongue to lick each taut peak until she was restless and moaning out my name. She smelled lightly of soap and fresh washed laundry and tasted even better. I was desperate to taste her all over and feel her warm soft skin against mine.

Creaking floorboards signaled that we weren't alone just as I heard my name. "Knox?"

I tossed the blankets over McKenna to cover her naked chest and jumped up. "Tucker? What's wrong?"

"My tummy hurts," he groaned.

"Okay, buddy. Come on." I led him into the bathroom, my heart pounding out of control. As soon as the toilet was in view, Tucker lurched over it and got sick. I stayed with him in the bathroom, sitting on the tile floor, just in case he got sick again.

A few minutes later, McKenna tapped on the bathroom door. I didn't know if she'd wanted to hide the fact she was staying overnight, but she stuck her head inside the door to see if Tucker was okay. "You need anything? A glass of water, maybe?"

I nodded. "Sure, that'd be great."

After a few minutes more, Tucker rinsed his mouth and crawled into my bed between me and McKenna. By that point it was nearly three in the morning and we were all exhausted. Tucker had insisted she stay and held her hand as he fell back asleep. I caught McKenna's eyes as she lay on the far side of the bed, a sick little boy sprawled between us, and as I watched her in the dim light, she seemed to understand that this was my life. Her eyes on mine and the small smile on her lips was her silent acknowledgement that she accepted each part. From my broken past to my responsibilities with my brothers. McKenna's constant presence here showed me that she could handle not only the fucked up side of me, but also my role as a brother and a parent. It was a huge feeling of relief. Realizing I wasn't alone for the first time in a long time, I feel into a peaceful sleep.

Chapter Six
McKenna

I had sent a quick text to Brian to let him know I wouldn't be home last night. And to my surprise, he hadn't replied. My phone had stayed eerily silent all night. A sinking feeling formed in the pit of my stomach.

After getting Tucker settled in his own bed with some dry toast and soda, Knox and I ventured to the kitchen where Knox set a pot of coffee to brew. I was working at the teen shelter today, but didn't go in until mid-morning, and Knox, with a sick little boy home from school today, was taking the day off to look after him.

Sitting down at the breakfast table, I watched him work. He seemed completely at ease in the kitchen, and for a guy as big and strong as Knox, it was a bit of an anomaly. One I very much liked. His domestic nature, despite being a rugged bad-boy, was just another thing I loved about him.

Luke and Jaxon entered the kitchen and gave me only a brief strange look when they saw me and realized that I must have spent the night. "Hey, McKenna." Luke smiled.

"Hey, Luke."

Jaxon grabbed an apple from the kitchen counter and began slicing it into chunks while simultaneously sizing me up.

"Fuck!" he cursed, dropping the knife and holding his finger up to inspect.

I jumped from my seat and crossed the room to where Jaxon stood. "Did you cut yourself?"

He shrugged, turning on the faucet to rinse his hand under cool water. "It's nothing."

"At least let me have a look." I took his hand, all but forcing him to let me see. These boys were so brave, so independent, that they didn't want to have to rely on anyone for anything. They'd been hurt so badly losing their parents. They were afraid to need anyone. The slice through the pad of his index finger wasn't deep, but was bleeding pretty steadily. "I think I can bandage this up pretty quick, it doesn't look too bad."

"Nah, I'm okay. Luke, hit me with that paper towel."

"Man-daid?" Luke asked, tossing a roll of paper towel across the kitchen to Jaxon.

Jaxon nodded and began wrapping several sheets around his bloodied finger.

"Man-daid?" I asked, watching their exchange.

"Yeah, like a Band-Aid, but for real men. Paper towel and duct tape." Luke smiled, tossing Jaxon a roll of duct tape from a nearby drawer.

Jaxon used the tape to secure the paper towel in place. "See?" He held up the digit. "All good."

I shook my head, giggling at their inventiveness. "What about your breakfast?" I asked, looking over at the discarded chunks of apple on the counter.

Jaxon shrugged. "I'll grab something later."

"Have a good day at school, boys."

Knox met me in the kitchen where I was tidying up after the boys.

He scooped me up in his arms, wrapping me tightly in a hug. "You don't have to do that."

"It's not a problem." I liked helping, feeling useful like this.

"About last night." His hand closed over mine, stopping me from wiping down the counter so I met his eyes. "Thank you for telling me about your parents."

I nodded. I hadn't wanted to tell him – not because I was set on keeping my past hidden, no, he'd been too open with me to do that. But because I knew he'd look at me differently once he knew. I'd seen it before – once people found out, their looks changed to ones of pity, of sadness. I couldn't stand the thought of Knox looking at me like that. But instead he'd just pulled me close and let me cry big soggy tears that rolled down my cheeks and stained his T-shirt. It had been exactly what I needed.

"Let me check on Tucker one more time and then I'll drive you home."

"Okay." I followed him up the stairs, wanting to say goodbye to Tucker myself.

We found him curled on his side, the trash can Knox had set next to his bed thankfully still empty.

"How ya feeling, buddy?" Knox sat down on the edge of his bed, handing him a stuffed teddy bear that had fallen to the floor.

Tucker wrapped his arms around the bear and closed his eyes. "The same. Tummy still hurts."

Knox pulled the blankets up higher around Tucker's shoulders. "I've got to take McKenna home and then I'll be right back. You need me to get you anything before we go?"

Tucker's eyes latched onto mine. He was like a mini-version of Knox, and even at eight years old, it was easy to see that he'd grow into a very handsome man, just like his older brothers. Seeing them together made my chest feel tight. Knox was so sweet, so gentle, and watching him care for his brother was the most wonderful sight. He was beautiful to me in that moment. It took me a second to realize Tucker was asking about me.

"Why does McKenna have to leave?" he asked, his features painted in confusion.

"She has to go to work today," Knox explained.

"But you don't, right?"

Knox shook his head. "I took the day off. I'm staying home with you today. We can watch a movie later if you want."

I bent down and placed my hand on Tucker's forehead, checking for a temperature. He didn't seem overly warm. "I promise I'll come back and check on you. Feel better, okay?"

He nodded, fixing on a brave face. "Bye, Kenna."

"Nikki's going to come over while I'm gone. Just in case, all right, buddy?"

Tucker nodded bravely.

Knox led the way downstairs and we dressed ourselves in coats and shoes, waiting by the front door for his neighbor Nikki.

Knox leaned closer, tucking stray strands of hair behind my ears. "I'm sorry we got interrupted last night. Maybe we can finish our conversation tonight?"

I wondered which part he was sorry got interrupted — our intimate moment or the conversation about my parents? I merely nodded my agreement. Moments later, his young neighbor Nikki let herself in the front door, her baby daughter Bailee balanced on her hip. The baby looked just like her mom — both were pretty with blonde ringlets and big blue eyes. I wasn't sure why, but I hadn't realized his neighbor was gorgeous. She eyed me carefully while Knox took the baby so she could remove her jacket.

"Hi. I'm Nikki." She offered me her hand.

"McKenna. It's nice to meet you. Your daughter's beautiful."

She took the little girl back from Knox. "Thanks."

I could tell there was something she didn't like about seeing me here with Knox. She probably wasn't used to seeing women here in his home, especially in the morning hours, and I briefly wondered if they'd ever had a fling.

"Tucker's upstairs in bed," Knox said. "I'd just stay down here if I were you. Keep both of you away from the germs."

Nikki nodded. "I will."

She crossed the room, sat Bailee down on the rug in the living room, and dumped a nearby basket of toys out in front of her, then planted herself on the couch with the TV remote. The twinge of jealously brewing inside me was unexpected. I knew Knox's past and worked hard to not let it get to me, but something about seeing this girl in his home, somewhere she was obviously quite comfortable, set me off. I pushed it from my mind as Knox led the way out to his Jeep.

The flu progressed from Tucker to Luke to Jaxon and I feared Knox was next, despite his insistence that he felt fine. He'd been taking care of everyone all week; surely he'd exposed himself to the sickness. I knew I was supposed to hang out with Brian that weekend, but Knox hadn't sounded well on the phone, so I'd put my date with Brian off, promising to make it up to him, and decided to go over and check on the guys once more.

The house was quiet. Too quiet. I suspected the boys were home, but they were either napping or doing quiet activities in their rooms. I climbed the stairs to the third floor and lightly tapped on Knox's bedroom door. Not waiting for an answer, I pushed the door open and stepped inside. The blinds were drawn, and the room was quiet, cool and dim. Knox was stretched out across his bed, his big frame limp against the mattress. I didn't even have to ask him if he was sick. It was obvious.

"You shouldn't be here," he said, sitting up in bed once he saw me. He looked miserable, and I'd guess it was a combination of a few things – lack of sleep being the main contributor. He lifted to his elbow to watch me cross the room. The sheets were strewn haphazardly around him and he was in a pair of loose-fitting gray knit pants and a white T-shirt. His feet were bare and his hair stuck up in several directions. "We're going to get you sick."

"Hush." I sat down beside him and brushed his hair back off his forehead. He felt warm and his cheeks were flushed. I might be in a house filled with germs, but that wasn't even hitting my radar. "I'm here and I'm staying. You can't do all this on your own, despite thinking you're Superman."

He chuckled, dryly, his throat obviously raw. "I don't think that."

I met his eyes. "You act like it sometimes. Working hard, raising your brothers, trying to right your wrongs. You're pretty amazing, you know that?" Something about seeing him this sick and miserable made me all sentimental.

"You think that, but it's not true," he said. I didn't argue, didn't want him to waste his energy debating his point. I knew he was amazing, despite what he thought. I just continued softly brushing back his hair, gazing down at him with reverence. "You've always thought that, haven't you?" he continued. "You always believed in me. Even before I believed in myself."

Of course I did. I was a counselor; I believed people could change, right down to my very being. I had to believe it. It needed to be true if I was ever going to be good enough to outdo the wrong that caused me to lose my parents. Or maybe I just wanted to believe that Knox could change because I'd felt such a pull to him right from the beginning. I'd wanted a little piece of this troubled man, even though it scared me. I needed him to be okay. So did his brothers. "Just rest. I'm going to go clean up a bit and run to the grocery store."

He smiled weakly up at me. "Thank you. There's some money in my top drawer." He looked over at his dresser in the corner.

He worked hard for his money, but I knew he wasn't any better off than me. If I could help out a little, I would. And there was enough in my bank account this week. I could afford bread and milk and basics for the boys. "Anything in particular sound good?"

He made a grimace, like food sounded awful. "Maybe just some soda."

"You got it." And perhaps some chicken noodle soup for once they all started feeling better. It was just what my mom would have made if I were sick. I'd get a big pot bubbling on the stove just in case. Fill the house with that yummy aroma in the hopes that would lift their spirits.

I headed downstairs and found Luke and Jaxon on the couch playing the least spirited game of Xbox I'd ever seen. They still looked glassy-eyed and pale, but they were out of bed and apparently well enough to sit and play, but not enough to engage in their usual banter and trash talking. "You guys feeling better?" I asked, slipping on my coat and shoes.

"Well enough to not be hugging the toilet anymore." Jaxon smirked.

"That's a good thing." I winked. "I'm headed to the store and I'm gonna make some chicken noodle soup later, it'll be ready whenever you feel up for eating."

"Thanks, Kenna," they both chimed in.

I would tackle the dishes and bathrooms when I returned. This house was in need of some serious TLC. After a week of four sick boys with no one cleaning up – it looked and smelled the part.

"McKenna?" Luke asked, glancing up from his game.

I paused, turning to face him. "Yeah?"

"Thanks for making our house feel like a home." He flashed a perfectly straight white smile at me and my heart melted a tiny bit in my chest. Without a family of my own anymore, I'd been unwittingly making myself part of theirs.

When I got home from Knox's place, I was exhausted. I felt like I hadn't slept in a week. I wanted nothing more than to crawl into bed and wrap myself up in the blankets, but first I wanted a nice hot shower. Brian wasn't home, thankfully, so I didn't have to field any questions about where I'd been all day. I knew he wasn't happy about me cancelling our plans to go and see Knox.

Under the steaming spray of water, I washed myself thoroughly, scrubbing away any lingering germs, though I'd been careful at Knox's, washing my hands and disinfecting everything I'd touched over there. Drying myself with an oversized towel, I padded into my bedroom and dressed in pajamas. I didn't care that it was only late afternoon. I felt like going to bed.

Crawling under the covers, I was asleep as soon as my head touched the pillow.

Chapter Seven

Knox

When my texts and phone calls to McKenna went unanswered, I decided to drive over to her apartment to see for myself what was going on. Just as I suspected, she'd come down with the flu. After an unpleasant exchange with Brian, I found her in her bed, curled into a tight little ball.

"McKenna?" I whispered.

Her eyes opened slowly, taking several moments to focus on mine. "Knox?"

"You caught it, didn't you?" I smiled down at her, brushing her hair back from her face.

"Uh huh," she nodded.

I knew there'd been no way she could have hung around me and the boys, as sick as we all were for four days straight, and not catch this nasty flu. Something tugged inside my chest seeing her so pale and listless. I wished there was something I could do, but unfortunately I knew this thing had to run its course. "Can I get you anything?"

She pulled the blankets up higher toward her chin. "I'm cold.

Maybe an extra blanket." She tipped her chin toward the chair in the corner where a fluffy throw blanket was folded.

I arranged the blanket over her and then crawled into bed beside her. "Here." I opened my arms. "I'll warm you up."

She snuggled into my chest. "Mmm. My own personal space heater."

McKenna dozed in and out of sleep while I lay there holding her. She stopped shivering after about ten minutes and soon her skin was growing damp with perspiration.

Now that my strength had returned and all the boys were healthy again, I'd returned to work. But if need be, I would stay here and care for McKenna, just like she'd done for us.

After a brief knock, Brian pushed open the door. Shooting him a scowl, I wondered if he invaded McKenna's privacy like this often. *Dickhead.* "Need something?" I asked. McKenna's eyelids fluttered, but she remained curled against my side.

"I'd prefer the door to stay open if you're going to be in her room with her."

Was he fucking serious? "Are you her father?"

Opening her eyes, McKenna looked up at me and frowned. My choice of words hit me at that exact moment. *Fuck.* "I'm sorry. I'll be right back."

I climbed from her bed and met Brian in the hallway, softly closing the bedroom door behind me. "What's your problem with me? Or is it with any man being with her that isn't you?"

"McKenna may trust you, but I don't. And I certainly don't trust you alone in a bed with her."

"She's sick. Do you really think I'm going to try something?"

He shrugged. "I don't know how you work – what you're capable of."

"I have issues, I'll be the first to admit it, but I'm not a fucking rapist. Christ." I shuddered. It made me wonder what McKenna had told him about me. Did he actually think I'd make her do anything she wasn't ready for? The truth was, McKenna had been the one driving the physical aspects of our relationship this entire time. Not that I'd give good old Brian the satisfaction of knowing that.

"She hasn't told you, has she?" Brian smirked.

"Told me what?"

"McKenna's still a virgin. At least I'm pretty sure she is."

All the air was ripped from my lungs. McKenna was untouched? That piece of information made me both deliriously happy and pissed off. How could she not have told me? What if I'd let things go too far the other night? "That's her business," I said, recovering.

Brian narrowed his eyes. If he wanted to believe I was the bad guy, that I was dangerous for her – too fucking bad. McKenna brought out new sides in me, made me feel things I'd never felt before. And I wouldn't hurt her, would never force her. He could think whatever he wanted to about me. I had zero problem knocking him on his ass again if the occasion called for it. And the way my blood was currently coursing through my veins, stirring up anger and resentment inside me, I wondered if now was that occasion. Instead, I took a deep breath and forced myself to calm down. "If we're through here, I have a sick girl in there to take care of." I headed into her room and closed the door behind me, signaling that she was mine to care for, not his.

Seeing her lying in bed again, there were a million things I wanted to ask her about. Brian had just dropped a huge fucking bombshell on me and I wanted to ask McKenna if it were true. If she was a virgin, we were on two totally different wave-lengths. What could she be thinking about wanting to enter into a relationship with me? Our conversations came roaring back me. The way she angled her hips to mine the other night, seeking, wanting… I couldn't be expected to control myself and go slow like she needed when she did shit like that.

I sat down on the edge of her bed and let out a heavy sigh.

"What's wrong?" she croaked, opening her eyes.

"Nothing, angel. Just rest, okay?"

She nodded and let her eyes slip closed again. We needed to discuss this, but the conversation would have to wait. One, because I had no fucking idea what I was doing, and two, because first she needed time to heal.

I pressed a kiss to her forehead and left moments later, reeling from the realization that for once, I was totally and completely out of my element with a girl.

Chapter Eight

McKenna

Monday morning I was finally well enough to get out of bed. I showered and changed into fresh clothes and then ventured out into the living room. Brian sat on the couch with his back toward me, essentially ignoring me. He was dressed and ready for work, but sat motionless with a mug of coffee. I grabbed a soda from the fridge and sat down next to him, wondering what I'd done wrong this time.

"You feeling better?" he asked, his eyes still glued to the commercial playing on the TV.

"Yeah. Sorry, the last few days are a complete blur." I opened the can of soda and took a small sip, the sugar and fizz tasting delicious after having nothing in the belly for so long.

"We were supposed to hang out this weekend."

So that's what this was about. Brian was giving me the cold shoulder because I'd had to cancel our plans. Did he really think I purposefully chose being chained to the toilet over hanging out with him? "Brian, I got sick."

"You spent all week working hard and then taking care of him." He shot me an exasperated look. "What did you expect to happen?"

I shrugged. When he put it like that, I couldn't argue. His anger was misplaced, but I supposed I had exposed myself to the flu.

"It's fine." He turned to fully face me. "It helps me see where I fall on your list of priorities. Dead fucking last."

Seeing how let down he really was made my heart ache for him. Brian always put me first – always. And he was right. He often ranked last on my to do list. Mainly because I knew he would always be there. My job and my volunteer work came first and Knox and his family were a close second. They were the only things that made me feel whole. Yet sitting here, facing him and looking into his sad blue eyes, I felt guilty. Not because I'd gotten sick and missed our weekend plans, but because I'd never feel the way about him that he did for me.

He'd changed his whole life for me. He moved away from his family and friends, he worked long hours at a tough Chicago accounting firm rather than the simple small town firm he probably would've ended up at had he stayed in Indiana. All because of me. And weighing on me most of all was the fact he didn't date. Like he was waiting for me to see him in a different light – waiting for me to be ready. I just wanted him to move on with his life so I could, too.

Knowing he didn't support my relationship with Knox was hard.

Brian had always been there to cheer me on through everything in life. He celebrated my small victories and praised my every accomplishment. This chance at something real felt like the biggest thing that had ever happened to me, and Brian didn't support it.

I took my soda back to my bedroom, feeling the need to withdraw into myself once again.

Sitting on my bed, I decided to call Belinda, feeling guilty for missing the last two Saturday group sessions – one because of the retreat, and this weekend's because I was sick.

Belinda disregarded my apology completely. "Things come up, McKenna. And you were under the weather. No need to apologize."

"Well, I'll definitely be there next Saturday and please let me know if there's anything I can do in the meantime."

"Perhaps there is something you could do. Amanda reached out to me on Friday…."

She explained that Amanda had yet to have any prenatal care and didn't have a vehicle to take herself to the doctor.

"Well, I'd be happy to take her, but I don't have a car, either."

"Hmm. That is a problem."

"You know what? It's not a problem. I can either borrow my

roommate's car or take the bus with her. Maybe just having someone reach out and offer to help will be enough. That way she doesn't have to navigate going to the doctor alone."

"I think that would help a lot. Very thoughtful of you, McKenna. Thank you."

"It's not a problem." It would give me something to do today, since I wasn't due to work at the teen shelter today. Though there was no way I would ask to borrow Brian's car. Not to mention he needed it to get to work. Hopefully Amanda would be okay with taking the bus.

Belinda took care of the details – contacting Amanda and arranging a time for us to meet up at her apartment. I got myself showered and dressed for the day and headed out to wait for the bus.

Amanda lived in a rundown apartment that she shared with three other girls. It didn't look like anyplace to raise a baby, but we'd hurdle one obstacle at a time. The first step was getting her well and making sure her baby was healthy.

"Thanks for doing this today." Amanda smiled at me as she buttoned her coat.

"It's really no problem. I didn't have anything going on today anyway."

She paused at the door, hesitating. "Was everything okay...the last group meeting you ran out of there pretty abruptly, and then haven't been back…."

I smiled at her reassuringly. "Everything's fine. It was just a slight misunderstanding…." I left it at that. I had to protect what Knox and I had.

"Fair enough." She nodded, clearly not one to pry.

Amanda, having moved here from southern Illinois, wasn't familiar with the city bus system. So while we rode, I showed her how to read the bus map and explained what the letters and numbers meant so she could learn to navigate the routes. To get to the free clinic downtown from where she lived, it required us to change bus lines twice, and I knew if she could master this, she could get herself anywhere.

"How have you been feeling?" I asked as we watched the traffic pass. Stealing another glance, I noticed her belly now protruded in a nice round bump.

"Actually, I've been having some morning sickness. But other than that, fine, I guess."

We rode the rest of the way in silence. I found myself at a loss for what to talk with her about. I knew about her issues with love and sex addiction from Belinda, but since she didn't seem to be in a talkative mood, I wasn't going to press her. She likely had a lot on her mind – with a baby growing inside her, no job, no car, and little support.

When we arrived at the clinic, we signed in and sat down in the waiting room. There were several other girls with pregnant bellies waiting in the chairs around us and a few who were most likely here for testing or birth control. Amanda flipped absently through a parenting magazine, not seeming to absorb a single word for how quickly she was turning the pages.

"There's something I feel kind of weird about and I should probably just tell you," she blurted after several minutes.

"What is it?"

"I, um, came onto Knox."

My eyes widened. "What? When?" I fought to control my voice. I couldn't go sounding like a jealous girlfriend right now. As hard as it was, I needed to be objective and professional. Amanda was opening up to me as part of her own treatment.

"In a moment of weakness…it was stupid, I know. He'd given me his phone number and I knew I supposed to use it to call him about recovery and kid-related questions, but one night I was sitting around feeling lonely and sorry for myself and I called him up and asked if he wanted to hang out and have a little grown up fun."

I nearly choked getting my next words out. "And did he?" If he'd lied to me about hooking up Amanda, so help me God, I'd lose it. I wasn't a violent person, but the wrath I'd rain down on him would rival the apocalypse.

She chewed on her lip. "No, he said he was trying to be done with random hookups and made it sound there was someone special in his life."

Wow. I knew I should respond, but I was rendered speechless.

"You're not mad, are you?"

It took me almost a full minute to realize she wasn't asking because she knew that Knox were sort of together, she was asking because she was supposed to be in recovery. My twisted emotions were going to blow this whole thing if I wasn't careful. "No, I'm not mad. I won't ever be mad for you opening up and sharing with me." I took her hand. "I'm actually proud of you, Amanda. You're growing. You might have slipped up a little, but you recognized that your actions were wrong." Her confession to me proved that. I released her hand and a smile blossomed across her mouth.

Amanda turned back to her magazine and tore out a coupon for baby formula, stuffing it into her purse. I decided then and there that I liked her. I was glad Belinda had asked me to help. Amanda was actually a sweet girl underneath her layers of hurt and despair. She was burdened by dark secrets just like me. I felt a sort of familiarity being with her, waiting here with her just so that she could have some company and not feel quite so alone.

As I looked around the waiting room, I couldn't help but notice the numerous posters plastered on the walls about birth control options. I'd never had to think about things like birth control, but as I sat there, my mind wandered to Knox, and I found myself thinking about birth control pills and condoms. I didn't know if or when anything might happen between us, or when Knox would be ready to take our physical relationship further, but I made a mental note to call and schedule an appointment with my gynecologist soon. Nerves danced in my belly at the thought of being intimate with him, but I knew I wanted him to be my first. Cold dread shivered down my spine. God, what would Belinda say? I shuddered at the thought. I was planning to have sex with one of our group members. Nothing about this situation was normal, but I didn't care because it felt right. And I was tired of being too careful, barely living these last few years. I wanted to be with Knox. Plain and simple. And I thought he wanted to be with me, too, as resistant as he'd been about taking our relationship further. We were making real progress and I wouldn't stop things now. And I'd need to make sure we were prepared so I didn't find myself in a situation like Amanda, with an unplanned pregnancy. Knox had enough mouths to feed. I wouldn't add a baby to mix.

I hadn't expected to go into the exam room with her, but when the nurse called her name, Amanda looked at me expectantly and waited for me to rise from my seat and join her. I could read the indecision in her eyes. She didn't want to be alone, and I couldn't blame her.

I held her hand while they performed an ultrasound and tears leaked from the corners of her eyes as she seen the tiny image of a baby inside her for the first time. The steady thump of the baby's heart was sure and strong.

The nurse estimated the baby to almost five months along, based on her measurements, which surprised Amanda. Her own calculations had been off. She was due in the spring.

"There's only one in there, right?" she asked the nurse, her voice high and almost panicked.

The nurse and I both smiled. "Yes, there's just one baby. And he or she looks to be growing just fine. Did you want to know the sex?"

"Yes, please," Amanda said.

"You're having a girl."

I held her hand while she cried, her eyes fixed on the screen. It seemed Amanda wouldn't be alone any longer.

Helpful deed done for the day, I dropped Amanda off at home and texted Knox as I sat on the bus alone. Being around someone even more alone and lonely than myself all day had inspired a visit. I missed him.

Chapter Nine

McKenna

When I arrived at Knox's place, Tucker had already gone to bed, but Knox, Jaxon, and Luke all sat together in the living room. While they were normally so good-natured, tonight the mood felt tense. I toed off my shoes at the welcome mat and ventured in to see what they were discussing.

Luke sat on the sofa with his head hanging in his hands. Jaxon and Knox were perched in the arm chairs facing him, all of their expressions sour.

"Do you want to talk about it or are you going to keep moping around like someone kicked you in the balls?" Jaxon asked, looking squarely at Luke.

"Cool it, Jax," Knox warned. "Luke? You wanna talk?"

Luke peered up, his eyes wandering over to mine and then back to his brothers. I sat down next to him. "Everything okay?" I asked.

He shrugged. "Just girl problems," he said, releasing a heavy sigh. "Mollie broke up with me."

I hadn't known that he had a girlfriend, but perhaps this was the reason he'd once asked me about how to make a girl's first time special. I still got a happy little feeling remembering how he'd opened up to me. "I'm sorry." I squeezed his hand.

"If Knox has taught us anything, it's that there are plenty of girls to go around. There's no sense getting your panties in a twist over this one. So pull your tampon out and man up," Jaxon said, rising from the chair. "And on that note, I'm going to bed. You guys are depressing."

Knox frowned, watching Jaxon retreat up the stairs. "Ignore him, Luke. Jax is an asshole."

Luke's twisted expression relaxed slightly. "How do you know when you're in love?" he asked Knox.

This should be interesting. I waited, breathless, to hear his answer.

Knox's brows drew together. "You just do." He hesitated for a few seconds, running his hand over the back of his neck, looking deep in thought, like he was trying to put into words whatever was churning inside his head. "I guess you know when you want to spend time with the girl, protect her, and take care of her."

My heart melted at hearing his description of love. We might not be there yet, but I hoped we were on our way.

"Like you are with McKenna?" Luke asked.

Knox's dark eyes met mine, and all the oxygen was ripped from my lungs. He didn't say anything else, he just watched me for several long moments while my heart pounded steadily. The warmth of hot adrenaline pushed through my veins. He was looking at me like he wanted to do unspeakable things to me and I was staring back at him, challenging him to take whatever he wanted. He already had my heart.

"Knox?" I asked, breaking the heavy silence. "Will you give us a minute?" I tipped my head toward Luke. I wanted to talk to him alone and I might spontaneously combust if Knox kept looking at me like that, all dark and hungry.

"Sure." Knox rose from the arm chair. "I'll just go check on Tuck."

Luke released a heavy sigh full of sorrow. I scooted closer to him on the couch. "You okay, bud?"

"Yeah." He flashed me a weak smile. "This love shit sucks, though."

"What happened with Mollie?"

He shrugged. "She acted like she was into me, we went on a couple dates, and then I heard at school today she was seeing this other guy the entire time."

"Then she wasn't worth your time. You're an amazing guy, Luke, thoughtful, smart, funny, and handsome. High school can be brutal, but you'll be at college soon and trust me, you'll be beating the girls off with a stick." I grinned wickedly at him.

He laughed. "Yeah, right. If I can even afford college. Every time I bring it up, Knox changes the subject. I've been applying to every scholarship I can find, but they're really competitive and so far, I haven't been offered a single one. I'm screwed without some financial help, no matter how good my grades are. My high school offers a scholarship to the valedictorian, which I have a good shot at – but it's a thousand bucks. What will that get me? Books for one semester?" He shook his head in defeat.

It crushed me to know that his future hung in the balance like that. "I wish there was something I could do to help," I pondered out loud.

"Just having you around helps. There's way too much testosterone in this house."

I couldn't argue with that. "Well, I plan on being around for a while. Someone's got to keep Knox in line."

Descending down the stairs, Knox glanced our way. "Did I hear my name?"

"Nope," Luke and I said at the same time, sharing a secretive smile.

"Well, I guess I'm gonna go up, too, "Luke said. "Night, guys, and thanks, McKenna."

"Night, Lukey!" I gave him a kiss on his cheek and watched him wander up the stairs before turning to face Knox. "How was Tucker?"

"Sound asleep." He sat down next to me. "Is Luke alright?"

I nodded. "Yeah. I just think there's a lot on his mind. Girls, how to pay for college…."

Knox blew out a frustrated breath. "Fuck. Tell me about it. It's been keeping me up at night."

I hadn't meant to add to his stress load, only to tell him how my conversation with Luke went. Knox hung his head in his hands and I moved closer so I could rub his shoulders. "Don't worry. It'll all work out somehow."

His head lifted until his intense gaze met mine. My fingers paused on his shoulders. "That's just it. Nothing just works out around here unless I figure it out. And I've been trying for the last year to figure out how in the hell I'm going to help Luke pay for college and so far I've come up with jack shit nothing, so unless you have an extra fifty grand laying around, it won't just magically work out." I could see the defeat written all over his features. He felt like a failure. He had three little lives depending on him and he wanted the best he could provide. "I'm sorry." His tone softened. "I don't mean to take it out on you." Considering that his usual way of taking out stress was by sleeping with random women, I would take sarcasm any day.

271

"It's okay. I know you're under a lot of pressure. I'm here to help however you need me." I couldn't imagine being in his position. I only had to budget for myself and even that was tricky in an expensive city like Chicago.

"Thanks, Kenna." He sat back against the sofa, pulling me closer. "It's good to see you feeling better. What'd you do today?"

"I took Amanda to the doctor for a prenatal appointment. She's having a girl. They said the baby is healthy and progressing nicely."

"That's good," he said, grabbing the TV remote.

"Why didn't you tell me the truth about Amanda?"

He glanced up at me, remorse flashing in his eyes. "I'm sorry. I should have. I just didn't want to give you something to worry about when I knew I had it under control."

"She propositioned you?"

He nodded. "There was no temptation there. None. I told you, I'm handling it. And I've got someone better I'm waiting for." He laced our fingers together, his palm resting against mine, warm and solid.

"Should we go upstairs?" I whispered, suddenly feeling bold and wanting some privacy with him.

"I thought we'd hang out down here, maybe watch a movie or something."

"Oh, okay." I tried to hide the disappointment in my voice, but failed.

Knox flipped through the selection of available movies for rent and let me pick a romantic comedy I'd been waiting to see for several months. I curled against his side and he held me while we watched the sugary-sweet interactions playing out on the screen. They seemed so far from real life. At least far-removed from my life and Knox's. In my experiences, real life and love were incredibly messy affairs. That was what I knew. Maybe that was why I was so comfortable with Knox. He'd been through hell and back, too, and we recognized those deep scars in each other.

Throughout the entire movie Knox kept things purely platonic. His arms were wrapped around me, strong and sure, but the few times I'd tried to let my hands wander to touch him, his stomach, his thigh…he would tighten his grip around me, holding me in place and effectively preventing me from touching him. It was incredibly frustrating and only left me worked up and buzzing unfulfilled energy inside me.

For two hours I lay there in his arms, his chest rising and falling steadily against my back, his breath warming the back of my neck. Various scenarios played out in my head. I imagined rolling towards him, unbuckling his belt and touching him again. What would he do then? The realization that he may stop me, that he might reject me, prevented me from making my move.

Once the credits rolled, I climbed from my warm spot next to him on the couch and stood, stretching. "Should we go up to bed?"

Knox stood up, watching me warily. "You're sleeping over?"

"Is that okay?" *God, why was he acting so weird tonight?*

He hesitated, looking down at the floor.

"Why are you acting like you don't want me here?"

He didn't respond, he just continued staring down at the floor between our feet.

"Knox?"

"This is hard for me, being near you and knowing I can't have you," he admitted softly.

I wanted to tell him he could have me, anytime, anyplace. I'd gotten brief glimpses of how good we could be together and I wanted more. "You have me," I whispered.

He crossed the room and pulled me into his arms. "I know. I'm sorry, angel. I have a lot on my mind and I don't want to fuck this up with you. That's all."

"Do you want me to go?" I looked up at him, blinking.

"No. Stay. Please?"

I nodded and let him guide me up the stairs.

Once I'd brushed my teeth and changed into a T-shirt of Knox's, I stood beside the bed, watching while he pulled his shirt off over his head and stripped out of his jeans. His body was a work of art, complete with sculpted lines and rugged muscles that I wanted to touch and lick. He evoked strange feelings inside me that no man had before. It was an almost animal attraction that brought out a new and viscerally sexual side of me.

"Knox?"

"Hmm?" He asked, folding his jeans and tossing them on top of his dresser.

I found my courage and took a step closer, tugging on the hem of my borrowed T-shirt. "When we said we were gonna do this, a real relationship…to me that meant everything that came along with a relationship." Several long moments ticked by while my heart beat thudded dully in my chest.

"Say we do this thing for real – then what?" Frustrated, his hands tore through his hair, leaving it in a sexy disarray.

"What do you mean? We agree to be there for each other, we both try."

"And if I fuck up? If I hurt you…." He stared blankly at the wall above my head. "I couldn't…I wouldn't chance that." I knew there was more he wasn't saying. I'd already been through too much with my parents. I was damaged and he wouldn't be part of contributing to my hurt any more than he already had. I hated that I could never seem to escape my past, no matter how hard I worked.

"Isn't that for me to decide?"

His eyes slid back to mine. "You believe in me way too much."

"Someone's got to, Knox. I've seen the real you. The one you keep hidden from everyone else. You're a good man, despite what you want me to believe."

"You refuse to see the bad in me."

"So tell me, then. What's so bad about you?" I was edging into dangerous territory. We'd never really covered his background in detail and I wasn't sure I could handle it, but I was putting on my bravest front to show him that I wouldn't be scared off. Who cared if prickles of sweat were forming against the back of my neck and my knees felt shaky? It was a conversation that needed to happen.

"You really want to hear the shit I've done?"

Suddenly losing my nerve, my lips parted, but no sound came out.

Knox took a step closer, his gaze hardening. "You want to hear that I fucked a mother and her eighteen-year-old daughter in the same day? That I broke up my buddy's engagement when I accepted a blowjob from his fiancée? That because of this sick need inside me I've pushed every boundary, every limit? That I enjoy anal sex and the occasional ménage? Is that what you want to hear? You can't handle me, angel. I can barely fucking handle me."

The air whooshed from my lungs, my confidence vanishing. For the first time I began to doubt him – us – my belief that this could work falling away like a veil in the wind. He would want things I couldn't possibility give him.

"Say something," he ordered, taking a predatory step closer.

"I get it, okay? You made your point. You're experienced. I'm not."

"That wasn't my point. Not at all." He hung his head, looking down at the floor, his hands returning to his hair once again. "I'm sick, not a man worthy of you," he whispered.

My heart broke for him. He deserved love and acceptance even if he couldn't see that. "The things you've done don't scare me. I just worry I won't measure up to your past."

He stepped closer, wrapping a hand around my hip to draw me nearer until we were just inches apart. It didn't escape my notice that he was dressed in only a pair of black boxer briefs. "You have it backwards. My past doesn't measure up to you." His voice was whispery soft and his mouth was brushing against my ear, sending delicious little shivers racing down my spine. He pressed a tender kiss against the side of my neck and my head fell back, my body craving more. His warm tongue slid against my pulse point, which was fluttering wildly. "I can read your fear, your uncertainty. You're not ready for this."

Finding my voice, I whispered, "So show me."

"You don't know what you're saying, what you're agreeing to."

We'd spoken only briefly about his dominant nature, but that word hung in the air all around us, its hidden meaning permeating my every pore. Maybe I couldn't handle his brand of physical affection. But what he'd shown me so far had been tender and intimate. Would sex with Knox really be so different? His tastes and desires were unknown to me, but most of me found that exciting. Nerves raced through my belly as he nipped at my neck. "If we do this, Knox…have a real relationship, you'd have to show me…." I breathed, finding my courage.

He squeezed me tighter. "If we do this, you have to tell Brian about us."

I giggled. Such an alpha male thing to say, laying his claim to me and wanting it known by all. "Of course I will. But stop avoiding this conversation. "

"What conversation are we having, McKenna?" He sucked the skin at the base of my neck, pressing sweet kisses against my collarbone.

"Sex," I murmured.

"You're not ready yet," he said. I pulled back and gave him a quizzical look. Was he serious right now? "I'll know when you're ready," he continued. "You need to trust me." His hands cupped

278

my cheeks and he pressed a kiss to my forehead. I didn't want to be treated like a china doll. I'd waited long enough for this moment in my life and I was sure.

"And you need to trust me." I might be damaged, but I was stronger than he was giving me credit for. I could handle this. Couldn't I?

He watched me with hooded eyes, taking stock of everything he saw – every emotion and stray thought racing through my brain. My entire body was alive and humming. It was as though he could see straight into me and read all my inner thoughts. It was the oddest sensation.

"Tell me what you want to know," he said, brushing the hair back from my face.

My stomach was coiled tight and nervous energy shot through my veins. Something was about to happen. I'd pushed him and now I needed to be sure I really was ready. "You seem so sure. And I don't know what I'm doing. I just need to know that's okay with you."

"That's a turn on, trust me. I can be a little dominating in the bedroom."

Finally, we were discussing the elephant in the room. "A dominant? Like…you want a submissive?" My entire body was tingling. I had to know what I was signing up for.

"Mmm, not exactly." His large palm curled around the back of my neck, his thumb stroking the skin there. "I just like taking charge. Nothing extreme, I promise."

My belly tightened. "I'm not into pain, Knox."

"That's not my thing at all, angel. You'd never have to worry about me hurting you." His voice was sincere, and his warm honey eyes were loving and kind, but that didn't stop the uncertainty raging inside me.

"What do you want, then?"

"Control. To show you pleasure."

His words sent a jab of lust straight between my thighs and I let out a whimper. Something about this man, his desire to bring me pleasure, lit me up from the inside out. If he had a trace of dominance, perhaps I had a trace of submissiveness.

"You like that, don't you, angel?" he asked. I nodded slowly, biting my lip as I gazed up at him. "Soon," he promised. "My self-control is almost non-existent where you're concerned."

"Everyone's had you. But I can't? How's that fair?"

"I'm giving you everything."

"By not giving me any?" I argued.

"Stop, McKenna. You don't know what you're saying."

"I do, though, that's the thing. I want this with you. And not this pseudo friend-zone you've placed me in. I want everything. I want to be loved, cherished, and made to feel like a woman, your woman, not your little sister."

"If you were my sister, I'd be put in jail for the things I want to do to you."

My heart stuttered. He did want the same things as me, I could see it in his eyes. "If I'm pushing you – if this is about your addiction, or because I'm your counselor…."

"It's not." He stepped closer.

"Then what is it?"

"Brian told me."

"He told you…." I paused. He needed to fill in the blank because I failed to see what Brian had to do with any of this.

Chapter Ten

Knox

McKenna was looking at me expectantly, waiting for me to explain. *Shit.* "When I came to see you when you were sick, Brian pulled me aside. He wanted to know what my intentions were with you."

A tiny crease formed across her forehead. "And…what are they?"

"I told him you were sick and I was simply there to take care of you. He thinks I'm a sexual sociopath. He was looking at me like I was going to shove my dick down your throat while you're sick, and I assured him I could keep it in my pants."

She chewed on her lip and waited. "What did he say?" she asked.

"He told me." She waited, breathless, her eyes locked on mine. "McKenna, are you a virgin?"

She sucked in a shuddery breath and her gaze fell from mine. I didn't want her to feel ashamed or embarrassed, and shit, I probably shouldn't have just sprung this on her, but we needed to discuss this. It didn't help that we were having this conversation dressed as we were – me in my underwear and her in just a T-shirt. But she needed to see that she wasn't ready for me.

"Does it matter?" she asked, clenching her fists at her sides.

"It does to me."

"So this *is* about my inexperience. I'm sorry to disappoint you."

She thought she was disappointing me, which made zero sense. "You don't know what you're talking about. I'm not disappointed. I'm fucking terrified. The thought of being the first to touch you, the first man to be inside you, to penetrate your tight pussy, makes me insane, but I'm scared I can't be what you need."

"What do you mean?" Sapphire blue eyes, wide with curiosity, blinked up at mine. "What do you think I need?"

"You need someone to be gentle and careful with you, someone who's soft and slow."

"You could try…." she murmured.

"I don't trust myself."

"I trust you." Those same eyes, now blazing with determination, stared into mine. "I'm here because I trust you."

She looked so beautiful, so soft and sweet, standing there in my faded gray T-shirt, feet bare and toes painted pink. And hearing her confess that she trusted me with something so sacred tugged at something deep inside me. Confessing some of my background has been a scare tactic. But the look in her eyes didn't match the

283

expression of a scared little girl. She needed to understand how fucked up I was. I couldn't let myself tarnish her perfection. And I would. I would take every last bit of her innocence and obliterate it just to quench my own desire.

Exercising my last ounce of self-control, I closed the distance between us and pressed a kiss to her mouth. "I'm not budging on this. I don't think you're ready yet." It was either walk away now or throw her down on my bed and have my way with her.

Her hands flew to her hips. "You also didn't think you had a problem with sex, and you fought me on getting STD testing done, and I know pushing you on both was the right thing. I get that you're scared, but Knox...."

I looked down, popping the knuckles in my fingers. "There's something else," I admitted. She looked at me quizzically. "I knew when you didn't say anything last time that you were probably inexperienced, because usually it's the first thing girls comment on...."

Shit. She still wasn't catching on. I was going to have to spell it out for her. "I'm, um, a lot bigger than average." I sounded like a cocky asshole, but I wasn't bragging. I wasn't trying to impress her. I was trying to warn her. To ensure she understood that this probably wouldn't be fun for her.

A slow smile uncurled on McKenna's lips. Not the reaction I'd been expecting. It made me wonder if perhaps she had noticed my size, either that or she was remembering it fondly now. But I wasn't trying to be cute. I'd had one girl actually tell me she needed to take a muscle relaxer before she'd let me fuck her. She was a little dramatic, but I wasn't kidding that nearly every woman I'd been with had commented on my size – I was a lot to handle, and they weren't virgins.

I hadn't been with a virgin since high school and I didn't exactly remember the experience favorably. I didn't take pleasure in causing pain. It wasn't something I wanted to repeat, but now with McKenna standing before me looking vulnerable and needy, I wouldn't reject her and I certainly wouldn't push her into the arms of another man. As much as I might have been fighting it, I knew it had to be me. If not tonight, then soon. Neither of us were good at waiting, it seemed.

McKenna pouted, her lower lip jutting out.

"Come here," I ordered.

She hesitantly stepped forward, her fingers still playing with the hem of the shirt.

"What do you have to do tomorrow?"

"I'm working at the teen shelter, but not until ten in the morning. Why?"

I smoothed my hands up and down her arms. "You'll probably be sore. I wanted to make sure you don't have anything too strenuous planned."

Her pulse thundered in her neck as if she realized for the first time that we really were going to do this. My dick had gotten the memo, too, lengthening in my boxers and growing heavy against my thigh. He would have to wait his fucking turn. I would do everything in my power to make sure McKenna was as wet and ready as possible before I took the precious gift she was offering. It was the least I could do. She was giving me something that could never be replaced. There were no do-overs.

I was never nervous before sex, but my own heart was thudding like a damn drum in my chest. The significance of this moment hit me hard. But I was like a hungry lion and she'd pushed me too far and now I needed a taste.

"I need to know your limits," I said, watching her fidget.

"My limits?" That tiny crease between her brow was back.

"I need to know if there's something you're uncomfortable with."

She chewed on her lip. There was something on her mind, but she was afraid to voice it.

"Tell me," I commanded, my voice steady.

She wet her lips, stalling for more time. "I don't like, um, oral sex."

"To give it or receive it?" I questioned, raising one dark brow. This was interesting, and not what I'd expected her to say.

"Receiving it," she managed to blurt out, looking down at the floor under my watchful stare.

"Why not?"

Her little hands balled into fists at her sides like she was afraid to admit whatever it was on her mind.

"Has anyone ever done that to you before, angel?"

She shook her head.

I sucked in a hiss of a breath and cursed. Shit, that only made me want to do it more. "Why do you think you wouldn't like it?"

"Be-because I can't imagine I'll taste good and…I would hate for you to think I smell or taste bad."

She was self-conscious, but she had no reason to be. I was certain she'd taste delicious, salty and sweet just like a woman should. I would enjoy showing her just how very wrong she was. I inhaled against the side of her neck. "I love your scent," I promised. "And I'm certain you'll taste delicious. Real males like that taste, McKenna." She sucked in a breath. "Let me worship your pussy," I breathed against her throat, causing her to break out in chill bumps. She shook her head. "That's unacceptable." She might have said this was something she didn't want, but it was the first thing I wanted to start with, limits be damned.

She opened her mouth to protest, then closed it with a squeak.

That's what I thought. "Anything else?"

"When you said you liked, um…." She heaved in a breath and held it, too uncomfortable to continue. I could only assume she was talking about my rant on enjoying anal sex.

"I won't be doing that with you. At least not yet." I wasn't sure McKenna was the kind of girl to ever be ready for that kind of total domination, letting me take her most private of places, but I wouldn't decide for her, not now. She constantly surprised me and perhaps between the sheets wouldn't be any different.

She nodded, relief washing over her features.

Leaning down to brush my mouth against her neck, I whispered, "If this is what you need, I'll take care of you. I wanted to show you I could wait, that this was more to me than sex."

She pulled back slightly to meet my eyes. "I already know this is more for you. You don't do relationships, or bring girls home to meet your brothers, and I'm guessing you don't often volunteer or go out of your way for a girl. You've already shown me with your actions what I mean to you. It's time for both of us to be brave."

I nodded. It was time to be brave. Grasping her hips, I walked her backwards to the bed and when the backs of her knees touched the edge of the mattress, she sat.

Wide blue eyes stared up at me as she waited, wondering what came next. Her gaze wandered lower, looking at the bulge in my boxer briefs.

"Do you want to touch me?" I asked.

She swallowed and nodded, her head bobbing up and down.

The urge to watch her pretty mouth around my cock pulsed inside me, causing an almost unbearable pressure. Now that I knew McKenna's intentions and desires, there would be no stopping now. We may not have sex tonight, but we were both ready for more. I nodded once, indicating that she could do what she wanted. McKenna hesitated, her hands twisting in her lap. I decided to play nice and help her out, tugging my boxer briefs down slowly. Her eyes locked onto my movements. My cock sprang free and she sucked in a shuddery breath. Using my right hand, I grasped my dick and stroked it slowly, showing her what I wanted her to do.

McKenna's hands uncurled in her lap and she gingerly brought them to my stomach, lightly tracing my abdominal muscles. I remembered back to the first time she'd touched me. She'd been so curious, yet so uncertain. It was an incredibly hot combination. With my heart pounding in my chest, I fought for patience, for self-control, when I was so used to exercising neither.

Soon, McKenna's hands wandered lower as her bravery blossomed. Biting her bottom lip firmly between her teeth, she finally closed her fist around me and a low growl escaped the back of my throat. Using both hands to stroke me up and down, McKenna did so slowly, as if savoring the feel of my cock in her hands. Her fingertips didn't close around me and I watched in wonder as she worked me over, using her palms, her fingertips, to pleasure me. It was the slowest, most erotic handjob I'd ever received. My knees trembled and my stomach muscles were clenched tight.

Her hands continued rubbing my cock, one hand even venturing under to lightly cup my balls. I could let her do this all day, but something inside me wanted to push her just a little bit more. And I knew McKenna wanted that, too. She wanted the full experience, to see my dominant side that I'd kept hidden from her.

"Get it wet," I said.

Her eyes snapped up to meet mine, confusion evident between her brows. She glanced to the bedside table, then the dresser, looking for some type of lubricant. "I – I don't have anything," she murmured.

"Yes, you do."

Realization flashed across her features.

I wanted to see her wet her palm with her mouth, or even hotter, the moisture that was certain to be between her legs, but instead she did something totally unexpected.

She brought her full lips to the head of my cock, and pressed a soft kiss there. I let out a ragged groan, fighting the desire to work myself deep into her throat. As much as I wanted to take control, I needed to let her do this at her own pace.

Satisfied with my reaction, McKenna did it again, this time letting the warmth of her tongue lave over my rock hard flesh, eliciting another moan from me. As she grew even bolder, she let her tongue wander the length of my shaft, doing just what I'd asked, getting me nice and wet. Her hands slid easily up and over me, pushing my pleasure to new levels.

Leaning forward, McKenna took me into the warmth of her mouth, her full lips suckling against my sensitive skin.

Fuck.

She might be inexperienced, but she certainly knew how to bring me to my knees. Maybe it was because of her lack of experience that I valued this so much. It meant even more. She was going out on a limb, pushing all her boundaries – for me. It did heady things to my ego. But tonight wasn't about me, it was about her. Lifting her chin with one hand, I fell free of her mouth, my dick glistening with her salvia and her lips damp and swollen.

"You're too damn good at that," I murmured, stroking her cheek.

She beamed up at me, clearly satisfied with my compliment. I wanted to make her feel comfortable and ready for all the new experiences I had in store for her.

"Lay back."

McKenna obeyed, scooting further up the bed, her T-shirt bunching up around her waist as she moved, the sight of her plain white cotton panties taunting me. She watched me with wide eyes as I slowly peeled her panties down her legs, exposing her most sensitive area, and dropped them on the floor at my feet.

I kissed her inner thigh and felt her shudder. Working my way up her body with gentle nips and kisses, I took my time, listening to her body's silent signals. The dip of her belly when my mouth tickled her hip bone, her undulating hips when I got close to her center. A few minutes more and I knew she'd be practically begging me to touch her there. But not yet. I removed the T-shirt over her head and continued tasting her skin. First mouthing the heavy weight of her breast, then a chaste kiss in the center of her breast bone. McKenna's frustrated whimper told me I wasn't focusing on the areas she needed me. Good thing I was about to give her everything she could handle. And then some.

I kissed my way to the tip of her breast and bit down, carefully using my teeth to tug the bud of her nipple. A surprised gasp pushed past McKenna's lips and I couldn't help the satisfied growl that escaped mine. Twisted need and desire spiked through me. She was finally beginning to understand that I was in control, that she'd given me her body and pushed me into this. I needed to do this my way.

I began licking her nipples in the same rhythmic pattern I wanted to lick her clit, eliciting soft groans and pants from her.

Every little moment with her, watching her discover the pleasure I could give her, was like a small victory. She was giving herself to me. Happiness surged through me. She squirmed, struggling against the mattress, her writhing hips making it difficult for me to give her breasts the focus they deserved. Even if her head didn't want my mouth moving south, her entire body disagreed.

Lifting my head from one breast, my eyes met hers. "Are you sure you don't want me to lick your pussy?" McKenna squeaked out something unintelligible and I chuckled against her neck. "Let me take care of you." I trailed my mouth lower, kissing her navel as I moved down her body. "Just a taste," I whispered against her pubic bone.

Her scent was maddening – purely feminine and entirely too tempting. I wasn't going to be able to go slow. My mouth closed around her folds and I sucked – hard – against her clit. McKenna's hips shot off the bed and her hands tugged at my hair. But I didn't let up. I rubbed my tongue against her until her muscles were trembling and her moans were almost loud enough to wake my brothers. I lifted my head just long enough to give her a pillow.

"Here. Scream into this if you need to."

Her cheeks flushed crimson. "Oh my God. Was I being loud?"

My grin was the only answer she got before I dropped my lips to
her sweet flesh again and gave her a gentle kiss. I considered
teasing her – pointing out that just fifteen minutes ago this had
been on her list of hard limits. And now I was pretty sure it was her
new favorite thing. But I kept that piece of knowledge to myself,
pride swelling in my chest.

After a few more teasing flicks of my tongue I bit down on her clit,
forcing a cry from her lips and the first orgasm to crash through
her, her body lightly trembling as she laced her fingers in my hair,
pulling me closer. I continued licking and softly kissing her as the
aftershocks pulsed through her. It was agony knowing how good it
would feel to be inside her when she came, her tight little body
throbbing around me.

"Knox…," she groaned, out of breath, "That was…."

"Shh." I pressed the tip of one finger against her opening, finding
her wet and ready. I wasn't done with her. Not by a long shot. I
eased my middle finger forward and watched for her reaction. Her
eyelids, suddenly heavy, began to fall closed. Inside, her body was
hot and silky and never in my life had I appreciated a woman
trusting me with her so completely.

Pushing slowly in and out, allowing her to get used to the

sensations, I carefully added a second finger. I felt her tense and a brief pinched expression flashed across her features. "Is this okay?" I murmured, kissing her inner thigh.

She nodded tightly.

She might have thought she was ready, but the way she was clamping down on my fingers assured me she needed more time. Knowing I couldn't take what she was offering tonight, my goal became to see how many times I could make her come.

Using the pad of my thumb, I circled her clit while my fingers continued pumping in and out of her. She clawed at the sheets, pushing her mouth against the pillow, and let out a long shuddering moan as another orgasm wracked her body from the inside out.

Chapter Eleven

McKenna

Blinking open heavy eyelids, I struggled to make sense of my surroundings. I didn't remember where I was, what day it was, or even my own name. I felt like I had been drugged. I stretched and turned my head and saw Knox's sleeping form lying next to me. Memories of last night came rushing back with vivid clarity. Knox's hot mouth on my most sensitive parts, his fingers pumping into me...I shuddered at the memory.

I'd opened up and told Knox my feelings on taking our physical relationship to the next level, and while we hadn't had sex, it felt like we'd grown closer. I was happy, if not a little dazed by the whole experience.

A quick check of the clock told me it was still early, just after sunrise, and I rolled closer to Knox, snuggling in beside him.

Draping a heavy arm over me, he pulled me tightly against him. "You okay, angel?" His sleep-laced voice was deep and husky.

"I'm fine," I whispered, breathing in the masculine scent of his chest.

"I'm sorry about last night."

I rolled onto my side and looked up at him. "Sorry about what?" From my perspective, I should be the one apologizing. He'd pleasured me until I all but passed out from exhaustion and I hadn't taken care of him at all. A fact I felt a little guilty about.

"Are you sore?" he asked, his eyes like warm molten honey on mine.

I shook my head. At least I didn't think so.

"I was too rough with you," he murmured, pressing a kiss to my forehead.

Memories of him biting me – my nipples and my clit – rushed back in full force. The press of his fingers roughly pushing into me. Knox thought I'd be upset, but I was relieved to see he hadn't treated me like a china doll. He'd lost himself in me, which was exactly what I wanted, considering I felt so out of control around him, too. Pressing my palm against his cheek, I returned his kiss. "You bit me," I said, fighting a smile.

"I know."

"You said you weren't into pain."

"Did it hurt?" The warmth and sincerity in his eyes nearly stole my voice. He was so beautiful, this confusing, troubled man.

"Well, no. Not really."

"I just wanted you to understand that you were mine."

"Oh." My heart galloped. I was his. Body and soul. And falling deeper every day.

"Was last night okay, then?"

I nodded, my head bobbing up and down while he studied me. "I liked it." Liking it was an understatement, but the furrow creasing his brow told me not to press the issue.

"Are you sure you're alright with this?"

I knew he was asking more than his words conveyed. He was asking if I was okay with his nature – his dominant, take charge attitude in the bedroom. The truth was, I was more than okay with it. With Knox I felt like a woman. I liked him making the decisions and pushing me in ways I never dreamed. He was opening me up to new experiences, just like I was doing for him. "Last night was perfect. I'm just sorry I fell asleep on you."

He smiled, the playful gleam I loved returning to his eyes. "Passed out was more like it."

I gave him a shove, but his body was a solid wall of immovable muscle. What he'd said was true, though, I'd all but collapsed from exhaustion after the three powerful climaxes he'd given me. If this was what a sexual relationship with him was going to be like, I would be one happy girl.

"I gotta get the guys up and ready for school." Knox kissed my lips and then climbed from the bed, treating me to a view of his firm backside as he moved across the room and began to dress.

I lazily stretched and then joined him, forcing my languid and relaxed body into yesterday's clothes before venturing downstairs.

I found the boys were already up and moving about.

"Dude, don't sit so close to the TV, Tuck," Jaxon said, nudging Tucker's shoulder. "You're gonna get a tan from that thing."

I chuckled as I watched them. The glow of the television was casting a bluish hue over Tucker's little face, but he obeyed, scooting backwards on his butt. Knox might have been worried about the second oldest Bauer boy, but I could see that in his heart, Jax was one of the good guys. Or maybe I just had entirely too much faith. I'd always believed the same thing about Knox, too. Yet I couldn't help the inexplicable feeling that everything good was about to come crashing down around me in a messy heap.

"What are these?" I asked, sniffing a huge arrangement of pink carnations on my dining room table.

299

Brian appeared in the doorway after changing out of his suit and tie and into jeans. He'd arrived home from work just a few minutes after me.

I picked through the pink blossoms, hunting for a card. There wasn't one and somehow I couldn't really imagine Knox sending me pink carnations. Maybe blood red roses, but not these. And when would he have had the time? I'd just left his house this morning and I knew he'd worked all day, too.

Brian watched me curiously. "They're from me."

"Oh. What's the occasion?" I couldn't recall Brian ever giving me flowers…except the bouquet he'd had sent to the funeral home at my parents' wake. But those had been white daylilies. For a totally different reason.

"No occasion. I just wanted to…." He stopped himself and exhaled heavily. "Come sit down with me."

"Okay." He was acting strange. I wondered if he'd caught the flu that was going around.

We sat side by side on the sofa, the TV playing softly in the background.

"I just wanted to apologize for everything lately. My behavior toward you, and fighting with Knox." He lifted my hand from my lap and held it. "I know you've been through a lot and I just want you to know I'll always be here for you. I'll be whatever you need, okay?"

"Okay. That's sweet of you, Bri."

Neither of us could deny that something had changed between us since Knox had come into the picture. I remembered Knox's request that I tell Brian about us, but somehow I knew the moment wasn't right. He was trying to apologize, to make amends. He'd gotten me flowers, which was sweet, but not necessary. Giving a girl carnations wasn't a romantic gesture, was it? Pushing all that from my mind, I thanked him for the flowers and headed into the kitchen. "Are you hungry?"

"Starved," he confirmed.

We were like two ravenous lions come dinner time. We'd been that way since we were kids. Searching through the cabinets, we settled on grilled cheese sandwiches. We worked together in the kitchen, him grilling the sandwiches and me slicing some tomatoes that were about to go bad. It'd been a while since we'd enjoyed each other's company like this and I was happy to see the previous tension between us was all but gone.

Over gooey, cheesy sandwiches, Brian shoved an envelope at me. "This came for you today."

The return address was a law firm in Indiana.

My stomach dropped.

I didn't want to open it, knowing it was somehow related to my parents' accident. But the letter taunted me, capturing all of my attention.

Brian's sheepish look apologized for something over which he had no control. I wondered if this was the real reason for the flowers. He knew this would upset me – take me right back to that dark place I was in four years ago. Running to Chicago hadn't been enough. My past would follow me anywhere.

"Are you going to open it?" he asked, pulling my thoughts back to the present. I looked down at my plate. I'd picked apart my sandwich into little bits. So much for my appetite. "What do you think it is?"

"Not sure," I said, finding my voice. "Probably something to do with their will."

He nodded and pushed away his own plate. It must be sympathy pains or something since I knew we were both hungry when we'd sat down.

I'd yet to settle all my parents' legal affairs, since dealing with it bought up too many painful memories. I'd done the bare minimum, the funeral was planned, and with the help of Brian's mom and a local realtor, I'd sold the house I grew up in. The movers had packed everything and it was all still sitting in a storage unit in my hometown. All the rest, pension plan, retirement accounts, and insurance policies remained on the back burner, untouched. Dealing with it all would be too final, and I just wasn't ready to go there. I especially didn't like this envelope with its shiny gold embossment on my dining table looking up at me, reminding me. It felt like two sides of my life were intersecting. It was childish, but maybe if I just refused to open the envelope, I could pretend that none of this was happening.

For all my running, all my volunteer work to make things better in this world, I still had to face that there was a bitter force driving me. It scared me to realize that maybe running into Knox's arms had nothing to do with love. It was about me throwing myself into something even messier and uglier than my own past. It was simply another place to hide.

"You're not going to open it, are you?" Brian asked, pulling me from my somber thoughts.

He knew me all too well. "Wasn't planning on it, no." I pushed the offending paper away, knowing it was pointless. I'd likely find it on my dresser later.

"Can I ask you something?" He glanced down at his plate, picking at the remnants of his sandwich.

"Sure."

"Have you and Knox…." His forehead creased. "Are you still…."

"Brian, that's none of your business."

"You are," he said, his voice certain.

I wanted to yell at him for interfering and telling Knox I was a virgin in the first place, but faced with the awkwardness of the conversation, I chickened out. Closing my eyes, I drew a deep breath.

"Wow. I'm surprised. Even after all those nights you've spent there?"

I released my breath in a huff. "I know you have a hard time believing this, but Knox really is a good guy. He would never do something I wasn't ready for. And he's been in recovery, so sex really wasn't on the table for either of us."

"But it is now?" His eyebrow quirked up. "And you're right, I do have a hard time believing that."

A heavy silence fell over us and I considered ripping open the envelope just for something to distract me from this awful moment.

Brian leaned closer, planting his elbows on the table. "So if you haven't fully given yourself to him, does that mean…." He hesitated, drawing a deep breath. "Do you think there'd ever be a chance for us?"

I wanted to set him straight, tell him once and for all it was never going to happen between us, but sitting there, looking into his bright blue eyes, something in me couldn't crush him. He'd done too much for me. Still, I didn't want to leave him with false hope. That wasn't fair to him. "Brian, I'm dating Knox. You should date other people, too." It was my subtle way of telling him he needed to stop pining for me.

"Your dad, your parents, they would have wanted you with me. You know that, right?" he asked. I swallowed a bitter lump in my throat. "They joked we'd get married someday from the time we were six years old, McKenna."

Fighting back tears, I excused myself to my bedroom while Brian called out my name. Bringing my parents into this wasn't fair. He knew my life's mission was to try and honor them in all things. My chosen career field, how I spent my time, but I'd never factored in who I dated. Realizing Brian was right sucked. My parents had adored him.

I fell back heavily onto my mattress with a thud. Today had been too much. I couldn't deal with the mystery envelope regarding my parents and Brian's declaration that I was dishonoring them by choosing the wrong man.

Part of me knew I couldn't hide in my bed forever, but most of me wanted to try.

Chapter Twelve

McKenna

The next several days passed in a blur. Between working, volunteering, and helping Amanda get around – everything from taking her to doctor's appointments to shopping for maternity clothes to buying prenatal vitamins, I'd barely had time to see Knox. And our alone time together had all but disappeared.

But tonight that was going to change, because Jaxon and Luke were taking Tucker out to dinner and then to their high school's basketball game, meaning Knox and I would have the house to ourselves for a couple of hours. It was exactly what I'd needed after a trying week.

I found Knox alone upstairs in his bedroom, sitting on the edge of his bed with his sketchbook open in his lap, looking deep in thought.

"Hi," I greeted him.

"Hey." He closed the book and crossed the room, drawing me into his arms. "Everything okay? You look exhausted."

Leave it to Knox to immediately pick up on how drained and crummy I felt. "I'm fine. It was just a long week."

"Yeah? And how many hours did you work this week?"

I quickly did the math in my head. "Mmm, somewhere around seventy, I'd guess."

"McKenna," he groaned, holding my shoulders and positioning me so he could meet my eyes. The dark circles lining them wouldn't help my case. But Knox couldn't understand how one simple letter from a lawyer back home could send me into a tailspin. It had been easier to work and volunteer than to sit at home with the constant reminder staring me in the face.

Knox pulled me over to the small sofa on the far end of his bedroom and we sat down. He looked at me intently. "What?" I asked finally.

"Just like you help me, I want to help you."

"What do you mean?"

"You've got to stop running."

"What makes you think that's what I'm doing?"

"You work seventy hours a week volunteering, you don't do anything for yourself. When's the last time you did something normal girls your age enjoy? Like go shopping or get your nails done?"

I stiffened at his implication that I wasn't a normal girl. "How's

308

that fair? When's the last time you did something a normal twenty-two year old guy would do?"

He smirked. "Not the same thing, angel. I have custody of three boys. Don't bring my shit into this. We're talking about you."

"I happen to like volunteering, and I like being here with you guys. I have no desire to go out and party it up like a twenty-one year old."

"But someday you might. And you might regret not doing all the things young people are supposed to do."

Was he speaking from experience? He'd certainly missed out on enough being responsible for his brothers. Though his sexploits more than made up for that deficit. "I'm not going to regret anything." I already lived with enough regret over my choices that fateful day I'd lost my parents. There wasn't room for more in my world. "Serving others is the only thing that keeps me sane. The only thing that makes me feel okay with being me," I whispered.

"I get that."

"Then don't ask me to change."

"I want you to find balance – that's all." Knox wrapped one hand around my knee and gave it a gentle squeeze. His touch was all that was needed to reassure me. He wasn't trying to force me to change or make me feel guilty about my choices.

"I want that, too," I admitted.

"One step at a time. Right, angel?"

I grinned up at him wryly. It was the same thing I'd said to him once about his addiction. "Right." I was suddenly feeling like the patient rather than the counselor. This was new.

"There's something that scares me, McKenna." Knox ran a hand through his wayward hair, meeting my eyes with a worried stare. "One day you're going to forgive yourself and let go of all this hurt you carry around. You're going to wake up and realize I'm all wrong for you."

Knox was the only one to call me out on my obsessive tendencies. I avoided my life. I avoided dealing with my emotions and grief. Not even Brian was brave enough to tell me the truth. I appreciated his honesty, but he was wrong. I'd always want him. He made me feel alive and secure. Like maybe I could finally stop running from my past.

"And when all that happens, you're going to want someone nice and normal," he continued.

"Let me guess, someone like Brian?"

"The thought has crossed my mind, yes. He's in love with you, McKenna."

The crushing weight of the knowledge that he was right hit me square in the chest. Knox was looking at me like he could see straight through me. I could not have felt more exposed if I'd been sitting there completely naked. How did he not only understand me so well, but also get my complicated relationship with Brian? Feeling vulnerable and needy, I curled into his side, needing his warmth, his protection from the muddled mess my life had become. Knox pulled me closer, lifting my mouth to his while my pulsed thrummed violently in the base of my throat.

I didn't try and explain away my feelings, I didn't even tell him that I wasn't going anywhere, but I did decide then and there it was time to show him how deeply my feelings for him ran.

Chapter Thirteen

Knox

Unable to resist the swell of her full mouth quivering so close to mine, I lowered my lips to hers.

A kiss that was meant to be innocent quickly turned heated. McKenna whimpered and opened her mouth to mine, our tongues tangling wildly as her hands pushed into my hair. She nipped my lower lip, tugging it with her teeth to pull me closer.

She was a woman in need and I was just a man. A man who hadn't been laid in God knows how long. I needed to feel her heat surround me. Gripping her ass, I lifted her from the sofa and moved her to my lap. She wrapped her legs around my waist, clinging to me like I was her everything. And maybe I was. It broke my fucking heart and something in me snapped.

With our mouths fused together, her tongue hypnotically rubbing against mine, I found my hands unbuttoning her pants. Rather than stop me, McKenna's hips pushed forward, her body eager for friction.

I needed her just as badly as she needed me. We were two lost souls fighting to cling to something real. But our first time shouldn't be like this – so desperate and full of anguish, mouths seeking, hands grasping, clutching for something to hold on to. We were a tangle of limbs and hands groping until each of us had shed the other of our clothes. I lifted a fully nude McKenna, strode with her across the room and lay us back against my bed. She straddled me and remained motionless for several seconds. The dim light in my room bathed her skin a faint golden glow. She'd never looked more beautiful to me than in that moment.

Pulling away from her mouth, I cupped her face in my hands. Hazy blue eyes slowly blinked open to meet mine. "Not like this, not for your first time," I breathed, my heart pounding.

"But this is how I need it. Make me forget everything else," she whispered.

I wanted her to know only my name, to know it was me inside her, but she deserved to be loved, cherished, and I had fuck-all of a clue how to do that properly. I only knew the physical aspects – I dealt in pleasure and orgasms and how many condom wrappers were on the floor the next morning. But real intimacy, taking care of all a woman's needs – let alone a woman as complex as McKenna? It was a sure shot at failure.

But right then, in that moment, McKenna was just a girl looking for closeness any way she could get it. If that ended with me inside her, so be it. It was the only way I knew. And it seemed neither of us was capable of waiting anymore.

She was giving herself to me, despite knowing what I was. The most beautiful gift she had to offer was mine. Feeling her damp heat against my belly where she sat, and my erection brushing against her ass, desire rocketed through me.

Everything in me wanted to take control, to lift her hips and position her so she could slide down on me, but I knew if I did that, I'd hurt her. And since that wasn't in the cards, I hauled her off me, forcing her to lie on her back.

Coils of desire raced through my bloodstream, and I had to physically force myself to go slow. I kissed McKenna, long and deep, claiming her with my mouth. Never had I spent so much time just kissing, but with her, I found it strangely satisfying and hard to stop. When she was squirming beneath me on the bed, I dropped to my knees on the floor between her legs, taking her ankles in my hands and planting her feet on the bed so that she was wide open for me. McKenna's head lifted from the pillow and she looked at me, poised above her with wide set eyes. With my gaze locked on hers, I lowered my mouth to the juncture between her thighs and inhaled. McKenna flinched, her belly dipping as she sucked in a breath. She needed to understand that I loved the feminine scent of her arousal. That sweet fragrance made me lose all sense of right and wrong, all rational thought. Parting her glistening pink flesh, I swirled my tongue over her clit until a sob broke from her lips. Her entire body trembled, begging for release, while I ruthlessly licked against her.

Her orgasm hit me like a sucker punch to the gut. I was becoming addicted to giving pleasure rather than taking it. Emotions tore through me and I took a moment, sitting back on my heels and wondering how it was this beautiful woman I'd only known a short time had completely undone me.

"Knox," she whimpered, reaching for me.

I crawled up onto the bed with her and McKenna immediately took my cock in her hands, rubbing and stroking just like I'd shown her. A dark hunger simmered inside me, pooling at the base of my spine, the need to be inside her overtaking me. I reached for a condom and rolled it down my length while McKenna watched and chewed on her lip. Hesitation surged inside me. Was I doing the right thing?

"Are you sure you're ready?"

Her hand curled around my eager cock, as if to feel the latex sheathing me. Every moment with her was a new awakening. It kept me grounded and in the moment like never before. "I want you." She pressed her lips to my throat, her hot breath rushing over my skin in the most reassuring way. She wanted this. Me. Even with all my shortcomings, she was choosing me.

And for the night, I was hers. Body and soul.

McKenna

After putting on the condom, Knox lay down beside me so we were facing each other on the bed. I rested my head on his arm and his other hand was between us, positioning his hard length against me.

Lying side by side like this wasn't the position I imagined. "What are you doing?" I asked.

"I want to hold you. Is this okay?"

"Yeah, but it's just…."

"This isn't how you pictured it going?" he asked.

"No. I thought you'd be on top." I remembered my embarrassing lecture to Luke about how to ensure a girl's first time was special. It showed how little I knew. I guess I never thought my first time would be with Knox, looking deep into his eyes. It sent a warm ripple of pleasure through me.

"We'll get there, but for your first time, me on top doesn't allow you to control the speed, angle, or depth, so I thought this might work better. I want you to be comfortable."

I relaxed my head against the pillow. I was comfortable. I was lying

316

on my side facing Knox and we were snuggled close. I could feel his warmth all around me and his scent sending me into my happy place. But warning bells were going off in my mind. Knowing Knox had a dominating side…I didn't want him softening this experience for me. I wanted to know he was right here with me, fifty-fifty, enjoying every moment, not sacrificing himself for something he thought I wanted. "But I thought you liked taking control, I want to be sure you're…."

His lips against mine stopped me mid-rant. "Not for your first time. This is about you." He leaned forward and pressed another kiss to my lips, softer this time. "Just try and relax, okay?"

I nodded and watched him.

He pressed the tip of himself against my opening. I tried to relax my muscles like he'd told me, but my body was anything buy welcoming to the blunt head of him. Lifting my top leg so I was spread apart, Knox cradled my calf in his big palm. I felt more exposed in this position, but when Knox's mouth went to my throat and began lightly nibbling me there, I forgot all about that.

He pressed his hips closer to mine again and I felt the very tip of him push inside me. Knox released a hiss through his teeth and pulled back. It wasn't working.

Dropping a kiss to my forehead, he looked deep into my eyes. "Do you want some extra lubrication?"

"Whatever you want," I murmured, hoping I wasn't doing something wrong.

His thumb stroked my cheek as he gazed down at me. "I like it tight, I just don't want to hurt you."

I was prepared for a little discomfort. "It's okay. I'm fine." I was a mess of nerves and my inner muscles trembled in anticipation, but I wanted this. I wanted him. Knox better not back out on me now. I couldn't have another failed attempt at losing my virginity. Using his hand to guide himself, Knox pressed harder, penetrating me, stealing the oxygen from my lungs, waking me up from the inside out. With his eyes locked on mine, he thrust deeper, several more inches slicing me open. My mouth dropped open in a silent scream.

With my body stretched to accommodate him, Knox moved slowly, using long measured strokes that I felt deep inside me – in a place no one had ever touched me before. But what I really savored was the look in his eyes. The way he was looking at me made my heart race and my body respond despite the pain. He was a man in need, dark hunger reflected back at me in his features. A warm shiver raced along my body.

I felt stretched to capacity, the sensation entirely new and slightly painful, but in the best possible way. Still, I didn't like the idea that Knox was holding back. I wanted to show him that I wasn't afraid of his dark side. Wrapping my legs around his back, I urged him closer. He released a guttural groan and buried his face against my neck. "More, Knox," I murmured. He obeyed, his hips slamming into me, forcing a cry to rip from my throat.

I worried for a moment that my weight was crushing her, but when McKenna's legs wound around my back, I lost all sense of rational thought. She squirmed beneath me, begging for more, and unrestrained need raced through my veins. Done holding back, I pounded into her tight channel without mercy. She cried out, all her muscles tightening around me.

A pang of guilt sucker punched me in the gut. I should be gentle with her, but that wasn't my style and I let my raw need to consume her overtake me. "Are you okay?"

"Yeah," she exhaled against my mouth, and I kissed her deeply, relief washing through me.

This might not have been my first time, but nothing about this was familiar to me. Sharing this with her meant something. It wasn't like all the other times when my mind shut down and I lost myself to the numbness of pleasure. I was aware of everything. Every heartbeat, every cry of pleasure, her hot breath rushing over my skin, the pull of her warm channel hugging me. She was intoxicating in the most sobering way.

I knew I was getting close, and since there was no way I was going off before her, I used the pads of my index and middle fingers to circle her clit and bent forward to kiss her breasts, latching onto one of her nipples and grazing it with my teeth. McKenna shuddered in my arms, crying out in pleasure rather than pain this time. I pumped into her with long, measured strokes, continuing to pleasure her, and soon felt her body clench around mine with her climax. I held her while little tremors passed through her body, slowing my pace to allow her to enjoy every pulse and sensation. That certainly hadn't happened the last time I was with a virgin. I remember her begging me to just finish and the blood stains on her sheets when we were done. Back then I'd been in high school, though, and not nearly as skilled and unfortunately not as in-tune with a woman's pleasure. But with McKenna, that wasn't an option. I was tuned in to her every breath.

Moments later, I lost myself inside her, gripping her ass and letting her milk every last drop of fluid from my body. I clung to her long after, each of us unwilling to let the other go.

Sex had never been like that before. I would have been up and out the door the minute I got off. With McKenna, I reluctant to let her go even to remove the condom.

"Did I hurt you?" I asked.

She shook her head, curling against me.

She was so quiet, I worried I'd done something wrong. "How do you feel?"

"Happy," she answered.

Releasing a sigh, I pulled her into my arms, drawing her even closer. "Not too sore?"

"No, I don't think so."

Relief washed over me. I knew I should apologize, I was too rough with her, but it was who I was, and if she wasn't complaining, then neither was I.

"Was everything okay for you?" she whispered.

I tipped her chin up to meet my eyes. "That's what you're worried about? That I didn't enjoy myself?" I fought back a smile while she nodded up at me. "It was perfect." I pressed a tender kiss to her mouth, hoping that quieted all her fears about not measuring up. There was nothing to measure up to, with McKenna occupying all of my brain space I couldn't have recalled a previous partner if I tried.

We lay together as the room grew dark around us. Never in my life had I savored a quiet moment quite like this one. McKenna's head rested on my shoulder, her tangled hair splayed on the pillow between us, and her warm, soft body molded to mine. A monogamous healthy sexual relationship was completely foreign to me. And knowing this beautiful, sweet girl trusted me made my heart beat erratically. She believed in me when no one else did. She saw the man I hoped I could become.

My brothers would be home soon and I knew we needed to get up and get dressed, I just didn't want to. "Are you hungry?" I asked finally. We'd skipped dinner and gone straight for dessert. The least I could do now was feed her.

"Why, are you going to cook for me?" The hint of a smile tugged at her mouth.

"Of course. Come on." I urged her from our warm little nest and we dressed and headed downstairs.

Just as we were finishing a casual dinner of soup and sandwiches, I heard the front door swing open, followed by the sound of voices. The guys were home. I sent McKenna into the living room to relax while I cleaned up. After greeting her, Jaxon and Luke wandered into the kitchen.

"How was it?" I asked, adding the bowls and spoons to the dishwasher.

"Good, Tucker had fun, but we had to duck out the back way at the end because we ran into an old fling of mine," Jaxon said.

Just great. I didn't want Tucker around Jax's booty-call drama.

"What's wrong with McKenna?" Luke asked, helping himself to the half-sandwich McKenna had left uneaten on her plate.

"What do you mean?"

"She winced when she sat down on the couch like she was in pain or something and her hair is all messy and out of place. She have a bad day at work or something?"

Shit. Jaxon's knowing gaze met mine and he shook his head. "Something like that," I bit out, my tone harsher than I intended.

"We should do something nice for her," Luke said, oblivious to the silent exchange happening between me and Jax.

"Yeah, good idea." I rubbed the back of my neck, completely at a loss.

"Maybe we could make her dessert or something," Luke said, rummaging through the cabinets. "What does she like?"

"No clue." I wasn't winning boyfriend of the year – that was certain. And the way Jax was looking at me made me feel like the world's biggest asshole. I needed to fix this, to take care of my girl. "I have another idea."

After giving my orders to Jaxon and Luke, they headed up the stairs. Next I needed Tucker to go hunting through the cabinets in search of my next ingredient. "Tuck," I urged him from McKenna's lap. "Come here, bud."

He followed me up the stairs while McKenna watched curiously after us.

We met the guys in the second floor bathroom where Jaxon was gathering up mounds of dirty clothes from the floor and overflowing hamper and Luke was kneeling beside the bath tub, giving it a long overdue scrub down. Seeing that everything was underway, I sent Tucker on his task, searching the hall closet for some type of body wash that could double as bubble bath while I headed upstairs to gather a few candles I knew I had stashed in a drawer in case of power outages.

I met Jaxon in the hallway. "Everything cleaned up in there?"

"It's getting there. Something happen tonight?" he asked, his eyes narrowed and locked on mine. For all the times I'd given him shit for his antics with girls, I knew his scowl was my payback.

"Nope."

"Liar," he muttered under his breath.

I wanted to tell him I would fix this and make things right, instead I released a deep sigh and went to finish the final details for McKenna's surprise. I might not be able to afford to buy her gifts or give her fancy things, but I hoped this small gesture would show her that I cared and that I was trying.

I considered running down to the corner store and picking up a bottle of wine or something until I remembered that the last time McKenna had drank she'd practically tried to jump me. No sense in encouraging that. She'd had enough for one night.

Instead, I had Tucker make her a cup of chocolate milk, which he brought up in one of our mother's china teacups.

Once everything was ready, I led a suspicious McKenna up the stairs by her hand. "What are you guys up to?" she asked.

I stopped at the threshold to the bathroom and turned her by the shoulders. When she saw the three boys and behind them the tub filled with bubbles, the edges lined with white candles, she sucked in a breath. Luke switched off the lights and Tucker, impossible not to love, thrust his arms out to his sides and shouted, "Surprise!"

"What's all this?"

"It's for you, angel," I whispered, leaning in close to kiss her temple. "The guys helped me. We thought you could use some relaxation."

McKenna silently gripped my hand in a wordless thank you. The expression on her face told me it had been a long time since anyone had done something nice for her. She served others all day long, and the unshed tears simmered in her blue eyes as she struggled to believe she was worth such care and attention.

"Clear out, guys."

McKenna stopped them on their way out, planting a kiss on each of their cheeks. "Thank you." Tucker threw his arms around her middle, squeezing her tightly.

When the door closed us in, I spun her to face me. Lazy steam vapors drifted up around us and the low flickering light of the candles gave everything a sense of calm. I pressed a kiss to her waiting mouth. "You lied to me. You're sore, aren't you?"

"Is that what the bath's for?"

I didn't answer, I just kissed her again. "There are fresh towels in the cabinet under the sink. I'll meet you upstairs when you're through."

She nodded and took my face in both her hands, bringing her mouth close to mine. "Thank you."

The warm whisper of breath on my skin was the only thanks I needed. "Enjoy, angel. Oh, and Tucker brought you chocolate milk." I nodded towards the cup on the counter beside the sink.

"I like the pink teacup. Nice touch." She grinned.

"It was our mom's favorite." I left her with a smile blossoming on her lips. "Take your time."

Chapter Fourteen

McKenna

After my bath I found Knox in bed, half asleep. I dropped my towel and climbed in beside him, curling my naked body around his. "Hi," I whispered, kissing the spot behind his ear.

"Feel better?" he asked.

I nodded, rubbing my lips against his neck. "Yes. That was lovely." I hadn't soaked in a hot bath like that in ages. And he was right, I had been sore. The warm water had soothed most of the lingering ache reminding me of where he'd been, deep within me. And the bubbles made from Knox's manly-scented body wash had made the experience that much better. I felt closer to him. Surrounded by him. I hadn't wanted to get out – and didn't until the water had started to turn cold.

I wished I could put into words what tonight had meant to me. Our lovemaking, him taking care of me like that...I'd never experienced anything like it. I was falling for this man, body, heart, and soul. Part of that scared me, but mostly I felt happy and safe. "Thank you, Knox."

"You're welcome, angel," he murmured.

"I love you." I hadn't planned on telling him – I had barely let myself think those three dangerous words, but before I could even process what I was doing, they were out of my mouth and lingering in the air between us. My heart pounded unsteadily and the calmness I'd found vanished in an instant.

Several agonizing moments of silence passed between us. I knew he'd heard me. I knew he was still awake. I also knew I probably just triggered every defense mechanism Knox had put in place. Dread churned in my stomach, twisting it into a painful knot. I was dying to know what he was thinking. Surely he felt the pounding of my heart against his back, the faint sweat breaking out over my skin. Knox gave my hand a careful squeeze, but said nothing.

The next morning, seated behind my desk at group, the weight of what I'd done came crashing down on me the moment Knox strolled into the room looking happy and carefree.

I'd lost my virginity last night to a man who was in sexual addiction recovery. I could lose my counseling license. I could lose everything I'd worked hard for – and for what? While I was falling deeper and deeper, I had no idea what it would lead to. Did Knox even love me? He'd told me time and again he wasn't capable of love. I was finally starting to see the ramifications of that. The risks I was taking for him could all be for nothing. My chest felt tight as I watched him take a seat across the room without so much as acknowledging me.

That week's group was the most awkward experience of my life. Each member shared the number of days since their last sexual encounter and when Knox said one – my cheeks flamed as memories of me unabashedly grinding against him in his bed last night came flooding back. I didn't know how to reconcile these two halves of myself – the counselor helping him heal and the girl who wanted to fall into his arms and give in to the pleasure of the moment.

It seemed like I'd lived a lifetime of new experiences since I'd first watched him saunter through that door just a few short months ago. So much had changed and yet nothing really had. I had Knox in my life now – but the threat of his past still threatened our future, I still had Brian playing the overprotective and slightly possessive big brother, and I'd yet to face my own past. Dread churned inside me. I had a strange feeling everything I held dear was about to collide.

There were times I thought we could really do this – forge a real relationship built on honesty and trust. Like when I'd been neck deep in bubbles last night, feeling pampered and cherished. Other times, like this moment sitting in sex addicts anonymous, or when Knox hadn't returned my *I love you* I realized I was living in a fantasy land and that this relationship had far more complications than I gave it credit for.

As the weeks passed, I became less and less sure about what I was doing. My life was spinning out of control further by the day. It made me miss my mother and her pragmatic advice more than ever. I was falling deeper and deeper for a man with an inability to love me back and my weekly group sessions were becoming something I dreaded. They were heavy and intense and I felt like a complete hypocrite.

Everything I did felt like a burden I could just barely carry the weight of and by the end of the day, I collapsed heavily into bed alone, my chest an aching hole. I thought I could do it, be with Knox on his terms, wait for him to come around and continue leading SAA, but I was quickly beginning to realize it was too much for me. I was emotionally invested in both – loving Knox and helping with his recovery – and I didn't even know where we stood.

I'd kept myself busy with work and volunteering in an attempt to give him a bit of space. I'd met up with Amanda a few times and we'd been scouring resale shops for pink baby clothes. Even Knox's neighbor Nikki had helped out – sending a big bag of Bailee's old clothes home with me for Amanda. But none of my distractions helped. I was consumed by my growing love for Knox and the undeniable guilt about the relationship we were carrying on.

Knox was picking me up from my apartment tonight since he'd become increasingly difficult about me taking the bus. I had my backpack slung over my shoulder with pajamas, a few toiletries, and clothes for tomorrow since heaven forbid I leave a few things over at his place. I didn't want to freak him out. I was sharing his bed, but I knew I wasn't occupying the space I really wanted to – his heart.

Brian watched me from the corner of his eye, disapproval written all over his face.

"I'll see you tomorrow," I murmured, stuffing my keys in my coat pocket.

"That lawyer called again."

Crap. I chewed on my lip, avoiding his eyes.

"You ever gonna deal with that?" he asked.

Not if I don't have to. "I will, Bri. Soon," I promised. Spotting the headlights of Knox's Jeep from the front window, I headed out the door.

"Hi," I murmured, climbing inside the darkened interior of the Jeep. The scent of warm leather and Knox's unique masculine scent of sandalwood washed over me and calmed me in an instant. Maybe things would all work out. I just needed to have patience.

"Hi, beautiful." He kissed my forehead before pulling out onto the road. "The guys have missed you."

Reading between the lines, I wondered if he had missed me and that was his way of letting me know. I craved his affection, craved honesty and realness from him, but I sensed he was still holding himself back from me. "I missed them, too."

When we arrived home I was accosted by Tucker, who seemed to grow an inch every time I saw him. "Hey buddy." I rumpled his hair. "How's school?"

"Good. Will you read to me tonight?"

"Sure." Casting a quick glance at Knox, I let Tucker take my hand and pull me upstairs to his bedroom.

After three books and a sleepy goodnight hug, I pulled the blankets up around Tucker and met Knox in his attic bedroom. He was sprawled out across his bed with his sketchbook balanced on his chest. "Tucker get settled in okay?"

I nodded. "Yeah, he's out cold."

He studied me for a second, watching the way I stood in the center of his bedroom, my eyes sweeping over the room. "What's on your mind?" he asked, patting the bed bedside him.

Take your pick. That letter I'd yet to open from the lawyer in Indiana concerning my parents' estate, Knox's failure to fully commit, my guilt over sleeping with a sex addict in recovery, or

Brian's recent admission that he wanted to be with me. I felt dizzy just thinking about it all.

I couldn't dump all of that on Knox right now. Releasing a heavy sigh, I decided to tell him the least painful part. "Brian asked a few weeks ago if he had a shot with me. He said it's what my parents would have wanted."

"And what did you say?" His face was impassive, but I hoped that maybe this would push him into action. I wasn't going to be happy with our arrangement forever. I wanted a real commitment, love, a relationship that I knew could eventually grow into something more.

"I couldn't say anything. My parents loved him."

"I see." I wondered if that was a twinge of disappointment or fear that flashed in his chocolate brown eyes. Before I could decide, his expression had turned stoic.

With Knox's cool demeanor – he was neither pushing me away, nor drawing me closer. I wondered if it was time to go back to Indiana and deal with my past once and for all.

"I don't know what this is, but you know how I feel about you, right?" I asked.

He nodded, but gave me no indication he shared those feelings. I wanted to push him for answers – to ask him to explain – but I feared hearing his answer, so instead I sat on his bed, quietly picking at the hem of my sweater.

"Tell me what else is on your mind. There's something more than just Brian's infatuation bugging you."

"This is too much for me. I thought I could do it – be with you and lead SAA, but I can't." The heavy sigh weighing on my chest ripped free. "I'm emotionally invested in both and I don't even know where we stand."

"That's fair," he said quietly, looking down at his sketchbook.

I hated how calm and cool he was about it all. What did he mean? What was happening to us? Whoever said sex changed everything between a man and a woman was right.

"I need to go back to Indiana. There's something I need to take care of. And I'm going to ask Brian to come with me."

He nodded. Piercing brown eyes gazed up at me, making my chest ache. "When are you leaving?"

I shrugged. I hadn't talked to Bri yet – with this being a spur of the moment decision and all. "Probably around the holidays. I know his mom will want to see me." With Christmas just a week away, it made sense.

"You're still staying over tonight, right?"

"Do you want me to?"

"Of course I do. I'll always want you here, McKenna." His voice was so sincere and the look in his eyes was genuine, but I still felt like something was missing. I'd gotten him to open up and I'd convinced him to let me share his bed, but I hadn't gotten what I really wanted – the real Knox, unedited and genuine. He was still holding part of himself back and that hurt more than I ever thought it would.

I headed into the bathroom with my backpack, planning to brush my teeth and change clothes. Instead, I sank down on the toilet lid and silently cried.

I cleaned myself up and emerged from the bathroom a short time later. I found Knox waiting for me in bed with just the soft glow of his bedside lamp to guide my way. I crawled into bed beside a man who owned my heart and made me dizzy with desire, yet offered me so little in return. Maybe this was some type of self-punishment I was putting myself through. Wouldn't Brian be the easier choice? He'd love unconditionally and without all this worry that kept my stomach in knots. But maybe that was just it. Anything worth having wasn't going to come easily. I knew without a shadow of a doubt I'd fallen in love with Knox, and I hoped me heading home to Indiana would give him some time to think about what he wanted.

Chapter Fifteen

Knox

I was losing her. And that couldn't happen. With desperation, I dragged her across the bed and positioned her beneath me, kissing her hard until I felt her respond, her tongue sliding against mine, her legs parting to let me press closer. I hated that this felt like goodbye and I was using the only coping mechanism I had – sex. But I couldn't open myself up for love again and be crushed in the process. This was what I had to offer and while I wondered if McKenna could accept that, her body seemed to be on board.

Her dancing around her talk with Brian and taking off for home meant one thing. She was keeping her options open just in case I fucked up again. She would need someone to fall back on, and Brian was her backup plan. I couldn't fuck up again or I'd send her straight into his arms for comfort. The realization terrified me. Because while I might be holding it all together right now, there were no guarantees that I'd remain on this path. And if McKenna was set on going home, I would show her exactly what she'd be missing.

I might not be able to tell her I loved her, but I could make her feel good. Moving from her eager mouth to her throat, my lips pressed against her pulse point, feeling her heart riot in response. Planting damp kisses and peppering her with gentle bites, I worked my way lower, removing her T-shirt to reveal her ample chest. I wasn't capable of going slow just now and McKenna's writhing, whimpering responses told me she was okay with that. I nibbled at the skin between her breasts, pushing them together and feasting on them greedily. I loved her tits. The way they rose and fell dramatically with her breaths, the moans that would escape her when I flicked my tongue across their peaks…she made me rock hard from her taste and scent alone, and then add in the sounds she made and I was done.

Pushing her pajama bottoms and panties down her legs, I positioned myself on top of her. I was rougher, more demanding than last time and I wasn't sure if it was my fear taking over or just that the need for her was consuming me from the inside out. Finding her wet and ready, I sheathed myself in a condom and took her roughly, plunging into her again and again until I felt her give way and I was buried to the hilt.

I pressed my face into her neck, needing to breath in her scent, needing to know it was just her and me. "Christ, angel, you feel like a hot little sleeve squeezing me."

"Knox…." She moaned out my name long and low and tightened her grip around me. Her nails scratched into my shoulders, but I appreciated the pain. That way I knew this moment with her was real. I pounded into her, again and again, taking from her. Taking

339

every bit of emotion she made me feel and using it as fuel.

She had embedded herself into my life, made me need her. I'd never needed a woman the way I needed McKenna. Her bright smile. Her giving nature. The sound of her laughter, the curse words she made up when she was playing video games with my brothers. She held complete power over me and that scared the shit out of me. I hated the idea of letting her go away with Brian, but saw no other choice.

Sex used to make me feel in control, but this was anything but controlled and organized. McKenna tore through all my layers, refusing to submit. She was an active participant, encouraging, panting, angling our bodies to drive me deeper, and hell if I wanted to stop her.

Soon I was fighting off the inevitable climax I could feel building at the base of my spine and I focused on bringing McKenna to the edge. I wanted her helpless and sobbing my name. Spreading her knees wider, I slowed my pace, dragging my length in and out of her slowly while simultaneously rubbing her clit over and over with the slick juices between us. Her eyes slammed closed and she groaned.

"Open them, angel."

Hazy blue eyes struggled to focus on mine and I continued rocking into her at my languid pace until she found my gaze.

340

"Be a good girl and don't come until I do."

Her eyes widened and she let out a soft whimper. I pumped into her hard and fast, slamming my cock into her warmth until my balls tightened against my body and pleasure was ricocheting through my bloodstream. I pulled out of her at the last moment, tearing off the condom and coming all over her tight little pussy. I marked her swollen pink flesh, using my cock to rub my semen against her clit. McKenna moaned out loud, watching as I pleasured her.

I brought her fingertips to her belly where some of my fluid remained. "Touch your nipples."

She obeyed, taking her breasts in her hands and using the moisture to rub her nipples. Watching her touch her breasts while I pleasured her was the most erotic sight. I rubbed her clit with the head of my cock, using the stimulation to bring her to orgasm. "Come for me, angel."

Her climax hit her hard. Her hips bucked off the bed and her nails bit into my thighs as tremors passed through her shuddering form.

We lay together for a long while, our bodies slick with sweat and sex, but neither of us caring. My cock softened and the evidence of our lovemaking dried long before I was ready to move. This felt like goodbye and I hated the idea of letting her go off alone and deal with her past, including whatever it was she needed to explore with Brian. I climbed from bed and while the water heated for the shower, I delivered a damp cloth to McKenna to clean to herself. Neither of us spoke a single word. Shit, we even avoided eye contact while we cleaned ourselves up and dressed for bed, crawling between the sheets a short while later. I wasn't sure what had changed, but I knew something had. McKenna had a choice to make on her trip home and I had to decide – if she came back to me – how to fully let her in.

Chapter Sixteen

McKenna

The events of last night had me reeling and the harsh light of morning did nothing to bring clarity. When I'd told Knox about Brian's advances and that I needed to go home, he'd been so indifferent. But then he'd taken me to his bed – our lovemaking rough and passionate. I couldn't help but wonder if that was his way of letting me go.

Last night had been so intense, so unexpected. Feeling him mark me with his hot semen made me crave him even more. Everything about Knox was addicting – from the way he took charge of my body and my pleasure to the way he commanded my heart.

I climbed from bed while he slept, hauling my backpack to the bathroom to wash up and change. When I returned to his bedroom, I wondered how I would wake him, how I could possibly say goodbye, but the bed was now empty. The messy blankets were the only evidence of our night spent together. But finding him missing wasn't what stopped me dead in my tracks. On the window beside his bed I saw three little words written with a fingertip on the frosty pane of glass. *I love you.*

Knox has left me a message, something he wasn't capable of telling me out loud.

I sunk down on the mattress, trying to process what this meant – why he'd left this for me to see and then fled the room. I wanted to run down the stairs, find him, and throw myself into his arms. But as I sat there staring at the words fading into the glass, I started to become angry.

I'd given him my virginity, my complete trust, I'd told him I loved him. I'd cared for him and his brothers when they were sick and I'd risked my entire career. And for what? A man who seemed so indifferent to me leaving? Who didn't even possess the courage to say back to me what I'd already told him weeks ago?

Feeling crushed, I glanced up one last time, and saw the words had faded into nothing. They were gone. Not even a trace remained. If Knox had really wanted me to see this...why would he have written it somewhere so fleeting?

I grabbed my backpack and headed downstairs. All four of the Bauer boys were in the kitchen, fixing breakfast while Knox fiddled with the coffee pot. He took his time, adding the filter and coffee to the machine, then crossing the room to add water to the carafe. Was he avoiding me?

"I'm gonna head out. Have a good day at school, boys." Three sets of warm brown eyes turned to mine while Knox focused on his task with a deep crease etched across his forehead. "Bye, Knox." I forced the words from my mouth when all I wanted to do was go to him.

"Bye, McKenna," he said softly, refusing to even glance my way.

Okay, then. I wouldn't build up our relationship in my mind into something it wasn't. He wasn't ready and only time would tell if he ever would be.

Chapter Seventeen

McKenna

"You about ready, McKenna?" Brian called from the living room several days later.

"Just about. My suitcase weighs a metric ton!" I tugged the unwieldy thing unsuccessfully across my room. I knew he wanted to be on the road early this morning and the main hold up was me.

"Here. Let me get it." Brian easily lifted the suitcase from the floor and towed it to the foyer. "Geez, you pack enough?" He chuckled.

Seriously, that bag had to weigh fifty pounds. But I didn't know how long I'd be gone. This time I was going to take care of my parents' matters once and for all. No more having my past hanging over my head. When I came back to Chicago, it would be with all the skeletons in my closet cleared out so I could finally move forward. At least that was my goal.

Being back in my small home town and back in the guest room at Brian's parents' house felt strange. I expected it to feel safe and comfortable, but it was anything but. I felt oddly out of place, like I

346

was trying to squeeze myself into a spot I no longer fit. And if I had to hear Brian's mom Patty ask me one more time how I was doing or tell me that I'd gotten too thin, I was going to scream. But it was Christmas Eve, so I was trying to be calm and put on my happy face for the sake of the holidays.

I was getting ready for the annual Christmas party Brian's family threw every year when I heard a knock at the bedroom door. Glancing down at my robe covered body, I quickly made sure all the important stuff was covered, then answered the door. "Hi, Bri."

He was dressed in khakis and the God-awful Christmas sweater his mom had made for him when he was in high school. It looked itchy and uncomfortable – not to mention hilarious. He was a grown man with red and green reindeer dancing across his chest and stomach.

"Don't say anything," he warned me, fighting off a smile.

I patted his shoulder. "You're a good son."

"Consider yourself lucky she didn't make you one of these things. When I told her you were coming home, there was talk of patchwork poinsettias in gold and red."

"Wow, I guess I dodged a bullet." It was nice – whatever this was – happening between Brian and me. It felt like old times.

"You sure you're okay with tonight?"

"Yeah, why wouldn't I be?"

He shrugged. "There'll be a lot of people you haven't seen in a while. If that's going to make you uncomfortable, you don't have to come."

Releasing a heavy sigh, I considered my options. Though I wasn't particularly excited about the party, sitting alone in my room sounded even more miserable. "And what would I do instead, hide out up here?"

"No. You and I would go out and do our own thing – catch a movie or something."

His offer was sweet, but no, I could handle this. I leaned in and kissed his cheek. "I'll be fine."

He smiled at me, a genuine heart-warming smile that put me at ease. "Okay. Choice is yours. If tonight gets to be too much, just say the word and we're gone."

As nice as it was knowing I had options, I needed to do this – if only to prove to myself that I could. "I'm good. Just don't leave me alone with Jimmy Shane. You remember how grabby he was in high school?"

"He tries to touch you and I can promise I'll remove every finger from his hand." He grinned. "Well, I just stopped by to see if you

348

needed anything from the store…my mom's sending me out for more eggnog before the party starts."

"Nope, I'm good. I just need to finish getting ready."

"Okay, see you soon then."

When a police officer stood at the front door an hour later, his face ashen and grim, my stomach plummeted to my toes. It was eerily similar to that fateful day two policemen had shown up at my door and told me about my parents. All those horrible feelings came rushing straight back. I gripped the arm of the man standing next to me, not caring in the slightest that it was Jimmy Shane.

I watched in slow motion as Brian's parents, Patty and Dave, stepped into the hallway with the cop. When Patty broke out in a loud sob and buried her face against her husband's chest, I crumpled into a ball, collapsing onto the floor. Something had happened to Brian.

The room around me spun, tilting and pitching violently. The police officer left, Dave got Patty settled on the couch, and then made some type of announcement. The blood rushing in my ears blocked out what was said. Or maybe I just wasn't ready to know yet. Party-goers began to filter out. I remained frozen to the spot I'd claimed on the living room carpet, too afraid to move, unable to think.

When Dave lifted me to my feet a short time later, I struggled to make sense of his words. The roads had been icy. Brian was in a car accident. He was at Mercy West in critical condition. He handed me my coat and was waiting for me to respond.

"Are you coming with us?"

Brian was alive? "Of course."

We piled into the car, my nerves completely shot. Even though Brian was alive, I couldn't let myself breathe just yet. My dad had survived his accident for two days in critical condition before the blood hemorrhage in his brain ended his life. And I knew Patty and Dave were probably thinking the same thing. They'd stayed by my side through it all, sleeping in hospital waiting rooms and eating out of vending machines right alongside me. It was only fitting that I be here now with them in their darkest hour. Hugging my arms around myself for warmth in the backseat, I watched as they held hands on the center console – gripping each other tightly. I felt scared and alone.

Brian looked worse than I expected. And even though I'd been down this road before, nothing could adequately prepare you to see someone you care about pale and broken in a hospital bed, punctured with tubes and hooked up to machines beeping about God knows what. But for his parents' sake, I tried to be the calm one and hold it together while they cried over his limp and battered body.

He had lacerations on his face and head from flying glass, a punctured lung when the airbag deployed after he'd struck the lamppost, a concussion and a leg broken in three spots. But he was stable and assuming he did well over the next couple days, he'd be downgraded from critical to serious condition. The doctors were taking every safety precaution, but believed Brian would pull through.

The next day was a blur – but in an all too familiar way. The constant worry and stress, the sterile hospital air, a stiff neck from sleeping in an uncomfortable chair, and the dark circles lining my eyes were all too familiar.

In the chaos of it all, I'd somehow forgotten it was Christmas Day. I thought of Knox and the boys and missed them with every ounce of my being. I wanted nothing more than to be wrapped up tight in Knox's strong arms and tucked safely away from all this heartache. But I supposed being near him brought a different kind of heartache. I wondered what they were doing today…if they had a Christmas tree in the living room with wrapped presents underneath, or if they were working together to make a big dinner later.

I looked up to see Dave dozing quietly in a chair beside Brian's bed and Patty flipping through a magazine for the twelfth time. "I'm going to go make a quick phone call," I whispered to Patty. "You want another cup of coffee?"

"Sure, hon, that'd be great."

It was all she'd eaten or drank since we'd arrived here yesterday.

Stepping into the hallway, I took a moment to gather myself. I had no idea what to expect calling Knox. We hadn't talked in eight long days. Not since he'd so thoroughly claimed my body and then let me walk away without a backward glance.

I leaned against the wall for support, drawing deep breaths as I dialed his number.

"McKenna…." he answered on the first ring.

The rough sound of his voice brought a thousand memories rushing back. "Hi."

"Are you still in Indiana?" he asked.

I swallowed the lump in my throat. "Yeah."

"What's wrong? Did something happen?"

I should have known he'd hear it in my voice. He knew me too well. "Oh God, Knox…." Tears sprang to my eyes and the tightness in my chest threatened to close my throat. "It's Brian…I don't know what to do…."

"Christ, what's he done now?" he barked.

"No, nothing…he was in a car accident. I'm at the hospital. I slept here last night with his parents."

"You weren't in the car with him, were you?"

"No. I was at his parents' house when it happened."

"Fuck," he muttered under his breath. "Is he okay?"

"I – I don't know yet." My voice broke and I chocked on my words, tears freely streaming down both cheek. It was the first time I'd cried since I'd found out about the accident. I'd held it together in front of his parents and the parade of doctors and nurses, but somehow the comforting familiar sound of Knox's deep voice sent me over the edge.

Knox waited while I sobbed, fighting for breath, never once rushing me. "He was banged up pretty bad, but they've repaired his lung and his leg, so as long as the concussion didn't do any damage, he should be okay."

"Breathe for me, angel. It'll be okay."

I drew a deep breath, struggling to regain my composure. The busy nurses and hospital staff shuffling past paid me little attention. Apparently a girl crying uncontrollably in the hallway was a normal occurrence. I forced myself to maintain my hard-won sense of self-control, focusing on the sound of Knox's steady breaths to calm me.

"I'm sorry...." I whispered.

"Don't apologize. Are you all right?"

"I think so. I just hate being back in this hospital, and I hate feeling so helpless. I mean, this is Bri...we've been inseparable since first grade."

"Hang in there, okay?"

I nodded and then smiled, realizing he couldn't see me. "I'll try."

"So I know it's the wrong time to ask, but the guys miss you. Any idea when you'll be coming back?"

"No clue. I've taken a leave from work. I want to be here for Brian, ya know?" I had requested one because I wasn't sure how long all of this would take, and now with the accident, I was even less certain.

"Understood."

Was that sadness in his voice? "He was there for me when, you know, so I should be here for him and his parents."

"Of course. I get it, McKenna. You guys have a past and he's been in an accident. It makes sense you'd want to be by his side."

"Yeah." I shuffled my feet, trying to think of something else to say.

I wasn't done hearing his voice.

"Merry Christmas, angel," he whispered.

I'd forgotten that was the reason I'd called in the first place. "Merry Christmas," I whispered back. "What are you guys up to today?"

"Nikki and the baby came over for a little bit. Tucker had gotten Bailee a gift. And now we're getting ready to head out. We're actually going to the soup kitchen to volunteer. We're cooking Christmas dinner for those with nowhere else to go today."

My throat felt tight again. "Knox…that's amazing."

"Yeah, well, there's this certain girl who sort of changed my way of thinking about things. Jax complained a little bit, but I think it'll be really good for the guys."

"I'm proud of you." I had to physically force myself not to say I love you. I loved him with my whole heart, but I couldn't stand the thought of being so vulnerable and hearing silence again. Little by little he was changing and growing into the man I always knew he could be. "I guess I should go. Brian's mom is waiting on me."

"Take care of yourself, McKenna."

"Bye, Knox."

I hung up the phone and cried like a baby.

When I'd finally composed myself, I ventured downstairs to the hospital cafeteria and got the cup of coffee I'd promised Patty. When I returned to Brian's room I found Patty sitting in the arm chair beside the bed, but Dave was gone.

"He went home to get a change of clothes for us. He'll be back in a little bit and you can borrow the car if you want to go home to shower or change," she informed me.

"Okay, thanks." A shower sounded heavenly, but I didn't want to leave on the chance that Brian woke up.

Patty hung her head in her hands, her expression pure agony. "I just keep thinking what if I hadn't sent him out, I knew the roads were icy…all over a carton of eggnog…." Her voice broke as she sobbed into her hands.

"Patty…." I crossed the room and stood beside her, placing one hand on her shoulder. "This isn't your fault. Accidents happen." In that moment, my clarity couldn't have been more apparent if I'd been struck by lightning. Seeing Patty's anguish and guilt made me feel so foolish for holding onto my own guilt for all these years. My parents' accident wasn't my fault. What I'd said to her was true. Accidents happened. They happened to good people and sometimes no one was to blame. Though I supposed that wasn't entirely true. In my parents' case. The drunk driver who'd taken their lives was very much to blame. "Shh, it's gonna be okay. Brian's gonna pull through." I continued rubbing her back, soothing her as best as could, but inside, my thoughts were swirling. My realization changed everything. I felt freer and more aware in an instant – more grown up. Little by little, I felt the dark shame I stored inside me slipping away.

My adolescent mind at seventeen wasn't mature enough to handle their deaths. I'd needed someone to blame – and I'd punished myself. But the twenty-one year old me was seeing things clearly for the first time and the results were astounding. Despite the horrible circumstances of the moment, I felt more in control than ever. We would all be okay. Once Brian was healthy, I would go back to Chicago and try to fix things with Knox. We were grown up enough to have a conversation about the scary *L* word. He either loved me and wanted to be with me, or he didn't. And I would have to accept his decision and move forward with my life once and for all.

Chapter Eighteen

McKenna

As the days turned to weeks, Brian's recovery progressed quickly and I had no choice but to finally face my fears. I'd set up an appointment and visited the lawyer earlier that day. I was still trying to process the shocking truth of it all as I sat quietly at my parents' gravestones.

I'd known that between their insurance policies, pension plans, and the sale of our house I'd been left a significant chunk of money, I just hadn't expected it to affect me so much. It felt so final walking out of the lawyer's office with a large check in my hands. It was a life-changing amount of money and just as I was starting to get things figured out in my own head, I knew it was going to change everything. It would change where I lived, how Knox viewed me...even what I did for a living if I chose... and unease churned inside me. I wasn't good at change.

Knox and I continued talking every few days – surface level stuff – he'd fill me in on the boys and I'd give him Brian's progress report. We never talked about us. I never told him how I missed him with every ounce of my being, and he felt more distant than ever. As hard as it was to imagine, I wondered if he'd slipped back into his old ways.

I was planning to return to Chicago while Brian stayed behind for physical therapy for his leg. No longer living on a few dollars a day meant I could rent a car and drive myself home.

I huddled into my coat as the chilly air swirled loose strands of hair around my face. The bitter temperature and icy barren ground matched the somber tone of this reunion with my parents. I tucked my mitten-covered hands into my pockets as I filled them in on Brian. I talked out loud, the sound of my voice my only company. As I told them about the events of the past few weeks, I realized that my parents had liked Brian and viewed him as a good match for me because he'd always treated me well and protected me. Knox protected and took care of those he loved, too. And he made me happy. At the end of the day, my parents would have wanted me to be happy. It wasn't lost on me that my lack of attraction to Brian was because there was nothing to fix. He was a perfectly nice, well-adjusted man from a normal, nice family. But it didn't matter the reasons — the attraction wasn't there and it never would be. I had to believe my parents would have accepted that.

Knox had been right about one thing — one day I would forgive myself and move on. Today had proven I was capable of that, in small doses. But he'd been wrong about himself not fitting into my life. Being near Brian produced no spark, no electricity, and I missed the warmth that Knox created in me. I knew that by the end of this week, I'd be more than ready to get back. I was even considering changing up my punishing routine – volunteering fewer hours a week, taking more time to take care of myself and enjoy the little things in life. If I'd learned only one thing on this trip, it was that life was short and could be ripped from you at any moment.

I was also starting to feel guilty for not acknowledging his handwritten *I love you* message left on the window for me. He was still healing and that was his way of trying. I needed to acknowledge his efforts and progress, not act like a spoiled child who needed everything her way.

If my parents were really out there somewhere listening to this, I wanted to think they'd understand that Brian would always be a constant reminder of what I'd lost. Brian was my past. Knox was my future.

Digging my cell phone out of my coat pocket, I dialed Knox.

Chapter Nineteen

Knox

Seeing McKenna's name flash on my phone made me ridiculously fucking happy. I rounded the service counter at the hardware store where I was working and headed for the stockroom, tossing the pair of pliers I was supposed to be price checking onto a shelf. The customer would have to wait.

I ducked into the dusty stockroom and closed the door behind me. "Hey, angel."

"Hi," she returned, her voice whisper-soft.

"Everything okay over there? Brian?" As much as saying his name grated against my nerves, the guy had gotten pretty messed up in that accident, so I didn't want to be a complete asshole and not ask how he was doing. Still, I'd be lying if I said it didn't make me insane with jealousy that McKenna had put her entire life on hold – put us on hold – to tend to him and stick by his side. I couldn't help but feel she'd chosen him over me.

I wished I'd had the balls that morning to take her in my arms and tell her I loved her. But instead I'd taken the pussy way out and scrawled it onto the window. There was a good chance she never even saw it. I sent her away into the arms of her very male best friend without even telling her how I felt. Basically I was a jackass.

"Brian's doing fine. I think he's annoyed at the slow pace of his recovery with his leg and his mom's constant hovering, but considering how things could have turned it, he's very lucky."

"And how are you?"

She hesitated for several seconds before answering. "I realized some things this week."

"And what's that?" I wasn't religious, but I prayed to God it wasn't that she'd figured out Brian was the better choice for her and she was staying in Indiana.

"My parents' accident wasn't my fault. It was the damn reckless, irresponsible drunk driver." Her voice wavered ever-so-slightly and she took a moment to compose herself. "I was talking to Brian's mom Patty after the accident and it all just hit me. My actions that morning may not have made a difference in the outcome. And for years I thought maybe I should have been with them. But I see now that I wasn't meant to go then. I'm here for a reason. I'm here to do good in the world."

"That's great to hear, angel. And you're right. You had nothing to do with the accident."

"I know that now. I can't image how someone could be so selfish, so negligent. I will never forgive the man who did this. I have zero tolerance for drunk drivers."

I was happy to hear her channel her anger into the right place – McKenna wasn't responsible for her parents' deaths. The man

362

behind the wheel was. But cold dread slithered down my spine realizing, I'd never told McKenna about my own drunk driving arrest. Would it be a deal breaker for me and her?

"I'm going to be coming home soon," she continued.

"Can I see you when you get home?"

"Yeah, and there's something I have to tell you when I get back."

"Something good or something bad?" I asked.

"Um, just something…different. About my life. I finally met with my parents' lawyer."

"Okay." I had no clue where this was heading, but I'd follow her lead on this one. "See you soon, then?"

"Yeah. Goodbye, Knox."

"Bye."

Chapter Twenty

Knox

"Do you want to talk about it or are you going to keep moping around here like someone kicked you in the balls?" Jaxon asked, glancing up from the TV.

"Are you going to watch the game or are we going to pretend this is Oprah?" I asked.

He smirked. "Fine. But the guys know something's up. You're not yourself. You've been acting like a dick ever since McKenna took off. Care to tell me what's really going on?"

The feeling that I'd lost McKenna churned in my gut. I couldn't sleep. Food didn't taste right and when I tried to drink to numb the pain, I couldn't even catch a buzz. Luke had taken Tucker to the public library, so it was just me and Jaxon at home today. "I talked to McKenna. She's coming home soon."

"That's a good thing, right?"

"Yeah, I mean, I think so. But she said we have to talk when she gets back. I think she's had some sort of realization about her past and finally accepted that her parents were killed by a drunk driver and not because of anything she did."

"And?" Jax drew out the word.

Apparently I needed to spell it out for him. "And she doesn't know I was arrested for drunk driving and that my sentence was what brought me into her class in the first place." Not mentioning it at the time was an omission — it just never really came up, but keeping it from her now felt like a deceitful lie.

"Shit. That sucks."

I blew out a frustrated breath. "Tell me about it."

Jax flipped the channel on the TV. "That's why I don't do love. As soon as you let your walls down, shit falls apart and then you're the one sitting there feeling like shit. It's easier to hit it and quit it."

"Nice, Jaxon."

He shrugged. "It's just the truth and you know it. You lived that way for years."

I couldn't argue; he knew my history too well. "Well, sometimes feeling something is a good thing. It reminds us that we're still human." I'd rather be having no sex with McKenna than be sleeping with a bunch of random girls, but I knew nothing I said would get through to him. He'd have to figure all this out on his own one day, too.

Jaxon rose from the couch and handed me the remote. "I know I'm not good at this shit, but you know you have to talk to her, right?"

I nodded. "Yeah. Thanks, bro."

I knew I needed to talk to her, but I wasn't sure that would make a difference. With her new-found clarity and anger toward the drunk-driver who killed her parents – what could I possibly say?

Chapter Twenty-One

McKenna

I couldn't wait any longer. After the four hour drive with nothing but the radio to keep me company, I couldn't resist going straight to Knox's place. With darkness settling in, I parked on the street and grabbed my overnight bag from the backseat before jogging to the front door. I'd been planning on coming home tomorrow, but as the morning had stretched on, I became more and more anxious to see Knox. I'd hastily packed, said my goodbyes, and hit the road. I wanted to surprise him.

Tucker answered the door a few moments later.

"Kenna!" He latched himself around me, squeezing tightly.

"Hi, bud. I missed you." I leaned in and kissed his forehead.

"I missed you, too. Are you back for good?"

"Yep. I sure am." Following him inside, the cozy familiar feeling of being home settled over me. A tower of Legos was half-built on the living room rug and the TV was playing cartoons. The house even smelled the same. I inhaled deeply, breathing in the scent of boys. "Where is everyone?"

"Luke and Jaxon went out somewhere, but Knox is here."

My heart picked up speed. I couldn't wait to see his deep soulful eyes, to kiss his scruffy jaw, inhale his masculine scent. I'd missed him so much. "Where is he?"

"Knox?" Tucker asked.

I nodded.

"He told me to wait down here. He brought a girl upstairs."

My stomach dropped like a stone and I broke out in a cold sweat.

"McKenna? Are you okay?"

I pulled in a lungful of air. "I'm fine." I couldn't let him see the blood rising in my cheeks or the sheer panic in my eyes. Turning from Tucker, I marched up the stairs. The journey up the three flights of stairs felt like an out of body experience. I floated above myself and watched my legs climb each step, my shaky fingers gripping the banister. My pulse thundered in my ears as I waited outside his closed bedroom door. With my heart pounding way too rapidly to be safe, I raised my fist to knock. Then stopped. And listened.

Low feminine moaning followed by Knox's voice giving some type of command.

Bile shot up my throat and I swallowed, forcing the sickness down. With tears clouding my vision, I reached for the door knob and pushed open the door.

What I found inside the room was the last thing I'd expected to see. I fell to the floor, my legs giving out beneath me as the adrenaline in my bloodstream rioted.

"McKenna?" Knox's confused voice asked in the distance.

The moaning hadn't stopped and I brought my hands up to cover my ears and squeezed my eyes closed. Footsteps crossed the room toward me and I felt Knox's strong arms close around me, and movement as he lifted me from the floor.

"Breathe, angel," he whispered into my hair. "Amanda, clear a spot on the bed…." I felt him place me on his bed and I began to thrash, trying to sit up, to move but his hands held me firmly. "Stay put. We need to talk." His low authoritative voice whispering my name was the last thing I heard before I let the blackness pull me under.

When I Break #3

by

Kendall Ryan

About the Book

In this third and final installment of the much-loved WHEN I BREAK series, Knox and McKenna's relationship has reached a critical impasse. The mistakes and secrets of their pasts have caught up to them and threaten their future happiness. Can McKenna trust that Knox's sexual addiction is behind him and make a life with this beautifully troubled man? And when Knox reveals the full truth about his past, will McKenna be able to put her own fears aside and accept him?

When We Fall is the conclusion to Knox and McKenna's story.

Chapter One

KNOX

I knew I needed to stay calm and assess the situation, but McKenna showing up here tonight had really thrown me off. And not to mention a very pregnant Amanda waddling across my floor, groaning in pain, was putting me a little outside my comfort zone. My head was spinning like a fucking top.

Think, Knox.

I checked on McKenna again. She was sprawled across my bed where I'd laid her down, and her body was limp and pale. She was breathing, but she wasn't responding to my voice or touch. She had passed out cold from the shock of finding me in my bedroom with Amanda. I would have to deal with the repercussions later. My guess was that McKenna had driven back from her extended stay in Indiana, and finding me with Amanda in my bedroom—along with the soundtrack of Amanda's moans—had McKenna assuming the worst. Next, I tried to get Amanda to sit down and rest, but she pushed me away, insisting that walking was helping.

Knowing I was seriously out of my element, I grabbed my cell phone and dialed my neighbor, Nikki. She had a baby; surely she'd know if this was false labor or the real thing.

"Nik, yeah. Hey, my friend Amanda thinks she's going into labor, but she's not due for another several weeks—"

Nikki cut me off, saying something about a guy named Braxton Hicks and timing contractions, but before I could hear the rest, Amanda let out a bloodcurdling scream.

"I'm peeing, I think I'm peeing! Am I peeing?" She squatted on the floor, her pants growing darker with a wet stain.

What the fuck? I cursed under my breath and crossed the room to give her a hand.

Nikki, overhearing the entire thing, laughed. "Her water just broke. Get her to the hospital. This baby's coming early."

Christ. "McKenna's here and passed out—I can't just leave her. And Tucker's here, too. Can you come over?"

"Sorry, I'm out of town at my mom's," Nikki said.

"All right. Gotta go, Nik."

"Good luck."

I hung up the phone and helped Amanda remove her wet pants and underwear, then gave her a pair of my sweats. I'd worry about cleaning up the puddle of water on my floor later. In all the commotion, Tucker had come upstairs and was now peeking around the open doorway. "It's okay, Tuck, you can come in."

He ventured inside the room slowly, looking around at the two women, his eyes as big as saucers. McKenna was still out cold.

"What happened?" he asked.

"Kenna's all right, I promise. And Amanda's going to have her baby."

Amanda let out a low moan and sat down on the bed next to McKenna. Doing the only thing I could, I picked up my phone and dialed 911. The paramedics could make sure McKenna was all right and give Amanda a lift to the hospital. While I waited for them to arrive, I sent Tucker downstairs to gather up some towels. He didn't need to be up here seeing Amanda in agonizing pain and worrying about McKenna. It wasn't healthy for his little mind to try to process all that was happening. I was having a hard enough time keeping my own stress level contained.

A few minutes later I heard sirens and ran downstairs to meet the paramedics. One man and one woman rushed inside and followed me and a wide-eyed Tucker up the stairs to my attic bedroom.

They assessed Amanda and determined that she was in active labor and got her ready for transport. Then they turned their attention to McKenna. I didn't breathe a full, deep breath until I saw her eyelids flutter and open. Her eyes met mine, and all the fear and anxiety knotting inside me relaxed just slightly.

"Hey, angel." I leaned over her on the bed and pressed a kiss to her forehead.

"What happened?" she asked, pushing up on her elbows to sit up.

Tucker edged himself closer, nearly climbing into her lap. It seemed I wasn't the only one who'd been worried about her.

"Tuck, give her some space."

McKenna took his hand and squeezed, showing him that she was okay.

"You came in and saw me and Amanda, and you passed out," I explained.

Her gaze shot over to where Amanda was sitting on the sofa with the paramedics on either side of her. "Oh my God, is she okay?"

"She's in labor. They're gonna take her to the hospital. She came here about an hour ago, complaining of a backache and contractions, and said she didn't have anywhere else to go."

McKenna chewed on her lip, taking in the chaos across the room.

"Sir?" One of the paramedics called me over and I kissed McKenna's forehead again, then went to them.

"How is she?"

"She's doing great but progressing quickly, so we need to get going."

Amanda grabbed my hand. "You're coming with me, right?"

I hadn't planned on it, but the fear in her eyes pulled at something deep inside me.

"I need someone," Amanda insisted. "I can't do this alone. Can either you or McKenna come with me?" Her voice was shrill, bordering on hysterical.

Shit. Amanda was right. And since McKenna had just driven five hours and then had a fainting spell, I didn't particularly want to send her off to the hospital for what could very well turn into an all-night process. "Of course I'll come."

While the paramedics brought Amanda downstairs and loaded her into the ambulance, I explained to McKenna and Tucker that I was going to the hospital. McKenna's crystal-blue eyes turned hazy and she blinked several times, looking away.

"Will you be okay here with Tuck?" I asked her. "The guys should be home soon."

McKenna nodded. "I'll be fine. And you're right, someone should be with her. We'll talk when you get back."

Unable to stop touching McKenna, I kissed her temple and told Tucker to take good care of her, then dashed down the stairs to grab my keys. I would follow the ambulance in my Jeep.

Chapter Two

MᴄKᴇɴɴᴀ

I'd imagined the worst when I heard the feminine moans coming from behind Knox's closed bedroom door. My heart had shattered and crumbled into a million pieces as I came to the conclusion I'd lost him in the weeks I'd spent away. I'd chosen to go to Indiana and stay there while my friend Brian recovered from his car accident, but the second I heard what I thought was sex happening on the other side of that door, and that I'd lost Knox for good, I wanted to take back every moment I'd spent at Brian's bedside.

Knox being in his bedroom with a laboring Amanda was the last thing I'd expected. And I knew that said something about the level of trust I had in him. If I wanted to be here, and see where things could go with us, I needed to work on my trust issues. But one thing at a time. I swung my legs over the side of the bed and tested my weight on my shaky legs.

"Should we go downstairs?" I asked Tucker. He nodded, taking me by the arm and helping me up from the bed. "I'm okay, buddy. I promise."

He was so sweet and chivalrous, and just eight years old. It was an adorable combination. "Do you want to watch the new Spiderman movie? I got it for Christmas."

"Sure, buddy. You get it started, I'll be right down." I wanted to throw the wet towels into the washing machine, figuring that the amniotic fluid currently soaking into the hardwood floors should be cleaned up before Knox got home.

After starting the wash, I met Tucker in the living room. He'd made a big nest of pillows on the couch for us and had the movie all cued up.

"Ready?" he asked.

I nodded.

Tucker grabbed the remote control. "I fast-forwarded it to the best part."

I chuckled at his efforts, not bothering to explain that I'd prefer to watch the movie from the beginning. His enthusiasm was enough. He hit PLAY and an action scene, complete with good guys and villains, played out before us. I decided it was actually rather thoughtful of him to fast-forward just to the good parts. Plus in the weeks since Christmas, I guessed he'd already watched this at least a dozen times.

I wondered how long Amanda's delivery would take and if the baby would be okay. She was delivering really early, but I knew she was well into her third trimester, so I hoped that meant the baby was developed enough to be all right. I was glad I had Tucker cuddled in my lap to distract me. Otherwise I'd probably be pacing the floor, completely stressed out and worried.

Just as the movie was ending, Jaxon and Luke arrived home.

"Hey, guys." I whispered my greeting so as not to wake Tucker, who was softly snoring against my shoulder.

Jaxon smiled crookedly. "You're back."

I nodded.

"Good. Knox was like a hormonal teenager when you were gone." Jaxon lifted Tucker from the couch and cradled his dead weight as he carried him up the stairs.

Luke sat down beside me. "Where's Knox? Does he know you're back?"

"Yeah. It wasn't quite the reunion I was expecting, though. When I got here, our friend Amanda from group was here and she'd gone into labor. Knox took her to the hospital." I left out the embarrassing part where I fell like a sack of stones, dropping to the floor from shock.

I knew it was wrong, but part of me wanted to grill Luke about Knox's activities while I'd been away. Had he behaved himself? Knowing he'd hooked up with someone would crush me, and since it wasn't right to use Luke's honesty against his own brother, I abstained. "How was winter break?"

Luke shrugged. "It was okay. I worked down at the hardware store with Knox most days, trying to build up a savings account for college. I'm going to keep working there a few days a week after school."

I loved his determination. It made me realize that I'd taken my own education for granted. When it was time for me to go to college, all I had to do was apply, and even then I'd complained about the endless essays and applications. My parents had set aside money for years so I didn't have to worry about anything when it was time to go. As much as I tried to put myself in Luke's shoes, I knew I'd never really understand the struggles he had to endure. "I heard you guys volunteered on Christmas," I said.

"Yeah. It was really cool. I think we're gonna start doing that every year, make it our new family tradition. Holidays just aren't the same without our parents."

"I know what you mean." I loved the idea that I might have inspired their new holiday tradition.

Jaxon returned from putting Tucker to bed, and stood in front of where Luke and I sat on the couch. "I think I'm gonna go out for a while."

"Stay in with us," I blurted. I didn't want to worry and wonder where Jaxon was and who he was with; I felt responsible for the boys tonight with Knox away. Maybe it was my nerves, or maybe it was because of what happened to Brian, but I'd feel a lot more comfortable with us all under one roof.

"You have to make it worth my while then." He smirked.

"Okay?" I hadn't meant to phrase it as a question, but I was curious what he meant.

"You know how to play poker?" he asked.

"A little." One of my college roommates had a boyfriend who was really into poker. He'd taught us both the basics.

"You have any cash on you?"

I nodded.

"Perfect. Come on."

Luke and I rose from the couch and followed Jaxon to the dining room table. Luke tugged on my wrist, meeting my eyes with a solemn gaze. "You don't have to play with him."

"It's fine."

Honestly, the distraction of a game of cards sounded better than sitting on the couch moping and waiting for Knox to get home. And I liked the idea of getting to know Luke and Jaxon a little better. I hadn't spent any quality time with just the three of us before. "Can we play with just three players?" I asked Jaxon, settling into the chair across from him.

"Yeah, shorthanded poker. Luke, Knox, and I play this way sometimes."

Luke rolled his eyes. "Knox and I don't play with him anymore. He's too good. Be careful, McKenna."

I laughed. I couldn't really see Jaxon trying to roll me for my money. I grabbed my wallet from my purse and set it on the table next to me. "I think I can handle myself."

Jaxon smiled at me, a devilish grin that showed off one dimple. "I like the confidence. Game on, babe."

Luke rolled his eyes and leaned back in his chair, folding his arms behind his head.

I watched as Jaxon pulled a roll of bills from his pocket that was several inches thick. *Whoa.* Where had he gotten that kind of money? There had to be several hundred dollars there, and as far as I knew he didn't have a job. Unless you counted breaking hearts and getting into fights. I averted my eyes from the stack of money he was shuffling through. It was his business.

Jaxon made quick work of changing my twenty-dollar bill into singles and passing the cash back to me. "Aren't you getting in?" I asked Luke.

He shook his head. "I don't play Jax for money anymore. Now we trade homework assignments."

I guess that made sense. Luke was good at school and it seemed to come naturally for him. "Oh. Well, what do you get if you win?"

A confused look twisted his features. "I don't know. I've never won."

I watched in awe as Jaxon shuffled and dealt the cards. The way his fingers glided over the cards with ease told me he'd spent a fair amount of time playing, a little hidden talent I'd known nothing about. It seemed the more I got to know about these boys, the more they surprised me.

"So, where is Knox anyway?" Jaxon asked, dealing the last card.

While I arranged the cards in my hand, I explained about Amanda and how her water had broken on his bedroom floor.

Jaxon made a face and shuddered. "Nasty." Luke's expression was more one of concern. They couldn't be more different if they tried.

I'd been dealt a decent hand—a pair of tens and a pair of sixes—and I tossed a few dollars into the center of the table. After seeing and raising, then noticing conspicuous looks from Luke, I called Jaxon and he turned over his cards for me. A full house. He took the bills from the center of the table and gave me a mocking look.

Throughout the game I continually glanced down at my phone, wondering what was happening at the hospital and when Knox would be home. I felt a little bad that I hadn't been the one to go with Amanda. I was sure she could have used a female friend there, but someone had to stay here with Tucker, and knowing the state I'd been in, it made sense that person was me. Watching Spiderman with a cuddly eight-year-old was much less stressful than being a birth coach, I was sure.

While Jaxon easily won hand after hand, Luke delivered salty snacks and cold beverages to the table, as if pretzels and chips would make up for me getting my butt kicked by Jaxon.

As it turned out, I wasn't as decent a poker player as I'd thought. Or Jaxon was just that good.

When my twenty dollars had dwindled down to two, I folded, laying my cards down on the table, then yawned. It was already after midnight. "You know there is such a thing as letting a girl win." I smiled sweetly, handing over more singles.

"I respect you too much to treat you like an unequal opponent," he said, sweet as pie.

"Yeah, sure you do." I winked.

"Let's just not tell Knox about this, okay?" Jaxon grinned, stacking his pile of newly acquired bills in front of him.

I chuckled. No doubt, Knox wouldn't be happy about Jaxon swindling me in a game of poker. "I'm beat, guys. I think I'm gonna call it a night."

One more quick check of my phone and still nothing from Knox. I considered calling him but decided against it. If he was helping Amanda during her labor, he'd have his hands full. Yet there was something that nagged at me. Her showing up here when she was in labor seemed a little odd to me. Maybe they'd grown closer while I was away. Pushing the thoughts aside, I rose from my seat and stretched. "'Night, guys."

Luke and Jaxon kissed each of my cheeks and I climbed the stairs feeling happy and complete. Being near them made me feel like I was getting my second chance at a family.

Crawling into Knox's bed alone felt strange. The bed was too big, too cold, and it made me yearn for his warmth. The one bonus was that the pillowcase smelled like him. Curling onto my side, I snuggled in closer, breathing in that delicious scent, and drifted off to sleep.

When Knox finally arrived home late the next morning, I'd already made a big pancake breakfast, cleaned up, and played an epic battle of superheroes with Tucker. Knox looked weary and tired, but most of all he looked traumatized.
I rushed to his side, cupping his cheeks in my hands. "Knox? The baby…?"

"Is fine. A little girl. Not quite five pounds. They have her in intensive care, but there's not a thing wrong with her."

"Wow. That's great news. And Amanda?"

"She's doing well. She was a trouper. It was a long labor. For all of us."

"What's wrong?" I took in his ragged appearance, the fine lines that seemed to have appeared overnight, and his pale skin tone. "You look…scarred for life." I chuckled, giving his chest a pat.

He met my eyes, deep worry etched into his honey-brown stare. "No man should see the things I saw."

I couldn't help but giggle again at his obvious discomfort. Giving birth was a natural process, but apparently Knox and his poor eyeballs felt differently. "Did something…happen?"

Knox swallowed heavily. "I just…the things I saw…I can't unsee that." He made a face.

I gave his chest a playful shove. "I think you'll live. Poor Amanda is the one who had to go through it all. Did she get pain medication?"

He nodded. "Yeah. She made it a good long while without any and then it got too bad. I called the nurse, and they put something in her back that made the pain go away."

I smiled. Knox had proven he was a good friend and a good brother. But what I really wanted to know was if he could be a good boyfriend.

"Thanks for staying with Tucker and the guys. Everyone good?"

I nodded. "All is fine. They were fun." I almost told him about Jaxon taking me for twenty bucks in poker last night and immediately decided against it. I knew things were already somewhat shaky between the two of them, and didn't want to pile on any additional stress. "I came straight here last night because I wanted to talk."

Knox nodded, bringing a big, warm palm to my jawline and stroking my cheek. "I know. We do need to talk, but I'm exhausted. I was up most of the night and the little sleep I did get was in a folding chair." His rough thumb continued its path, softly rubbing my cheek. "Can I take a rain check?"

"Of course. I guess I'll go home. Unpack. Shower. Water my sure-to-be-dead plants."

"Okay. Thanks again for last night. I'll call you later."

All the excitement I'd experienced when I pulled up to Knox's house last night had vanished. I still needed answers, but for now it seemed, they would have to wait.

Chapter Three

KNOX

McKenna surprising me last night should have been a good thing. But it was more than just the situation with Amanda that was giving me pause and had me asking for a time-out today. I knew the conversation we needed to have—about McKenna's painful past and my own drunk-driving arrest. But every scenario I played out in my mind ended with her in tears and my heart broken. I just wasn't ready to go there yet. I needed her. My brothers needed her. She'd only just showed back up in our lives and I didn't want to lose her.

After greeting the guys and checking on the house, I fell into bed, drifting off to a deep sleep almost immediately. When I woke several hours later, I felt groggy and disoriented. Checking the time on my phone, I realized it was late afternoon and reluctantly crawled from bed. After a much-needed shower, I felt more alert and ventured downstairs.

Jaxon was sitting on the couch with a brand new laptop balanced across his knees.

"Where'd you get that?" I asked.

He looked up from the screen at me. "I won some money at a hand of cards."

I frowned. "I told you I don't want you gambling." Jaxon had enough bad habits without adding another to the mix.

"Relax, man. I had a good hand and I bet appropriately. It's not a big deal. And besides, I got it for Luke. I thought he could take it to college with him next year. He's gonna need a computer."

I couldn't argue with that. Jaxon's intentions were in the right place. "Fine. But I'm serious about the gambling." I headed toward the kitchen before halting mid-stride to face him again. "And don't be looking up porn on that thing. I don't want Tucker stumbling across your search history."

Jaxon chuckled. "That's the entire reason I shelled out six hundred bucks for this, dude."

I shot him an angry scowl.

He laughed again, closing the laptop and setting it aside. "I'm kidding. If I want pussy, I have three dozen contacts in my phone. All I have to do is text one of them. I'm sure you know how that works."

My blood pressure shot up. The little shit was right. Which made me realize I should probably delete all those numbers. I didn't want McKenna finding them and getting the wrong idea. Or worse, I didn't want to chance succumbing to temptation if this thing between me and McKenna didn't work out.

"Where are the guys?" I growled.

"At the park," Jaxon said. "And speaking of pussy…I'm going out." He grinned.

I rolled my eyes. Perhaps he was a lost cause. The sooner he was out on his own, the better. He would have to make his own mistakes and learn his own lessons, just as I had.

I made myself something to eat and sat alone at the kitchen table. The house was picked up and more organized, and I wondered if that had been McKenna's touch last night. There was no denying our house felt like more of a home because of her—her light, feminine scent that hung in the air long after she was gone, the sense of calm she instilled in me and the boys, the home-cooked meals she occasionally spoiled us with. God, I'd missed her.

As I ate, my mind wandered to McKenna. She'd been a vision standing in the doorway of my bedroom last night, her skin flushed and her heartbeat racing in her neck. I couldn't even imagine what she thought was going on inside my room. Finding Amanda in labor was probably the last thing she expected.

Anticipation coursed through me at the thought of seeing McKenna tonight. She had said there were some things she needed to tell me. Which meant I needed to delay pulling the skeletons out of my closet. That would have to wait. Tonight was about her.

As I cleaned up after my meal, my mind went to the events at the hospital last night. I shuddered remembering Amanda's guttural cries when she pushed the baby out, along with a rush of fluid and blood. I didn't care what anyone said; there was nothing natural about that process. It made me want to kick the ass of whoever put Amanda in that position and left her to deal with the consequences alone. He was a coward, whoever he was. Watching her hold her baby girl and sob just as hard as the tiny thing in her arms was a harrowing experience, and one I'd probably never forget. The baby was born prematurely, and though nothing major appeared wrong, she'd be under close watch for some time to come. I imagined both McKenna and I would be back at the hospital to visit both of them soon.

But right now, it was about me and McKenna.

––––––––––––––

When I picked up McKenna an hour later, she jogged down the stairs before I had the chance to go up and get her. Exiting the Jeep, I crossed around the front and met her beside the passenger door. She stood silently waiting for me to open it. But I wasn't in any sort of rush.

Taking her face in my hands, I brought her lips to mine. "God, I missed you." I held her close, drinking in her breath, the warmth I felt just having her near. "When you left, I thought…"

"What?" she murmured, her mouth brushing against mine.

"That I'd lost you. I thought you were choosing Brian and a

391

normal life back home over me and all my mountains of baggage."

Her eyebrows pinched together. "How could you think that?"

Moving my hands from her jaw to her waist, I tucked my thumbs into the back of her jeans and stroked the smooth skin of her lower back. "That morning you left...I shouldn't have let you go like that."

McKenna's mouth lifted in a smile just before my lips claimed hers. Not needing any more prompting, she pressed her lips to mine, running her tongue along my bottom lip until my lips parted and her tongue swept inside, gently stroking mine. What began as a sweet hello kiss turned into something much more desperate. She felt it. I felt it. This time apart hadn't been easy on either of us.

It was a damn good thing she was back. After getting a taste of how sweet and sensual she was, I knew I was ruined for all other girls. There was only McKenna.

I growled in satisfaction, a low rumble emanating from the back of my throat. "What are you doing?"

"Distracting you," she said, her voice breathy.

"It's working." I pressed my hips into hers, letting her feel the hard ridge she'd inspired in my jeans. "We should go before I get arrested for public indecency."

She giggled. "Where are we headed? Your place?"

I shook my head. "I might have something planned."

This information earned me a smile. Good, because I'd planned my very first date and something in me liked the recognition. I'd never dated, and McKenna understood what this meant.

If it were summer, I could take her to the Navy Pier and ride the Ferris wheel, or to the beach where we could sit and watch the waves of Lake Michigan crash against the shoreline. Instead, I helped her inside the warmth of my Jeep. The frigid temperatures dictated we'd be doing something indoors.

I drove us to the downtown restaurant I'd researched online. Never had I spent so much time planning a meal. But this wasn't just any meal; it was a second chance for us. Knowing it would take a small miracle to find parking even reasonably close to the restaurant, I pulled to a stop in front of the valet sign. McKenna shot me a curious glare. "We're eating here?"

I nodded. I might not have much to offer her, but one nice meal out wasn't going to break the bank. McKenna had done so much for me and for the boys. I wanted to treat her to something special and show her how important she was to me.

After I handed my keys to the valet, we headed inside the quaint Italian restaurant, Cucina Bella, and were guided to the table I'd reserved near the fireplace. McKenna's answering smile was the only reassurance I needed. It was good to mix things up now and then.

We sipped our drinks—sparkling water with lemon for her and a draft beer for me—and made small talk. She'd hinted that there were some things she needed to talk to me about, and as insanely curious as I was, I allowed her to gather her courage without prying. When the server approached our table for a second time, I looked to McKenna. "Shall we decide on dinner?"

She nodded.

"Just a few more minutes," I told the apron-clad server. He turned on his heel and strode away.

After flipping open her menu, McKenna scanned the length of the page before her gaze jerked to mine. "This place seems kind of pricey...are you sure this is okay?"

"Of course. Order whatever you'd like." There were various cuts of steak and several types of seafood dishes.

She chewed on her lower lip. "I can pay for myself, don't feel like you have to..."

Leaning in toward her, I placed my hand on hers. "I brought you because I wanted to enjoy a nice night out with you. One without loud, nosy boys, video games, and stale pizza."

McKenna's mouth pinched closed and she gave me a tight nod.

I had no idea what she was thinking, but if she was so worried about money, I could open my wallet and show her we wouldn't be locked in the kitchen washing dishes to pay for our meal. I could afford a nice dinner, for Christ's sake.

Once we had ordered, I pushed my chair closer toward her and leaned in. "Are we going to talk about what's on your mind?"

McKenna swallowed the piece of bread she'd been absently nibbling and placed the rest on her saucer. "Okay."

Watching her chew on her lower lip again, I suddenly had a sinking feeling about whatever it was she was going to tell me. Like a schmuck, I'd planned a romantic date, and by the sour expression on her face, she was going to break up with me. Just my fucking luck.

"I had a moment of clarity in Indiana and realized you were right about some things." She took a deep, fortifying breath. "I can't keep up this pace. It's not healthy, and my parents wouldn't have wanted this for me."

"What are you saying?"

"This is too much for me, Knox. I thought I could do it, be with you and lead Sex Addicts Anonymous, but I can't. I'm emotionally exhausted and it's not something I can continue."

"You don't want to lead group anymore?"

She shook her head.

"And us…are you saying…"

"I feel like I probably rushed you. You were in treatment and I just…wedged myself into your life, your home…your bed." A playful smirk lifted her mouth.

"I had no complaints."

The truth was, the aspects to our physical relationship moved at a much slower pace than I was used to, but our emotional relationship was what had sent me spiraling out of control. That loving side of me had died a long time ago, on the day I'd watched my mother be lowered into the cold, hard earth. But if there was anything that gave me hope that maybe I could get that part of me back, it was McKenna.

"So you were worried about telling me you're leaving group?" I asked.

She nodded. "And there are a few other things, too."

"First, I'm happy that you're realizing your schedule was too full, and I think it's good you're taking a step back. Besides, my days at group are done anyway. It's no longer court appointed for me. I passed through all the sessions with flying colors."

"Why was your therapy court appointed?" A crease in her forehead lifted her brow as she apparently realized it was something we'd never discussed.

Fuck.

"We'll get to that." Later. *When hell froze over, hopefully.* I needed to man up and grow a pair, to tell her about my secret past, but knowing there was a chance she wouldn't be able to live with my actions, I wasn't willing to do that just yet. I wanted her to know how I felt about her first, and since the idea of telling her I loved her made my body break out in a cold sweat, I figured I needed a little time. She probably didn't realize it, but I'd never said that to a woman before. It was a big fucking deal to me and not something I just tossed around.

"Tell me what else is on your mind," I said, my voice low and more commanding than I'd intended.

She took a deep, shuddering breath, her nerves rising to the surface. "I finally settled all my parents' legal affairs."

"And?" What did that have to do with us?

"I inherited some money." She cleared her throat. "A lot of money, in fact." With her eyes darting up to mine, McKenna licked her lips. "Enough to take care of college for Luke."

I bit down and tasted blood. "Absolutely not."

"W-why?" she asked.

"Because the Bauers pay their own way. And your parents left that money for *you*. This is another one of your do-good charity routines and avoiding facing reality. They left that money for you and only you. They didn't set up some scholarship fund for needy kids. They wanted you to take care of yourself, have a nice, comfortable life. And I won't have you shoving this cash at Luke just to avoid that."

McKenna drew a deep breath as anger flashed in her eyes. She could argue all she wanted, but she knew I was right. This was just another of her damn avoidance techniques. She said she'd grown during this trip home, had realized a few things; well, it was time to see if she was telling the truth. Because there was no way in fuck her parents worked hard and saved their whole lives just to see their only daughter give away their life savings to pay someone else's way while she lived like a pauper in a tiny apartment and took the bus. Fuck that. The more I thought about it, the angrier I became.

"Is this money the reason you offered to pay for dinner tonight?" I asked through clenched teeth.

McKenna lowered her eyes, her chin falling to her chest.

Great. Not only was I not good enough for her, now there was some type of financial divide between us, too. A low growl emanated inside my chest. "Let's just go." Feeling defeated, I reached for my wallet and tossed more than enough money down on the table to cover our bill before I stood.

She rose to her feet and followed me to the exit, her eyes still trained on the floor.

Once inside the Jeep, I tried to shake off the sting of defeat I'd experienced back there in that restaurant. I'd tried to do something nice for her, show her that she was my girl and I could take care of her, and it had all backfired in my face. She didn't trust me to pay for a simple meal, let alone take care of my own family. *Fuck*.

Noticing the way her arms were curled around her middle, I cranked the heat to high. "Are you warm enough?"

She nodded. "I'm fine."

Damn it. I was being a prick. I took a deep breath, fighting to calm my raging emotions. "Hey…" My tone softened and I reached for her hand. "I'm sorry."

Gazing out at the headlights of the oncoming traffic and the snowflakes floating in the night sky, I knew this wasn't her fault. Her intentions were pure, as always. And she had no way of knowing that one of my hot buttons was when people assumed I couldn't take care of the boys. It had happened numerous times over the years. I caught suspicious glares or outright accusations about how I could afford to provide for them from teachers, guidance counselors, and even my own lawyer at the custody hearing. McKenna had touched on a sore spot for me, but her involvement wasn't like the others. She wanted to help, plain and simple. And I'd all but jumped down her throat. Not that it changed my stance any, but I knew I'd overreacted.

McKenna watched the traffic pass, looking deep in thought. "It's okay. It wasn't my place."

I didn't say anything further, I just laced her fingers between mine and squeezed her hand in the darkness. "You're always thinking of others. I just want to see you take care of yourself with that money."

She nodded. "I know. I will, I promise."

"And I think your first priority should be buying yourself a car. I don't like you taking the city bus."

She nodded again. "I know. I've thought about that, too."

I released a deep exhale. Good. We were getting somewhere. I knew I shouldn't have freaked out earlier and ruined the entire night. But she was still here and she was holding my hand, so maybe it wasn't completely ruined.

"I thought you'd say the first priority was me moving out of my place with Brian and getting my own apartment."

Shaking my head, I glanced over at her. "No. Contrary to what you might think, I like you living with him, with someone there to protect you in case of a break-in. I wouldn't want you moving out until you're ready to move in with me."

Glancing her way, I checked for her reaction. McKenna's mouth dropped open and she stared blankly straight ahead. I might not have said the L-word yet, but judging by her reaction, that clued her in to how I felt. She wasn't just some random hookup to me. But something told me McKenna needed to hear that in words, and not just through my actions.

I parked in front of her building and brought her hand to my lips, pressing a tender kiss there before releasing it.

Chapter Four

McKenna

"Do you want to come inside?" I asked Knox as we sat in silence outside my apartment building. I might as well take advantage of the fact that Brian was out of town and I still had the apartment to myself. Plus, before our argument over money, Knox had said that tonight's date was supposed to be just us, and I wasn't ready for it to be over.

Wordlessly, Knox turned off the ignition and his dark gaze met mine, causing a warm shiver to rake across my skin. "Brian still gone?"

I nodded. He was thinking the same thing I was—that with Brian out of town, this was one of the rare times we'd have true privacy from the boys. Delicious anticipation raced through my veins.

Knox was out of the Jeep and opening my door within seconds, causing my lips to curl up in a grin. He was every bit as eager for this reunion as I was. We still hadn't talked about the elephant in the room—our relationship—but I was trying to give him the time he needed. I'd told him I loved him, and weeks later he'd scrawled the same message to me on the frosty pane of his window. Hearing him say those words to me was what I craved, what I needed, but I was going to be patient with him. For now.

His arm curled protectively around my middle as we trekked up the two flights of stairs to my unit. Feeling his big, warm hand at my rib cage shouldn't have caused such a thrill to course through me, but it did. I was addicted to his touch more than was even remotely normal. I'd lived twenty-one years without the touch of a man, and yet right from the beginning I'd been hungry for his. My time away had only made this need inside me more acute. And Knox's thrumming pulse and barely there restraint told me he felt it, too.

My shaking hands fumbled to get the key in the lock, but once I did and the door pushed open, Knox towed me inside, slammed it closed behind us, and pressed my back against the door. The air whooshed from my lungs as my back hit the door and his solid body closed in on me. His eyes flashed on mine, dark and hungry, seconds before his eager mouth found mine.

A startled gasp escaped my throat as my body struggled to comprehend where the mild-mannered Knox of earlier had gone. He kissed me deeply, his tongue taking command of mine, his firm body pressing me harder into the door. My hips pushed back against his, seeking friction between us.

His fist twisted in my hair, angling my mouth to his as his tongue hypnotically stroked mine. Molten heat dampened my panties, my body every bit on board with where this was headed. His thigh wedged between my legs, pressing the seam of my jeans against my clit, and I let out a ragged groan, remembering our first erotic encounter began this same way. There was something naughty and taboo about being in the entryway to my apartment, as if we couldn't be bothered to take the three seconds it took to get to the bedroom.

Before I had time to process what was happening, Knox's hands were under my butt, lifting me up and spreading my thighs wide. I secured my legs around his waist so my core was positioned against his firm cock. A gush of moisture caused me to clench my legs, and I tilted my head back, exposing my throat to his exploring kisses and grazing bites.

His hot breath against my neck made me whimper and grind my hips even closer to his. Suddenly stalking away from the door, Knox carried me toward my bedroom. Gripping his shoulders as we moved down the darkened hallway, I felt my heart thrum in anticipation of what was to come next.

After tossing me none-too-gently onto the bed, Knox then dragged me by my ankles across the mattress. My heart jumped into my throat. I wanted to kiss him, to touch him, but the dark gleam in his eyes told me that he was in charge. And that thought alone caused a hot shiver to race through my veins. I liked his dominant side. Knowing I was his did insane things to me.

Unbuttoning my pants, his fingers slid into the waistband of my jeans and he tugged them down my legs, bringing my panties down with them. I squirmed on the bed, desperate to feel his rough hands against my skin, anxious for the release I knew he could give me. It had been too long; we'd both suffered too much.

"Knox…" I whimpered.

"Sit up," he ordered coolly.

I obeyed, rising to a seated position that conveniently put me eye level with his belt buckle. Temptation spiked within me.

"Unbutton your top."

He wanted to watch me undress myself. My fingers fumbled with the buttons on my cardigan, finally freeing the last one, and let the top fall off my shoulders. Knox found the hem of my camisole and tugged it up over my head, his fingers expertly unclasping my bra so I was left completely bare and exposed in front of him.

He leaned over me, brushing his cheek along mine. "Beautiful," he murmured.

With him this close I could smell the warm, musky scent of his skin. That familiar smell of warm leather and Knox sent a rush of endorphins skittering through my bloodstream. The brush of his rough cheek against my collarbone as he lowered his head hardened my nipples into points. The promise of what he could do with his mouth taunted me and I whimpered helplessly.

"Patience, sweet girl. Are you going to let me taste you this time?"

I nodded eagerly. It turned out I had no reason to be self-conscious with Knox. I had to remind myself he'd done everything and then some; nothing shocked him. I might as well go with it and enjoy the pleasure he could so expertly deliver.

Blinking up at my dark angel, I frowned. He was still fully dressed and watching me with an amused expression. Gazing down at his erection, I chewed on my lower lip. I wanted to touch him. I'd missed the solid feel of him in my hands.

"You want this?" He adjusted the rather large bulge protruding from the front of his pants.

I reached for him and unbuckled his belt, determined to push him to the same frenzied state he'd driven me to. His hands found mine and he made quick work of stripping, shoving his jeans and boxers down his hips and stepping out of them before pulling his shirt off over his head. A chiseled six-pack of rock-hard abs wasn't something I was strong enough to resist.

Need coursed through me. I wanted to touch him. Reaching one hand tentatively toward him, I paused, hesitating, before dropping my hands to my lap and looking down at the floor.

Using two fingers, Knox tipped my chin up so I'd meet his eyes. "Let go of your shyness and insecurity. This is just me and you. And trust me, you can't possibly do anything wrong."

I swallowed down the sudden wave of nerves and nodded. Leaning forward, I pressed my lips to the warm skin over his solid abdominal muscles, inhaling the scent of him. His muscles tightened gloriously as I trailed kisses from his navel downward. He released a helpless groan as my lips hovered just above his eager cock. Pride and happiness surged through me.

I gripped him in my right hand and stroked the smooth, velvety skin, enjoying the feel of his engorged length in my hand. Knox's head fell back as he turned his body over to the sensations. I trailed my free hand up his thigh, my fingernails grazing the fine hairs. I wished I had the skills to make him feel as out of control with desire as he made me.

Leaning forward, I opened my mouth wide, taking him in and delivering a slow, wet kiss to the head of his cock. A breath of air hissed through his teeth and I repeated the move, this time lightly cupping and squeezing his balls, the weight of them in my palm both foreign and enticing. While continuing to rub him with my hands, I moved my mouth up and down, taking him farther down my throat with each thrust.

Soon his hips were rocking forward to meet my mouth and his hands were fisting in my hair. "Shit, angel," he choked out, stepping back from me with a twisted expression.

I blinked up at him, trying to understand why he was stopping me. I'd just found my rhythm.

His elongated cock glistened enticingly and his chest rose and fell with each ragged breath as he fought for control. "No more being insecure. You're fucking good at that."

I fought off a smile, feeling oddly proud.

"Lay back," he ordered.

I scooted up the bed and laid back, my head on the pillow, but my gaze still on him. I decided that I liked having him in my bedroom. His presence was so large and overwhelming that the soft comfort of my own space eased the experience.

He reached for his discarded pants and found his wallet, withdrew a foil packet, and tore it open. I wondered if he'd planned on us reuniting physically tonight, or if the condom was simply a remnant of his old life. Pushing the thought away, I watched him roll the condom down his length and my breathing hitched in my chest. He was big, even bigger than I remembered, yet I craved the feeling of every hard inch invading my body.

He joined me on the bed, then dragged me by my waist until I was on top of him, positioning me so I was straddling his hips, my knees on either side of his thighs. Knox's amused expression caused a smile to tug against his mouth and he rested his head against the pillows, crossing his arms behind his head.

"W-what are you doing?" I stammered.

"Giving you control. Showing you I'm yours. Do what you want, angel."

He was giving me control? Now? Summoning my courage, I raised my hips and lifted his cock from his body, positioning the tip at my entrance. Lowering myself slowly, I felt him begin to impale me and I stiffened above him. What if I wasn't good at this?

"Take a deep breath, relax your muscles."

I released an exhale and let myself sink down farther, savoring the feel of him stretching me, entering me so deeply.

"That's it."

Knox might have said this time was for me, but it seemed he couldn't resist bringing his hands to my hips, his fingers gripping me tightly, biting into the skin. His face was a mask of concentration, his eyes locked on mine and his jaw tense.

"Like this?" I asked, pressing my knees into the bed so I could lift up and down on him slowly.

"Fuck, yeah, baby. Ride me. Just like that." His voice was a rough, gravelly plea and I couldn't help but obey, rocking my hips against him over and over.

As I grew accustomed to his size, the pace built faster. I sensed a shift in Knox and soon he was no longer okay with lying back and letting me take control, he was clutching my butt and raising his hips with thrusts of his own that pushed into the very core of me.

Guiding my mouth to his with one firm hand on the back of my neck, Knox kissed me. Desperate to feel his warm lips on mine and the heat of his breath wash over me, I returned his kiss greedily. He groaned helplessly underneath me, pushing his thick cock deeper and deeper inside me with each thrust.

Without breaking our connection, his pace increased, slamming my hips down onto his lap and claiming my mouth with deep, hungry kisses. I might have been the one on top, but I was no longer in control. My body was like a rag doll being used for his pleasure, and subsequently my own. The pulsing sensation of an unexpected orgasm crashed through me, my head dropping back and a low desperate murmur clawing up my throat.

Knox growled something in response to my body's tightening and slowed his pace, his expression twisted in pleasure or agony, I couldn't be sure. "Fuck, angel. You're so perfect." His tight grasp on my hips loosened, as though he realized he was probably bruising my skin. I didn't care. A deep, all-consuming orgasm like that would be worth whatever bruises and soreness I had tomorrow.

Once my inner walls had finished trembling, Knox withdrew amid my protests and lifted me off of him, laying me on the bed next to him while he positioned himself above me. Keeping my legs together and my knees bent and pushed up to my chest, he held my calves in one of his hands and used his other to guide himself back inside me.

My back arched involuntarily off the bed and my hands scrambled for him, gripping his thighs as he rocked forward again and again, pummeling me with long, purposeful strokes. I clung to him desperately while he worked himself inside me, pumping his hips and keeping my legs in place.

He bit out a string of curse words and I felt the moment he gave in, his body jerking and his cock swelling inside me, filling the condom he wore.

Knox released his hold on my legs and pressed a soft kiss to my mouth. He got up just long enough to remove the condom and grab me a handful of tissues, wiping between my legs carefully before returning to the bathroom to dispose of it all. I made a mental note to take the trash out before Brian got back. I didn't need him seeing the evidence that my virginity was indeed gone and make some comment about it.

Knox crawled into bed beside me, pulling the quilt that was folded at the foot of my bed up and over us.

"You're trembling," he whispered, brushing the hair back from my face.

I nodded. "That was intense."

He smiled and pulled me closer, tucking me against his side and draping a heavy arm over me. "This feels so good, holding you like this."

Panting to catch my breath, I curled onto my side and let him hold me. His big, warm palms smoothed up and down my body, lightly stroking me and soothing me until all my muscles were relaxed and I felt sleepy.

As I dozed off into a light sleep, feeling complete and happy, I made mental notes of all the things I needed to do. Check on Brian. Check on Amanda and her baby. And find a way to become an anonymous donor for a college scholarship and be sure that Luke was the recipient. But for now, I just relaxed and let Knox hold me snugly in his arms.

The way he'd been himself—so uninhibited and fierce, taking me over the edge with each punishing stroke—was the sexiest thing I'd ever seen. He'd claimed my mouth with deep, hungry kisses, seeking love, acceptance, and belonging. He might not have said the actual words yet, but it was only a matter of time. I felt his love in each kiss and whispered compliment.

He kissed me once more on the forehead and then rose from the bed. "I need to get home to check on the guys."

I nodded and got up, pulling on the pink bathrobe hanging on the back of my door.

Knox stepped into his jeans and tugged his shirt on over his head. Once he was dressed, he pulled me into his arms, lifting my mouth to his and looking deep into my eyes. I didn't know what he was trying to tell me, but I felt his love and concern all the same.

But he had told me he'd loved me, hadn't he? Not in words, but with his body. The tender way he'd made love to me for my first time, his protectiveness over me, the way he read my body and gave me exactly what it needed. It was closer to love than anything I'd had before.

"Thank you for the date tonight," I whispered against his lips. I'd felt so cherished and thoroughly cared for that I wanted to tell him I loved him, too, but I didn't. I just pressed my mouth to his and felt his lips curl in a smile.

"Thank you for everything. For staying with the boys last night. For giving me time. For being you. I don't even want to think what my life would be like without you."

I knew just what he meant. We were good for each other, plain and simple. Knox pushed me out of my comfort zone and made me believe I was worth something. And I forced him to deal with the pain in his past and examine the damaging coping mechanisms he employed. My life felt fuller and more meaningful than it had in years.

"I'll come by tomorrow night after work," I murmured.

He nodded. "See you then."

After walking him out and locking up, I fell into bed, my body heavy and relaxed, and let sleep pull me under.

Chapter Five

MCKENNA

The following morning I was up early, feeling eager to jump into my new life. Of course I had my job at the counseling center and my obligations volunteering, but I was also firm on keeping some of the resolutions I'd made myself and Knox. Beginning with putting myself first. I made an appointment at my gynecologist's office for later that morning and then drove to a local salon, one of the benefits of still having the rental car. I knew I needed to return it and think about my long-term plans for transportation, but something about having a car in the city felt so decadent after surviving for so long without one.

After getting my hair cut, colored with caramel highlights, and styled into flowing waves, I couldn't stop touching it and stealing glances at myself in the rearview mirror as I drove. My hair felt so much softer with all the spilt ends cut off. It had taken nearly three hours at the salon, and while that normally would have made me feel guilty and like it was a waste of time and money, today it felt like therapy—something I was supposed to do to take care of myself. I decided my mom would be thrilled seeing me happy like this. All these years I'd told myself I should keep up my punishing schedule for them, to make sure their deaths were not for nothing. But today, for the first time, I realized both of my parents would have hated the girl I'd become. They would have hated seeing me spent and exhausted, the dark circles under my eyes. I never knew indulging myself could feel so good.

When I arrived at the doctor's office, I fought off the wave of nerves I experienced walking into the waiting room. I was a twenty-one-year-old woman who needed birth control. This might have been new and scary for me, but I reminded myself that the doctor had probably seen and heard it all before.

After filling out a stack of forms, a nurse called my name and brought me back to an exam room, where she took my weight and blood pressure, and then asked me to strip completely and dress in a paper robe and wait for the doctor.

I did as instructed, folding my bra and panties and hiding them under my folded jeans, then climbed up onto the exam table, arranging the stiff robe around me.

The doctor knocked once and entered. She was tall and gorgeous with honey-colored skin and long, dark hair. She could have been Beyoncé's sister, and I felt self-conscious sitting there in my paper outfit. But she immediately put me at ease, explaining that she'd conduct a vaginal exam and Pap smear, and then we'd talk about birth control options.

I leaned back on the table and placed my feet in the stirrups where she directed.

After several seconds and a little pinch, she stood up and removed

416

her gloves. "You look very healthy."

I didn't know what a doctor might say while looking at my lady parts, but I supposed healthy was the best thing.

"What kind of protection are you using today?" she asked.

"Condoms."

"Are you in a monogamous relationship?"

"Yes." I nodded. I felt confident for the first time since Knox and I had begun seeing each other that this statement was true. I didn't know if it was possible to be completely cured from sex addiction, or if he still had occasional dark thoughts or struggles, but I felt certain I was the only woman in his bed and in his arms these days.

We discussed the birth control patch, pills, and the shot. I decided to go with the shot, knowing it lasted for three months and wouldn't be something I had to think about every day. The nurse came in and administered the shot, then I redressed and left, feeling confident and in control of my life for the first time in a long time.

After working my shift at the teen center, I drove to Knox's place around dinnertime. The boys were gathered around the table, eating when I arrived, and Knox set out an extra plate for me, loading it up with a piece of chicken and potatoes. I loved being here with them and as I ate, I enjoyed their banter. The noise volume was a sharp contrast to my own quiet apartment.

KNOX

While we ate, my gaze kept wandering over to McKenna. Last night had been incredible. It had started a little rocky when she'd brought up wanting to give away her inheritance to fund Luke's education, but it had ended perfectly. Watching McKenna's confidence grow as she moved above me in bed had been life changing. It had broken something inside me and as worried as I was about admitting my drunk-driving arrest to her, I had to believe that all this would work out.

"Stop playing with your chicken and eat, Tuck." I shot my youngest brother a warning glare. The chicken leg I'd put on his plate was currently performing a can-can dance.

Tucker giggled, glancing up at McKenna, and took a big bite. The little shit. He was flirting with her. She choked on a laugh of her own, covering her mouth with the napkin.

"Have you filled out your applications yet?" I asked Luke.

He set down his fork, a serious crease between his brows. "What's the point, Knox? We can't afford it."

I squeezed my fists at my sides. "Get your damn applications filled out and turned in. I told you I'd worry about the expenses." Luke needed to do his part and I would figure out a way to do mine, damn it. I was tired of them all doubting me.

McKenna stared down at her plate, looking deep in thought.

Shit. I was being selfish. McKenna had the money—she wanted to help—and my own insecurities were holding Luke back. This wasn't about me and my damn ego. Besides, I knew I had bigger things to worry about. My future with McKenna still hung in the balance, if I was being honest with myself. Pushing my plate away, I realized it was time to open up.

After we'd finished dinner and cleaned up, McKenna followed Tucker upstairs, promising to play superheroes with him before it was time for lights out. It gave me a chance to think about how to put into words what I needed to tell her.

Luke sat at the table with Jaxon's new laptop, unhappy but filling out his college applications. Jaxon had left, saying he was going out for a couple of hours. It was a school night but he was eighteen now; it wasn't like there was a lot I could do. As long as he was going to school and getting good grades, I didn't really care.

I found McKenna perched beside Tucker's bed. The bedside lamp glowed softly, illuminating a beautiful sight—a peacefully sleeping little boy, and a woman I adored tucking the blankets securely around him. My heart swelled watching her. Tucker might not know a mother's love, but I was thankful he had McKenna.

Sensing my presence, she glanced back at the doorway and spotted me. I crossed the room toward them and kissed Tucker's forehead. "'Night, buddy," I whispered. I reached for McKenna's hand and pressed a kiss to the back of it before pulling her up to stand.

Without releasing my hold on her hand, I led her up the stairs to my bedroom. "How many books did he make you read him this time?" I asked.

"None, actually. He just wanted to talk."

That was interesting. What could my eight-year-old brother want to talk to her about? I followed her to the edge of the bed and sat down beside her. "What about?"

"He asked if you and I were going to get married and if I'd be his mommy."

Holy shit. "What did you say?"

Her gaze met mine. "I told him the truth. That I didn't know, but I would always be there if he needed me."

I nodded thoughtfully and released a sigh.

"What else could I have said? We haven't talked about us since I've been back."

It had only been a few days, but she was right. It was an overdue conversation. Still, she was putting me on the spot and she knew it.

420

Her hands were clasped together and her knee was bouncing up and down with nerves. McKenna putting me on the spot took guts; I'd give her that. And I wanted to talk about all this, I really did, I just thought I'd have more time to plan out what I wanted to say. I still had no fucking clue how she'd react to my drunk-driving conviction.

"I've told you how I felt," she continued. "I've been very open with you."

Taking a deep breath, I settled my nerves. I laced her fingers between mine and kissed her temple. "I know. And I shouldn't have let you leave last time without telling you how I felt. There are things I want to tell you, things I need to say... Fuck." I tore my hands through my hair, fighting for the right words. Why was this so damn hard for me? It was just as hard telling her about my arrest as it had been telling her about my past with sex. I didn't want to lose her. Couldn't.

McKenna rose from the bed and paced the room, seeming to draw strength and determination with each step she took. "When I met you, I figured you were some sex-loving player, a guy always on the prowl, just looking to hook up with whatever willing girl crossed your path."

I winced; she wasn't far off the mark.

Stopping at the end of the room to turn around, she continued marching past me. "But then I got to know you—and the boys—and I realized that you weren't that guy. I discovered you were this broken man looking for love and affection, but going about it entirely the wrong way."

She turned again on her heel, looking deep in thought.

Where was she going with all this? I wanted to tell her that loving part of me died. I wouldn't even know how to get him back, but I knew she was right.

"McKenna, let me say a few things." I rose to my feet, facing her.

"No. You can't control everything all the time, Knox. Love is fucking scary. It's an unstoppable wave that has the power to pull you under and drown you completely. You don't always choose it, it develops, slowly at first or sometimes all at once. And other times it's ripped from your life way too soon. Like with your mom. My parents. But that doesn't mean we can give up. Love is the most beautiful thing in the world. We all deserve it. And when we lose it, we deserve a second chance. And a third. Give it a chance."

A slow smile uncurled on my lips. "You just swore. That was your first curse word. We need to celebrate." I grinned at her and she swatted my chest, giving it a playful smack. "I love you, McKenna. With every part of my heart. And you're wrong, it doesn't just scare me, it fucking terrifies me. The thought of losing you…" I shuddered involuntarily, knowing that was a very real possibility once I told her the truth. "I love everything about you—your giving nature, your outlook on life, the way you are with my brothers. Your heart's too damn big and you're way too good for someone like me, but as long as you want me, I'm never letting you go."

Unshed tears shimmered in her eyes as she looked up at me.

My thumb swiped against her bottom lip as I cupped her face in my hands. "I love you, angel," I repeated.

Blinking back tears, she drew a shuddering breath. "I love you, too."

"I should have told you sooner. Did you see my note on the window that morning before you left?"

She nodded, confirming she had.

"Why didn't you say anything?"

Her shoulder lifted in a shrug. "I don't know. For being a man with dominant tendencies, you sure know how to keep a girl in suspense. I guess I didn't want to take the lead in that aspect of our relationship. It was important to me to hear you say it."

I nodded. She was right. Again. Christ, when was I going to learn? "So you like it when I take control?"

She licked her lips and nodded.

I chuckled low under my breath, unable to hold it in. This girl was perfect for me. "C'mere, angel." I lifted her face to mine and kissed her deeply.

McKenna responded immediately, her arms winding around my back and her hands wandering under my shirt.

"Slow down," I whispered against her ear. "There's still more we should talk about."

"There is?" she asked, gazing up at me with a crease lining her forehead.

Shit. I might have been tough in other aspects of my life, but I wasn't brave enough for this shit. I couldn't rip apart a relationship I was just building with her. "I like your hair. Is it different?" I said finally, running my fingers through the long, silky locks.

She laughed out loud, tipping her head back. "I was waiting for you to notice."

"You're always beautiful."

She beamed up at me, her smile white and innocent. "Remember how we talked about me taking better care of myself?"

I nodded.

"Well, today I went to the doctor and then went to the salon and splurged on getting my hair done."

"Good girl." I pressed a kiss to her mouth. "Everything okay…with the doctor?"

"Yeah. I, um, got put on birth control."

This time I couldn't help the smile tugging on my mouth. My wide grin told her this knowledge made me very happy. Knowing I could be inside her without any barrier produced a caveman-like response in me. I'd always used condoms. Always. But McKenna was trusting me, giving herself to me fully. The thought was intoxicating.

"That's…" I choked on the words and this time McKenna was the one laughing at me.

"You like that, don't you?" she teased. "Good, because I got a shot in my butt today for you."

Bringing both hands down to her backside, I rubbed her ass cheeks gently. "My poor girl." Nuzzling into her neck, I gave her a few slow, damp kisses as I moved closer to her mouth. "I'll take good care of you tonight," I murmured against her skin. It occurred to me she didn't have any of her stuff here—nothing to sleep in, no toothbrush. It made me realize I needed to take better care of my girl, make sure she felt comfortable here.

She dropped her head to the side, giving me better access to her neck, her fingers still tracing little circles on my back, underneath my shirt. "You said we needed to celebrate. What did you have in mind?"

My lips curled in a smile as I planted a kiss on the spot just beneath her ear. "You sure you can handle it?"

She nodded eagerly.

My fingers found the hem of her shirt and I began to lift it over her head, my body all too ready to show her all the ways she was mine.

"Wait." Her hands stopped me. "You said there was more we needed to discuss."

I faltered, swallowing a lump in my throat. "Yeah. Ah, I wanted to tell you, you wanting to help Luke…if it's what you want, that's cool with me."

"Yeah?" she asked.

"Yeah," I confirmed. "You and him work out the details. I trust you."

"You're being so good tonight." She patted my chest. "Very cooperative."

God, it had been too long since we'd had a night like this, one where we could be playful and just enjoy each other. There had been too much shit swirling over both of us lately, and though I knew I should say more, something in me couldn't. We deserved tonight. We deserved to just enjoy each other.

"Now, where were we?" I pulled her close so our bodies were pressed tightly together and took her mouth in a hungry kiss, gripping the back of her neck to hold her close to me. McKenna moaned into my kiss, angling her mouth to mine. She was so responsive, so needy, and the dominant lurking inside me fucking loved it.

My cell phone vibrated in my pocket and McKenna let out a soft whimper as the buzzing device pressed against the front of her jeans.

I chuckled at her response. She liked that. Good to know. "One second, baby." I released her and tugged the phone from my pocket. I was going to toss it on my dresser, get rid of the interruption, but Jaxon's name flashed on the screen.

Shit. Nice timing, asshole. "You better be dead or dying," I bit out as I answered the call.

McKenna swatted at me again. "Be nice," she mouthed.

"Close," Jaxon croaked. "I'm at Regency Hospital. In the ER. Can you come get me?"

"What the fuck? What happened?"

"I got jumped. I'll explain when you get here."

Motherfucker. "On my way."

427

"What's wrong? What happened?" McKenna's worried gaze met mine.

"Jaxon's in trouble again. Can you stay here with the boys?"

Her hand flew to her mouth and she nodded.

Adjusting my raging boner, I fled down the stairs.

When Jaxon and I arrived home, I didn't care that he could hardly walk or see out of eyes nearly swollen shut—I made him march up the stairs to his room. I didn't want him sleeping on the couch and the sorry sight of him to be the first thing Tucker saw when he woke up in the morning.
"Get to bed. We'll talk about this in the morning."

Jaxon huffed. "If I don't get them their money, there will be nothing to talk about. I'm telling you, man, this crew is ruthless."

I fisted my hands at my sides, fighting the urge to punch the wall. "We'll figure it out." I had no idea how, but of course the responsibility would fall on me.

Apparently we'd made enough of a racket that we'd woken McKenna. She peeked inside the room, gazing in with wide eyes. "Oh God." Her hand flew to her mouth. "Jax..." She crossed the room and pressed one hand to his cheek. He winced at the contact and she withdrew. "What happened?" A lone tear rolled down her face and I took a deep breath, fighting to calm myself down.

"He was beaten within an inch of his life over a gambling debt. They dropped him off at the emergency room and promised this time was just a warning if he doesn't pay back what he owes," I answered for him.

McKenna's gaze left mine and searched Jaxon's. He looked guilty. I knew he felt as terrible as he looked, which was the only thing helping me contain my rage.

"Jax…why?" she asked.

"I was trying to help."

I cursed under my breath and pressed my fingers against my temples.

Jaxon hobbled closer, scowling as he met my gaze. He looked every bit as pissed off as I felt. "I'm not a kid, Knox. I know you're struggling with the money for Luke's college, and that shouldn't be what ruins this for him. Or for you and McKenna. You're a dick when you get stressed out and you make stupid fucking decisions. You're happy, like actually happy for the first time in a long time, and Luke…Luke deserves to go to college. I was doing my part. You're not the only one who can take care of this family."

"This was your way of taking care of things? Fuck. Next time, get a job. You know, something actually legal that's not going to end up costing me money to bail your ass out."

"Don't be mad at Jax," McKenna chimed in. "He was trying to help. Even if it wasn't in the right way, his intentions were in the right place."

"He's fucking eighteen years old, McKenna. He's an adult. He knows better."

Jaxon collapsed onto his unmade bed, lying back and releasing a heavy sigh. "If I don't pay them back…"

"I know." I clenched my jaw. I knew the group of guys he'd bet and lost against. A local street gang of thugs. Even if I didn't like the idea of caving to their demands, I knew he was right. They wouldn't stop until they had fucked us over, and this beating was the tip of the iceberg in terms of what they were capable of. I couldn't have them going after Luke or Tuck. We needed to take care of this.

"How much do you owe?" McKenna asked, her voice whisper soft.

"Twenty-five thousand," Jaxon said, not meeting my eyes.

"Fuck, no, McKenna. This isn't on you to fix." This was not what I envisioned when I told her she could help Luke.

Luke entered the room and closed the door behind him. "You guys need to lower your voices unless we want to turn this into a family meeting." He grimaced when he saw Jaxon. "Shit, bro."

Christ, the last thing we needed was Tucker getting up. Although if I was being honest, I knew Jaxon's injuries would look worse tomorrow. His eyes were already nearly swollen shut and his lip was busted apart and huge. By morning the bruises would begin to turn purple. He clutched his ribs and toed off his shoes. McKenna knelt beside his bed to help him.

"Everyone out. Jaxon needs his sleep." Luke and I started for the door when McKenna's hand flew up, stopping us.

"Wait." She swallowed and straightened her shoulders. "I have the money. I was going to give it to Luke for college…"

Luke's gaze flew to hers and a smile blossomed on his mouth.

"But…" she continued. "It sounds like at the moment, making sure Jax doesn't end up dead is more important."

Luke's smile fell and he shot a murderous look at Jaxon. Jax closed his eyes, obviously unable to watch the disappointment looming in Luke's expression.

"We don't have health insurance, so this little adventure at the hospital tonight is going to cost us, too," Luke added.

Shit, he was right. As much as I hated the idea of McKenna bailing us out, I realized we had little choice. I might have been okay with her helping Luke out, giving him money toward his education, but I hated the idea of her throwing away her money toward Jaxon's criminal enterprises. I would pay her back every penny. And I would make sure Luke still got to go to college too. Somehow.

"We'll figure this out tomorrow."

My tone was final and McKenna nodded. I doubted sleep would come tonight, as wound up as I was, but we headed up the stairs and climbed into bed, deafening silence hanging all around us.

Chapter Six

McKenna

In the morning, the harsh reality of the situation with Jaxon pushed itself into the forefront of my brain. I rolled over and tugged the blankets up higher, snuggling into Knox's side, trying to pretend for a few minutes more that all this wasn't happening. A quick peek at Knox told me he'd been awake for hours. He was lying still but staring straight up at the ceiling, looking lost in thought.

I sat up in bed, looking down at his dark, troubled expression. We needed to do something, not just cave to this gang's demands. "Knox?"

He glanced over at me, the crease between his brows softening just slightly when he met my eyes.

I took his hand, giving it a squeeze and letting him know we were in this together. I was here and I would help in any way I could. "We should call the police. They jumped Jaxon. And we can't just turn over this much money." Now that it was morning, I was thinking more rationally about the situation.

Silence hung heavily in the room around us. "No police, angel," he said. "These guys will just retaliate if we get the police involved. Last year something similar happened—a guy who owed them payment for gambling debts talked to the police when they got too

rough with him, and the next day they put a bullet in his head."
Knox looked back up at the ceiling, his mouth pulling into a tight
line. "I won't put any of us at risk. Money isn't worth any of our
lives. And I'll pay you back every cent, I promise."

I started to wave him off; this wasn't about money. I didn't care
about Knox paying me back, but the grim expression etched across
his face told me now was not the time to argue. I gave an
imperceptible nod. "Okay," I whispered. We'd do things his way.
This was his family, and I knew he'd protect them the best way he
knew how. All I could do was be there for them.

I dressed in yesterday's clothes and kissed Knox good-bye, and
after heading home to shower and change, I went to the bank. It
turned out getting twenty-five thousand dollars in cash was a lot
more difficult than I expected. After meeting with a teller, an
assistant manager, and then the bank branch manager, I headed off
to work. They would have my money by the end of the day. It
would take them several hours to get it all together.

I sent Knox a text. I didn't know if something would happen to
Jaxon in the meantime, but I figured the men who had threatened
him would give him some time to get the cash together.

> Me: *I'm coming over tonight with the money.*
> Knox: *I don't like this.*
> Me: *Me neither. But we have to do it.*

He didn't respond and unease churned inside me all day long. I hated thinking that he'd try to take matters into his own hands today, try to persuade the guys who'd done this to Jaxon. I couldn't have something happening to Knox, too. Brian was barely healed and now Jaxon was lying in bed, broken and beaten up. We just had to bite the bullet and pay the gang off. This had to work.

Thankful I still had my rental car, when I left work I drove straight to the bank again. The bank manager looked at me as if I were crazy when he handed me the backpack full of stacked bills. He asked again and again if I was okay. I think he thought I was being bribed or threatened into withdrawing this money. Well, I was, sort of. Someone I cared about would be badly hurt if I didn't fix this.

As I headed back to Knox's, Brian called to let me know he would be back in the morning, but I could barely concentrate on what he was saying.

When I arrived at Knox's place, he looked ready to murder someone. He was pacing the floor in the living room and his brows were drawn together, his eyes hard and fierce. I'd never seen him so worked up.

I held up the backpack. "I brought it."

He nodded and crossed the room toward me, then immediately gathered me up in his arms and pressed a firm kiss to my forehead.

I hated to admit it, but he was scaring me. My knees trembled and my stomach felt queasy. I had no way of knowing if this was all going to turn out okay and I couldn't lose another person I loved. I couldn't. The desperate need to never let him go, to stay by his side tonight, clawed at me. "I'm coming with you."

He shook his head. "Not happening."

"Knox—"

His mouth closed over mine and the rough edge to his kiss killed my protest. He was a desperate man, doing what needed to be done to protect his family. But it was obvious there'd be no negotiating this. I realized he had no choice taking my help with the money, but it was obvious that was where my involvement ended. I didn't want to argue and push him when it seemed like he was already at the edge of his control. I knew what happened when he lost control; I wouldn't push him there willingly. If staying behind at the house was the way I could protect him and preserve his sense of calm, I would do it.

"I want to keep you safe. Stay here with Luke and Tucker."

I released a heavy exhale and nodded. "Okay."

"Lock the doors and don't answer if someone comes knocking."

I nodded again, my stomach cramping with nerves. *Jeez.*

"If anything happens to us, call the police."

Oh God. I couldn't handle something happening to Knox. Tears filled my eyes.

"Hey, shhh, it's okay," he whispered, brushing his knuckles along my cheek. "We'll be all right. Stay strong."

He was right; I needed to pull myself together. I didn't want to alert Tucker that anything was wrong. I blinked the tears away and fixed a neutral expression on my face. I just had to have faith.

Jaxon looked even worse today. I had no idea what story they gave Tucker, but Jaxon looked every bit like he'd been jumped and brutally beaten. His eyes were swollen and puffy, heavy blackish-purple circles lining each one, and he was limping slightly, holding a hand to his side. His ribs were either bruised or broken, and part of me didn't even want to ask.

I wanted to rush to him and take him in my arms, but I merely met his eyes with a sympathetic stare and he gave me a tight nod. Even though this was pretty much the world's crappiest situation, it brought me closer into this family, and I had to say I loved that.

Watching Knox converse in hushed tones with Jaxon and Luke, I was struck with a pang of shock. Before I met Knox, I was so naive. I never knew even half of the things that went on in this world. I had been living in my own bubble of misery, volunteering and just existing. Still, I wouldn't trade this for anything. Even though times were tough, I had a family again. A big, messy family, complete with love, heartache, and worry. My emotions were right at the surface today and everything felt so raw and new. I was out of practice with this whole family thing, and felt vulnerable and exposed.

Luke and I watched them prepare to leave, exchanging equally worried expressions between us. Luke, seeming to realize he was now the oldest brother in charge, came to stand beside me and placed a comforting arm around my shoulders, giving me a squeeze. "It'll be okay, McKenna. Knox will handle this." His voice sounded calm and certain, but he had no way of knowing the outcome, any more than I did.

I just nodded. I trusted Knox; I just didn't trust this shady neighborhood street gang. Once they'd gotten this money from us, would they really leave us alone?

Shrugging on the backpack, Knox crossed the room and kissed me full on the mouth. He rarely did that in front of his brothers, but I met his kiss with my own fierce edge, letting my tongue briefly rub against his. His hands cupping my face trembled ever so slightly. "I love you," he whispered.

I nodded. "Love you, too." My eyes screamed at him to stay safe and come home to me in one piece.

He nodded in silent acknowledgement of my request. "We'll be fine."

My stomach dropped to my toes and for the first time, I could relate to Knox's fears and hesitations when it came to love. If I didn't love them all so much, this process wouldn't be nearly as scary. I gripped Luke tighter and said a silent prayer that Knox knew what he was doing.

Several hours later and everyone was in bed, but I was way too amped up to sleep. I paced Knox's bedroom, my heart heavy with worry. *Where were they? What was taking so long?* I checked my phone for the hundredth time and fell back onto his bed. I curled into the pillow that held Knox's unique scent, inhaling deeply. Warm leather and male musk, a delicious combination.

A short time later, I awoke to the sound of someone climbing the stairs.

Knox was back.

I sat up in bed, rubbing the sleep from my tired eyes. *Oh, thank God. He was okay.*

Knox stood in the doorway, smiling at me like everything was right with the world, and the tense knot that had taken up residence in my stomach uncurled in an instant. His brilliant smile melted my heart and the hardened shield I'd erected in his absence.

He tossed the backpack onto the bed and it landed with a dull thud. It was still full. I lifted it to my lap and unzipped it. The cash was still stacked inside.

"What happened…how did you?"

Dread sank low in the pit of my stomach. They hadn't succeeded tonight. Which meant the gang was probably coming for us. My mind was already running through scenarios of us five holed up in my apartment. I needed to buy groceries, milk, get more towels…

"McKenna." Knox's warm hands cupped my cheeks. "Look at me."

My gaze drifted back to him and I took a deep breath. *Just breathe.*

"You didn't think I was just going to watch them walk away with Luke's college fund, did you?"

That was exactly what I'd assumed. That was the plan, wasn't it? I wouldn't have offered the money if I hadn't thought it was the only way. "I don't understand."

I listened with bated breath while Knox filled me in on how he'd contacted his lawyer and provided the tip that this exchange was going down tonight. His lawyer agreed to inform the police; that way the call could never be traced back to Knox. Several members of the gang were wanted on various charges, and once the cops had the time and meeting place of tonight's exchange, they showed up and apprehended the bad guys. Knox and Jaxon took off running—well, hobbling in Jaxon's case—and hid out until the police had made their arrests and taken the gang members away to keep up the ruse Jaxon and Knox weren't responsible for involving

440

the police. Once the scene was clear, the money was returned to Knox.

I shook my head in disbelief. I couldn't believe he'd put himself in danger, orchestrating that entire thing without me knowing. I felt sick thinking about what could have gone wrong. It was probably better that he hadn't told me about his alternative plan; my head would have been spinning with *what ifs*. Saving this money was not worth the risk.

"Knox, you guys could have…" *Been killed*. I couldn't even bring myself to speak the words. Hot tears leaked from the corners of my eyes. Why would he take such a risk? I couldn't lose him.

He took my hands and held them. "That is your money to do what you want with. Your parents worked hard to earn that, saved for years to make sure you would be okay. Even if I don't love the idea of you giving it to Luke, I get it. It's who you are. It's one of the reasons I love you. That money is yours to do what you want with. There was no way I was just handing it over."

"But how did you know this would all work out? That you could trust this lawyer and the police to—"

"Shhh. It's over now." He kissed me softly on the mouth.

My whirling thoughts and racing heart felt anything but comforted. "Are you sure it's not going to come back to you? They could find out you set this up. How do you know this lawyer, anyway?"

Questions tumbled from my lips as my brain fought to catch up.

His gaze slid away from mine. "It's been a long night. We'll talk about that later." Opening his arms, he urged me closer. "Come here."

I sensed there was something he wasn't telling me, and a flicker of curiosity bloomed inside me, but I let it go and curled against his side, savoring the feel of his firm body against mine. Knowing how close I could have come to losing him tonight quieted me and I clung to him, desperate for skin-to-skin contact.

Chapter Seven

KNOX

I tugged McKenna closer, pushing my hand under the T-shirt she wore to bed, unable to resist running my hand along the soft curve of her ass. Tonight had been stressful—leading Jaxon into a situation like that and involving the police, which totally went against my gut and had put me on edge. But there was no way I was letting McKenna take the hit for Jaxon's mistake. That money belonged to her. I wasn't about to let it fall into the hands of a street gang. She deserved to be in control of her parent's inheritance, and even if she wanted to use it to fund Luke's education, it was hers to do with what she wanted.

"What are you doing?" She giggled as my hand squeezed her ass cheek.

"Just exploring," I growled near her ear. I hoped she wasn't too tired, because I needed to feel her around me. Tonight more than ever.

"How can you be thinking about sex right now?" she teased, wiggling her ass farther away from me. "You could have been killed tonight."

"But I wasn't." I tugged her close again. No way was I letting her escape that easy. "And now I want to celebrate by getting my cock wet in your sweet honey." It was crude, but I wasn't in the mood to sugarcoat my mood with pretty words. I hitched her bare leg up over my hip so she could feel that I was already semi-hard for her.

"You and your insatiable boners." She rolled her eyes for dramatic effect. Her playful mood was exactly what I needed to relax. And studying me in the dim light, McKenna seemed to understand that. "The things I do for my sex-addicted boyfriend." She sighed.

Boyfriend. I liked that word coming from her lips. "I'm addicted to your tight, hot pussy. And I'm not going to apologize for that."

"So, what are you going to do about it?" she challenged, a lively spark in her eyes.

I pulled her over the top of me so she was straddling my lap. I loved the weight of her against me, the sight of her sitting on top of me. Tugging her panties to the side, I touched my fingertips to her pussy lips, finding them glistening with her moisture, and my cock swelled even more. "I want to feel your heat squeezing my cock."

McKenna let out a helpless whimper.

I continued rubbing her, spreading her apart so I could stroke her clit in a little circular pattern that made her hips rock slightly against mine, and nestled my cock nice and tight between her ass cheeks.

"Careful, angel. I'm tempted to bury myself inside you, and if that happens I don't know if I can hold back tonight."

She breathed my name, her head dropping back as she pushed her hips closer, greedy for more friction against her pleasure spot. A firm grip and a twist of the fabric and I tore the panties from her body, tossing them aside. "Oops," I deadpanned.

She watched me with wide eyes, her pulse frantically thrumming at the base of her throat. She liked this side of me. *Good girl.*

Lifting her weight with one hand, I pushed my cotton boxers down my thighs with the other, freeing my cock to rest between us. Rocking her hips against me, her wet pussy slid along my shaft, coating me in her juices. A growl rose from my throat. I cursed under my breath, my hands clutching into fists at my sides. Restraint was not my strong point, and she was making me crazy with desire. I was about three seconds away from pounding into her, brutally taking everything she was offering.

"You better stop me now, angel, unless you want me to fuck you bare." I knew her birth control hadn't kicked in yet, but shit, in that moment, I was willing to risk it. I needed her. Just her, with no barrier between us. She made me want things I never thought I'd want. She made me crazy with the desire to not only fuck her, but to consume her from the inside out.

"Give it to me," she breathed. Her confidence and husky tone caused a drop of fluid to leak from my tip.

Positioning the head of my cock at her entrance, I pushed forward slowly but steadily, easing past the tightness of her inner muscles and not stopping until I was completely buried deep inside her body. McKenna let out a low murmur of discomfort. I knew I was testing her, pushing her limits, but I also knew she liked it. And I loved the feel of her stretching around me.

"Ride me, angel," I encouraged, placing one hand against her side, my thumb lightly stroking her hip bone.

She rotated her hips, drawing me even deeper and savoring the feel of me buried so completely, before lifting and lowering herself back down in tiny increments as she adjusted to my size.

Watching her hips move against mine, seeing her eyes slip closed as an expression of ecstasy overtook her features was too much. *Fuck.* She was my everything.

I gripped her hips, lifting her up and down while I planted my feet against the mattress and used the leverage to thrust into her. Unable to hold back, I pounded into her tight little pussy over and over again, loving the way her chest bounced as I plunged into her.

All too soon, McKenna was exploding around me, murmuring my name and gripping her breasts to rub her nipples as she started to come.

The sight of her, coupled with the intense way her body gripped at mine, wrenched the last of my self-control away. Tingles at the base of my spine drew my balls tight against my body as my own release began. Hot jets of semen pumped into her. McKenna clung to me helplessly and I lifted up on my elbows to kiss her. Her walls continued pulsing around me for several seconds as our breathing slowed and our kiss turned deeper, slower.

One thing was certain: I did not deserve an angel like McKenna. The only explanation for her presence in my life was that my mom had sent her from heaven to look after us all. It was the only thing that made sense. I'd known she was my angel right from the very beginning.

I wanted to make love to her over and over again, taking my time like it might be my last time touching her. The last time I had the privilege of holding her naked body against mine. Because when she found out about my connection to the lawyer, I was all too aware that all of this could end.

Chapter Eight

MCKENNA

Amanda and her baby girl, AnnMarie—named for both of her grandmas—were being released from the hospital today. And since I felt so guilty that I hadn't even visited once, I'd offered to pick her up and give them a ride home. Just as I was stepping into my shoes and shrugging on my coat, Brian opened the door to our apartment.

"I wasn't expecting you until later," I said with surprise. "Did you drive yourself?"

He lifted his arms out to his sides. "Good as new. Not even a limp. I can operate a car and everything."

Much-needed laughter bubbled its way up my throat. The last few days had been too tense, and it was good to see his smiling face.

He gathered me in his arms for a hug. "Damn, it's good to be home," he said.

"It's good to see you on your feet."

"Where are you off to?" he asked, taking in my appearance.

"I was actually going to pick up a friend and her brand new baby from the hospital, then drive them home."

"You still have that rental car?" he asked.

I nodded sheepishly. "I was supposed to return it days ago. But it turns out I like having my own wheels."

Brian chuckled. "How about this. I'll follow you to the rental lot so you can return it, and then I'll give you a lift to the hospital so we can get your friend."

I nodded. "If you don't mind, that would be really helpful."

"Are you kidding? I've been in a bed for almost a month. The last thing I want to do is sit inside alone and watch more TV."

He dropped his bags in his bedroom, used the restroom, and then we were on the road within minutes. As promised, Brian followed me to the rental lot and waited while I returned the rental car and paid the bill, then we were en route to the hospital.

"So…you and Knox…" he started.

When I was in Indiana for all those weeks, Brian knew my relationship with Knox was on the rocks. Now he was fishing for information, but I couldn't blame him. He had to be curious, and I'd been pretty closed off about my relationship.

"We're back together. I love him, Bri. I love being with him and his brothers. And I think my parents would have wanted me to be happy."

He nodded silently, looking out at the road. "Yeah, they would have," he said after several minutes of silence. "They would be really proud of you, you know."

It was the first time I'd heard him acknowledge that, and irrational tears filled my eyes.

"Guess it's time I let you go," he said softly. "Shit, I've had a crush on you since the first grade. You can't say I didn't try."

I chuckled lightly. "You put in a valiant effort."

He reached over and took my hand. "Knox is lucky to have you."

"Thanks, Bri."

His injury and time recouping seemed to bring him a new sense of peace and clarity. It had given him a lot of time to think. And my leaving him while he was still recovering to return to Knox must have sent a stronger message than I realized. I'd chosen Knox over him in every way possible.

When we arrived at the hospital, we checked in at the security desk and were directed to the third-floor maternity wing. I thought Brian might just wait for us in the waiting room, but he insisted on helping, saying there would probably be bags to carry.

I decided I liked his new helpfulness and sense of peace about our friends-only status. We paused outside Amanda's room and I gave a knock on the door.

"Come in!" she called, her voice sounding clear and happy.

I poked my head in and made sure she was dressed. She was wearing stretch pants and a cute top, and had a big smile across her face.

"I have my friend Brian with me…that okay?" I asked.

She nodded. "Of course. Thanks for coming." She waved us in.

We entered the room and I gave Amanda a big hug before peeking inside the bassinet holding the tiny baby.

"Aw…" I gushed as a rush of emotions hit me at once. Amanda was a mom. And AnnMarie was so tiny and pink. She was absolutely precious. A miracle baby in more ways than one.

While I held the baby and cuddled her in the nearby rocking chair, I was vaguely aware of Amanda and Brian getting to know each other. *Oops.* Apparently I'd forgotten my manners along with making formal introductions as soon as I'd seen the baby. But Brian was standing with his hands in his pockets and a big grin on his face, and Amanda was laughing at something he'd said, so I focused on the sweet little thing in my arms again. She was so light, I could hold her forever. Her little pink face turned up to mine, and she lazily peeked open one eye and yawned. I couldn't help but giggle.

"So she's all good, despite being born early?" I asked.

Amanda nodded, pulling her attention away from Brian. "Yeah, she's good to go. She had a hard time regulating her body temperature, which is why we had to stay a couple extra days, but she's completely healthy. She's almost five pounds already, and eats like a horse."

The pride in Amanda's smile touched something inside me. It seemed we were all growing.

"So I hear we're here to spring you out of here," Brian said, looking at Amanda again.

"Yes, I'm more than ready to leave. It's impossible to get a decent night's sleep with nurses coming in every couple of hours and turning on the lights, poking this, prodding that."

I handed her daughter back to her. "I hate to tell you this, but I think your nights of sleeping are over."

"Yeah, I know." She smiled down at the baby in her arms. "But she's worth it."

"May I?" Brian asked, stopping in front of Amanda and looking down at the baby.

"Oh, sure," she said and passed him the infant.

Watching Brian hold the baby only made her look tinier. He cooed something unintelligible down at her while Amanda and I swooned. What was it about a man and a baby?

While Amanda bundled AnnMarie up in the car seat, Brian and I gathered up her bags. "Do you have everything you need at home?" I asked. I knew the birth had been a surprise, and aside from our thrift-store shopping a while back, I didn't know if she was prepared to take the baby home.

"I have a bassinet for her to sleep in, diapers, wipes, and some clothes. I'm breastfeeding because it's, well, it's free and I can't afford baby formula. Besides, it's not as bad as I thought it'd be. So yeah, I think we have everything we need."

I nodded. "Okay." It sounded like she had the essentials covered. I realized babies really didn't need much. Despite all the plastic gear and baby products on the market, Amanda was embracing the simple side of things.

Brian's brows scrunched together. "If you need anything else, you let us know. Any friend of McKenna's is a friend of mine."

Amanda smiled up at him. "I will."

His offer was sweet. I wondered if his demeanor would change if I told him how I knew Amanda, and that she was an addict in recovery I'd met in group. Or maybe his harsh criticism was only reserved for Knox. Either way, I let it go. Today was a happy day, and it felt like everyone was heading in the right direction.

Chapter Nine

McKenna

With the drama of the last few days behind us, I wanted to make the most of my time with Knox. We needed to be alone, to just reconnect. I loved that he'd planned a date for us, and deciding that I quite liked having a boyfriend, I wanted to return the favor. I wanted to go somewhere we could both relax and enjoy the day together. And I'd told Belinda that despite returning to Chicago after my extended leave of absence, she should give my Saturday morning sex-addict group to my replacement permanently. Which meant both Knox and I were free on Saturdays now. My new schedule felt positively decadent. Having time to actually pursue a relationship was something new for me. The old me would have felt guilty. The new me was going to enjoy every minute of it.

When Knox picked me up later that afternoon, I slid into the warmth of his Jeep, inhaling his masculine scent and instantly feeling happy and secure.

"Are you okay with me being in charge today?" I smiled at him.

His gaze jerked over to mine and an unexpected jab of lust shot straight between my thighs at the wicked grin on his lips. "I think I can handle that. Where to, angel?"

454

"Downtown," I answered. "Park somewhere near Lakeshore Drive."

He was dressed in a warm-looking thermal tee and a black fleece, and since it wasn't totally freezing out today, my plan should work.

Once he'd parallel parked on a side street just off Lakeshore Drive, I laced his fingers with mine and led him down to the walking path bordering the lake. It was the middle of January, which meant we were completely alone on the beach. Just me, Knox, and the endless blue water stretched out before us, gently lapping at the sandy shoreline.

We huddled into our coats and almost by instinct, our joined hands squeezed tighter. It was just us. No kids. No Brian or Amanda. No drama. I breathed in a deep, refreshing lungful of fresh air and sighed happily.

We walked side by side in silence for a few moments, and though it looked like there was something heavy on his mind, when I questioned Knox, the tension in his features fell away and he dropped a kiss to my mouth.

"Everything's perfect, angel," he assured me.

Perhaps it was still lingering worry over Jaxon. Either way, I dismissed it. Knox was by my side and that was all that mattered. I was learning to let the past go, to stay in the moment and enjoy.

I nestled closer into his side, inhaling his intoxicating scent.

"Are you cold?" he asked, leaning down to press a kiss against my temple.

Not with his big body to shield me from the wind. "Not really, no."

"So, are we gonna talk about things now that you're back?" he asked.

"Like?" I prompted.

"Like your many volunteering jobs, where you live, and when you're going to buy a car and stop taking the bus." He raised an eyebrow at me.

I remembered feeling protected and cared for right from the first time I'd gone to Knox's house—he was so against me taking the bus across town on my own. He'd insisted on personally escorting me home. He'd wormed his way into my heart right from the beginning, even if I didn't see it at the time. All the signs were there. He was a good man. Or maybe I was the exception, since I was pretty sure he hadn't always treated women with such care and respect.

I glanced over at him to address his questions. "As for volunteering, I'm no longer leading the Saturday morning group." I was guessing he'd figured as much since I hadn't in a couple of months now. "A car is on my to-do list. Brian said he'd help me look."

"I'll take you, McKenna." His look said not to argue.

Okay then. Knox will help me get a car.

I nodded and continued. "And what about where I live?" I paused, waiting for him to give me some clue about what he'd meant. My apartment with Brian was in a safe part of town. I didn't see what issue he could possibly take up there.

He stopped walking and turned to face me. The sunlight glinting in his beautiful eyes showed off shades of moss green and warm brown. He released my hand, only to bring both of his palms up to cup my face. "When you were away, I realized something about myself. I love you, McKenna, and I don't want to be without you. I want you to move in with me."

The air felt trapped in my chest as I processed his words. He wanted me. He loved me. His offer was much more significant than he could have known. He was giving me my family back. The piece of me that had been missing for all these years. A warm home filled with love and activity. Tears welled in my eyes.

"Knox…" I sobbed, inhaling ragged breaths.

"Shhh. Don't answer now. I know it's a lot to process, something you probably want to think about. But I promise you one thing—

I'm never going back to the man I was before. You've changed me. You came into my life and completely fucking gutted me. I thought I couldn't love again, but you were right all along. Love was the exact thing I was missing and searching for in all those women."

I flinched slightly at his words. Being reminded of his past wasn't easy, but his thumb brushed across my bottom lip, deliciously distracting me.

"I was looking for you the entire time. And it took a downward spiral for me to find you. My angel," he whispered.

I wanted to tell him yes, of course I would move in, but my lips were busy attacking his. I kissed him with a brutal force that he matched with swipe after swipe of his tongue against mine. He hauled me closer, one hand still cupping my face, and the other pressed against my butt to align our bodies together. Suddenly being in public seemed like a terrible idea.

"Knox…" I breathed against his damp lips.

"Yeah?" His voice was a rough growl that sent delicious vibrations spiraling through me.

"Let's go somewhere."

"My house," he answered.

Yes. Please. Anywhere but here. Preferably somewhere with a bed. "Wait." I pulled back. "Won't your brothers be there?"

His hazy eyes found mine. "They know we fuck, McKenna." He pressed his erection against my belly and rubbed it against me.

A whimper fell from my parted lips and I couldn't argue. I nodded quickly and he led me back to his Jeep. I almost laughed as I tried to keep up with Knox's pace. His long legs ate up the sidewalk and I pranced alongside him. We'd made it fifteen minutes into our date before we cracked and needed to be alone. But there was no denying my entire body was humming with need. He'd created this side of me. And I was all too happy to go along with it.

We climbed inside the Jeep and Knox wasted no time cranking the ignition and pulling out into traffic. A silent glance in his direction caused a knot to form in my stomach. He was still rock hard in his jeans, the rigid weight of his erection clearly visible through the denim. Desire pulsed through me, hot and uncontained.

"Knox..." I murmured.

His hand curled around the back of my neck, guiding my mouth to his while he maintained eye contact with the road. "Not long, baby," he assured me, his lips brushing against mine.

I pressed my thighs together, squirming in the seat as his warm tongue licked against my bottom lip. I knew what delicious, naughty things his tongue could do to other parts of my body. A flash of moisture dampened my panties.

I'd survived so long without physical affection and sex, maybe now

I was making up for lost time. Either that or Knox alone had unleashed something in me that refused to be contained. Especially now that I knew how good he could make me feel.

When Knox broke the kiss, I found myself unable to resist. I reached across the center console and curled my hand around the hard ridge in his pants, eliciting a soft groan from him.

I rubbed his firm length up and down, loving how big and masculine he felt in my hand. I wanted to make him feel good and lose all control like he did to me. I wanted to see him come apart.

"Shit," he cursed, his hands gripping the wheel until his knuckles turned white.

I wanted to unbutton his pants, tug down his zipper and free his cock, feel its warm weight against my skin, in my mouth, but I settled for lightly stroking him over his pants.

The raspy breath shuddering in his chest was the only encouragement I needed. Using my fingernails, I lightly raked across him, squeezing and caressing him. I might have said this was for him—meant to turn him on and drive him wild—but it was just as much for me. Touching him, knowing I was bringing him pleasure, made me feel sexy and powerful. Not to mention how it drenched my panties with my own arousal.

Thankfully, we soon pulled to a stop in the driveway behind his house and Knox turned to face me.

"You're going to regret teasing me, angel."

The husky tone of his voice and ragged breathing, coupled with the sight of his raging erection, made my stomach flip. I was playing a dangerous game, but there was no way I was stopping now.

He sucked in a few deep breaths, and adjusted the monstrosity in his pants before climbing from the Jeep.

Unlocking the back door, he led me inside. All was peaceful in the house. Tucker and Luke were in the living room, Tuck watching cartoons and Luke busy typing away on the laptop.

Knox and I crept up the stairs without so much as a hello. I felt a little villainous, sneaking off to do naughty things with him, but it was a feeling I liked. I was embracing the bad-girl side of myself that only Knox brought out.

Once we were safely tucked inside his bedroom, with the door locked and closed behind us, Knox's hungry gaze caught mine and I felt trapped. I was his. Completely at his mercy. He stalked toward me like he was the hunter and I was the hunted.

Not bothering to cross the room to the bed, he pinned me against the wall, his large frame swallowing mine as he pressed his body close. He rubbed his large erection against my belly.

"You wanted to tease me, make me want you, but not let me come... That wasn't nice, angel."

I let out a helpless whimper. I hadn't meant to be mean.

His mouth caught mine, taking my bottom lip between his teeth and tugging it gently. "Naughty girls like you need to be taught a lesson."

"Are you going to punish me?" I whispered, my lips brushing his.

"I'm going to make sure you never forget who's in charge." He lifted my shirt from over my head and tossed it behind him, then he found the clasp on my bra and removed that next. The cool air nipped at me, sending goose bumps across my belly and puckering my nipples. His gaze slipped lower and landed on my breasts. "So pretty," he said, his thumbs lightly stroking the sensitive pink flesh. A gasp stuck in my throat. His hands were warm and I savored the rough feel of his fingertips against me.

"Knox," I breathed.

"Shhh. You forgot already, angel, I'm setting the pace today."

A frustrated whimper escaped my lips and I leaned forward to kiss him. If I could drive him wild, maybe I could get him to move things along faster. I reached for his belt buckle and his mouth moved against mine in a low, throaty chuckle.

"No way, sweetheart. You're not playing with my cock again until I'm ready for you to. Hands clasped behind you."

Fighting the urge to roll my eyes, I laced my fingers behind me, which only caused my breasts to stick out more.

Knox's wet mouth closed over one nipple, and with his eyes on mine to watch my reaction, he sucked and licked my nipple until it was distended into a firm peak. Then he flicked his tongue back and forth across the other while I watched in agonized pleasure.

His fingers worked at the button of my jeans, then he slowly lowered the zipper and tugged them open to push them down my hips. My panties went next as Knox roughly shoved them down my legs until I could step out of them. I stood before him completely undressed as the chill of the room nipped at me and desire burned hotly inside. The effect was dizzying.

Keeping my fingers laced behind me, I raised up on my toes, needing to be closer to him in any way I could. I nuzzled against his neck, stroking my nose against his rough skin and inhaling his scent. "Can I kiss you?" I murmured.

"Of course."

I captured his mouth in a hot, hungry kiss, my tongue lightly stroking his while his hands curled around my hips, squeezing as though he was just barely holding back from taking me right here, right now. To which I'd have no objections.

Using his grip around my hips, Knox lifted me and I wrapped my legs around his waist, enjoying the sensation of the hard ridge in his denim pressing into my bottom as he carried me over to his bed.

Finally.

He tossed me down onto the mattress and looked down at me for just a second before pulling his shirt off over his head. I loved studying the dips and planes in his abdominals and pecs. I could stare at this man all day; he was a work of art. So masculine and strong, both inside and out. His hands caught his belt and I watched as if in a trance as he slowly undid the buckle and pulled his cock free. He was thick and swollen with need, a large vein running the length of him.

Unable to resist, I rose on my hands and knees and brought my mouth to him, running my tongue along that pulsing vein, teasing, licking, and tasting his smooth length. A low murmur escaped his throat and my core clenched with need. I gripped his shaft, rubbing both hands up and down as my mouth continued to hover over him, licking and sucking all along his steely cock.

His fists gripped my hair, moving it away from my face, and his hips rocked forward, plunging him deeper into my mouth.

"Christ, angel." He cursed low under his breath and tilted my chin up so I'd meet his eyes. "You like doing that to me, don't you?" He brushed a knuckle along my cheek and I nodded. "Does that taste good?" he asked, teasing me.

I smiled wickedly and licked along the head of his cock again, tasting the salty bead of fluid leaking from his tip. His cock twitched and he moaned something unintelligible again.

"Lie back," he ordered.

I lay down against the pillows, watching him, waiting for him to make his move, but he seemed entirely unrushed and content to just take in my naked form, a slight smile curling at his mouth. For a sex addict, he seemed much too in control, and the thought made me smile. He was mine. All his past troubles and all the worries we'd overcome made this moment that much sweeter, like it meant more because we'd worked to get here.

Knox lay down beside me, covering me with the warm weight of his body, and sank inside me slowly, letting me acclimate to him an inch at a time.

Chapter Ten

KNOX

Holy shit, she felt amazing. It took several minutes to work myself completely inside her, but the patience was worth it. My eyes slipped closed the moment I was fully buried inside McKenna's warm heat. She might have been prim and proper outside the bedroom, but my angel liked to get a little dirty between the sheets, further proof that she was the perfect girl for me. I whispered dirty things into her ear as I fucked her slowly—telling her how tight she was around me, how good she felt, and she let out tiny whimpers each time I did.

Everything about her was incredible, and I knew without a doubt that I was a very fucking lucky man. Her pussy was like crack and I kept up an easy tempo, enjoying the feelings flooding through me.

"I can feel you tightening around my cock. Do you want to come?" I asked, letting my lips brush past the shell of her ear.

"Yes," she said and moaned. The hint of desperation in her voice told me that while I'd been waiting for her, she'd been holding herself back, waiting for me. And since I knew she'd been turned on and wet since our ride home, I wanted to take care of her.

I pressed my thumb against her clit, eliciting a soft cry from her, and began lightly rubbing as I continued the even rhythm of my strokes, pushing in and out of her. McKenna flew apart, convulsing and squirming in my arms, repeating my name over and over again until the last of her orgasm pulsed through her body and left her limp and sated in my arms.

Not yet done with her, I pulled her hips to mine, entering her deeply. Her back arched off the bed at the unexpected invasion. Her eyes had that glassy, faraway look, and I could tell she was undone. I wanted to flip her over, to sink into her from behind and watch her ass wiggle against my thrusts, but I knew I was too close. And McKenna was worn out.

"I'm almost there," I murmured, kissing her neck.

Pumping into her again and I again, I felt my balls draw up close to my body as her tight muscles gripped me. A shuddering moan pushed past my lips as she milked my cock deep inside her body. "Kenna…" The broken groan rumbled deep in my chest and I collapsed onto the bed on top of her, gathering her in my arms and holding her tightly against my chest.

As our heartbeats pounded together, I knew I couldn't put off the truth about my past much longer. It wasn't fair to her. She'd given me everything—her heart, her devotion, her virginity, for fuck's sake, and I couldn't even tell her the truth. McKenna had given me a chance at true happiness, and the boys had a loving female in their lives for the first time in years. I was being selfish hiding this from her and it was starting to eat at me, to wear a hole in my newly mended heart. It wasn't fucking healthy.

I held her securely, breathing in the scent of her shampoo as a million thoughts swirled through my brain. She'd healed me, made me a better man, yet none of that could erase my past. I held on to hope that since she'd forgiven me once before, she could find a way to do it again. If only there was a way to show her how sorry I was, she could understand my dark past was truly behind me.

Chapter Eleven

KNOX

"Guys, come on, we're going to be late." I corralled my
brothers toward the front door and they groggily obliged, slipping
into shoes and coats.

"If this is lunch, why do we have to be up at the crack of dawn?"
Jaxon yawned. His face looked a hell of a lot better since the beat
down, just the hint of a shadow darkened his left cheekbone.

"Because," I said. "There's training beforehand and we need to
have everything ready for one hundred fifty people by noon. Come
on."

I'd arranged for us to volunteer at a church today to serve lunch to
a Mothers Against Drunk Drivers group that was having an all-day
retreat. McKenna was meeting us there later. I knew it was fucked
up that I hadn't told her the truth yet about my own past with
drunk driving. I guess this was my own twisted way of trying to
make amends.

When we arrived at the church, we parked in the back and tramped
down the stairs to the basement and into the large kitchen.
McKenna was already inside, and a large smile spread across her
face when she saw us.

"Hi!" She bounded across the room and flung herself into my

arms. "This was such a good idea." She kissed me warmly on the mouth. It was more than I deserved and a twinge of guilt flashed through me. *Shit*.

"Hi, angel," I murmured, pressing a kiss to her forehead.

She greeted each of the boys in a similar fashion, with hugs and kisses on their cheeks. She was so good to them, filling the void left behind when Mom died, that my chest tightened and I had to turn away.

"So, where do we start?" I surveyed the large kitchen.

McKenna had gotten there early and met with the church kitchen staff. We were making lasagna, salad, and brownies, and she gave each of us an apron as she explained the tasks.

Tucker and I teamed up on the brownies, Jaxon was going to make the salad, and McKenna and Luke were going to prepare the main dish. It would take us a couple of hours to prepare the huge batches of food, plus cleanup time afterward.

Putting Tucker on dessert probably wasn't the wisest idea. He kept stealing the pieces of chocolate I was roughly chopping. I glanced over at Jaxon, who was chopping tomatoes into slimy little chunks, and almost chuckled at the disdain on his face. Public service was good for him. Maybe this would get him to open his eyes and see there was more to life than gambling and girls.

McKenna and Luke gathered their ingredients and were beginning to assemble pans of lasagna noodles and sauce.

"You sure you want me to have all that money?" Luke asked her, a questioning look in his eyes. He wasn't any more used to handouts than I was, and that made me proud.

"Of course I'm sure. It would make me very happy to see you off at college. That's the best use of the money I could think of."

"You're too good to us." He playfully tossed a noodle in her direction.

McKenna caught it and smiled at him. "Yeah, well, I kind of have a thing for your brother…"

He laughed. "Trust me, I noticed." His expression grew thoughtful for a few moments as he layered cheese over the bed of noodles. "It's just really cool of you to forgive him."

"Forgive him?" she questioned, peering up from her task to meet his eyes with an inquisitive expression.

My stomach turned sour and dropped like a stone.

Chapter Twelve

MCKENNA

Luke and I were elbow deep in noodles and tomato sauce, and I was trying to understand what he meant about me forgiving Knox. I knew Knox's background as a sex addict, but since I'd forgiven that a while ago, something told me there was more Luke was referring to.

Using my clean hand to push a lock of hair behind my ear, I turned to face Luke. "What do you mean?"

He swallowed and his gaze wandered over to Knox's. Knox looked like someone had punched him in the stomach. His shoulders were rounded forward and his face had gone pale. Knox shook his head at Luke, and his mouth pulled into a frown.

My hands felt shaky and I gripped the edge of the counter for support. "L-Luke?" I stammered.

The entire kitchen went still and silent as the weight of this moment bore down on us. Something was about to happen. Something Knox didn't want me to know, if his reaction was any indication.

"It's time, Knox. She needs to know. No more hiding, right?" Luke said, his voice barely above a whisper.

I licked my lips and faced Luke again, my eyes begging his for the truth.

Without any further prompting, Luke took a deep breath and began. "All of this—Knox cleaning up his act, us being here today, volunteering for a drunk-driving cause—it's Knox's way of trying. Listen to me. He loves you. Don't forget that."

I nodded slowly, fighting to comprehend where this was headed. "Tell me, Luke."

Luke's gaze shot over to Knox once again. "You gonna do this, or should I?"

Knox dropped the knife he'd been holding onto the chopping block. "I will."

Escorting me to a back hallway, Knox's fingertips at the small of my back felt cold and lifeless. He was terrified for me to learn whatever he was about to tell me, and I was equally as scared. Just as my life had begun to stabilize, I sensed everything I thought I knew was about to change. The feeling was disorienting.

Knox and I stood in silence for several heartbeats. I was torn between wanting him to tell me the truth about whatever it was he'd been hiding, and living in blissful ignorance for a while longer.

"You know I love you, right?" he started.

I nodded slowly. The sentiment that sometimes love wasn't enough pushed itself to the forefront of my brain, and I steeled myself for whatever he was going to say next.

"You never asked about the reason I showed up at that first sex addicts meeting. And I never offered the information."

He was right. I didn't know why it never occurred to me before, but now I was filled with curiosity. What had prompted him to take that step? I recalled he'd said that he was there at the request of his counselor. "You were in counseling," I offered.

"Yes."

"Why?" I asked softly. I could only assume it had something to do with sex, and I shuddered at the thought. Had he hurt someone? Done something awful?

"We should talk about this later, when we have more—"

I shook my head. I needed to know. "I know about your past, what more could you possibly tell me?"

"You don't know everything." He hung his head.

"You're scaring me. Did you father a child you never told me about?"

"No. But I have a feeling that might be easier for you to stomach."

"Knox. Just tell me."

"All right," he said, running a hand roughly through his hair so it stood in odd directions. "Promise me one thing. That you won't run."

I nodded. "I'm here. You have me."

Agony twisted his features. "Before I met you, I was a mess. Weekends were my escape from reality, and I used them to their fullest. I drank too much, fucked too often, and didn't really care about the ramifications."

I waited for him to continue, the sound of my own heartbeat thundering in my ears.

"One night last summer, I got a little too fucked up. And instead of walking home like I should have, or calling a cab, I drove my Jeep home. Or at least, I tried to."

My hands clutched at the cement wall behind me, fighting for something solid to hold on to.

"I was pulled over and arrested that night for drunk driving. I had no business being behind the wheel, and I spent that night and most of the next day in jail. My brothers were terrified something horrible had happened to me. I'm all they have, and it was a huge fucking wake-up call that I couldn't abandon them like everyone else had. I knew I could never do something that reckless ever again, but the damage was done. I was convicted of drunk driving, sentenced to community service, and ordered to see a counselor for anger management after smarting off with the judge. The counselor I saw diagnosed me with sexual addiction rather than anger issues, and referred me to SAA."

I felt betrayed in the deepest way. Knox's past had collided with my own, and the wreckage was overwhelming. "Why didn't you ever tell me?"

"When I asked you about how you became a sex addiction counselor, I'd wanted to hear about your sordid past, maybe learn that you'd overcome this addiction yourself and turned your struggle into helping others. But instead, you were simply a good person who was stepping in to help. It made me feel like a fucking charity case. I couldn't tell you then. And since I wanted to see where this was headed, I didn't."

Part of me understood why he didn't open up with that information right away. But later, once we were together and he knew about my parents, there was just no excuse. And now him being here today, volunteering at a drunk-driving charity, it felt like a sorry excuse for an apology. I felt tricked and cheated. The man I'd come to love with my whole heart had hidden part of himself from me.

"Tell me what you're thinking," he said, his voice whisper soft.

"I'm going to need some time."

Knox nodded, acknowledging my need for space and time to sort through the conflicting feelings inside me. I hated drunk drivers, despising the reckless, careless attitude that put them behind the wheel and endangered others. And I'd just learned the man I loved was one of them, and not only that, but he'd hidden it from me for months.

Tears streamed down my cheeks. "I need to go…"

He nodded. "Okay. I'll tell the boys you had to leave. Just don't give up on me, McKenna."

"'Bye, Knox."

In the moments before I told McKenna, her blind faith in me made it all the more painful. She'd watched me with those wide blue eyes, waiting for whatever I was about to say. And I knew it was going to fucking crush her. There was nothing worse than the feeling of hurting her. She was so sweet, so pure. She didn't deserve the shit I put her through.

My troubles with the law—my court-appointed counseling sessions, the entire reason I'd met her—all of it stemmed from drunk driving. I'd just completely shattered her world. And I hated the sight of her face going completely pale as all the blood drained away. It wasn't fair asking her not to run. Of course she was going to run. I was a monster of the worst kind. I couldn't even be honest with the woman who owned the deepest part of me.

I headed back into the kitchen in a daze to face my brothers.

"What happened?" Jaxon asked, concern lacing his features.

"She's gone, isn't she?" Luke asked.

I nodded, confirming the worst. It was what I'd expected, but it stung more than I thought it would. The urge to hit something flared inside me. My hands curled into fists as I tried to calm the deep, searing anger burning inside me. I'd found the perfect girl—given her my heart—and it was all for nothing. Maybe this was punishment for all the girls I'd used and tossed aside over the years. Karma was a motherfucking bitch.

And now I needed to put on my happy face and be there for my brothers. Our little adventure today suddenly seemed so trite—we were fucking volunteering at a drunk-driving benefit. How in the world I ever thought this could make up for my lack of honesty with the girl I loved, I had no idea.

"Knox?" Tucker's little voice broke my concentration from the spot I'd been studying on the floor. His brown eyes were flooded with worry.

"Everything's gonna be okay, bud. I promise."

I had no fucking clue if that was true, but I couldn't admit that to him. If it wasn't true, if she couldn't forgive me, I was going to head into the nearest bar for liquor and pussy to numb myself with.

Chapter Thirteen

McKenna

I was in love with a man I could never be with. We'd successfully hurdled his sexual addiction and that was the easy part. But this...I had no words. I never dreamed our shared, shattered pasts would be what stood in our way. We'd come too far. Lost too much. The universe was playing some sick joke on me, seeing just how far I could be pushed before I snapped. Well, this was it. I'd reached my breaking point. The score was the universe: one, McKenna: zero.

Knox hiding this from me the entire time hurt worse than finding out he'd been convicted of the crime in the first place. The very crime that killed my parents. My life was rocky enough. I needed a man who was capable of complete honesty, someone to build a stable foundation with. Someone I could trust and rely on. I couldn't share my life with someone with dark secrets, living in constant fear of what he'd reveal next. Because something told me if I knew all the ways Knox had messed up, I'd run away screaming, no matter how big my heart was.

But of course it wasn't that easy. I loved him. I couldn't just turn that off. And there were the boys to think about, too, sweet Tucker and Luke, and heaven knew Jaxon could use a positive role model. I hated the idea of just disappearing from their lives.

Two long and hard days had passed since Knox told me. And now that I knew the full extent of his past, the decision was mine. Either forgive him and let it go, and move forward with our future, or let it destroy everything we'd built.

Through my work at the teen center, I'd counseled woman and girls who were codependent, who felt worthless and rejected without a man in their lives. Women who were depressed and even suicidal over their relationship status. I never in my wildest dreams thought I could be like those women. I had listened to their troubles, asked all the right questions, probed gently and offered the advice I'd learned to give them in my training, yet I felt emotionless and detached from their problems. I was just doing my job.

It was only now that I finally understood. Only since Knox had invaded my life and taken over my every waking thought. Sex and love had the ability to consume you, and it terrified me. I felt desperate and needy and wanted him to love me, to draw me into his arms and never let me go. I didn't know how I could ever look those sad women in the eye again and tell them to move on. There was no moving on. Not once you'd met your true match. Something told me Knox had left an imprint on my heart, in my psyche, that would forever be there.

There was no choice. I had to find a way to move past this. Not that I wasn't furious at him for hiding the truth from me for all these months—I was. It was going to take some time for me to adjust to that. But I knew I would forgive him. How could I not? My love for him was too desperate, too all-consuming for us to be apart. Despite all his mistakes and dark secrets, I loved that man with my whole being. It wasn't a choice.

Gathering up my courage, I texted Knox and asked him to come over and talk. I felt safer having this conversation in my own space. Plus when Amanda had called earlier and asked if I wanted to come over and help out with the baby, Brian had volunteered to go in my place, leaving me alone in the apartment.

Knox confirmed he would be here as soon as he'd fed the boys dinner. I used the time to tidy up my room, too restless and on edge to sit and relax.

When the doorbell to my apartment buzzed a short time later, I nearly jumped out of my skin with the anticipation of seeing him again. I knew that no matter what happened, tonight would be big for me. I had worked on forgiving myself, moving past my parents' tragic deaths, and now it seemed that God had a sense of humor because I was being tested for a final time with forgiving Knox.

His somber expression greeted me when I opened the door. Dark circles lined his eyes as if he hadn't slept, and his hair was messy, standing up in several directions.

"Come inside." I motioned him forward into the foyer, thankful that Brian was gone to help out with Amanda yet again. He'd been so helpful over the last few days, driving her and the baby to their doctors' checkups and to the store for more diapers.

I led Knox into the living room, but we were both too tense to sit down. The mood surrounding us was sobering. I'd never seen Knox look so broken and defeated. Not even when Jaxon had been beaten and threatened by that gang.

Knox shoved his hands into his pockets and looked up at me through dark lashes. "There's no excuse for what I did. And not telling you earlier was—"

"I know," I offered. I could see the sincerity and regret written all over him.

"I'm sorry," he said simply.

"I know," I said again. His features were twisted in agony, and even though I'd decided to forgive him and move past it, he didn't know that yet. I decided to use that to my advantage. "Where did you see this headed? You and me?"

Pressing his fingertips to his temples, he briefly closed his eyes and then opened them again, fixing me with a desperate stare. "I love you like I've never loved anyone. I wanted you to move in, to be with me forever. I wanted to marry you, angel."

His admission completely stunned me, and I stood there motionless trying to process his words. I knew Knox wanted me to move in with him, something we hadn't even fully discussed, but now he was telling me that he wanted to marry me, too. My heart swelled three times its normal size in my chest and I briefly closed my eyes.

I struggled to put into words all the emotions I was feeling. But I knew I couldn't answer him now. "I need time to think, Knox."

He nodded. "I get that. Completely." He stepped closer, closing the distance between us, and tipped my chin up to his. "But don't forget that you're the one who taught me about vulnerability and letting others in. I know I'm damaged goods, angel, and that this is a huge leap of faith for you...but please believe me when I tell you I love you. All of you. And I always will."

I nodded. I did believe that. Knox was a changed man, inside and out. He was my everything. He and his family had become my whole world, and I loved each and every one of them. I just needed some time to clear the thoughts swirling in my head and do this my way.

"We'll talk soon," was all I said.

I knew Knox would be mad that Brian was the one taking me to get my first car, but I also knew he'd understand. As long as I got something safe and reliable and wasn't depending on public transit anymore, he'd let it go. Besides, I wanted to do this for myself, and inviting my oldest friend along felt like the right thing to do. Especially since I needed to tell him something big, something that would forever change the dynamic of our relationship.

I hadn't spoken to Knox since he came to my apartment several days ago. And even though I missed him with every ounce of my being, it felt good taking control of my life and getting things in order. I'd put that off for far too long.

Brian and I toured the car lot, and I selected a slightly used silver sedan to test drive. Once the salesman had made a photocopy of my driver's license, Brian and I were seated in the air-freshener-scented interior, ready to take a spin.

Gripping the wheel at ten and two, I waited for a large break in the traffic and pulled out onto the road. "So you've been seeing more of Amanda these days," I said as I drove. It wasn't a question, and Brian merely glanced up at me without responding. "That's a good thing, right?"

He nodded, a smile barely visible on his lips. Good thing I knew him so well.

"How is she doing?" I asked.

"She's great. She's an incredible mom. It's a big burden being a single parent, but I've never heard her complain once."

"You like her."

He chuckled at me. "I do. She's a sweet girl."

"What about the fact that she has a baby. Does that scare you?"

He looked thoughtful for a moment, but shook his head. "Not at all."

It was the same way I felt about Knox having custody of his three brothers. If anything, the responsibility only deepened him and enriched our relationship. There was a whole other side of him to love. They were never a burden. Well, except when we wanted alone time, but I was getting distracted. "So are you guys, like, dating?"

Brian nodded. "Yeah, I think so. We haven't technically been on any dates yet. She has a three-week-old daughter, you know? But I bring her dinner, we watch movies, and I really don't mind pitching in to take care of AnnMarie. She's a good baby."

"You're a good guy, Brian." I felt proud of my friend. He was growing up and moving on, just like I was. "I think I'm going to get this car."

"It's a great car for the money and seems to run well."

I nodded. I hadn't brought him with me to talk about cars or Amanda, so I gathered my courage for what was really on my mind. "Bri?"

"Hmm?" he asked, gazing out the passenger window.

"Knox has asked me to live with him."

I felt his gaze turn toward me, but like the chicken I was, I continued staring out the front windshield.

"Oh yeah?" he asked.

I nodded. "Yeah. And I've decided to move in with him."

"Wow. That's a big step, McKenna. Are you sure you guys are—"

"I'm sure. He's my everything."

"I get it. I could tell from the first time I met him that there was something major between you two."

It was nice to hear him acknowledge that. He understood that Knox and I were a package deal.

We sat in silence for the duration of the trip back to the dealership, and I wondered what he was really thinking about all this. When I pulled back into the parking lot and went inside to sign the paperwork, Brian lingered on the car lot. I watched him through the showroom windows, walking around to look at the new cars, and unease churned inside me. He wasn't going to make some last desperate plea for me, was he?

Finally I met him outside with my new car keys and found him lingering beside his car.

"Hey," he said.

"Hey."

"Get it all squared away?"

I raised the keys in my hand and gave them a jingle. "You're looking at the proud new owner of a Volkswagen Jetta." I grinned.

"Good for you." He returned my smile, but the worry line creasing his forehead was still present.

"Brian, what's…"

"McKenna, listen…"

We both paused, laughing at the other.

"You go first," I said. I braced myself for whatever it was that he was going to say. I was strong enough to handle it. Even if he tried to tell me that my parents wouldn't have approved of Knox, I was certain that wasn't true. They would be proud of any man who stepped up to raise his family and took good care of me, too.

"Amanda's living situation isn't ideal. She has two roommates, plus her and the baby in a small apartment. She and AnnMarie share a room, and I was thinking…" Brian paused and earnest blue eyes met mine. "I know it's sudden and not like me, but with you moving out, I'd like to ask Amanda to move in with me. We can set up your bedroom as a nursery for the baby. There'll be more room for toys and all the gear that comes with a baby, and I really like Amanda. Like, I really, *really* like her. I want to make this work."

His admission stunned me. I had no idea he liked Amanda so much. But honestly, I should have pieced it together. He'd been at her apartment almost every day since I'd introduced them at the hospital, and he'd come home with a big dopey grin on his face each time. It crossed my mind that Brian might not know about her past with sex addiction, but I knew that was a conversation he and Amanda needed to have. It wasn't my place.

"I think that's amazing news." I pulled him in for a hug. "Have you asked her yet?"

"No. Not yet. I've been thinking about asking her about getting our own place, but I didn't want to just leave you behind. Now that I know you're moving in with Knox…it just makes sense. It feels right, you know?"

Something told me Amanda would say yes. She'd texted me a couple of times mentioning how sweet my roommate was. She was falling for him, too. "Go tell her. I'm going to head over to Knox's place."

Brian nodded. "Okay. I think I'm gonna stop on the way and pick up a gift for AnnMarie. What do you get for a three-week-old baby?" he asked.

"Diapers?"

He chuckled. "You're probably right."

As he turned for his car, my hand on his forearm stopped him. "Bri...thanks for everything."

His eyes met mine. "Anytime. You know I'm always here for you. I'm always going to be here, no matter where we live or who is in our lives."

I nodded. I did. And it was a comforting feeling. "Text me later and tell me what she says."

"Will do. Have fun with the boys."

I hadn't told Brian about my fight with Knox, or his drunk-driving arrest. I merely nodded. But inside, my stomach was coiled tight. It was time to go face the music.

Chapter Fourteen

McKenna

A few hours later, I showed up on Knox's doorstep with a duffel bag slung over my shoulder, wondering what I'd find on the other side of the door. Could he have given up on me already and moved on? It was too painful to think about. I had to believe, with blind faith, that this would all work. I was out of options. Knox and I hadn't spoken in a couple of days, not since I told him I needed my space. But now that I'd told Brian he could move Amanda and the baby into my old room, I was out of choices. This had to work.

Just like he did the first time I came to this house, Tucker answered the door. "Kenna!" he shouted and flung himself into my arms. It immediately made me feel guilty about staying away for so long.

"Hey, buddy." I ruffled his hair and glanced around. Jaxon and Luke were in the living room, staring at a game of basketball on TV. Knox was nowhere to be seen, and dread churned deep inside me. "Where's Knox?" I asked, my voice coming out shakier than I intended it to.

Throwing an arm around my waist, Tucker led me inside. "He's working right now, but can you stay over and hang out with me?" Big brown eyes blinked up at mine. He was impossible to say no to. Just like his big brother.

"Of course I'll stay." I set my bag down in the living room and joined the boys on the couch.

Luke and Jaxon both nodded their hellos, not bothering to break eye contact with the TV until halftime. But I supposed if I was going to be living here, all of this was going to be my life. Boys, boys, and more boys. I nearly giggled at the thought.

"Do you know when Knox gets off work?" I asked.

Luke's dark, expressive eyes met mine and I knew he was remembering the volunteer event where he'd practically forced Knox's hand at telling me the truth. Luke had taken a risk, and I appreciated his honesty. His heart was in the right place. I hoped my small smile conveyed my thanks.

"He's closing up at the hardware store, it should be about another hour."

I caught up with the boys. Jaxon had cut out gambling, Luke was waiting to hear about the college applications he'd submitted, and Tucker was just Tucker. Loud, animated, and excitable like an eight-year-old boy should be. Thankfully, with Tucker to entertain me, the minutes passed by quickly.

"Have you guys had dinner yet?"

"Nope," they chimed in unison.

Unable to sit and wait any longer, I ventured into the kitchen to see what I could make for dinner. The cabinets and fridge were pretty much bare, but I pieced together bread and cheese for grilled cheese sandwiches and a couple of cans of soup. I hope Knox wasn't expecting a gourmet chef with me moving in. But I somehow knew he wouldn't be. The guys had been taking care of themselves for many years already. They wouldn't expect me to fill the role of maid or cook; I could just be me. The thought made me smile. The soup bubbled away on the stove and I added the last of the sandwiches to a big platter, carrying the whole thing out to the dining table.

"Boys, dinner!" I called.

I realized the extra commotion I heard from the living room meant Knox had arrived home. My stomach somersaulted and suddenly food was the last thing on my mind.

Knox entered the kitchen and his weary expression found mine. "McKenna?"

"Hi."

"What are you…"

"I made dinner."

His gaze ventured to the table. "I see that."

"Boys, come and eat up while it's still hot. I'm just going to talk to Knox," I instructed them. It was all the encouragement they needed. They descended on the food like a pack of hungry wolves.

"Guys, save some for McKenna," Knox said before shooting me an apologetic look.

We headed into the kitchen while the guys busied themselves with the food I'd made in the dining room.

"Sorry about them. You'd think they've never seen food before," he joked.

I smiled. "It's okay."

"What's going on, angel? I take you didn't come here just to make dinner."

"No. I didn't. I'm here because you were right. Your past was hard for me to accept, but it's also the thing that led you straight to me, and I can't help but think it was fate or maybe some divine intervention."

His forehead creased and he took a step closer, obviously trying to understand what I was telling him.

I took a deep breath and continued. "The exact thing I was running from led me to Chicago and pushed you straight into my path. I'm not going to lie and say this isn't hard for me. It's the hardest test I've ever had to overcome. Harder than coping with life without my parents. Harder than leaving my hometown behind. But loving you isn't a choice. And it's worth it, Knox. You're everything to

494

me. You, your brothers, this home and family you're offering me. I want it. I want all of it. I won't allow my past to rob me of any more joy. You messed up, but you've changed. You're not the same man who got behind that wheel. And I understand the life circumstances that drove you down that path. I know there will be bumps and bruises as we figure this out together. But I'm not going anywhere. You have me. You've had my heart right from the beginning."

Without a word, Knox gathered me in his arms, tugging me to his chest and lifting my feet from the floor. I buried my nose in the crook between his neck and his shoulder and inhaled the scent I'd missed so much. "God, it feels good to hold you, to have you back," he said.

"You have me. And I'm planning on staying if you still want me here."

He pulled back to meet my eyes, still holding me so my feet didn't reach the floor. "For good?"

I nodded, a big dopey grin overtaking my mouth.

"I don't know how I could possibly deserve you, but I love you, McKenna."

"I love you," I returned, "and your entire rowdy family." We could hear the boys arguing over how to divide up the food in the other room.

He grinned down at me and kissed my forehead. "Should we go tell the boys?"

I nodded.

Back inside the dining room, I saw that the entire plate of sandwiches was gone except for stray pieces of crust, and only about an inch of soup remained in the pot. I guess I'd underestimated the appetites of three growing boys. I'd have to remember that next time I made them dinner.

"Guys, I have some news." Knox's hand found mine and he linked our fingers together, tugging me closer. "I asked McKenna to live with us and she said yes."

Luke's face immediately broke into a wide grin and all three of them looked surprised, but happy. I wondered if they'd ask deeper questions, like what this meant for the relationship between Knox and me, or logistical ones, like how we would divvy up bathroom time and share household chores. But the room remained completely silent and still.

Until Tucker passed gas.

Loudly.

Okay, so apparently they're comfortable around me.

Everyone broke into fits of laughter, me included.

"I think you should consider yourself christened. Welcome to the family," Jaxon said.

"Rule numero uno, no farting at the dinner table, dude." Luke frowned at Tucker, who in turn stuck out his tongue.

"On that note, should we go upstairs?" Knox asked.

I nodded, not wanting to stick around and experience the smell that had already caused Jaxon and Luke to run for cover while Tucker laughed hysterically.

"I will feed you, but first I just need to be alone with you," Knox whispered near my ear as we started up the stairs.

I wondered what he had in mind for this alone time.

"What do you want for dinner?" he asked, once we were all alone in his bedroom. Our bedroom. I wondered if *cock* would be the wrong answer. My recovering sex-addict boyfriend was turning me into a raging sex addict. And I liked it.

"I'm not really hungry for food just yet." I met his deep brown gaze and bit my lower lip. I had no idea if my sexy stare was appealing, but the low growl that rumbled in his chest and the way he stalked toward me caused my stomach to coil into a tight knot. I wanted him. I wanted everything—our future—all the pleasure he could give me, and I couldn't wait another second.

I had a new addiction: loving McKenna. The fact that she was here at all, let alone telling me that she still wanted to be with me was amazing, and that she was moving in...well, she continually blew my mind with her willingness to forgive. She inspired me in so many ways. There would be no going back to that lost and broken man I was before her. I believed what she said was true. We were brought into each other's lives at just the right moment. McKenna secured her hands around the back of my neck, her fingers curling into my hair. I lowered my mouth to kiss her sweet lips, but held part of myself back. Sex wasn't the right way to show her how I felt about her, but in that moment, I didn't think she cared. She rubbed herself wantonly against my groin, causing my dick to harden, which wasn't abnormal around her. My cock had been in a semierect state since the day I met her. She'd become my everything. There was no turning back now.

I'd lived without the gentle, loving touch of a woman for so long, though, that I wasn't about to stop McKenna. Her fingers continued toying with my hair while our mouths moved together.

I'd loved my mother so much. I wasn't afraid to admit it. I was a momma's boy growing up. Losing her took a piece of me that I wouldn't get back, a piece that no woman could ever replace, no matter how hard I'd tried. And trust me, I'd tried. I fell into bed with girl after girl, looking for some kind of connection. But since my hardened heart believed that love only ended in pain, I never got my happy ending. It was something I thought I'd live without. Until I met McKenna. I had to love and forgive myself before I could open myself up to another. Opening my zipper wasn't enough. I knew McKenna would give me some line about how it was normal, how sex addicts substituted sexual experiences for emotional intimacy, but it all finally clicked.

"Knox…" She breathed out my name, then inhaled against my neck. A jolt of desire shot straight to my groin, hardening me the rest of the way.

"Yeah, angel?"

Her hands found the tense bulge below my belt and she gave him a gentle squeeze. "Don't make me beg."

Christ, how could I say no to that? Big blue eyes met mine, urging me on, making me want to give her whatever she asked for.

"I need to say a few things first." I fought to control my pounding heartbeat that I could feel pulsing in my cock. *Damn.*

McKenna waited, blinking up at me silently. God, she was beautiful. I didn't think I'd ever get used to her natural beauty—to her blue eyes that showed her every thought and emotion, to the soft curves that swayed when she walked, to her too-big heart that caused her to take care of everything and everyone in her path.

Taking her left hand, I guided her to my bed, lowering us both onto the edge. I stroked her naked ring finger, dreaming about the day I'd make her mine. I wanted to be the one to tuck her into bed each night, the first one to see her sleepy smile in the morning, the only man to listen to the gentle sounds of her breathing as she fell into a deep sleep. I wanted to be the only man to make love to her. And I told her all that and more, the words rushing out from me as I watched her eyes grow teary.

"Shhh, don't cry. Just tell me you want all that, too."

She nodded, her misty blue eyes looking happy despite the tears. Using my thumbs, I brushed the dampness from her cheeks.

"Will you marry me, angel?"

McKenna's voice broke in a tiny whisper and she flung her arms around my neck, repeating the word *yes* again and again. Never had one little word sounded so good.

I felt like pumping my fist in the air, but settled for squeezing her tight in my arms and peppering her neck with kisses while she continued to sob quietly. Actually, I wasn't sure if it was crying or laughing since her mouth was curled up in a pretty smile.

"Say something, baby. Is this too fast for you?"

She shook her head. "It's perfect, Knox. I want to be with you always." A crease pinched her brow.

500

"What is it?"

"I just…I don't want a big wedding. With my parents gone…"

I understood completely. Big events and holidays were hard without a family around you to celebrate with. But I knew we would make new traditions as the years passed. "Whatever you want."

"Maybe just the courthouse—with the boys there, too."

"Whatever you want," I promised again. "But you will wear a pretty dress for me, and we will celebrate."

She nodded, her smile blossoming wider.

Knowing I couldn't stave off my raw need for her any longer, I pressed her back against the mattress, bringing my mouth to hers in a searing kiss.

Removing her clothing piece by piece, I trailed my mouth down her body, licking and biting her succulent flesh. My teeth grazed her rib cage, earning me a tiny shriek as I moved lower, leaving damp, sucking kisses along her belly. McKenna squirmed, her hips undulating, and her chest rising and falling rapidly. Pushing her panties to the side, I swept my finger along her silken center, earning me a small whimper of pleasure. My own groan of satisfaction followed. I loved making her feel good. She didn't even have to touch me. Well, that wasn't entirely true. If I didn't come soon I'd probably have a massive case of blue balls later.

"You want me to kiss this sweet pussy?" I murmured, my lips just millimeters from her smooth core.

A helpless groan and her fist in my hair were apparently the only responses I was getting. I pressed an innocent kiss against her pussy lips, before spreading her apart so I could run my tongue along the length of her. Her fist tightened in my hair, holding me right where she wanted me. With my mouth curling into a smile, my tongue found her clit and I licked her over and over, timing my tempo to the sounds of her moans. It was easy to read just what she liked.

When she was close, I pushed my index finger inside her, pressing against the spot deep inside on her front wall, and I felt her body contract as she started to come. Adding my middle finger, I continued fucking her with my hand while my mouth latched onto a nipple. "You like when I kiss your sexy tits, huh, baby?" She rode my fingers, pumping her hips as her eyes locked onto mine.

The force of McKenna's orgasm caused her to clench around my fingers and cry out in bliss. Fuck, I needed to think about soundproofing my bedroom. I loved how hard I could make her come, though. Watching her cheeks and neck color with blush as the blood rushed to the surface of her skin was a huge turn-on. I loved the effect I had on her.

Stripping myself of my clothes in three seconds flat, I gripped my eager cock, stroking it slowly and moved alongside her. "I need to be inside you so bad."

"Yes…" she said and groaned.

Her pussy was still hypersensitive from her orgasm, and not to mention incredibly tight as I tried to penetrate her. "Relax for me, baby," I reminded her. McKenna drew a deep breath and worked at relaxing her muscles, allowing me to slip inside several more inches. She felt like a hot molten fist squeezing me. It was a testament to my control that I didn't immediately come.

Tensing my muscles and clenching my ass, I pumped into her hard and fast. The next time I would go slow, but I needed to spill myself inside her. I couldn't explain it, not even to myself. But I needed to give in to this raw, primal connection we had to show myself it was more than sex. I loved her and I knew she felt it, regardless of whether the sex was sweet and slow or hard and fast.

I met her eyes and kissed her again, unwilling to break our connection in any way. With her blue eyes on mine, her tongue lightly stroking my bottom lip, and my cock buried deep inside her, I found the meaning and connection I'd been looking for all along. Sex with the woman I loved was better than I ever could have imagined.

Forcing myself to slow, if only to draw out her pleasure and mine, I felt her begin to contract around me again. I dragged my cock in and out slowly, grinding my groin against hers to put pressure directly on her clit. Her tight little pussy clamped down hard around me as she climaxed. *Fuck it.* I was going to come.

My own release hit me like a punch to the gut and I cried out her name, burying my face against her neck as I spilled myself inside her.

McKenna's phone chimed from the bedside table and she reached for it, checking her text messages. The sheet dropped away from her chest, and though we'd already gone twice, my body didn't fail to notice her luscious curves.

"Who is it?" I asked, trailing a hand along the curve of her spine.

"Brian." She grinned.

"I just gave you three orgasms and you're smiling about a text from Brian?"

She frowned and slugged me on the shoulder. "Hush. You and I both know there's not a thing wrong with your ego."

She had me there. I knew how to make my girl insane with desire.

"Amanda said yes," she continued. "She's moving in with him."

"Wow. Those two? Really?"

She nodded. "They hit it off. And I guess when you know, you know."

"Believe me, *I know.*" I smirked and gave her butt a playful swat. We'd had a bumpy ride, but I knew that would only make us appreciate the good times more. And something told me there were lots of good times in store for us.

McKenna was my addiction.

But somehow I knew that was an addiction she'd approve of. All-consuming need coursed through me and I hauled her over top of me.

"Again?" she asked, her voice rising in surprise to see I was already hard for her again.

"Never question my cock's stamina when it comes to you, angel." I nudged at her wet opening and a soft, whispery whine was her only response. "Not too sore, are you?"

"Not yet."

I sank inside her slowly, knowing she was all I'd ever need.

Epilogue

McKenna

Two years later

"See you tonight, buddy." I kissed Tucker on the cheek and then watched him board the big yellow school bus waiting at the curb. I stood there for a moment too long, watching him pull away and enjoying the feel of the sun sinking into my pores.

It had been a long winter, made longer by the fact that Jaxon had been in jail for dealing drugs for the past several months. He'd been released last week and had spent the time at home with us, rediscovering himself and preparing for a new life—one away from drugs and gambling and girls. He would spend the summer at a rehabilitation ranch, working and learning to live as a better man. Knox had been quiet and withdrawn when Jaxon had left. It had taken me some time to get through to him, to get him to see that we were all responsible for our own choices and that Jaxon was going to make things right. I also had to remind him that we had a lot to be thankful for, the least of which were Luke's achievements at college. He was doing phenomenally well. That seemed to soothe Knox. But I knew it wasn't easy for him being the head of this household. He loved without regard, worried from time to time and was fiercely protective. It was just one more thing to love about him.

I headed back inside, giddy at the thought that Knox and I were

506

both off work today while Tucker was at school. One thing I never counted on since moving in two years ago was the lack of true alone time. I could count on one hand the number of times when Knox and I had the house all to ourselves.

I found him in the kitchen, sipping orange juice straight from the carton. I shook my head and made a tsking sound. Try as I might, there were just some habits I'd never break these boys of.

"Hey, Mama," Knox said, stuffing the carton back into the fridge as if I hadn't just witnessed his violation of it.

I giggled at the nickname. Tucker had started calling me Mama Kenna shortly after I moved in and Knox, who thought it was adorable, often used the nickname too, since he knew it always brought a smile to my lips.

"Did you get that boy off to school?" He leaned back against the counter, letting me take in my fill of his naked torso.

Momentarily distracted by the ridiculous six-pack staring back at me, it took me a moment to answer. "Uh-huh," I managed.

Knox grinned at my reaction. "Over two years later and I still get her weak in the knees."

"Do not!" I couldn't let him know how easily he got me worked up. I didn't want that knowledge going to his head. He already knew he was a complete sex god with command over my body, heart, and soul. Jeez, a girl needed to keep a few secrets.

He pushed off the counter and stalked closer. "What do you want to do today?" His gaze wandered down my body while his fingertips grazed my hip bone. A zing of electricity darted through my center.

Damn it. There was no denying I wanted him. I shrugged, trying to play it cool. "I don't know. I was thinking of going to the mall, getting some summer shopping done for me and Tucker. He won't fit into any of his shorts or T-shirts from last year…"

Knox's gaze locked on mine and his fingers tightened as they curled around my hip. "You have exactly three seconds flat to get this fine little ass up those stairs and undressed," he growled. "One…"

I swallowed heavily and met his intense gaze, loving this dangerous game I was playing with him.

"Two…"

I darted around him, but not before I felt the sting of his palm connect with my butt, and jogged for the stairs.

McKenna was breathless and fighting to push her jeans down her thighs when I entered our room. I struggled to keep the smile off my face as I watched her. My angel liked being told what to do in the bedroom; she loved it when I took charge. Which was good because I loved it, too.

Once she was stripped down to just a pair of blue cotton panties, McKenna stood in front of me. Her jog up the stairs had winded her, and her tits were rising and falling deliciously with each breath she drew. I approached and carefully circled one sensitive nipple with the pad of my index finger, rubbing the soft pink center until it pebbled under my touch.

"Do you want my mouth here?" I continued rubbing and circling her nipples. Her breath hitched in her throat and she murmured some unintelligible sound. I knew that kissing and sucking on her tits got her nice and wet for me, and I couldn't help teasing her.

Lowering my mouth to her chest, I pressed a tiny kiss to the tip of each breast, her skin erupting in chill bumps in the wake of my breath. "Why are these still on?" Working my fingers into the side of her panties, my fingers found her warm center. Slick and wet, just like I predicted.

I pushed the fabric down her legs until the panties pooled at her ankles and she stepped out of them. Running my fingers along her bare folds, I found her clit and lightly rubbed. McKenna's knees trembled and she reached a steadying hand toward me, grasping my bicep as I continued my assault.

Then I bent to her ear and whispered, "Get on your knees, angel."

I took her hand and helped her lower herself to her knees, then unbuttoned and unzipped my jeans, tugging them down just enough to free my cock. It greeted McKenna, begging for her mouth.

Taking the base of me in one hand, she guided me to her mouth. Big blue eyes met mine as she sucked against the head of my cock. *Holy fuck.* Watching her suck my dick was almost as good as the sensation itself. She might not have had experience before, but her passion for me and for this came through loud and clear. She devoured me, pushing as much of my length as she could fit into her mouth, salivating around me and pumping her fist up and down while her other hand cupped my balls. I was hers. She was the only girl who could make me come in about three minutes flat just by sucking me.

I tipped her chin up to mine and her eyes latched on again. "What do you think you're doing?" I growled, my voice rough with desire.

Considering her mouth was currently full of my cock, she didn't answer, but her eyes implored mine.

"You're a greedy little thing this morning. Why would you try to make me come in your mouth when you know I want to be inside you when I go off?"

She swallowed and the sensation cut straight to my balls where I had to fight off a moan.

"Get on the bed."

McKenna rose and scrambled up to the bed, lying down on her back and widening her thighs so I could see her pretty pink folds.

Shit, that was a beautiful sight. I drew a couple of deep breaths to calm myself down, or this was going to be over in a damn hurry. Needing a moment to recover, I took my time licking and kissing a trail along her body, spending extra time nibbling the creamy flesh at her inner thighs until she was writhing and groaning beneath me. I flicked my tongue against her clit, bringing her right to the edge of her orgasm before placing a chaste kiss against her pussy and crawling up her body.

When she let out a groan of frustration, I said, "Same thing you did to me, angel. Fair's fair." The truth was, there was no way she was coming without me inside her. I needed to feel her tight walls clench around me when she came. I fucking craved it.

As I positioned myself against her and eased inside slowly, my eyes slipped closed and I went to my happy place. The place where I felt content and loved and accepted. McKenna wrapped her legs around my back, tilting her pelvis to meet mine, allowing me to thrust deeper. She could now handle all of me, which sent my cock to his happy place, too.

Dragging my length in and out of her, I cradled her face in my hands and kissed her full mouth, telling her I loved her over and over again.

Knowing that this beautiful girl loved me for the man I was, it made our relationship and our intimate connection that much stronger. We hadn't gotten around to making it official yet, but it was just a matter of time. Maybe this summer on the beach.

"Knox, I'm close…" she murmured, tightening her vice-like grip on my dick.

Fuck.

McKenna let out a short cry and her fingernails bit into my ass as she pressed me closer. I drew out her orgasm, kissing her mouth, her neck, and her breasts as she clung to me, her pussy throbbing deep inside.

I shuddered once and started to come, hot jets of semen pumping out of me and into McKenna as our bodies fought to get even closer together.

Afterward, we laid tangled together in the sheets, our skin dewy from exertion and our hearts still beating too fast. We made plans for the rest of our day together—going out to lunch, and then down to the lake to walk along the beach. I smiled at the secret knowledge that sex one more time before Tucker got home from school would probably be on the agenda, too.

I tugged her closer, drawing her to my chest, thankful that I had at least a million more days like this to look forward to. Before McKenna, I thought I was incapable of love—and maybe I was. But she'd changed something fundamental inside me just by her presence in my life. Her sweet and giving nature, her big heart that had plenty of room for not only me, but also my brothers, and her ability to forgive were all things I loved about her. And I made sure to tell her every day. Now that I'd found her, I would do everything in my control to show her she was the love of my life.

Curling into my side, McKenna released a happy little sigh. Knowing that she felt the exact same way was something indescribable. I felt a deeper connection to her than any other person in the world. She was my everything.

Acknowledgments

Thank you so, so much to the readers who have followed this series and this family in their journey to their happily ever after. I had a good (but exhausting) time exploring the dynamic and relationship between a sex therapist and a sex addict. It was a concept that wormed its way into my brain and begged to be written. I also loved getting to know the Bauer brothers and will miss them now that this series is done, but am hard at work on something new. I want to sincerely thank you for your enthusiasm and support for my books.

Once again, thank you to Pam Berehulke for your guidance, wisdom, and editing expertise. You're a lifesaver.

Thank you to the bloggers who so diligently followed this series and reviewed every book. You guys are made of awesome. Truly a writer's wet dream. ;)

A big ole hug to my early readers for your feedback and excitement: Rachel Brookes, Sarah Larson, and Emma Hart. You are each wonderful.

Other Titles by Kendall Ryan

Unravel Me

Make Me Yours

Resisting Her

Hard to Love

The Impact of You

Working It

Craving Him

All or Nothing ✓

Hard to Love

A New York Times & USA Today bestseller ~ Available Now!

Cade's always taken risks...

Cade takes care of his sick younger sister by doing what he does best—cage fighting and starring in adult movies, his newest moneymaking scheme designed to pay for his sister's growing medical bills. But when his latest gig finds him admitted to the ER sporting an erection from hell, thanks to the little pill given to him by the director, he can't get the pretty little nurse who treated him out of his head, even though he knows she's so far out of his league it should be illegal.

Alexa's always played it safe...

Tired of being pigeonholed as the sweet, innocent one, hardworking nursing student Alexa has been looking for ways to break out of her goody-two-shoes image. When her friend suggests the outlandish idea of losing her virginity to the sexy and sure-to-be-skilled porn star, Alexa is mortified. But then when Cade refuses her proposition, she finds herself pissed off and embarrassed. When she tracks him down to give him a piece of her mind, she isn't prepared for what she finds. Watching him care for his little sister tugs at her heart, and suddenly it's no longer just about losing her virginity, but about helping Cade. Because Lord help her, she might actually be falling for a porn star.

Resisting Her

A New York Times & USA Today bestseller ~ Available Now!

Agent Cole Fletcher lives for his job at the FBI, and he's more than ready for his next assignment—raiding a cult compound and putting their leader behind bars. But he isn't prepared for Savannah and her knock-you-on-your-ass good looks. At nineteen, she's too old for foster care and too damaged to live on her own. Against his better judgment, but knowing she has nowhere else to go, Cole takes her in. But helping her out won't be easy. He helps her through screaming nightmares and lingering fears, and that's the easy part. Her preference to sleep cuddled up next to his warm body, and her desire to please him in every way, makes her harder and harder to resist.

Visit Kendall Ryan at:

Website: *www.kendallryanbooks.com*

Facebook: *Kendall Ryan Books*

Twitter: *@kendallryan1*

Printed in Great Britain
by Amazon